Hidden Treasures

by

Kathleen Buckley

Cover Art by *Teddi Black*

The Wild Rose Press, Inc.
PO Box 708
Adams Basin, NY 14410-0708
Visit us at www.thewildrosepress.com

Publishing History
First Edition, 2024
Trade Paperback ISBN 978-1-5092-5785-0
Digital ISBN 978-1-5092-5786-7

Published in the United States of America

Dedication

Mrs. Swanson, my high school guidance counselor in Fairbanks, Alaska, told me that if I wanted to write, I should get a factory job rather than a more challenging professional one. If I'd taken her advice, I might have written dozens more books by now.

Chapter 1

Late December 1739, Passevant Magna, Kent

The steward's office was warmed by a good fire in the hearth, its mantel wreathed in bay and ivy because Mr. Salt enjoyed the trappings of the season. Allan Everard heard of his father's death when a Passevant footman thrust his way into the room and held out a letter sealed with black wax.

Salt took it without a word and broke the seal. The message was short, but he did not speak at once, merely frowning down at the sheet. "His lordship, Augustus Passevant, fifth Baron Passevant, is dead. His lordship, the sixth Baron Passevant, has instructed me to turn you off." To the footman he said, "You may go. I assume Baron Passevant does not require an answer."

"No, sir, but I'm to stay until Mr. Everard clears out."

Allan stood up and gave a curt nod. "I'll not be long packing." Neither his father's death nor the dismissal were unexpected: he had known and dreaded them for several years. The only surprise was that Julius Passevant had not even waited until their father's body was cold to issue the order.

"Where will you lodge? In case I should have questions about one of the matters we have been working on," Salt inquired.

Before he could reply, the footman cleared his

throat, "Begging your pardon, sirs, his lordship don't want Mr. Everard in Passevant Magna nor Passevant Parva neither."

"Until I secure a new post, you'll find me at the Blank Shield in Wellstone, Mr. Salt." Hardly more than an ale house, it was sure to have a room for him.

"I will miss your assistance, Everard. You have handled so many of the tenants' matters so efficiently."

The praise warmed him, despite worry about his future.

The footman, whose name Allan could not recall because he was one of the more junior ones, spoke. "I'm right sorry, sir."

Allan gave him a friendly smile to show there were no hard feelings. "We all knew it would come to this. I'll be down in a few minutes." The office was the front room of the steward's good-sized cottage. One of the smaller bedchambers had been Allan's home for the last ten years.

Salt put the sheet aside in the stack of papers to be filed away. "I'll tell the boy to hire the cart. You'll need it for your trunk."

****

The Blank Shield in Wellstone was far enough from the Passevant lands not to buzz with talk about the baron's death. The local folk had business and gossip of their own and took more interest in the Earl of Barlyon, only three miles distant and always a topic of gossip. The late Lord Passevant's attorney found Allan in the alehouse two days later, reading and sipping a mug of small beer.

"Mr. Everard?"

Receiving an affirmative reply, the fellow

introduced himself. William Hart's neat bob wig, plain suit, paunch, and sharp eyes could have been a successful merchant's, but his air of gravity belonged to the law. Allan invited him to sit.

"I will while I drink a tankard of the ale, which is said to be excellent," he said. "Then I should like to speak with you in private. 'Tis fortunate you told Salt your direction, but then, he'd know I needed it." Hart proceeded to ask him about his work for Passevant's steward. *Curious.* Was he being interviewed for a position on Salt's recommendation?

His position at Passevant had never been comfortable. Everyone knew he was Augustus Passevant's bastard. The villagers were civil because he was the steward's assistant and Salt was a power in the community, but they were not friendly. Fear of the heir and Lady Passevant accounted for that. Once, when the family's party had arrived at church later than usual, the baron's heir had noticed Allan in the last pew and muttered to his sisters, "That curst by-blow's here. Don't look." But of course they did.

He could have left after learning as much of property management as Salt could teach him. The steward gave him a reference but asked him to remain as Baron Passevant desired it. Allan had agreed: his education and training qualified him for a position, but would they weigh against his bastardy? Inevitably a prospective employer would inquire about his family connections, and he had none to offer. Besides, Salt was aging and needed the help. A widower with no children, he needed the companionship, too. Allan would manage somehow.

His ale gone, Hart asked if Everard would accompany him to the Wheel and Whip, the coaching inn where he had hired a private parlor.

The small, oak-paneled room was cozy on a chilly day. Hart ordered a bottle of claret instead of punch "for we must keep clear heads, Mr. Everard, which we are more like to do with wine than a punch bowl." Once they were alone, he said, "Now, to business. I don't know if you're aware your father's will was read yesterday."

"I did know Lord Passevant was buried, though I did not try to attend. I wasn't summoned to come to the reading." And hadn't expected to be. His father had made sure he was educated enough to support himself. Given the late Lord Passevant's retiring nature and the assertive characters of his lady and heir, Allan had cherished no hope of receiving anything more. No one could know the fifth Baron Passevant for as much as a week without understanding he dreaded discourtesy, brangling, and unkindness. He could face no argument except about scholarly matters. The wonder was how he had ever come to beget a child on the wrong side of the blanket. Had Allan's mother, whoever she was, seduced him? He would never know. By the time he had learned he was Passevant's bastard, he was old enough not to blurt out such a question. Especially as he had never been alone with his father the few times they had met. He had seen his progenitor only three or four times since being turned over to Salt, and those occasions had scarcely qualified as meeting. Allan had been present but ignored by the late baron except for a brief, unreadable glance.

"Have you made any plans, Mr. Everard?"

"I hope to find a post as a steward or bailiff. I'm qualified to be either. I've not found anything in the London newssheets yet, and there's nothing locally. I don't think it would be wise to continue in this district, anyway."

"I'm sure you are correct. A petty, vindictive man, the sixth baron. I don't believe you need seek a post immediately. What you must do is accompany me back to London. Lord Passevant charged me with the task of instructing you to see a certain solicitor in town to, hmmm, 'learn of something to your advantage.' " A quirk of the lips and raised eyebrows made comment upon the theatrical phrase. "I perceive you are surprised."

Allan supposed his expression gave him away. He was dumbfounded. If Hart had been quoting, Passevant had possessed unknown depths.

"His lordship very sensibly did not want the Passevant family attorney—myself—further involved in the matter. I'll introduce you to the solicitor, and he can advise you."

The following day found Allan sharing a traveling coach with William Hart, Esq., on the way to London.

****

To Allan's surprise, Peter Wilde was no more than thirty to Allan's eight-and-twenty. In the man's office, with a file box at hand and the door closed against any intrusion, Wilde explained, "The fifth baron made certain arrangements with my father not long after your birth, which would provide you a small income. Not as good a settlement as some would make for a natural child, but there were circumstances which would have made it awkward to leave you more."

Lady Passevant.

"Then about two years after your birth, Lord Passevant won an inn here in a game of hazard. He transferred it to this firm in trust for you until his death

5

or until your majority if you were under age when he died."

Allan murmured, "Good God."

All gentlemen played at cards or dice, but the baron could not have been a hardened gamester. If he had lost, the amounts had been too small to affect the estate's income. Presumably any winnings would have been correspondingly small.

"I confess I know very little of the late Lord Passevant, but from what my father told me, the win must have been fortuitous. That random stroke of luck permitted him to make a good provision for you without anyone in his family learning of it."

That would have been essential, from what Allan knew of Passevant's dread of confrontation.

"At his lordship's instructions, this firm has dealt with the tenant, taken the lease payments, and deposited them. The lease expired several months ago and was not renewed by the tenant, an elderly man who seems to have become incapable of continuing in business. The property is not currently in use but had been let out in rooms for many years, with a cook shop taking up the kitchen and dining room. It's empty now. I inspected it when the lease ended, and 'tis in need of work. But it has one great advantage."

Allan wished he might know what it could be; an empty inn needing to be repaired and rented out sounded like more trouble than it would be worth. "And that is, sir?"

"It's freehold."

Freehold. Allan would own the land on which the inn stood. Much of London was held by wealthy speculators who built homes and shops and leased them out. Even a small piece of land might be valuable.

"Even if someone in the family did learn he had transferred the property to you, he or she might assume an old inn all but falling to pieces was of little value. Gifting instead of willing it to you was a clever strategy, however. Avoiding legal unpleasantness is a good thing, when possible."

"They'd have sued to get it back."

"Precisely," Peter Wilde enunciated. "The closest scrutiny of the barony's and the baron's ledgers would not reveal the baron receiving the inn as he won it. To keep the expenses relating to it out of the account books he had my father open a bank account which he initially funded from pocket money. That's how the land tax and my father's fees were paid. The lease payments went into the same one."

"Pocket money," Allan echoed. He could appreciate how it was done. Men of means kept amounts of cash about them which would support a poor family for a year; few would question what a gentleman spent it on. A mistress, wagers, cards or dice, drink, clothing, amusements, or trinkets and trifles.

"There were some expenses when the lease ended: new keys, a gate, a caretaker's wages. Nothing significant, given the accumulated income." He named a sum.

Accustomed to dealing with the finances of a barony, he was still impressed. He need never work again and could still live like one of the lower gentry. He could marry. As the steward's assistant he had not earned enough to support a wife. Even if he had and could court a suitable girl, he could not have started a family in a place he would have to leave when his half brother inherited.

Wilde went on, "It is empty now only because Lord Passevant was aware he had not long to live and thought it best to keep it empty but for a reliable caretaker, so as to leave the choice to you. And as I said, to make it appear not worth fighting over. I advise against making a decision until you have seen it."

"I may not know then, either. I've never lived in London and know little about commercial property in town."

"I'll be happy to advise you. A good deal of my work has to do with leases of that sort. Now, I have a set of keys for you." He unlocked a desk drawer and brought out a great ring with a surprising number of keys.

"Upon my soul, has the inn so many chambers?"

"Did I not mention 'twas once a coaching inn?"

"No, Mr. Wilde, you did not. I had imagined no more than half a dozen bedchambers." A coaching inn! A substantial property, then.

"The key with the ribbon tied around it opens the little gate."

The attorney had mentioned a gate, but Allan had given it no thought in the torrent of other information.

"Lord Passevant thought it best to close off the entrance into the yard to prevent damage. There was a heavy double door from ground almost to the top of the coach entrance, of course. Not enough room even for a sweep's climbing boy to wriggle through. A bar secures it inside. A small door with a grill has been added on the right side. Your property is the Three Greyhounds in Aldersgate Street."

****

The inn did need repairs. Still, his heart gave a little

leap at the size of the place. It had possibilities, though not as a coaching inn. A newer one buzzed with activity on the same street.

The key turned easily in the lock, but as he pushed it open, a stocky man emerged from the right arm of the U-shaped yard.

"Your name, sir?"

Allan stared at him. The graying brown hair, powerful shoulders, and pugnacious chin reminded him of someone. Before he spoke, the fellow said, "Ah, Mr. Allan Everard. Welcome."

"Tom Chappell?"

"Ay, former coachman to his late lordship. The heir's lady took against me for not groveling enough. By then, his lordship knew his time was short, but he saw me right, making me the caretaker here."

"I'm glad for it."

"His lordship was a good man."

Allan acknowledged the comment with a nod.

"Will you step in and lock the gate behind you, sir?"

They sat in the room from which Chappell had come, the inn's office, while the man showed him the list he had prepared of necessary work to be done. No one had asked him to do so, but he reckoned the attorney and clerk who'd come to look at the Three Greyhounds wouldn't notice any but the most glaring needs.

"A-course, you wouldn't have to do it. There's plenty would be glad to rent rooms just as they are. Terrible hard to find a place to lay your head here in town."

His wife brought them ale and biscuits.

"On t'other hand, renting rooms to a pack of poor people—families, many of 'em—is no work for a gentleman. I had to throw out the last of the old man's tenants when he went at the end of the lease."

"Lucky I'm not a gentleman, then."

"Beggin' your pardon, sir, we all knew who your father was. And a credit to him, too."

Embarrassed, Everard muttered, "Thank you." He ate the last of a very good coriander seed biscuit. "Mr. Wilde suggested selling the inn or leasing it to someone who would rent out the rooms."

The coachman said, "You could. If you sold, you'd have money in hand, and I reckon you'd know how to invest it. If you leased it to someone, or rented out the rooms, well, it's like having farm land with tenancies. Lodgings in London are expensive. There's plenty of decent men like clerks that would be glad of a room here, and my Molly's good cooking. Either way the money would keep coming regular."

A member of a nobleman's family would turn livid at receiving unsolicited advice from a servant. As a bastard, Allan had no right to scorn anyone. Besides, Chappell had a point. Allan's rented room had seemed monstrous expensive, considering its shabbiness and the landlady's nonchalance in the matter of cleaning and service.

They'd drunk the last of their ale.

"Would you like me to take you around, sir? Or maybe you'd rather look it over by yourself."

"Give me the tour, please, as you must know the inn well."

"Every rat hole and bit o' fallen plaster," Chappell agreed.

The office, dining room (ha! An elegant name for a long room with rough tables and benches), and kitchen took up half of the right wing's ground floor, with bedchambers occupying the rest. The far end housed some storage for the stable yard which lay through another gate. The wing to the left of the coach entrance held more rooms. Stairs at either end of the yard led up to the galleried first and second stories. A tattered piece of cloth hung as a curtain in one window, and lines to hold laundry were strung between several of the posts.

They went through all the bedchambers, storerooms, and the stable. The dormer windows above the second story belonged to the servants' rooms, those employed by the Three Greyhounds when it had been a coaching inn and those of the passengers who had maids, menservants, footmen, and the like. Noon had come and gone by the time their inspection ended in the kitchen. Soup simmered over the fire, and Chappell's wife was rolling out pastry.

"Near time for dinner," Chappell said, "if you'd care to share our meal. Molly's a good cook."

"I guessed as much from the biscuits. Thank you. I'd be happy to join you. Afterward I've a few questions."

"You can ask while we eat if you want. Molly has some notions of her own."

The inn had once been handsome. During his inspection, he began to appreciate the proportions of rooms and windows, the elegance of the pillars and balusters. He had thought the dining room unappealing when he first saw it, and indeed the furniture was rough and better suited to a village ale house than a good coaching inn. But the fireplace mantel was expertly carved. He could imagine the jingling of harness and ladies and gentlemen dining here.

When he finally left the Three Greyhounds, Allan

had reached a decision: he would not sell the inn. The place possessed an odd charm. Someone had inscribed his attempt at an epigram—in English—on one of the window panes. One could deduce two things: the fellow could afford a diamond ring to do the etching, and he was no poet.

Allan would never be landed gentry but owning a piece of London, the greatest city in the world, ay, that was something.

Chapter 2

Early February, Stanbury Manor, Wiltshire
When their groom pelted into the morning room to inform Rosabel and Oriana their father had collapsed in the stable yard as he dismounted, Rose sat stunned. Their father was not old, not yet fifty years, and in rude good health.

Ory's first words before Rose could speak or move were "But who will take care of us?"

"I will until Papa is well." She had mothered her sister since she herself had been twelve and Ory six.

Cook, the despot of their kitchen since before Rose's birth, followed Jem into the room, fingers twisting her apron. Their butler came to stand behind her, white-faced.

She had been mistress of the house for almost eight years, making sure Papa paid the coal merchant and the farrier, managing their social life, and visiting the tenants. More recently, she had told him they must begin to plan for Oriana's future.

Her responsibilities had given her some confidence. She said, "He must be brought in and put to bed. Send the stable boy for the doctor, if you haven't already done so. Cook, do you have any—"

Jem broke into speech. "John Coachman says he's dead, mistress."

Oriana, frozen where she sat with her embroidery,

let out a cry.

Rose took a steadying breath. Papa had suffered several episodes of chest tightness, which he dismissed as muscle strain. "We must have the doctor anyway, in case he is mistaken. Send the boy, and then you and Sam carry my father up to his chamber."

The shock and the need to take charge held the tears off until the doctor had confirmed Paul Stanbury was indeed deceased, a fact she had suspected as he was laid in his bed. Even then, she had duties to perform: comforting Oriana and directing the butler to see to the usual mourning rituals, whatever they were. Rose had been too devastated to notice or remember what had been done at her mother's death. Then just as she thought she was free to hide in her bedchamber for a while, Mistress Howard said, "You'll need to talk to Parson about the funeral." At twenty years of age, Rose was not only the lady of the house, she was now the head of the household.

As she sealed a note for the stable lad to take to the vicarage, she realized she must write her father's attorney as well to ask what legal actions were required.

About ten days later, a terse note acknowledged her communication: Attorney Lucian Brand had the estate's matters in hand. A second communication a month later brought startling news.

...I apologize for taking so long to respond, but I have been your family's attorney only for the dozen years since my partner died, although this firm has represented your family since your grandfather's time. Your father's will as revised after your mother's death named you Miss Oriana's guardian, assuming that you would have attained your majority before she needed one.

Thus I found it necessary to go through your family's entire file to ascertain whether there is any male relative who might act as guardian to your sister and yourself which would be preferable to being wards in Chancery. Then too, in the absence of a male heir, the property would escheat to the Crown.

On reviewing the file, I found mention of a Horace Stanbury, your grandfather's nephew and therefore your father's cousin, who is the recipient of an annuity funded by your said grandfather. I wrote to him in care of the bank which disburses the payments, having no other address for him. It might take weeks for a reply if he lives at some distance from the bank or goes in only infrequently. I wrote also to your maternal grandfather, General Sir Oliver Milton, but have not received a response.

I should add that as no other guardian was named in your father's will, you young ladies both being over the age of seven, are eligible to choose your own guardian by application in your own hand to the diocesan Consistory Court. I append a copy of the language to be used if you wish to choose a guardian.

"Do we have a cousin?" Ory asked. "Papa never mentioned him."

"Father's cousin would be our cousin once removed. I'm sure I never heard of him. And if Mr. Brand did not know about him, Papa and Cousin Horace may easily have lost touch. Come, let's look in the Bible."

The family Bible reposed on a table in the family parlor. Their father had read aloud from it on Sundays when the weather made the low-lying road to church impassable except on horseback. Papa's readings were usually more interesting than the vicar's, as at any mention of an animal, his agricultural interests led him into anecdotes about the manor's animals, or animals he had hunted, or someone else had owned, hunted, or failed to purchase. References to crops brought forth similar recollections.

On a blank page at the front, the births, marriages, and deaths of several generations of Stanburys were recorded. The girls bent their heads over the crabbed script, the older entries faded to brown.

"Father was Grandfather's only surviving son." Rose's finger moved up. "But Grandfather had a brother, and he had a son named Horace.

"How strange we never heard of him," Ory said.

"Great-uncle Stanbury died when Horace was only a child," Rose pointed out. "Perhaps his mother remarried and moved away."

Perhaps their grandfather had given Horace an annuity because he had been left in poverty either by his papa or by his mother's remarriage. Family was one's only source of safety.

She hoped Grandfather Milton would agree to be their guardian. She remembered him fondly though they had visited him in town only three times, the last almost five years ago. Papa thought the general rigid, and although he had not said so in her hearing, Rose suspected her grandfather considered Papa careless. She admitted there was some truth to that judgement: her father did give short shrift to anything that did not interest him. Never his land or tenants: she was as sure of his devotion to them as to his daughters. But he had little use for what he regarded as empty conventions, and he put off doing anything that bored him. That he had revised his will on their mother's death was a surprise, but perhaps Attorney Brand had browbeaten him into doing so. Paul Stanbury might have declined to name an alternative guardian on the grounds that he himself was in excellent health and Rose would be of age in nine years.

She broached to Oriana the question of who they would like as guardian. "I would prefer our grandpapa. You may hardly recall him, but I liked him very well. 'Tis a pity he is not a great correspondent." An understatement when he had replied neither to her letter informing him of their papa's death nor to Attorney Brand's. And why had he not? He must surely have received one or the other. "But he is kind. Peppery sometimes but with a smile in his eyes."

"I remember him a little. He gave me caraway comfits, and he had a little cannonball on his desk. He let me roll it on the floor. I wouldn't mind him as guardian."

"He is quite old, and we should include another choice in case Grandpapa should die while we are still minors, though I'll be of age in six months. We have not met Cousin Horace and know nothing of him," Rose said, "but we do know Mr. Brand. Our long-lost cousin may not welcome the responsibility of being our guardian as he knows no more of us than we of him. That is, assuming he is still alive."

After some discussion, they agreed that their attorney, being a known quantity, would do very well as an alternate, and they set to work writing out their requests to the diocesan court.

****

The funeral was long past, and the wood anemones were blooming. Disbelief and their first grief passed, and their day-to-day lives went on much as they always had, except for missing their father.

They had all but forgotten the question of guardianship by the time they received Attorney Brand's next letter.

I received a letter from Mr. Stanbury about three weeks since but put off writing to you with the news as I anticipated hearing from the diocesan court shortly. I had written Sir Oliver a second time and received a curt note declining guardianship, based on Sir Oliver's age and ill health, but as you had indicated I was your second choice, I expected to be appointed. The court's decision reached me yesterday, and to my surprise, they have chosen Mr. Stanbury on the ground that he is related to you, the property is entailed and will be his, and as you will be living there, he is the logical choice. I was able to talk with him today and he seems to be a serious, well-conducted man. I will bring him to Stanbury Manor next week to meet you…

Horace Stanbury and Attorney Brand duly arrived, after sending a message to the manor to let Rose know they would stay at High Stanbury's inn for propriety's sake. They would call the following day, as the afternoon was far advanced.

Ory was all fidgets until the following morning when Brand and Horace Stanbury arrived. There was no obvious reason to dislike their cousin, yet Rose could not feel quite at ease with him, perhaps because his manner was somewhat stiff though he spoke pleasantly and observed the customary civilities.

His breeches, coat, and waistcoat of dark green wool were suitable for the country, though Rose did not think any country gentleman of her acquaintance would wear an edging of lace on his wrist ruffles and his neckcloth when casually dressed. He could not be in straitened circumstances: she knew little of gentlemen's fashions, but she recognized fine tailoring.

If he did not look quite like a country gentleman, he was certainly not what her father had disparaged as a "town beau," dressed with finickal care and full of compliments and idle chat. His air of alertness or perhaps watchfulness, reminded her of Grandpapa, though not of a military man. She did not know what basket to sort him into.

Paul Stanbury having employed no bailiff, one of the grooms accompanied Horace on a tour of the estate though their cousin seemed disconcerted at the prospect, perhaps because he was not dressed for riding. In their absence, Brand told them what little he knew of the heir: he was a gentleman living in London, not purse-pinched. This seemed little enough, considering he had met with Stanbury before bringing him to Stanbury Manor.

Ory said, "I am sure we will come to love our new cousin. Does he have a wife and children, sir? I often think how pleasant it would be to have brothers, though Rose is the best of sisters."

Brand's brow puckered. "He has not mentioned either. He is a rather reserved man, however, and men often do not talk of their family connections when discussing business matters."

Men! A female would have learned what he did in town, his favorite pastimes, whether he was married or a widower, if he had children and their ages and names, any number of personal details.

Before Rose could remark on the slightness of the attorney's knowledge, he continued, "I do not know if he will wish to live here as he has some business interests in town. Otherwise we could have come sooner. I suppose he will hire a bailiff to oversee the manor. He may decide you must move to town."

Rose would have liked to visit London, but unless Cousin Horace were married and moved in good society, she would hardly be able to meet eligible men. And if he was in business rather than merely invested in some genteel enterprise, he would not have the correct social connections even with a wife.

When Stanbury returned from viewing his inheritance moving awkwardly, Ory inquired, "Are you well, Cousin Horace?"

"It's been some years since I rode much. There's no need for it in town."

Brand suggested he might prefer a brandy to tea, an offer that was accepted gratefully.

"If you mean to move to Stanbury Manor now you are a landed gentleman, I expect you will soon become accustomed again," Brand remarked.

Twin furrows appeared between their cousin's eyebrows. "I suppose I must live here part of the year. Certainly I must make this my residence while I acquaint myself with the property."

This lack of enthusiasm for their handsome and productive manor made Rose bristle inwardly. In fairness, she admitted she would have been equally offended if he had been jubilant at his good fortune, coming as it had from her father's death.

Ory's head swiveled toward Rose, on the brink of making some comment. The chances were against it being tactful. Rose gave a minute head shake.

How would he deal with their tenants? Unfamiliar with country ways and without appreciation for the manor, she hoped he would hire a good bailiff to manage it. Would he know a good bailiff from a bad one? She would have to advise him.

The idea he would live at the manor even part of the year was not comfortable, either. But as the heir he was entitled to make his home with them. No, she corrected herself: they would be living with him. Stanbury Manor was no longer theirs.

Rose passed the plate of ginger biscuits. She had not said much, taken up with studying her new relative and her own thoughts. Either their cousin was a serious man, or else he maintained a sober demeanor because theirs was a house in mourning. The fact he had not written a letter of condolence weighed against him.

"I'm sure your family will enjoy the clean air and the countryside."

"Family?" Stanbury echoed the word as if translating it from some foreign tongue. His response came a trifle slow. "You are my only remaining family as far as I am aware. My parents are long dead and were estranged from my grandparents. I was young and never thought to ask about other connections."

Wouldn't most men as almost as old as her own papa think of marriage and children first rather than of parents and grandparents? Cousin Horace was about forty years, she thought. She stole a look at Brand. His face told her nothing. Man-like, he might have missed its oddness.

"How much of the year do you think you would spend at Stanbury?" Brand permitted Rose to pour him another cup of bohea and accepted another biscuit.

"Perhaps the summer."

Even Rose knew anyone who could desert London

during the hot, smelly months did.

Now Brand looked troubled. "Mistress Rose and Miss Oriana have been living here on their own since their father's death, having no female relative who could stay with them. 'Tis the country, too, where the usual conventions are sometimes ignored. But if they are to continue living here, some suitable older female should be employed to lend them propriety. If you prefer they should move to town, they would still need a chaperon, but the advantage would be the greater ease of Mistress Rose meeting some eligible man. Once she marries, she could take charge of Miss Oriana's introduction into society in a few years."

"That had not occurred to me. I will have to decide what's best to do."

Stanbury's bland face did not change. Nevertheless, she sensed he had been caught off guard. If he had never married or had to make provision for dependents, the thought might be daunting.

"He's very ordinary, isn't he?" Oriana observed when they were alone. "I expected him to look like Papa. Or more like Papa than he is, at least."

"He is not as tall and sturdy and that makes a difference. And you and I are not similar in looks." Stanbury was lean as a whip and sharp-featured, not a look she admired.

"Perhaps I am a changeling." Ory giggled. "I suppose you are correct about Cousin Horace. Did you notice, his skin is as pale as yours?"

"Paler, I would say." Rose too often forgot to wear a hat out of doors. Horace either spent his time indoors or was as careful of his complexion as a fine lady.

On Sunday, Rose introduced him to the parson and

her family's friends and acquaintances after the service. Cousin Horace was all grave urbanity though he said little. Easy to overlook when the parishioners had plenty to say and exclaim over.

At dinner that day, Stanbury announced he would send for his belongings.

"A companion should be hired for the young ladies before you take up residence in the house, Mr. Stanbury."

"Surely no one could object to girls living with their cousin, Mr. Brand. As you pointed out, in the country the rules of behavior are not as strict."

Neither she nor Brand could argue the point though he was only rather a distant relative, previously unknown to them. Rose was used to a good deal of freedom and did not welcome the suggestion of a chaperon, but even she suspected their living with a single man of his age would cause talk when no one had ever heard of their having a cousin before.

The attorney stretched his stay two days longer than necessary to discuss various legal points with Rose and Stanbury, then finally took his leave, privately admonishing her to write if she had any questions or if difficulties arose.

She and Cousin Horace were no better acquainted after a week than they had been at their first meeting, making it impossible to warm to him. Their new cousin's conversation revealed no personal details: not likes or dislikes, how he passed his time in London, where he had grown up, what he did for amusement. His most revealing remark was on the May Day festivities—"A mob of prancing clodhoppers celebrating some old heathen custom"—from which she gathered he was contemptuous of country people and customs. The second part of the remark might indicate Dissenter tendencies, as the Puritans had called the traditional Christmas mince pies "superstitious pies." Rose and Oriana missed the maypole and morris dancing in Low Stanbury, but they could not have attended so early in their mourning even if their cousin had permitted it, as she was sure he would not. That, at least, was not a point of contention between Rose and their guardian.

The sum of Horace Stanbury's possessions, a single leather-covered trunk, arrived by carrier's wagon. He did not have much in addition to the portmanteau he had brought with him. Good! He must mean to stay only another month or two. But when she asked, he replied that his decision would depend upon the manor's finances and the difficulty of finding a bailiff and a chaperon for Rose and Ory, dashing her hope he would return to London and leave them on their own.

Chapter 3

Allan discussed with Chappell the daunting list of repairs necessary before the Three Greyhounds could be offered for lease or as lodgings. Seeing Allan's expression, the former coachman said, "There's plenty of 'em I could do easy enough. Augustus, Lord Passevant, paid me well for taking care of the place. I'd have done more to fix things, but I'd have needed supplies, and it wasn't thought needful to make improvements, only to fix enough to keep the building from falling down. I wouldn't charge you for my work."

Chappell feared he and his wife would lose their employment and home if Allan leased the inn to someone, and he might be correct. A lessor might require only the most minimal repairs, which would be less expensive. The former coachman probably hoped Allan would turn it into a lodging house which would need their services, hence his willingness to do some of the work.

"I learned some carpentry from my foster father's hired man." Raymond Willis could only afford a cottage with a few acres and servants because Augustus, Lord Passevant, had settled money on his former tutor to bring Allan up. "Some of these things would not be beyond my abilities." He tapped the list. "I'd hire men to repair the roof and to sweep and repair the chimneys."

"And a glazier for the windowpanes that are broke,"

Chappell pointed out. "Mr. Everard, an idea I had that's not about repairs, is, if it's let out as rooms, you could maybe rent out the stabling as well. That's terrible high in town."

A second gate led into the stable yard from the alley on one side of the inn, as well as the one from the courtyard. When Chappell told him how much it cost to keep a horse in London, Allan blinked. New to the city and never having owned a mount, the cost of stabling had not crossed his mind. "A very good notion, Chappell. Thank you."

In the end, no single matter influenced his decision. The possibility of doing some of the work without extra expense, the additional income from stabling, and the wish to keep the Chappells employed all played a part.

"I think I may as well live here as I will be helping with the work. 'Twill be cheaper than the room I'm renting now even if I must buy some furnishings."

"There's a few bits and pieces left behind. It's only to move them to one of the rooms. I don't reckon you'd need more than a new mattress."

And so it was settled. He gave his landlady notice the same day.

****

In his oldest breeches and shirt, the sleeves rolled up to his elbows, Allan wiped the sweat from his brow. His hair was straggling free of his hair ribbon, and he took a moment to retie it. The past week had exercised muscles unused since leaving Willis's home to work for Salt. The morning's project was completed. As he could not begin the next task until Chappell returned from the ironmonger's with some needed hardware, he would investigate his bedchamber's second door.

Allan had chosen one of the larger rooms for his own because it contained a tester bed too big for anyone to bother stealing. With the new mattress, a table and chair, and a wash stand, the chamber was as comfortable as his former lodging and more private. He had paid no attention to a door in one of the side walls during his initial tour, and on his first day of residence, Allan was too tired to investigate after helping Chappell saw boards to replace rotting stair steps and nail them in place. The next day he attempted to open the door only to find it locked. None of the inn's keys would open it, and as he had no time and little curiosity, had let the matter go.

The door to the west of his own along the gallery gave access to a much smaller apartment, likely meant for a body servant traveling with the lady or gentleman who would have occupied the one he now used. To his surprise, it had no second door.

Or did it? A tall, crudely made clothespress stood where the connecting door should be, a mystery solved. The door must have been blocked to make another space to be rented. Shoving the press toward the exterior wall would give the little chamber access to his own, though he supposed he would have to get a locksmith in to replace the lock if a key could not be made. The smaller room could serve as his office.

He pushed the end of the cabinet which creaked and barely shifted before refusing to move farther. Putting all his strength into another attempt to move it, he might as well have pushed a mountain. He could take it apart, of course. But the curst thing would be useful if he continued to live here and putting it back together would be more work than it was worth.

He strode to the window, opened it to let in whatever

breeze might be available, and gazed out at the alley that ran along the south side of the inn. Distant cries from a woman selling fish door to door and another of "Fresh 'spargus" carried to his ears. Not a bad neighborhood. The inn might still be thriving if not for mismanagement. The last owner, elderly and too fond of gin, sometimes forgot to record the rents he collected when he remembered to collect them.

When he turned back to his task, sunlight fell on the end of the clothespress. The bottom was wedged against a floorboard that sat higher than the others. So much trouble over a little cause but easily mended.

The board was near half an inch higher at the end, and its nails were still in place. He gave the cabinet a shove back before leaning with both hands on the protruding edge. That failed to bring it level. Neither did a sharp tap with a hammer fetched from the tool chest. If it would not go down, the board must come up. He pressed his fingers against the raised edge. If it would come up a bit farther when he pulled, he would use the crow. Wasn't that what carpenters used to pry things loose? The board came up so suddenly he fell on his backside. The nails on the raised end had been cut off almost level with the bottom of the plank. With his fingers under it near the other end, another jerk freed the board.

A box was wedged in the cavity between the floor and the ceiling of the room below. The lid had not quite closed, preventing the floorboard from seating. His first thought was that of the boy he had once been: *a pirate's hoard*. It would be empty, of course. He enjoyed the idea anyway as he lifted the casket out.

The gathered mouth of a leather bag had been caught

under the lid, preventing it from closing, which prevented the end of the floor board from lying level. Probably whatever was inside the pouch was worthless, a servant's trumpery belongings too important to him to be left where someone might steal them.

Frowning, he hefted the bag's weight. The contents were lumpy and shifted, the sound and feel of them suggesting metal. The leather thong that should have been drawn tight was loose, suggesting the pouch had been put away quickly and carelessly. He wanted to open the mouth wider and examine whatever it was. He resisted the impulse.

Allan pulled the strings tight, stuffed the bag into the box, and set it back in the hole. Then he carefully replaced the floorboard. He would put off seeing what he had unexpectedly inherited until his day's labor was done, anticipating the revelation as if 'twere a sweetmeat after dinner.

At supper, he told Chappell and his wife he had discovered the adjoining room but not about what he'd found.

"Ay, those big corner rooms all have little chambers for a maid or manservant, I expect. For old ladies or men who might need help in the middle of the night. Didn't occur to me you didn't know and I didn't think of the door being behind the press or I'd 'a mentioned it. Right sorry about that, Mr. Everard."

"No need to apologize. We were looking for things that needed repair."

Later Allan retrieved the pouch, worked the thong loose, and carefully poured the contents onto a handkerchief spread on the rickety little table he used as a desk. The long summer evening's light illuminated glowing red, green, and blue, dazzling him. With finicking care, he separated the pile into its components.

Rings, necklets, earbobs, brooches, and bracelets, set with gems or great, misshapen pearls, lay before him with a double handful of English, French, and Spanish gold coins. He knew little of jewelry, but these pieces did not look like those ladies wore currently and the pouch's dry, stiff leather hinted at its age. The coins were old, none later than 1638. A pirate's hoard, indeed.

Had this been left by his father to increase the value of the property? No. Unlikely for many reasons. Allan might have immediately sold the property, which would be valuable enough for its land. Even if he kept it, he might never have found the bag.

Then there was the age of the leather and his father's nature. The baron's sister had told someone when neither was aware of a listener, "Augustus has no more backbone than a hop vine while my sister-in-law has enough for the Life Guards." He could not imagine the baron coming to a place like this without at least one or two attendants or companions, let alone prying up a board to leave the bag. And where would he have got the jewelry and coins without leaving a trail in the account books or diverting Passevant family heirlooms?

Amazing enough he had been able to give Allan the inn. But then, no one could have kept him from doing so, as long as they did not learn of it. In fact, his lordship had managed not only to avoid recriminations and shouting in his lifetime, but for his legitimate son, daughters, and widow not to learn of it even after his death, protecting Allan from the same and worse: legal action.

The gift of the inn had been generous. The unexpected treasure trove made it a fortune if he could find a way to conceal his windfall. Now he was gone, he was dismissed from the family's minds as he had been dismissed from his position and from Passevant lands. Yet if it came to their ears he was prospering, they might wonder. He had no intention of setting himself up as a gentleman, so how would anyone in their circle come to know of his situation here? He doubted Attorney Hart would speak of it. He had obeyed the late baron's instructions regarding Allan and was unlikely to betray that trust even though his loyalty now was to the current baron. Besides, if Hart revealed he had sent Allan to Peter Wilde on the late baron's instructions, the Passevants would blame him.

He sat pondering while the sky turned to rose and gold before he returned his treasure to the pouch. When he placed the bag in the box, however, he discovered a folded sheet of paper in the bottom. Written in an old-fashioned hand, the letter was unfinished, with no date and no signature and half the page blank.

Madam,

I thank you again for your kindness to me, your unworthy and unfortunate grandson. With what you have given me, I shall survive until it may be safe to return, which I pray will not be too long delayed. I go now to arrange passage on the first ship to sail for some more hospitable land. Once I know what my destination is to be and set foot upon the vessel, I will have Seth deliver this to you. He has no need to depart these shores and no wish to do so.

What had become of the writer and of Seth? Whatever their fate, there was no use speculating. They were long gone.

In the pocketbook he used to note repairs made, their

cost, and things to do, he added: *See Peter Wilde*. Who better to give advice than his own man of business?

"Bless me!" was Wilde's first comment on hearing of the discovery. His second was "I perceive your difficulty. Men inherit from relatives or earn a fortune in some commercial endeavor or even win one at cards or dice. Those are all understood sources of wealth. Money that appears from nowhere is questionable and leads to talk."

"I do not plan to figure in the beau monde," Allan said. "Bastards are not welcome unless their fathers are royal. Mayhap a duke or marquess's by-blow might be accepted if acknowledged. Why attract unwelcome attention by trying to shoulder my way into society?"

"First we need to determine your treasure's value, then it can be sold and the profits invested."

"How can I do so? Word of it must not reach Lord Passevant. Would a jeweler be able to resist wondering where I had got such a collection of antiques?"

"A jeweler, one patronized by society, could afford your unexpected treasure," Wilde remarked, "but he would be a bad choice precisely because he deals with the upper classes."

"Then how can I dispose of my windfall?"

"There is a dealer in precious stones who may be interested. If he buys them, it's likely the gems would be recut as these are of a very old style. The settings would be melted down and newer ones made."

"Is he trustworthy?"

"I believe so. To be certain, I suggest using Solomon de Toledo as an intermediary. He's a moneylender, and I would trust him with my money. I have frequently sent clients to him, and they have benefitted from his advice, whether he lent them money or not. The importer is his brother, and I believe would treat you fairly anyway."

****

"You have a valuable collection here, though most of the stones could be better cut." Samuel de Toledo peered at the sapphire brooch with a pendant featuring a cherub, its torso formed by a baroque pearl. "I'll be happy to buy the lot from you, if Solomon will lend me a bit." He grinned at the fourth man in the room.

"Of course, little brother."

Then it was merely a question of details: Solomon's cheque made out to Samuel and Samuel's made out to Peter Wilde, who would invest the money on Allan's behalf. Bows all around; Samuel and Wilde made the deposits and returned. Allan handed over the jewelry. After a celebratory glass of claret and more bows, Samuel and his brother departed. Solomon and his hulking bodyguard, who was idling out on the street, would see the gem merchant safely home.

Allan breathed a sigh of relief.

"Have you decided what to do with your inn?"

"I don't want to sell it." To explain a decision that was less practical than emotional, he decided on the truth. "It's not a manor in the country, but it's still property and can't vanish the way money can."

"I'm in favor of property ownership, myself," Wilde agreed.

Chapter 4

Their cousin had a talent Ory found fascinating: a wonderful ability to sketch. Oriana loved to draw and was more accomplished than expected of a young lady, but she was not satisfied, never having had lessons. Rose had no talent at all and could not help her improve. One evening in the parlor after supper, Horace bent over a lap desk, glancing occasionally at Ory, who was embroidering a pair of pockets. Rose, passing his chair, saw the drawing and exclaimed, "Cousin, you have captured my sister to the life!"

He looked up at her briefly. "Yes, I think I have." Tardily he added, "Thank you."

"Oh, are you drawing me?" Ory stopped in mid-stitch. "May I see?"

"I suppose so." He rose and displayed the sheet.

She squealed with delight. *She is still so young*, Rose thought, and made a mental note to remind her young ladies did not squeal.

"I wish I could draw like that, Cousin Horace. Could you, would you, give me lessons?"

"If you wish." While he did not sound enthusiastic, he did smile slightly.

Perhaps this might be a way of becoming better acquainted with their guardian. "Do you paint, too? Would you paint a portrait of Oriana to hang with the pictures of our mother and father and Stanbury grandparents?"

A little pause: then he replied, "My father did not approve of boys wasting their time in such feminine pursuits. I taught myself to draw, but the use of paints is beyond me. I will do another more formal sketch, if that would suffice."

She agreed, pleased to think they had made some progress in breaking through his reserve. He began Ory's lessons the next day. He proved an excellent instructor, always with an encouraging word for her sister's efforts.

Stanbury proved to have a fine tenor voice when Rose heard it for the first time several Sundays after his arrival. Perhaps he had needed to become accustomed to the hymns. What had they sung in his previous parish? Or had his branch of the family belonged to some nonconforming sect rather than the Church of England? If so, it would explain why he had not attended university as Rose had guessed from his reply to a neighbor's jocular comment that he supposed Stanbury was a Cambridge man. He had evaded the implied question by inquiring, "Is it my waistcoat makes you think so?" This made the fellow laugh. Then Stanbury asked if there were a local hunt, which was surprising as he was not an accomplished rider. Take part in a fox hunt? He'd be off at the first fence or hedge. Perhaps he expected to improve with practice, or perhaps he knew Mr. Smythe was hunting mad and would forget his curiosity about Stanbury's university.

The first intimation of real changes in their lives came while he was out one day. He had not mentioned his destination. He might be unused to having anyone to apprise of his comings and goings.

Rose went to the study to replenish her escritoire's

supply of paper, intending to write to the head of the St. Osyth's ladies' charitable committee, asking what clothing was most needed for the poor, as she and Oriana could do some sewing while in first mourning. The study door was locked. She asked Stanbury about it later.

"Of course I keep it secured in my absence. The household money is kept there. Also I have not yet finished with the ledgers and do not care to have my notes disturbed."

"Father never thought it necessary to lock the door," she observed.

Her cousin raised his thin eyebrows. "You will forgive me, I hope, for pointing out that the late Mr. Stanbury was not always as careful as he should have been."

This was not quite fair. The bills were always paid promptly despite Papa's dislike of what he called "fiddling paperwork."

But on one occasion when Ory burst into the study without knocking to relate that a fox had got into the chickens' pen and carried one off, she found him going through a document box. "Why would Cousin Horace bother with those old papers? They can't be of any importance. I never saw Papa so much as open it."

Neither had Rose. Several of the boxes had rested ignored on the lower level of the shelves that filled one wall.

"He may feel he has to, in order to be completely informed about the manor and our tenants," Rose said fairly. So serious a man, and involved in business, too, might well be conscientious. Yet she could not respect him for it; somehow it seemed intrusive.

Ory accepted her suggestion without hesitation.

A few days later, Stanbury appeared suddenly in the door to the family parlor while an elderly widow was paying a call on Rose. He entered and was civil when Rose introduced Mistress Francis, but Rose suspected he had heard at least part of her friend's statement, "I'm sure you will soon get used to each other's ways and then be more at ease." She hoped he had not heard her own complaint that elicited that advice.

The following Sunday, Stanbury hurried them into their coach after the service. Like most of the congregation, they had usually lingered to chat with friends and exchange news with those they had not seen since the previous week. They did not learn whether the blacksmith's daughter had given birth yet, or whether the old man who tended the graveyard and dug the graves had benefitted from a new remedy for his rheumatism. Cousin Horace had always seemed uncomfortable in the informal gatherings: polite but distant. He must have decided to avoid the encounters. Oriana thought him shy with strangers. Rose suspected he preferred not to let anyone know him well.

At supper one evening Rose happened to remark, "You are a better correspondent than most gentlemen, Cousin." He received a surprising number of letters, far more than her father had and wrote an almost equal number of replies as Rose knew from their groom who took them to the receiving office in High Stanbury.

By a certain tightening around his mouth, he did not appreciate the comment. She should have known better. She would not pry into a casual acquaintance's or stranger's affairs, but after all he was a family member…even if he was still almost unknown to them.

"I have some investments, Rosabel, but financial

dealings are no concern of a lady. I am also attempting to find a good bailiff and a female to act as your chaperon," he went on after a hesitation.

She had heard that men disliked having their judgement questioned by females. Her father's free and easy manners had not accustomed her to the reality. Even a casual observation was enough to annoy their cousin.

Oriana liked him, grateful for the drawing lessons. His casual compliments about the improvement in her sketches, or her grace or her tiny stitching made her inclined to forgive or excuse much. For that reason, Rose tried not to dislike him.

Ory said, "He must know best," when he decided based on advice from someone—unspecified—they should not attend the ladies' charitable committee meetings or pay visits to neighbors and tenants while in mourning. He did not forbid them to receive callers, but after Mistress Francis, there were no further visits.

"He's been so kind to teach me to draw correctly, Rose, when he has so much to do with the estate. You know my drawings are much improved."

"They are indeed. Your portrait of Pansy was a very good representation. Her eyes were just where they should be." This earned a giggle, as in one of her earlier attempts Pansy's eyes appeared to be on the same side of her head, which would be unusual for a horse.

Oriana's elfin smile faded. "Rose, if only you did not argue with Cousin Horace, we could all go along comfortably. You know how the parson praises gentle, modest women."

"I don't argue with him. I have only tried to keep him from making mistakes, as he is not familiar with managing country property and tenants." Horace

Stanbury was still ignorant of those things because he did not listen to her tactfully worded suggestions.

"Men do not care to be corrected by females," her sister pointed out. She sounded exactly like a certain matron of their acquaintance who was famous for her pronouncements.

But when Stanbury decided to sell their horses, apart from the coach horses and a hack for his own use, Ory was moved to protest mildly, "But how will Rose and I pay visits, when it is suitable for us to do so, Cousin?"

"In the coach, of course, like the young ladies you are. To be jauntering around the countryside on horseback is not at all the thing. Surely you would not pay calls on our neighbors in your riding habit."

His objection to visiting in riding dress made no sense. They and the neighboring ladies all did so unless they were too old or infirm to make riding easy. Even Mistress Ogilvy, a grandmother six times over, rode.

If Rose thought this would significantly shake her sister's opinion of the man, she was mistaken. Later, when they were alone in Rose's bedchamber, Ory sighed, "I wish it had not been necessary to sell our horses. I will miss riding and Pansy especially. But we must make the sacrifice if there are debts. At least I have my watercolor of her for a remembrance."

There had been no debts before their cousin took over, and Rose was sure he had not incurred any, or not enough to require selling their riding horses. He turned off the stable boy and second groom, pointing out that with only three horses, the remaining groom could manage the little work the boy did, and if he did not choose to do so, why, there were plenty of men glad to get a place as a stable hand.

No: Cousin Horace's purpose had been to make it difficult for either of them to visit friends or the village. While he claimed they might make calls upon friends in the carriage once their first mourning was over, her request to be taken to the mercer to buy material for a pair of new gowns for Ory whose old ones were now too short and tight in the bosom, was refused. She could lengthen them, but adding gussets in the bodice would be far more difficult. She did not care to mention that problem to Horace.

"I fear one of the horses is lame in his off foreleg. However, if you will tell me how much fabric you need, I will ride in to get it."

Apparently he had a good eye for such things as he returned with a pale rose cambric and a blue muslin, with ribbons to match both. Oriana blushed with pleasure. The colors were unsuitable for mourning, not that anyone outside the household was likely to see her. Rose said nothing, however, deciding to pursue a policy of appeasement. Her sister might still suspect she had not been won over, as Rose was not normally docile. If so, Ory was able to ignore it. Perhaps she also feared that their respective opinions of Stanbury would drive a wedge between them.

As they drank tea in the drawing room after supper one evening, Horace announced he had completed his examination of the household and tenant ledgers.

"I fear more economies will be necessary as the accounts are not in as good order as they should be." He took a sip of tea.

She knew this to be untrue. She had written the checks for their suppliers or paid the smaller local accounts in coin ever since her mother's death, a task

Papa tended to put off because he always found something more interesting to do.

"The rent from most of the tenancies is low, with the amounts being fixed for decades at a time by your grandfather and continued by your father. It barely covers your living expenses. There is nothing put away to pay for repairs to this house or the tenants' cottages or any other improvements."

Reluctantly she admitted to herself there was never much left over although somehow her papa had managed to scrape up enough coin for maintenance. But the occasional leaks in the roof were repaired piecemeal. If it needed to be replaced, or if the stable or barn burned, or a tenant's house suffered serious damage…*It hasn't happened so far and maybe never will.*

"Your pin money will have to be reduced. Worse, and I dislike telling you this, you have no dowries."

"But my mother often spoke of the money set aside so we could make good marriages. What happened to it?"

His vexation told Rose he did not appreciate her question, which sounded accusing even in her own ears.

He answered anyway. "Two thousand pounds were set aside before your birth to provide dowries for whatever daughters were born. Your grandfather's means were comparatively modest.

Because he established that annuity for Horace, Rose reflected, as their cousin went on, "There would have been a little growth from interest, and it was expected by both your grandfathers that your father would add to it from the manor's profits as he could. The year before you were born, your father took an opportunity to double or triple the principal. The 'South

Sea Bubble' investment scheme, as it was called, burst soon after your birth. The money was lost."

Even Rose had heard talk of the financial disaster that had ruined so many and led to the suicides of some.

"However, Oriana at least will not need her dowry for several years yet, and by then I may have worked out a solution to the problem."

The following day he turned off Bray, the butler. Bray's eyes shone with tears when he told Rose. He would have worked another ten years, he told her, and was sorry to leave them. She and Ory felt as though they were losing a family member. Bray was almost like another grandfather.

Griggs, their father's valet, had been kept on while he sought other employment, their cousin having declined his services. Horace gave the men references, though they were short and lacking in warmth. Rose wrote characters for both explaining that the new heir had not had time to form a true opinion of their services. She did not mention this to either Horace or Ory.

Papa had specified in his will that longtime servants should be pensioned when they were ready to retire, so Rose also wrote to Brand to make sure they received their pensions, as at their ages it might be difficult to find positions. Thank God there was money available for that, at least.

She had not thought when writing the letter that the action must come to Horace Stanbury's attention sooner or later. He never did speak to her about it or show any awareness of the pensions being paid.

But when Rose was steeling herself to inquire about their as yet unpaid pin money after the next quarter day, he summoned both girls to the study and announced that yet more economies were necessary. He had transferred their legal work to his own London attorney to save money. The second housemaid and the kitchen maid must also go. They were unnecessary when the family could not entertain during mourning. Rose pointed out they did need edible meals.

"Then I suggest you and your sister help the cook. 'Twill be good training for marriage." Her cousin dipped his quill in the standish and resumed penning a letter.

Oriana was able to shrug off the loss of help in the stable but not the reduction in the house servants. The latter dented Cousin Horace's halo when she discovered that she and Rose would actually have to labor in the kitchen and take on the dismissed housemaid's duties.

There was no help for it, Rose knew after speaking with Cook. Mistress Howard, learning that she was losing her helper, apologized and said she would be seeking a new position. "Jed Turner will hire me to cook at the Blue Boar. Not as good as work in a gentleman's house, but I'll have help and mayhap I can make his bill of fare one to be proud of."

"I will assist you."

"You, ma'am? A lady can't do kitchen work."

"I must, rather than lose you. Judging by his choice of the new stable hand, 'tis unlikely my cousin would employ a competent cook." Jem, their remaining groom, had given his notice and been replaced. They now had a clumsy dolt caring for the horses at lower wages, their coachman doing his best to train the fellow.

The woman puffed out a breath. "That bunglesome lad was never next or nigh a horse before he came here, if I'm any judge." The cook twisted the corner of her apron, then dabbed at her eyes with it. "I wouldn't like to leave you in the lurch…"

"I'll do what I must." With a faint smile, she repeated what Stanbury had told her. "Experience of cooking will prepare me for marriage."

"Ay! And that's what you should do, Mistress Rose, and escape from this place."

She had thought of it. She was near one-and-twenty and then could marry without her cousin's consent, but who? She had attracted no gentleman in the neighborhood. Her features were even and her complexion clear (if somewhat brown because she would forget to put on her hat before going out of the house), but she did not have the inner glow that prompted people to remark on Oriana's angelic beauty. There was a widower or two in the neighborhood who might marry her for her common sense and breeding years, and a merchant in comfortable circumstances who would welcome a connection with a wife of good family. Showing her interest in any of the men would be difficult when they did not linger after church and could not attend social events. Still, one of her friends, Mistress Francis, perhaps, could drop a hint to prepare the ground for a marriage as soon as she was able to do so.

Then her sister could live with them. *If our cousin permits it. Ay, there's the rub.* Would he? He might be glad to return to London and not have to bother with them. She feared not. Cousin Horace liked to be in control. She suspected too that his reason for dismissing so many of the servants had been that he did not trust them because they took Rose's part.

To be sure of securing Oriana's guardianship, she would have to snare a rich man, preferably with a title, who would be willing to go to law to overturn Horace's guardianship. She knew a few aristocrats, but none was a likely prospect. Even if one had been, she would not dare write, as all letters must now be given to her cousin to be taken to the receiving office by his groom.

"I cannot marry unless I can take Oriana with me." She could not bear to leave Ory with their guardian although Stanbury was invariably pleasant to her if not to Rose.

"You'd think a gentleman as inherited property and has no wife wouldn't want to be responsible for a young girl. I know for a fact a guardian needn't have the child with him. My sister works for a lady as has her son and little girl living with her, and the guardian lives two counties away and only sees them once a year."

"Do you think Mr. Stanbury would agree to let my sister live elsewhere?"

"I don't rightly think it," the cook admitted. "He has odd humors, your cousin, if I may make so bold, and likes to be master."

Chapter 5

Oriana surprised her. On their mother's death, Rose had made a cosset-lamb of her. Now she was fourteen, blonde, lovely, fragile in appearance, and rather timid. Perhaps Rose's anxious care for her was responsible; nothing had ever been expected of the child except to learn her lessons. The idea of Oriana sweeping or dusting was ludicrous.

But when Rose mentioned she would do the kitchen maid's work and help the housemaid as needed, Oriana protested she could do one or the other herself. By tacit agreement, Cook and Rose assigned her to help the housemaid with the lighter tasks. They must somehow manage until...the thought stuttered to a halt. Until what? She and Oriana must simply endure for the time being, but they could not go on as they were indefinitely. Something would have to change.

Stanbury must notice how the standard of housekeeping had declined. The remaining housemaid laid the fires, emptied and cleaned the chamber pots, and carried hot water up to Rose's and Ory's chambers and then to Stanbury's in time for him to wash and shave. Rose rose at five to assist Mistress Howard, then scrubbed, collected Stanbury's and their own laundry, and returned to the kitchen to help prepare for dinner and supper. The housemaid and Rose together would turn and air the mattresses when necessary. Oriana dusted, swept, and tidied all the rooms they used: parlor, dining room, drawing room, passages, and bedchambers. No one was permitted to do the study except in Horace's presence—and then he insisted the remaining maid do it.

Rose, like her sister, might have assumed Stanbury was simply unused to managing a household. He probably lived in lodgings in London. He might have been concerned about the manor's finances on his first arrival, but he had admitted the rents covered their living expenses even if there was little to fall back upon if some major expense arose.

Brand thought him comfortably situated, and while Horace dressed plainly, the maid reported he had a coat heavily embroidered on the front edges, cuffs, and pocket flaps and brocade waistcoats. They sounded like the clothing of a wealthy man. Now that Stanbury Manor was his, he could afford to pay for repairs. Or could he? Gentlemen did not always pay their bills promptly or sometimes at all. Living on credit would account for his clothing.

In that case, perhaps a saving of fifty or sixty pounds a year in wages might really be necessary.

****

Stanbury had no manservant, and yet his clothing continued to be well maintained and his shoes and boots polished. Had he not grown up in a gentleman's house with someone to care for his clothing? Or had his family's straitened means left him accustomed to caring for his own, except for his shirts, neckcloths, and handkerchiefs, which were laundered by the local washerwoman each week, and ironed by the maid?

Rose's curiosity about their odd cousin turned to suspicion while she changed his bed linen one morning.

Hurrying to finish that task and get to the scullery, Rose dropped one of the candles she had brought to replace those burned down to stubs in the bedroom. *Oh, pshaw.* With the natural perversity of things, it rolled under the bed. She replaced the others, added the old ends to her basket of brushes and cleaning rags, and lowered herself to her hands and knees.

Light from the windows made it just possible to see the pale cylinder which had come to rest against some kind of box. Her cousin's? He could have had it stored in the attic with the other luggage, unless it held something he needed to keep by him. If so, one would think it more convenient to keep it in the dressing room rather than pushed so far under the bed. She reached for the candle and felt something else under her fingers. She stopped, hardly breathing.

The object lay behind the candle. Gently, using her fingertips, she rolled the candle toward her. Once it was out of the way, she saw a ring a few inches from the left corner of the box. Without questioning why she was doing so, she studied the ring's position before drawing it out from under the bed. By its weight, the heavy band was gold. The pink stone glowed in a beam of sunlight when she held it up.

Some signet rings were engraved with the wearer's coat of arms, others with initials or another pleasing design, or perhaps a classical subject like a Roman god. This pretty stretching cat was an unusual subject for a signet. If Rose had misplaced such a thing, she would have informed the whole house. Then again, if she kept it put away and seldom wore it, she might not have noticed it was gone. She had never seen Stanbury wear the ring and if he did not wear it, how had it come to rest under the bed?

Transfixed, she stared at it. How, indeed? A rabbit or other small creature might freeze in just the same way on sensing a predator nearby. Had some premonition warned her to make certain of the ring's position before she removed it? The explanation of its presence under the bed might have come from a novel, a class of literature of which she was fond, though she was not fanciful as a rule. Her first thought, that it was a trap to catch a searcher, struck her as farfetched until she remembered the locked study, the unnecessary dismissals of servants, and half a dozen other peculiarities in Stanbury's behavior.

If it were moved, Stanbury would know someone had looked under the bed. She gave an irritable click of her tongue. Had he forgotten a maid would clean under the bed at least occasionally? Mayhap a man might not think of how and where a servant cleaned. Then again, if a maid had found it (rather than herself) she would have set it on the bedside stand or dresser, and likely have told the housekeeper or butler of its presence. Rose replaced it as near as possible to its original position.

She could no longer pretend away her doubts about her cousin. There were two neighbors within easy walking distance for a country-bred lady. Rose could make her visits over two or more days. She would contrive to visit one of them somehow after dinner at one and before helping with preparations for supper. The latter was not an elaborate meal even before her father's death. Soup if the weather were cool, leftovers from dinner, perhaps barley gruel with currants, egg yolks, white wine, and cream, salmagundi, or a fricassee of eggs.

Their situation was now so troubling to her that she must confide in someone outside their own household. She had to let someone know their situation and to confirm that her suspicions struck others as justified.

****

The Hargreaves were a middle-aged couple whose youngest daughter had been Rose's good friend before she married and moved away. Her mother exclaimed over Rose's work-roughened hands and recommended a soothing salve. Her father pointed out that they were minors, and their cousin was their guardian. They must be good, patient girls and obey him. Somehow their conduct had offended their relative, who was of a stricter disposition than their late papa. Anyone who encouraged them to defy their appointed guardian, Mr. Hargreaves said sternly, would be at fault. He had no doubt Mr. Horace Stanbury knew what was best for his wards, and he was now the head of their family as well.

Rose saw nothing to be gained by explaining they had been patient and tried to propitiate Stanbury and thanked her friend's father for his advice. Mistress Hargreaves encouraged her to visit often.

"I will try, but I may not be able to get away from my duties at home, with so many of the servants dismissed, and our horses sold."

This finally impressed Hargreaves. "What, all of them?

"Our butler, my father's valet, the under-housemaid, the kitchen maid, the second groom, and the stable lad. The remaining groom gave notice, and now we have one who is not very skillful," she ended tactfully.

Hargreaves tutted and said, "I meant the horses, Rosabel," as his wife exclaimed, "But how are you managing with so few servants?"

"Oriana does the light cleaning, and I do the under-housemaid's work and help Cook."

"Intolerable!"

After a frowning pause, her husband said, "I am sure Mr. Stanbury has a good reason. We met him at church and found him well-conducted and sensible, if somewhat puritanical. Depend upon it, he will moderate his treatment when he has settled into his new position."

Rose took her leave soon after.

The following day, Mistress Ruth Francis was appalled at their changed situation.

"My dear Rose, he must be forced to such drastic shifts. I hardly like to suggest this, but is it possible your father had debts you did not know of? Some men do gamble either at cards or dice or in their investments. You might not be aware of those in spite of paying the household bills."

"I help—helped—with the estate ledger, too, the last few years. His sight was not as keen as when he was younger, and he found it tiresome to have to squint, so I made the entries and totaled them. I never saw anything in that account book or in correspondence from the bank to suggest there were debts." She feared her face had flushed at her evasive response. The tenants' rents had not increased in years, although she had heard of other estates raising rents. Undeniably her father had lost the dower monies: Horace shown her the documents.

"Oh, dear. Living with a difficult relative is a trial." Mistress Francis sat pondering.

Rose had intended to be more forthcoming with Ruth Francis, who was almost like a grandmother to her, or what she supposed a grandmother must be, though she had none of her own. She lacked even an aunt except her uncle Milton's wife whom she had met only once or twice.

In her visit to the Hargreaves, she had not felt able to talk of her more nebulous suspicions of her cousin: the signet ring perhaps used as a snare, the instinct that their secretive cousin was keeping them away from their neighbors and friends.

The widow went on slowly. "He was perfectly gentlemanly that day I called upon you and he presents himself well at church. He is elegant, his manners are good, and he speaks very feelingly of his concern for your welfare. I did think it strange he requested that no one trouble you with calls as Oriana is still distraught over your father's death."

"She misses Papa as I do, but she has not gone into a decline nor is she subject to the vapors. I don't know why Cousin Horace has cut us off from our friends and neighbors." And from anyone who might aid them.

"From one or two things I have been told—is it not shocking how everything is gossiped about in a village? One would think we have nothing better to do—he is seldom met with, and if he has paid a call on anyone except our dear vicar, I have not heard of it." She paused before making an observation that impressed itself upon Rose. "His conduct toward you may result from lack of confidence. No one else seems to have noticed, but there is something in his speech which makes me wonder if his origins are quite humble. As if his branch of the family had declined into tradesmen. You may not recall that my husband made a hobbyhorse of studying dialects and even wrote essays on the subject which were collected into a book." She smiled apologetically.

"I do remember." In spite of her worry, Rose laughed a little at the memory from happier times. "He amused us by mimicking different kinds speech, like the old chapman who used to come through several times a year, and the Scot who stayed at the inn once."

"Fancy your recalling that, when he died when you were only eleven or twelve." They both laughed then, envisioning Mr. Francis hunching over as if under the weight of a pack, imitating the foreign peddler with his pins and needles and French lace and baubles and gauds of all sorts. "What a wag my husband was. I learned a great deal about our English dialects from listening to him. Something in Mr. Stanbury's speech gives me to believe your cousin grew up in Lancashire, perhaps in Liverpool. I think if Mr. Stanbury's branch of the family has declined into tradesmen, he may feel unsure in his new position and try to make up for it by high-handedness."

"A queer-tempered man, our cook calls him," Rose said, and they both laughed.

This visit left Rose wondering. Horace Stanbury had always seemed different from the other gentlemen she knew, whether they were old or young, county gentry or the occasional London visitor come to rusticate for a month or two. The old lady's suggestion would explain some of his strangeness. If he had prospered in his trade, perhaps he could afford to dress richly and as a successful merchant or tradesman, he might well worry about the manor's expenses. Yet his secretiveness seemed excessive even if he wanted to conceal an ungentlemanly connection to trade.

****

Despite mourning her father, Rose might have

enjoyed spring as she usually did if she were not so tired and if her sister had not grown so quiet. No doubt her melancholy resulted from her new household duties as she now took art instruction from Stanbury only occasionally rather than every day. She had vegetables to gather for Cook or her regular light cleaning to do, or stockings to wash, those not being given to the laundrywoman who came once a week to boil the dirty clothes. In the evenings after supper she had little to say, concentrating on mending. She disliked such activities as much as she loved drawing, causing Rose to wonder and worry at the alteration in her behavior.

She did not immediately ask Ory what was wrong, first telling herself that the child was merely worn down by her labors. Then Rose thought she would wait until Horace rode out, for if he were anywhere in the house, they might be overheard. Stanbury could move as silently as any cat, appearing without warning. Finally she admitted to herself she was afraid to ask Oriana what was wrong. After putting it off another day, she followed her sister to her room when they went upstairs to bed, on the pretext they should consider making themselves plain gowns. "I believe I recall some lengths of dowlas in the attic. That would spare our better clothing. Come, let me take your measurements before you retire."

"It's so coarse, and when are we to have time to cut and sew them?" Ory complained as Rose closed the door behind them. Even Horace would not enter their bedchambers unannounced.

"We won't, of course. But discussing it made a convenient excuse for my not going directly to my own room in case our cousin was paying attention." He was almost always watching them as if he did not trust them any more than Rose trusted him. "Now pray tell me what is wrong, dear, for something is." She perched on the edge of the bed and her sister sat beside her.

Ory's gaze fixed on her lap while she began to pick at a rough place on one nail.

"Ory?"

"Rose, I truly thought Cousin Horace would deal better with you when you stopped questioning his decisions. I told him I wished he would be reconciled with you and not treat me better than you."

"I can't imagine he was pleased about that."

"He only laughed and swore he held no grudge and would be happy to give you drawing lessons too, if you wished."

"I don't resent his giving you drawing lessons and complimenting you on your talent. I have no interest in sketching."

"He's given me things, Rose. It's not fair I should get a gift if he doesn't give you anything."

"He bought the dress lengths for you because I told him you needed new gowns as you were growing."

"He gave me some salve for my hands, and some lovely soap, much nicer than what we buy in the village, too. He said it was important to keep my hands and skin pretty and white."

"It is." Rose avoided glancing at her own work-roughened hands. "We won't always be drudging."

"N-o-o-o."

The word might have been squeezed out of a prisoner on the rack. Rose reflected she was become foolishly fanciful.

"He says he plans a fine marriage for me, and so I would not have to work around the house much longer.

He told me not to mention it to you as nothing is settled yet."

"You are too young to marry." Not in law, perhaps, with a parent or guardian's permission, but she was hardly beyond childhood.

Ory ignored her reassurance, such as it was. "Cousin Horace says things that—oh, I don't know how to explain. They're strange, that's all. Besides, I don't want to marry yet. I want to go to London after our mourning is ended and meet gentlemen there. So I said as you are older, you should marry first."

"Thank you, Ory, dear." Not likely when she could not leave Ory alone with Horace.

Her sister failed to notice her ironical tone. "He means to arrange something for you, too, though it might take a little longer." She blushed and studied her nails assiduously.

Probably because Stanbury had pointed out Rose was nearly on the shelf and besides, only passably pretty, as well as being a managing female. She could hear him saying it. *A marriage arranged by Horace Stanbury?* She hardly knew whether to laugh or cry.

"I will think of something to prevent your being married soon." They would have some warning of an impending betrothal when the possible suitor came to meet Oriana. "I would speak to him about this, but as we know, he does not take advice from females."

"And he would know I had told you, when he swore me to secrecy. It was to be a surprise for you, he said," Ory added in a small voice. She did not sound much reassured.

Looking back, she could not recall when her sister's usual buoyant spirits had been in evidence, not very recently, anyway. Her worry about Horace Stanbury had blinded her to Ory's distress. Could Attorney Brand or their grandfather do anything if she wrote to them? Mistress Howard would take the letters to the receiving office on her half day if Rose asked her. But she had written to her grandfather after he declined to be their guardian, requesting only that he write as he was the only close family left to them. Her letter had gone unanswered. There was no reason to suppose he would reply this time. Brand might be willing to aid them, but their cousin would immediately suspect him. Too, how would they receive a reply from him, even if he could suggest a way to help them? The inn at High Stanbury served as the receiving office. Stanbury's man picked up the mail and delivered it to his master.

She racked her brain and prayed for some solution to occur to her before Stanbury brought a suitor to the manor. Then Rose observed Horace Stanbury's narrow-eyed scrutiny of her sister one evening and knew she must get her sister away soon. Nothing good lurked in that measuring gaze.

****

Their opportunity came unexpectedly when she heard him tell Henry Davis to put the horses to the coach in the morning to take him to Bath. He meant to meet a friend there, remain two full days to rest the horses and transact some business. He would bring his guest back the following day. Rose's policy of meekly obeying their cousin's requests (or orders, not to put too fine a point upon it) proved a lucky one. Evidently believing she was docile, at supper that evening he told her to prepare a guest chamber as he was expecting a friend to visit.

"I've told Cook to be prepared to serve the best

meals she can, as the viscount will expect to be well entertained."

"Your friend is a nobleman?" Oriana asked, eyes wide. "Is he handsome?"

Rose cared less about that than about how Sally Howard and she would produce elaborate dinners when a simple family dinner of only one course might consist of five dishes. Considering the season, they might serve a dressed lamb's head, a baked pudding, and roast mutton, accompanied by kidney beans and sliced cucumbers. She considered the lamb's head. Perhaps they should instead substitute a soup. Not the sort of meal the viscount or Cousin Horace would expect!

"He's thought to be a well-looking man," Horace said judiciously. "And his title goes back three hundred years."

Why was she worrying about what the guest would think of dinner when this was their chance to get away?

That night she told Oriana to pack a change of clothing, and she did the same. "We will wear our black gowns. They will not show the dust as a color would. Pack one of the pretty new ones as they fit you. The older ones don't."

"Shouldn't we keep to our mourning, Rose?"

"I think we should have something pretty to wear in London." Ory found black clothing far more of a trial than Rose did, her artistic bent giving her a love of both soft and vivid colors.

Rose thanked God that neither the Hargreaves nor their servants nor Mistress Francis's servants had gossiped about her visit or that if they had, word had not reached Cousin Horace's ears.

The housemaid no longer had time to maid them and

was too busy to discover each had concealed a small valise in her wardrobe. Apart from a change of clothing they would take only the things they would regret abandoning. They had miniatures of their parents and a few cherished mementoes and trinkets. Mama's jewelry was locked away in the office strongbox. By good fortune, she had kept the letters from Attorney Brand in her chamber. They added nothing to the weight of the bag and might prove useful.

They had money left from the sums Papa had given them at each quarter day, there being little on which to spend it even in High Stanbury. Rose thought they could get to London with some left over. A useful book in the library listed London's coaching inns, the towns they served, hackney fares, and other information helpful to visitors. Stow's *Remarks on London* was kept on one of the upper shelves. Horace was unlikely to notice its absence.

The nearest stage had three coaches a week, a stroke of luck as some routes had only one, but they would need to get a ride to Salisbury. She could rely on Cook. Rose asked Mistress Howard if she knew anyone with a cart or wagon who might take them to the coaching inn and not tell anyone.

As soon as Stanbury left for Bath, Cook bustled off to the Blue Boar, whose publican had offered her work. She had refused only because she would not leave the girls alone in the house. "If he wants me to cook for him, he'll get you to Salisbury with none the wiser if you leave at dawn tomorrow. That's plenty of time to get there when the coach leaves at ten."

They would have to put up at an inn overnight on the way to town, but they should be in London in the afternoon of the following day. Stanbury would return from Bath a day later but probably not reach the manor until evening.

"Jed Turner won't mention he's taken you to Salisbury, not for anything. He's sometimes got business there anyway, so no one will think it strange."

The sky was only pink-tinged when the innkeeper's wagon stopped in the lane that ran along the side of the property nearest the house.

Mistress Howard would worry until Rose was able to write to her in care of the Blue Boar, and even then Rose would not provide their address. If Stanbury discovered it, he could insist on their return, and the law would support him.

Chapter 6

Almost before they climbed down from the stagecoach at the Angel on the backside of St. Clement Danes church, a middle-aged woman, plump and neatly attired, asked if they had come looking for work. She had an old aunt that needed a pair of decent, honest girls, and the work wouldn't be too hard. Her voice and expression were kind. Her eyes were like a pair of raisins in the crust of a loaf: small, dark, and hard.

"Thank you, mistress, but we've come to live with our grandfather," Rose replied without hesitation.

"Surely you'll want a bite to eat first. I know how tiring it is to ride on the roof and barely time to eat at the changes. Let me buy you a morsel and a hot drink."

She saw hope in Oriana's eyes. Cook would have packed a basket with food for them, but Rose feared Stanbury's hulking "groom" would notice how much had gone. He was always sneaking around the kitchen and servants' area, to Mistress Howard's and the housemaid's annoyance. Thank God he never ventured into the front part of the house or upstairs. They had taken a little food from the kitchen at Mistress Howard's insistence as she pointed out that inn food was terrible costly. Their meal this morning had consisted of an apple and an apricot-sized lump of cheese each. Aching in her heart as much as in body, she thanked the woman again and added, "He is expecting us on this stage, though he could not meet us, being lame from the gout."

Beside her, Oriana twitched in surprise. Rose gave the woman a pleasant nod, hooked her free arm through her sister's unresisting one and stepped out briskly.

"Why did you tell that good woman Grandpapa expected us?"

"I didn't trust her. Her smile did not reach her eyes."

"I wish we had accepted her offer," Oriana murmured as they trudged along. "There couldn't have been any harm in eating before we went on."

The reproach pained her. Of course Oriana didn't understand why Rose had refused. "I'm sorry. But we weren't interested in taking work as maids, and it would have been wrong to waste her time and money. We'll have something to eat when we reach our grandfather's house. Dear, I looked back as we walked away, and she was speaking with that other young woman who was on the roof with us."

"Even one servant would be a help for her aunt until she could find another."

How to explain the conviction that they would never have reached Grandfather Milton if they had taken a meal with the helpful woman? Rose could not understand it herself. Oriana had never had to fend for herself or been denied anything until their cousin's arrival. Neither had she, but Rose was accustomed to dealing with domestic crises and tradesmen. She was not as trusting as her sister.

They bought two buns at a bakeshop and devoured them on their way, for what was yet another ungenteel action?

****

Heart pounding, Rose stood outside the neat three-story house near Hanover Square, an arm around her sister's shoulders. The door had been closed in their faces. Should she knock again and insist on seeing her uncle? Her aunt by marriage would not help. The memory made her almost ill with anxiety and anger.

They had waited outside until the footman fetched their aunt. She and Ory had curtsied without receiving so much as a nod.

"Aunt Martha, we are pleased to see you again."

Seeing no warmth in her face, she added, "I am Rose Stanbury and this is my sister, Oriana. I'm not surprised you don't recognize us. We were years younger when we met last."

No acknowledgement; nothing but a hard stare.

"As our father is dead, we have come to visit our grandfather. May we come—"

The hatchet-faced woman looked them up and down. "You're no kin of our family. Granddaughters of General Sir Oliver Milton dressed like scullery maids and all on your own? Be off!"

"But—"

The door slammed inches from Rose's nose.

Oriana trembled. "Rose, what are we to do?"

What were they to do? Dear God, she had no idea. They had had enough money to take the stage by riding on the roof, to stay at an inn overnight, and to pay for a hackney to their grandfather's house, but they were reduced to their last few shillings. She must try again. After all, Aunt Martha's error was understandable. Even their genteel speech could not overcome the impression given by their hair being untidy under their caps and hats, their badly dyed gowns black, wrinkled, and dusty, and Rose's hands at least work-reddened and rough. Oriana's were still almost soft and white, spared by Horace's salve. If Rose could only make her aunt listen for a moment, she could explain their plight.

As she raised her hand to lift the knocker, the door opened. The same footman who had summoned his mistress said, "You'd best go and be quick about it, or she'll send for the beadle. The master might have given you a few pence, but he's ill. You look like you can work. There's always work for kitchen maids." The door closed but less emphatically this time.

Despair washed over her. She had brought her sister to London to save her and instead she had doomed them both to starvation or infamy or both. She turned away from the door, wishing she knew what to do, or had a private place in which to cry. But she couldn't reveal her terror to her little sister.

"Rose," her sister ventured, "Could we rest for a little while before we go on? On the church steps?"

They had noticed the handsome church with its pillared bell tower when they approached Grandfather's house. It was not far. Maybe with a few minutes' rest and time to compose herself, she could think of something. "Of course, Ory. We will plan what to do next."

Rose sank down on the steps, grateful for the respite from moving. If only she were not so weary. But even a few moments' rest supplied an answer. They would go to Attorney Brand. He would help them. Could they afford another hackney fare?

She opened her valise and pulled out *Remarks on London* to review the section about hackney fares. An hour's time was one shilling, sixpence, and no shorter period of time was shown, so she had resigned herself to paying that to travel from the coaching inn to Hanover

Square. But hearing their destination, the driver said the fare was a shilling "…being as the Angel is near St. Clement's Inn, and from any of the Inns of Court to Westminster, if 'tisn't beyond Tuttle Street, that's the price as set by Parliament."

And confirmation of the hackney driver's explanation was there in black and white, except that the fare was more to some streets and the Tower of London. If they walked back to the Angel Inn, a hackney to Chancery Lane should be another shilling, which would leave them three shillings, tuppence. At the most, they would pay an extra sixpence. Limp with relief, Rose put away the guide book and said, "We have to go back to the Angel to get a hackney coach to Chancery Lane."

"Can't we find one here to take us there?"

Explaining that if the journey took more than an hour, they'd be charged for an additional hour whereas if they left from near St. Clement's Inn, they would save sixpence seemed overwhelming. "Come, the distance cannot be much over a mile and a half. We've walked farther that at home and thought nothing of it."

"Can we have something to eat first?"

"If there's a bakery or cookshop on the way, the money we save by walking will buy us something. When we reach Mr. Brand, he will give us supper."

"How long will it take, Rose? For I'm sure it's already suppertime."

"Not as late as that," she began and stopped. By the sun's position in the smoke-hazed sky, Ory was right. "Oh, no."

"I'm sure it must be. We did not arrive until after midday."

Rose swallowed bile. "You're right." By the time

they could reach Brand's office, it might be closed. She shut her eyes as if that would make their problem vanish. *Take a deep breath.* How much would a night's lodging cost? Too much in this neighborhood, probably. Some place cheaper, perhaps a boarding-house near the Angel?

She understood why Ory had hoped they might take a coach. Rose ached in her bones from being jolted around on the stage, and she was hungry, too. Ory was not panicking, but that was because she did not understand how little money they had left and how expensive London was. Or else because she had always depended on Rose, who had taken the place of their mother.

Oriana sat close beside her for comfort perhaps, while watching the people, carriages, and sedan chairs pass. She either had the confidence of youth or its heedlessness.

When she decided she must get her sister away from their cousin, she had failed to take into account the difficulties two young females with limited coin and without an escort would face. All she had recalled of London from their last visit was its size, dirt, and hordes of people and vehicles. Papa had taken care of all the arrangements.

"We must return to the Angel's neighborhood to find a cheap room for the night." If they could. "Tomorrow we will go to Chancery Lane."

"Is it very bad?" Ory asked, timidly. Rose had forgotten how quick she was to sense Rose's state of mind.

"I've made too many mistakes, Ory. I did not consider the possibility that we would not be welcomed at Grandpapa's home, and I should have, given his not having answered our letters. We should have gone to Attorney Brand's office first."

And what if he were out of town, visiting a client? When the opportunity to escape Cousin Horace had come, there had been no time to write to make sure Brand would be there.

Even she knew how dangerous London could be. Salisbury, merely a market town, had night watchmen now. The enormity of their peril overwhelmed her. After the anxiety of the last few months and today's disappointment, Rose's tears came as suddenly as a spring shower.

"Oh, Rose." Ory put her arm around her shoulders as Rose buried her face in her handkerchief.

"If Brand is not available to help us, what will we do?" She had not intended to tell Ory what she feared, but the question erupted as unexpectedly as her tears. They lived in no parish in London so they would not be eligible for charity. Would they be taken up by the watch as vagrants and cast into prison? Would they end in the workhouse?

"We could look for kitchen work, Rose."

The question recalled her to her responsibilities. She could not fall apart with her sister's welfare to consider.

"We can try." Assuming they did not starve or find themselves in the workhouse, what were the chances they would both be needed in the same house or even the same part of town? Did she dare let Oriana work by herself? Every adult woman knew female servants were in danger of being seduced or raped by the men in the house. But what else could they do but take any work they could get?

She was still sniffling and mopping her face when a

gentleman's voice said, "How may I help you?"

She almost wept again, half at the kindness in the man's voice and half because she had humiliated herself by her uncontrolled behavior. Before she could reply, Ory spoke.

"Sir, we came to London to live with our grandfather, but he is ill, and we couldn't see him, and our uncle's wife didn't believe we are his grandchildren, and now we have no place to go."

Her blush at Ory's too-frank speech to a total stranger might go unnoticed, considering her teary face. She gulped back a sob and said, "Thank you for your concern, sir." And wished whoever he was might be able to aid them, knowing she dare not trust him, not after their encounter with the woman at the inn. He was probably a rakehell. Gentlemen did not otherwise concern themselves with females of the servant class, as they must appear to be, clad in their dusty, countrified clothing.

Blinking away her last tears, she was tempted to revise her opinion. His plain black suit, slight body, and untidy hair suggested quite another sort of man. His eyes twinkled when she met his gaze. "May I introduce myself, ma'am? Wilfred Simmons, curate, St. Giles-without-Cripplegate. If you and your sister have nowhere to stay, your situation is serious. London is a hard place even for men if they have no work and no money. A female without resources risks danger to both body and soul. Please let me assist you."

She bit her lip. Mr. Simmons appeared to be respectable. He had a gentleman's voice and was no more than four-and-twenty, she guessed. Beside her, Ory sniffed dolefully.

"You are wise not to be too trusting. I have friends who will vouch for me inside." He smiled at her expression. "Ma'am, no one has ever been abducted from St. George's Church, Hanover Square."

Inside, two clerical gentlemen and the verger informed them that Mr. Simmons was indeed a curate of the Church of England and involved in various charitable works besides. After that, everything happened in the twitch of a cat's tail.

Chapter 7

He took them by hackney to a borderland between a poor but decent neighborhood and what Rose suspected was a very bad one. In Queen Elizabeth's reign, the half-timbered house must have been a wealthy family's home. The curate said Bethlehem House now housed orphans and women who had been left destitute from one cause or another, some with children. "No relation at all to Bedlam," he assured them.

"The almshouses can take only so many, and those are usually the elderly with no family or those too crippled to work," Mr. Simmons told them. "The workhouses separate families, which I consider an abomination. This establishment provides education for the children, pays for apprenticeships for them when possible, and trains the women for service or some other occupation. There is still much to be done." He added deprecatingly, "Lecture concluded."

The matron greeted them cheerfully, growing serious only when Simmons explained their circumstances.

"Mr. Simmons, we're as full as we can be. There's not a decent room to spare, even if the young ladies belonged in a place like this. Isn't there anywhere else they could stay?"

Rose's heart sank. She had been so sure Simmons had solved their dilemma. "We went to our grandfather's home but were turned away by our aunt-in-law. I suppose we did not make a good impression. We had dyed our oldest gowns for mourning."

Mistress Eccles surveyed them. "No one appears to good effect when they've been traveling, but did your aunt not recognize you?"

"We have not visited our grandfather for several years, and I suppose we have changed a great deal."

"I think she just didn't want us," Ory declared.

Rose cast her a look that said, *Hush.* "Our attorney wrote to Grandfather, who is General Sir Oliver Milton, when Father died, and so did I. We received no reply. He is said to be ill."

The curate tutted. "Mistress Eccles, there's no place I can think of. But if you have no decent room, have you an indecent one?" he asked, a twinkle in his eye.

"I'm sure I don't know what the church is coming to, sir." She laughed. "There's that room in the attic, the one with a leak, that we keep for the ones as has the most need to hide." The woman hastened to explain, "There's women as need to get away from their husbands or others that's hurt them. We take them in, no matter how crowded we are. And of course, some women and older children get work and leave, so places open up. But these misses won't be used to such mean living."

Rose would have blurted out, "Anyplace that isn't on the streets would be acceptable," but Ory spoke first.

"Rose has been working in our home's kitchen and scullery and doing the heavy cleaning. Her hands are as red and rough as our cook's, because she did the hardest work to spare me, but I've dusted and swept and done the light cleaning."

Rose added, "We lost a number of our servants so

we've been doing some of the work."

"Most of the work except cooking," her sister added under her breath.

"Mistress, will you explain how it is you decided to come to town rather than remain in your home, which would almost always be a better choice? 'Tis cheaper to live in the country than in London. Or was there debt which required the property to be sold?"

Mr. Simmons, no fool, had detected the flaws in their account. Would he send them back to Stanbury Manor?

"Our property was entailed, and the heir is only a distant cousin we'd never even heard of. There was no debt. I know, because I paid the bills. No creditors approached us or our attorney after Father's death. But our cousin claimed we must be thrifty and dismissed almost all of the servants."

Simmons frowned. "Is he your guardian?"

He would send them back rather than break the law by letting them stay. Then Rose's heart rebounded as she remembered something Mistress Eccles had said. The charity protected women.

"He said he was arranging my sister's marriage. He is clutch-fisted, though I suppose he must once have been poor, if he is not now, which might explain it…" She must stop gabbling. She swallowed and said, "I cannot think why he would suggest it when Oriana is far too young to marry. She's not fifteen."

"For the settlements, most likely," Matron Eccles remarked. "It's a way of repairing a family's fortunes or paying their debts, if they have a beautiful daughter. Such doings!"

"I know the law gives our guardian authority over

us, but please don't make us go back." How could she explain what she feared when she did not really understand it herself? If they insisted she and Ory return to Stanbury, Rose would have to find some way of escaping. And what would they do then? She had no idea.

The matron clucked, and Simmons shook his head, smiling, "Ma'am, a magistrate would insist we send many of the women here back to cruel and even murderous husbands, and yet we do not. We observe man's law as much as we can in good conscience, but we don't think God's law requires us to put women and children at risk of harm or death. For a short time, Matron, the attic might do. The charity intends to add another house soon," Simmons said.

"No matter what the Bible may say," Mistress Eccles muttered. She patted Oriana's hand.

Simmons cleared his throat. "Our board of governors has many resources. Perhaps they can find some reason for the Court of Chancery to change the guardianship."

Attorney Brand had thought Stanbury a moral man. But he might have mistaken lack of warmth and a sort of austerity for principles.

"In the alternative, they'll be able to make other arrangements for you."

Rose breathed again.

Simmons said, "Your cousin will be searching for you. He will hardly think of looking here for you...but it might be well not to use your own names."

"Mr. Simmons has the right of it. You wouldn't be the only ones, neither."

"I've always liked Hortense for a name," Oriana

said. Shortened to "Horrie," it would sound like her own nickname on the lips of the residents. Rose had always been Rose to her sister and close friends, but Horace Stanbury knew her only as Rosabel.

"We'll use our grandfather's last name." And that was how Rose and Horrie Milton began their new lives.

Their country home had been peaceful before their father's death and grimly silent after Horace Stanbury had all but emptied the house of servants. The noise and bustle of Bethlehem House seemed like all of London distilled into one mansion, and that one overcrowded. Children cried or whooped, women called back and forth, pots clanged, feet thumped on the creaking stairs. Bedlam often reigned inside, and even in the middle of the night, the street was not silent. Night-men's carts creaked past, men reeled home from public houses singing or arguing.

Ory was helping with the youngest children by her second day at the charity. Rose hardly knew what to do with herself at first beyond tidying the room she and Ory shared, not that it required much effort, being so bare of furnishings, and lending a hand wherever she could. She felt useless and idleness gave her too much time to worry.

She had intended to beg a piece of paper and the use of a pencil from the matron to write a note to Lucian Brand but hesitated. If it occurred to Cousin Horace they might have gone to their family's old attorney, Brand would be in an awkward position, having either to admit they were in London or else lie. And what could he do to conceal them even if he were willing to break the law?

Then Mistress Eccles approached her after breakfast, saying, "When you came, I hadn't much time to talk to you, but I recall you kept house for your father and had charge of the household ledgers."

"I did and helped our cook after the servants were gone."

"Mostly I spend my days finding work in London for women who aren't in danger from their men or in other places for those that are. Sometimes I teach a woman how to do a char, like how to remove stains from clothing or how to iron, unless one of the others can teach her. The bookkeeping keeps me up at night when I'm done with everything else. If you'd be willing to take over the accounting—" Mistress Eccles began the question hesitantly, as if she thought Rose might be above working for her keep as the other women did.

She cast aside good manners to interrupt. "I'd enjoy doing it. I like numbers. They're reliable and never deceive." Unlike some people.

Dealing with the ledger, she was contributing something in exchange for her board and lodging, although it took very little time each day. The matron had no other tasks to give her, and the cook refused her offer of assistance with horror.

" 'Twouldn't be proper, ma'am. You're a lady and won't never have to work in a kitchen. The girls what helps me need the training so they can be kitchen maids."

"…but I'll never be able to go back to my old life," Rose told Anne, a former governess, when she mentioned this exchange. "I can't stay here forever and must somehow support myself and my sister."

As sheltered as Ory had been, Rose feared she might shrink from the hubbub and the rough women around them. Instead her sister grew accustomed more easily than Rose, who did not know whether to be grateful or worried. While she was glad her little sister was blossoming, she worried about the effect of this ungenteel environment on her.

Rose had never felt stiff or awkward with their tenants, servants, and laborers or the shopkeepers and artisans in the village, and many of the women here were as decent as those, though fallen on hard times through various mischances. Here she was also exposed to a different class, making her realize she had led almost as sheltered a life as Ory.

Hearing one of the women explain how she had come to Bethlehem House "acos me sister's man kept a-wapping of me" Rose assumed she meant her sister's husband had hit her. Men of that class often were quick with their fists, and perhaps in his cups he had resented his sister-in-law's presence in his home. If she had not perfected an impassive face in dealing with Cousin Horace, Rose feared she would have been gaping and speechless when the speaker went on to explain that the "wapping" having resulted in a bun in her oven led her sister to turn her out of their lodgings "…which I don't think she would but for it being her man's get."

The former governess, the most like her in background, soon became her closest friend. One day she poured out her fears about her sister's future and her own. Anne would understand: who would hire a governess with a child or a housekeeper with a sister, even if those positions paid enough to support a dependent? How could she ensure Ory's future, if not her own?

Anne eyed Rose speculatively. "Do you think you could teach children and perhaps some of the women how to write? Several women are able to teach reading and counting, but not writing as they were never taught. Why, if they learned to write, they might send letters to the newspapers deploring their living and working conditions."

"God forbid the laboring class should complain," Rose said piously, suppressing a laugh at Anne's ironic tone. "I'd be happy to teach writing." She knew she could, having taught Ory to do so. Anne already instructed those who might become upper servants in correct speech, grammar, and deportment, and tried to teach a little history and geography to the older children, but she hadn't much time left for anything else.

"Do the ones you train to be upper servants find work when they are trained? For I'd suppose they would need experience and a recommendation."

"Some of the charity's benefactors take them into their households for a time to give them practical experience and are then able to write them a character."

She added, "Until I came here, I had no notion of charity being anything but giving the 'deserving' poor occasional gifts of food, castoff clothing, and lectures about accepting their station in life, or supporting the indigent elderly or crippled in an almshouse. One would almost think Bethlehem House had been founded by someone with experience of poverty and destroyed reputation." Sorrow shadowed her composed face briefly and was gone. "Some of the women would benefit from lessons in how to keep household accounts, but I never had an opportunity even to help Mama manage the household. Would you also consider—"

"Teaching them? Yes, of course. I'd be grateful for more to do." Acting as an instructress here might earn her a recommendation as a housekeeper or governess, too. Another worry: she and Ory were safe for the moment, but where would they go when they were thought ready to leave? Bethlehem House was not a permanent home. Younger residents were apprenticed if possible. Others were placed as servants with carefully chosen households. Women in danger from their husbands or lovers were found places well out of London.

She might be able to get work with a family of the middling sort: not wealthy but able to afford enough servants to need a housekeeper to supervise them. Or would she be thought too young for such a post? But what about Ory? Would she be able to support her sister in a boarding house?

She posed the question to Anne.

"She does pose a difficulty, Rose. I don't think whatever post you found would permit your sister to live with you unless they also needed a nursery or kitchen maid and hired her. But I can't think a girl so lovely and so trusting would fare well as a servant of any kind."

The idea chilled Rose. Her sister would be at the mercy of any predatory man in the house.

Anne had suffered the fate of many pretty servant girls while working as a governess. Her three-year-old boy was in the nursery while she served as the matron's aide-de-camp. During one of their conversations she said, "I did not think you would accept your situation so easily. I didn't, until my father replied to my letter with a refusal even to help me travel to the home of a connection of my mother's. My great-aunt would have taken me in though Father couldn't, of course, being a rector. Only think of the scandal!" was her tart conclusion.

"I worry for my sister, Anne. Unless there are no men of any sort in the house…"

They exchanged glances. Ory would be ruined within months, either by the master or by a male servant.

"That thought had occurred to me. We needn't worry about her yet, however."

"But when it's time for me to be employed, she will be on her own here, although I'm sure you'll look after her until you go." By now, Rose had watched a number of the women leave for positions, some to distant parts of the country where they and their backgrounds were more easily concealed.

"I won't be leaving Bethlehem House. I'm employed by the charity. The board of governors could not be sure of having another resident governess or finding one willing to work here. Thus I am indispensable. Bethlehem House is bursting at its seams, but you are an asset neither Mistress Eccles nor I are eager to part with. Your sister may eventually be found a safe place elsewhere, but there's no cause to think about that for the foreseeable future."

Relief overwhelmed her. She had begun by thinking she and Ory could return to polite society once she herself was of age. Within a week or two, she knew she could never banish from her memory all she had seen and heard since coming to London. Indeed, their flight from their home unchaperoned was enough to ruin them both, and their presence in Bethlehem House would be a scandal if known. Neither of them would be able to return to polite society, but at least Ory was safe from Stanbury's schemes. The world of Stanbury Manor receded more every day.

Ory had no thought of their future. She was full of

the amusing things her new friends and the little ones said. When Ory recounted one lad's tale of how he had escaped being abducted to be sold as a sweep's boy, Rose had laughed with the others but spoke to her privately in their little attic room.

"Dear, please do not refer to children as kinchins or kids. Mistress Anne tells me both are cant terms used by criminals or at least by the lowest sort."

"Oh! As gentlemen do not say bad words in company with ladies? But many here use words like that."

"Yes, but we must not. Mistress Anne doesn't."

Ory's face cleared. "Neither does Mistress Eccles, does she? Except when she forgets and something slips out. I'll try to remember."

Chapter 8

The inn smelled of new plaster, the vinegar used for scrubbing, and the beeswax used to polish the fireplace mantels and paneling. With work on the inn complete, Allan visited coffee houses near the Three Greyhounds and farther afield to find one that suited him. Each attracted a certain sort of patron: writers, men in the shipping trade, footmen and butlers, bankers, or those of a particular political bent. Some inns, particularly coaching inns, had coffee rooms, but while their customers were far more diverse, the bustling surroundings were not restful.

He visited the Green Tree and felt at home. Its tables were full of the lower gentry visiting London or gentlemen of modest means who lived in town. He did not stand out and during the afternoon he spent there, the talk was mostly of London, country matters, horses, politics, and the theater. No one asked about another's family connections. Such men would inquire only if marriage with a member of their family was contemplated. Judging by their clothing and manners, none of the Green Tree's patrons aspired to be taken for anything but what they were or to marry above their station. The third time he visited, he arranged to receive his mail at the coffee house, as it was closer than Peter Wilde's offices.

He made friends. One worked in some minor

government office, another cheerfully admitted he represented his cit father-in-law in dealing with the titled, another held a position with the East India Company. They and their friends were less concerned with social standing than with making a living. Two or three came from lower origins but had raised themselves by their own efforts and were accepted. Allan still felt he was playing a part among them.

One night, he and several others attended the theater—the pit rather than the boxes, of course. Looking up at a burst of laughter in an upper box, he froze to immobility on recognizing Julius Passevant with two ladies and an older gentleman. His half brother did not see him and why should he? Allan was in the pit some distance away, surrounded by others. Among so many, he was anonymous to those who could afford a box. Maybe he had worried needlessly about the sixth Baron Passevant, who would hardly bother to notice Allan now he had been sent away.

Exploring London on his own filled in a few days. His new acquaintances told him of the sights not to be missed by a visitor: St. Paul's, the Haymarket theater, the Tower, Covent Garden (after dark), the Royal Exchange, Don Saltero's Coffee House in Chelsea with its collection of curiosities and gimcracks. They also recommended the best brothels and warned him against the places where one was most likely to be cheated at cards or dice.

One pleasantly warm day, he visited the Perilous Pond off Old Street, with the marshy Finsbury Fields beyond it, a bit of countryside cheek by jowl with busy streets and closely packed buildings. Trees shaded the pond and spared a chance passer-by the sight of half-naked young men. On a hot day, the tangled roots and reeds bordering the pond sometimes killed a swimmer tempted to cool off in the spring waters. His foster father would have called this a reminder of the folly of succumbing to the desire for amusement.

Then Peter Wilde sent a message requesting Allan to meet him to discuss an inquiry about leasing the inn. Over a glass of sherry, Wilde described the potential lessor, a charity which housed and educated orphans and needy women and their children.

"Can they afford it?"

"The charity is funded by wealthy patrons and by small contributions. The board of directors includes a clergyman known for his activities in service to the poor, a prominent man of business, and some gentlemen not ashamed to be connected to such an effort. One thing I must mention, which may affect your decision, is the reason they are particularly interested in your property. The gates into the courtyard and stable yard provide more security than most of the buildings suitable for their purposes. Some of the women are fleeing violent men or pimps. Many landlords would refuse to let a property to house them."

Allan lifted one eyebrow satirically. "What right do I have to object to them? Many decent folk scorn me for my birth. I am willing to consider their offer."

"They will wish to inspect the inn. They have seen it only from outside the gate."

He and Wilde met with the two men in charge of the negotiations. Simon Hayes, the charity's man of business and one of its directors, and the Reverend Mr. Wilfred Simmons. The former handled the affairs of several wealthy aristocrats and a number of prosperous merchants, as well. The latter was a mild fellow with humorous eyes, devoid of self-righteousness. With them was a female, plainly clad and remarkable only for being a young lady. Allan wondered her people let her involve herself in such a charity and accompany the men without a chaperon.

"It was thought sensible to get a female's opinion of the premises," Hayes explained. "Mistress Milton is here to represent the future matron of our new residence."

She curtsied and murmured a greeting. He supposed she was a member of the charity or a relation of one and initially wondered what use she would be in evaluating a home for unfortunate women and children.

The men's eyes widened slightly as they walked through the rooms. Hayes sketched the inn's plan in a notebook with approximate dimensions and notes in tiny, exact script. The clergyman chatted with Chappell, who acted as guide while Allan drifted along on the group's periphery, as did the young lady. Allan only realized he had been studying Mistress Milton and ignoring the charity's representatives when Chappell gave him a curious glance, then tactfully looked away. Why was he drawn to her? Lust was part of it but not all.

In the kitchen, she had talked and laughed with Molly Chappell as if they were equals and asked what seemed like sensible questions about the furnishings and apparatus. The remainder of the tour, Mistress Milton spoke little but studied everything with sharp interest. As she opened and closed windows, tested that every catch was secure, and pushed and tugged at the grills over the ground floor windows, his opinion altered. She was making sure the building would be safe for its occupants, as safe as if she herself would live there.

He had met or observed a few genteel ladies in his work for the Passevant family. She might have belonged to a different species: she spoke no trite or frivolous word, yet she clearly was a lady despite her plain blue gown. In a lightning flash of inspiration, Allan imagined marriage to a woman like Mistress Milton, if only he could find one like her. On a sigh, he forced his attention back to the tour of the Three Greyhounds.

"What is done with the slops?" Mistress Milton asked as they descended to the yard after going through the upper stories.

"There are necessary houses in the stable yard. Chamber pots are emptied there. The privies haven't been cleaned since the last lease ended as there's been so little use. Having the night-soil men in to empty them regularly would be an expense."

"A necessary one," Simmons remarked with a grin as they returned to the inn dining room.

Hayes said, "The building is in very good condition," a prelude to admitting they could not afford the lease price, no doubt.

Allan had discussed terms with Wilde beforehand. He might make more money renting out the rooms, with decent lodgings expensive and hard to find. The counter argument was that some tenants might prove to be undesirable, and others might not stay long. Chappell should not be expected to collect the rents, deal with the tenants, and do the repairs. Allan had thought of hiring a manager to take care of those matters and decided that would create its own problems. The fellow might cheat him or rent to unacceptable tenants merely to keep the rooms filled.

"Will the residents here use the privies in the stable

yard during the day, meaning the gate to the stables would have to be unlocked, or will they use close stools day and night?" Mistress Milton asked.

The stable had not been included in the proposed lease. On Chappell's suggestion, Allan had intended to rent it out for stabling. Hayes and Mr. Simmons traded worried glances.

"We don't need a stable," Simmons began.

"Where are the children to play in wet or cold weather?" Mistress Milton asked suddenly. "Bethlehem House has that long gallery where the children play Blindman's Buff or leapfrog or run off their fidgets in bad weather."

Hayes opened his notebook and studied the floor plan he had made. "In the common room? It's the largest."

"Running and playing ball and marbles among the tables between meals?"

"Perhaps not," Simmons said, and sighed.

Allan foresaw their tentative agreement to lease the Three Greyhounds being withdrawn.

"I'll include the stable in the lease at no additional cost. The idea of lively children penned up inside on rainy days makes my blood run cold. The stalls would have to be removed and you might want to put a wood floor in."

The lady frowned slightly. "The stable has no fireplace, I imagine, and would be cold in the winter."

Mistress Chappell brought ale for the men and tea for the lady, and a plate of buns.

The property belonged to him. He supposed he had decided against turning it into a lodging house early on, perhaps after he had seen the workmanship that had gone into the building. Or mayhap after he'd done some of the work himself.

In low voices Hayes and Simmons discussed the amounts charged for comparable buildings, "…not that there are any," Simmons pointed out.

"I will lease it to your charity," Allan announced abruptly, "with the stables included, and I'll have a fireplace put in, if you have the stall partitions taken out and wood flooring put down if you wish." As the interest from investment of the inn's accumulated earnings and the sale of the jewels provided him a more than adequate income, he could afford to offer them generous terms. "There are two other conditions: I wish to live here in the large room in the southwestern corner and its adjoining closet, and Chappell and his wife must be kept on. He's done an excellent job, and I can attest to his good character. And his wife cooked for gentry before they married."

Hayes and Simmons exchanged a glance, but Mistress Milton was the one to speak.

"The buns are very good and are a kind I've never seen or heard of." She flicked one finger toward the last square of tender dough coiled around sugar, spices, and currants. "Do you know, are they her own invention?"

From her companions' expressions, they were surprised by the question.

"I don't know. We could ask," Allan said.

Wilde answered. "No, she has copied the kind that are made by a bakehouse in Chelsea. His Majesty's family has visited the Bun House to enjoy them."

"Can she cook thriftily?" As an afterthought: "If you know."

"She can and does."

"Would she be willing to teach cooking to some of the residents if the charity should decide to lease this place?"

On the question being posed to Chappell's wife, her answer was a cheerful affirmative. Mistress Milton gave her companions a minute nod.

Chapter 9

Rose was instructing several of the Bethlehem House children in the mysteries of addition and subtraction, using lengths of straw as counters when one of helpers came to the door and squeaked, "Please, ma'am, Matron says, will you come to her office."

She smiled at the girl and nodded before addressing her class. "Tomorrow, we'll go on with bigger numbers, and one or two of you may be ready to go on to multiply and divide."

Polly scurried away while Rose collected her straws and followed more slowly, wondering what was amiss. The matron was seldom to be found in the office unless she was administering a scold or congratulating some lucky resident on being placed in a position.

At her tap on the door, Mistress Eccles called, "Come in."

She had visitors in her little room. Billy, a boy of ten or eleven who sometimes did errands for them stood by her desk, eating a slice of bread and butter. A man, who was not one of the porters employed to do the heavy work and protect the house and women, rose from one of the two armchairs as she entered. Billy ducked his head and stuffed the remainder of his treat into his pocket. The man closed the door behind her. The scent of the dried lavender in a little chipped bowl on the desk was heavy in the air.

"Rose, this is a friend of Bethlehem House. He and Billy have brought us some news."

Having waited for an introduction which did not come, Rose dipped a curtsy a little tardily, murmuring, "How do you do, sir?"

He did not look like a gentleman, and yet she had greeted him as if he were, or nearly so. His reddish-brown hair was pulled back but not pomaded, his neat clothing was well kept but not new, the buttons plain, and he wore no jewelry. His face arrested her attention: aquiline, somewhat darkened by days spent outdoors, with clever eyes. "Call me Barlicorn. I'm no one to call 'sir.'"

The matron waved her to the other arm chair and looked to the visitor, who began, "Billy will tell you his end of it."

The boy chewed his lip. "See, I stays around here acos my mam and sis's here, so's I can watch out for 'em. I runs errands and holds horses sometimes." The boy could have lived in Bethlehem House with his mother and sister but had refused, on the ground he was old enough to earn his living.

"And gives his mother as much of his earnings as he can spare," Matron Eccles added.

Billy shrugged. "You lets me sleep in the kitchen when it's cold."

Rose silently blessed the charity for that. Many children did support themselves when no older than ten years, or even younger. Some of them had no real shelter in the cold.

"I know you're very quick and reliable when you're sent to the shops," Rose said.

He rewarded this praise with a flashing grin. "I

knows the neighborhood. T'other day, a Captain Sharp comes up to me—"

"A military gentleman?"

"A bully or cheat," Barlicorn translated.

The boy nodded impatiently. "Ay, and he promised me a guinea if I found a pair o' rum morts. A guinea! Give me a pitchure, he did." He paused, great with news.

The visitor's grin revealed slightly crooked teeth giving him an endearingly roguish appearance. "Sorry to spoil your lay, Billy." He unfolded a sheet of drawing paper and passed it to Rose.

She swallowed, staring at the sketches. There were three or four of Oriana: head back, laughing, carrying a basket of vegetables, reading a book. Two more were of Rose herself, bland-faced in one, pinch-lipped with annoyance in the other. When she could speak she said, "He's found us."

"He's searching, but he hasn't found you yet," Mistress Eccles replied.

Billy chimed in, "No, acos I asked the cove a deal o' questions, like if they was his dells or was they filching morts. He told me they was close kin of a gentleman and was lured away by a bad man, and he wants to save them. Their phizzes is being passed out all over, and the first to find 'em and report gets the guinea."

She looked to the matron, who replied, "I've told our friend how you came to be here."

"Does Mr. Simmons know of this?"

"I've sent him a message, but I think he'll say we will be wise to leave the matter to this gentleman."

Barlicorn grinned ironically at her description of him and said, "Thanks for your help, Billy. You can go now." He tossed a penny to the boy, who snatched it out of the air.

"Allus a pleasure doing business wif a gent, Barlicorn." He gave a saucy salute and was out the door, ferret quick.

"What am I to do?" If Cousin Horace found them, a magistrate would turn them over to him. She was not foolish enough to suppose her concern about Horace's motives would weigh against his kinship and rights as their guardian.

"Before we can answer that question, I need to know more about your relative. He's some distant relation of yours? What can you tell me of him, Mistress Milton?"

"He is my father's first cousin, making him my and Horrie's first cousin once removed. After Papa died, our attorney discovered Cousin Stanbury's existence and—"

"You did not know of him before? Your father had not appointed him your guardian?"

"No." She explained why his existence had come as a surprise.

"What impression did you have of your cousin at your first acquaintance with him?"

"We thought him a gentleman of leisure in town, though a rather stern one. Our attorney considered him strict in his notions of propriety, like a Dissenter, you know," Rose added, and saw him wince.

"Did you change your mind? As you say 'thought' rather than 'think.' "

How perceptive of the visitor, when she herself had not noticed how she had phrased it. "I did, though I hardly know why." She cast back to the first weeks after his arrival and remembered details she had forgotten or dismissed. "When he first came, he did not ride well, as if he had never lived in the country. Then there were the many letters he received. I saw some of them when our own footman was still fetching the post. The penmanship ranged from that of gentlemen to barely literate. Mayhap he was managing a shop or manufactory by post. But if his business was so large, would he not have left someone in charge? He was displeased when I asked about his business interests, which might have been because gentlemen do not have connections to trade, or because they do not discuss business with ladies. And he sold our horses and kept us from visiting our friends. I began by finding him odd and difficult and ended by fearing him when I learned he planned to arrange a marriage for my sister, who is not yet fifteen."

"Did your sister share your doubts or did you discuss them with her?"

"She still has the trusting nature of a child. She liked our cousin, who was always pleasant to her. I couldn't be sure my suspicion of him didn't come from my dislike of his manner until I found the ring."

"The ring?"

She described finding the signet and her fear that it had been left as a trap. "I know this must sound ridiculous, but by then, nothing he did would have surprised me."

"Could you describe the ring?"

"The design seemed an odd choice for a gentleman, being a stretching cat. Do you know how a cat extends her forelimbs on the floor while her rump is still high?"

"I do." He took a notebook from his pocket, turned to a blank page and scratched away with a stub of pencil. "Did it resemble this?"

She took the little book and stared at the flirtatious stretching cat. "That is very like."

"It is the emblem of a certain business." Returning book and pencil to his coat pocket, he said, "If your Cousin Horace is associated with it, as seems likely, 'tis not good news. You had a fortunate escape." Barlicorn's grim tone suggested the matter must be worse than she had feared.

She waited mutely for an explanation which was not forthcoming. Instead he asked, "What is his appearance?"

"He is just ordinary. Middling tall, thin, brown hair, gray eyes."

"No distinguishing features?"

She most vividly remembered the first time she noticed him watching Oriana. He had been lounging, chin resting on his fist, staring out the window to where her sister was cutting flowers. "Everything about him is narrow." She searched for more words to describe him.

"Can you draw his likeness?"

Rose shook her head. "I can scarce draw even a straight line. That is my sister's talent." Seeing his eyes sharpen, she protested. "You cannot ask her. If she knew he is searching for us, she would be terrified."

"Then let us reserve that matter for later. You say she liked Stanbury. Did she cease doing so at some point?"

"She began to keep her distance from him after a while." She recounted their conversation, ending, "That did not seem like enough to upset her so much, when she has always expected the best of people and life."

"I think we must ask her to tell us. If you will permit?" He waited for her reluctant nod. "Mistress Eccles?"

Stanbury's drawing had vanished by the time Oriana

entered with Matron Eccles.

Barlicorn rose to cede his chair to her. Once she was seated and grew less nervous after greetings and a few casual questions, he asked, "I think you came to be worried about something your cousin said or did. It would be helpful to know what it was."

Ory darted a look at Rose. "I told Rose."

"I've told Mr. Barlicorn about Cousin Horace's plan to arrange your marriage and maybe mine. But I don't think that was all of it, dear, was it?"

Ory twisted her fingers together where they were laced in her lap. "Not, not really. I liked Cousin Horace, but I couldn't understand what the letter could mean, and it worried me, and I didn't want to upset you more, and, and...." She gulped.

Letter?

Rose covered Ory's writhing hands with her own. "You may feel better if you talk about it. I think you know now he did not have your welfare at heart."

She squared slender shoulders and took a deep breath. Rose had never been prouder of her little sister, who had always seemed so fragile.

"That day when Mistress Howard sprained her wrist and you cooked breakfast..."

"I'm sorry you had to clean the grates that day, Ory."

"I didn't mind, really I didn't. But when I was sweeping out the hearth in his chamber I found a bit of paper at the back that hadn't burned."

Rose struggled briefly with her conscience. "Of course one should not read another's letters but if you unintentionally noticed something that disturbed you..." *Please tell us what it was.*

"I did, and I know it was wrong to read it, but I couldn't help seeing a few words. I couldn't stop wondering what they could mean."

"Knowing might tell us more about your cousin, Miss Ory." To Rose, Barlicorn's casual remark suggested lively interest.

"They referred to horses, and they were curious, that's all." She straightened as if reciting a lesson. "They said, '…will pay you a good price for your filly, but the mare's no use…' We hadn't a filly or mare in the stables. He'd already sold ours, except for the coach horses and an old hack. I didn't think he owned horses in town, because he was no sort of rider. Why would someone write him about buying a horse, if he doesn't have any?"

Barlicorn and the matron exchanged identical cynical glances, justifiably, as Rose did not for a second think Horace was even mildly interested in horses.

Now this fragment joined her previous vague concerns about him. But her sister's innocence should be preserved as much as possible, though from what, Rose did not know, though she suspected Mistress Eccles and Barlicorn did.

"Do you think Rose was correct all along to distrust Cousin Horace?"

"Was finding the paper the first thing that caused you to doubt him?" Barlicorn inquired.

"I did not like his idea of arranging a marriage for me, but he said it would secure my future, like being made to drink the apothecary's horrid potion to get over an illness."

Mistress Eccles slanted a look at Barlicorn.

"I believe if I were a lady, I would be unwilling to let Mr. Stanbury make a match for me." Barlicorn's airy tone turned serious. "He would expect to profit by it."

Replying to Oriana's questioning look, Rose said, "Through the marriage settlements, you know," though she herself was not sure how such things worked.

"Mistress Rose, you were wise to remove yourself and your sister from his control."

She wanted to ask what he thought Stanbury had intended but held her tongue in her sister's presence.

"Having a picture of your cousin would be very helpful as I've friends who could watch for him at the coaching inns and other places if they knew what he looks like."

Before Rose could speak, her sister said, "I can draw him. Cousin Horace said I drew as well as some men who are paid for their sketches."

"Ory…"

Hearing her protest, Ory glanced at Rose. She nodded permission reluctantly. The man had maneuvered both of them: Ory into offering and Rose into agreeing. To be fair, Ory did not seem in the least overset by talking about their cousin.

No more than five minutes later, she passed the visitor a sheet with a speaking likeness of their cousin. Seeing it brought Stanbury alive for Rose. She had remembered the thin face but had forgotten how sharp and narrow his eyes were, and how the mole high on his right cheek was almost like a patch such as some ladies wore.

Barlicorn studied it, frowning. "I've never met him."

That did not surprise Rose. The man was unlikely to move in the same circles as the fastidious Stanbury. But a faint emphasis on the word "met" made her wonder if

Barlicorn knew something about their cousin, even if he had not been introduced.

"Am I correct that his complexion is pale?"

"Yes, sir. At first, he hardly ever rose before noon and spent most of his time in the house." Ory, an early riser like most country dwellers, could not understand sleeping during the best part of the day.

"Thank you for your assistance, Miss Ory. Would you wait in the parlor for your sister, please?"

The smile Rose could not remember seeing in weeks, the smile of a carefree angel, lit her face. "Thank you, sir. I feel much better, knowing Rose was right." She went off cheerfully, almost like her old self. But she had grown up a little.

Once the door closed behind her, Rose demanded, "What is it you suspect?"

"Only that he is a man with secrets and has connections that make him more dangerous than the ordinary gentleman."

He was keeping something from her, which was infuriating. On the other hand, his questioning of Ory had somehow lightened her little sister's heart.

The matron spoke, startling both of them.

"Barlicorn, I think she must be told. Rose is a sensible young lady, not like most of the gentry-morts that wilt so easy."

"I know you are correct, though a decent man would not speak of this to any lady. Here it is, then, Mistress. I suspect Mr. Stanbury's correspondent was inquiring about buying Miss Ory."

"Buying Ory," she echoed when she could draw a breath. She collected her wits with an effort. "I never heard of such a, such a…"

"That was why I was reluctant to tell you. But Matron Eccles is correct; you need to know what danger you stand in."

"I must be very stupid."

"No. Any well-bred young lady would be equally unaware."

"How could that be legal or even possible?"

"What else but a sale is a marriage arranged for a girl by her father to a man she does not wish to marry but which will benefit her father?"

"But how could our cousin explain permitting the marriage when she is so young?"

"As her guardian, your cousin has almost complete power over her. He might say he felt it in her best interests, and who would challenge his decision?"

"He must know I would fight him to the death to prevent it."

"You would fail." The words dropped like stones. "May I ask how old you are, ma'am?"

"Twenty years, sir. Almost one-and-twenty."

"Then he is also your guardian, and you have no rights either. He could marry you to whomever he chose."

"Then if Ory is the filly, I must be the mare in which the author of the letter had no interest."

"Not very complimentary, but no doubt your cousin would have found a man who wanted you."

For some reason, something in that statement rang false; perhaps Barlicorn did not believe it himself. Why should he? There was nothing extraordinary about her: passably pretty but with neither the lively manner some men found attractive, nor the gentle, meek behavior that others preferred. A man bewitched by Ory would not give a snap of his fingers for her lack of dowry. Only a large dowry would make Rose appealing. The idea of her little sister being married so young, willy-nilly, was appalling.

"I cannot like the idea of my little sister marrying when she's not yet fifteen...but might she be better off as someone's wife than in Horace's power?"

"That," said Mistress Eccles to Barlicorn roundly, "serves you right for talking so mealy-mouthed, Barlicorn. Makes me wonder, it does, where you learned such gentrified ways."

The matron's observation disconcerted Rose as well as Barlicorn. At first he had sounded like a tradesman or clerk. Now she thought he had been speaking like a gentleman for some minutes. How odd. Was he too masquerading?

He hesitated before answering. "I've known gentry-folk enough to know what offends them."

The matron clucked and eyed him. "I'll say it if you won't."

"I'll do it. Ma'am, Stanbury might have meant marriage. Miss Ory said he talked to her about making a match for her and for you, too. But he might instead have been planning to sell her as a concubine to someone who prefers young girls."

Heart pounding, she blurted, "Surely he could not do such a thing even if he is her guardian. How could he explain her disappearance?"

"He could say he'd sent her to a ladies' seminary for a few years to gain polish. Eventually he could tell anyone who asked that she had made a runaway marriage from there or claim she had died of some illness or accident."

Before she could utter a word or even remember to breathe, he went on.

"And brothels will buy decent young women to improve their stock in trade."

"Virgins, he means," Mistress Eccles said. "Some men fancy a virgin."

Heart pounding, she could only stare at them, her cheeks flaming. She had not considered herself as sheltered as many unmarried girls. She had once begun reading a book called *The Fortunes and Misfortunes of the Famous Moll Flanders* which she had taken for a romance. When she realized her mistake, she had slipped it back into the bookroom while her father was occupied elsewhere. Since, she had met unfortunate women in Bethlehem House. Somehow none of that had been real to her until now.

The matron gazed at her pityingly. "A cup of tea is what you need. Come along now, we'll go see Cook."

Chapter 10

As Allan let himself in through the little gate at midmorning after a visit to the Green Tree, Chappell came out to greet him.

"Going to be a busy day, sir. I'm told we expect a load of furniture and goods soon. Mr. Hayes is here to make sure the delivery is put where it should go, as it was decided sudden-like and only half the rooms are ready. He's wishful to speak with you beforehand."

Hayes came out of the common room then.

"Mr. Everard, good day."

"Mr. Hayes, I understand you expect a carrier to bring some of the furnishings." He had formed a good opinion, endorsed by Peter Wilde, of the charity's man of business during the lease negotiations. "Pray let me know how I can be of assistance."

"Thank you. Perhaps you can, though not by helping move the furnishings...probably! Come, I should like to speak to you privately. The room to the right of the gate will do. I want to be nearby when the wagon comes."

In the former waiting room for coach passengers, Hayes positioned himself by one of the barred windows in the outer wall, like a cat at a mousehole. "I've come about a matter of security."

"Is there any way in which the Three Greyhounds is lacking? I realize it must be a consideration, given the residents' situation."

The man's intent gaze and slightly pursed lips hinted he was trying to find a way to explain. Allan asked baldly, "Why this agitation over a delivery of furniture, sir?"

" 'Tis not the delivery itself. The man who is most involved with the safety of those in the charity's houses will accompany it. He will discuss certain arrangements with you."

"And you worry he will not be pleased with the premises here? Was he not consulted before the charity leased it?"

"Of course, and was satisfied with it, too. The reason for his visit is a little unusual. Recently something has come up of which you should be informed."

Brows elevated inquiringly, Allan waited.

"As you mean to reside here, you are part of the charity's community and thus to some extent involved. He will explain."

"I shall look forward to it." Owning a property was more full of surprises than training as a steward, an occupation which Allan had previously found fascinating.

Hayes continued, "I must tell you he will be on the wagon. In disguise. He is somewhat unusual."

"I see." A very private gentleman, evidently. Though of course many a gentleman might prefer not to be associated with a shelter for poor women and children, most of them of the lowest sort. " 'Do good by stealth'?"

A reluctant smile greeted this quotation. "I agree with Pope's advice and so does our benefactor, but he's not, ah, gentry."

"Neither am I," Allan replied.

Hayes ignored Allan's dry admission. "However, he is strictly…" The man of business searched for a word. "Strictly fair and devoted to the safety of the charity's clients."

"I see." A Captain Hackum with a heart of gold? He looked forward to meeting the fellow.

Outside, a team turned toward the gate, and a man sprang down. "Ah, there he is." Hayes was already on his feet and striding for the door.

The gate bell rang, but Allan and Hayes reached the gate on Chappell's heels. He pulled the heavy bar up while Hayes pulled the first gate panel open as Allan dealt with the second. The drayman drove the low, sideless wagon into the yard, bringing it to a halt near the end of the inn's left wing. Chappell and Allan swung the gates shut, and Chappell dropped the bar into the brackets.

Hayes had gone to the dray on which several large crates had been roped down. The second man was already on the ground when Allan turned away from the gates. He wore a disreputable broad-brimmed hat and an enveloping greatcoat as the day was overcast and chilly.

Allan did not approach. The degree of secrecy implied in the visit suggested Hayes and the stranger would wish to conduct their business in privacy. Then both looked toward him and exchanged a few words. Hayes beckoned him over.

"Mr. Everard, this is Barlicorn."

"I'm right glad to meet you, Mr. Everard."

His voice was at odds with his dress and words. He was tall and lean, and a queue of russet hair hung under his old hat. Everard revised his previous expectation of a ruffian looking like bull-beef. Face to face, his eyes brimmed with intelligence and a trace of humor. His greeting was what any laborer might say, but his tone and diction belonged to a slightly higher class. A clerk, perhaps, but a prodigious confident one.

"How do you do, Mr. Barlicorn?"

His grin showed white, slightly crooked teeth. "I'm no one to be calling 'Mister.' Barlicorn's only a nickname. You're welcome to use it, sir."

"Because it's not your name?"

"Using my name would do the charity no favor."

"I'll see to the…unloading…now," Hayes said.

"Good, best to do that quick. Mr. Everard and I will talk in the common room." With a gesture toward the other wing, Barlicorn invited Everard to proceed him as if he were the host.

"We'll sit in the corner farthest from the kitchen for privacy, Mr. Everard."

When Mistress Chappell appeared surrounded by the aroma of something savory to offer refreshments, Barlicorn thanked her and refused. "Best we not be interrupted." He did not continue at once.

The man's gaze weighed him in a manner which would have been insulting if Everard had not sensed an authority nearly as absolute as a nobleman's or a judge's. It sat oddly on a man many respectable folk would have distrusted on principle.

"If we paid you a fair rent for your chamber, would you move to lodgings elsewhere?"

"Why?" No objection to his living there had been raised in the negotiations.

Barlicorn steepled his fingers. "Since we leased the inn, a problem has arisen. If you are living here, you may become embroiled in it whether you or we wish it or not."

Allan steepled his own fingers. *We*, the fellow said, as if he were a principal of the Bethlehem House charity. "I am comfortable here and would be reluctant to move in the absence of a compelling reason." If he agreed, where would he live? He could afford rooms in the sort of lodging rented by unmarried men of moderate means. The drawback would be that in such a place he might meet men of the landed gentry and second or third sons of the aristocracy. It wasn't likely any of them would know him, but unless he shunned them, sooner or later he would be asked about his family connections, what school he had attended, a host of questions he could not answer.

"There might be some danger."

"I think you must tell me more about this problem of yours."

"Two of the young ladies who were recently admitted to Bethlehem House came to us from better circumstances than most of the women."

"Ladies?" If they were ladies, they must indeed be something out of the ordinary for the home.

"They were left to the guardianship of a distant cousin they had never heard of. The elder sister began to fear for the younger's safety." A pause to see if Everard understood.

"Like that, was it?"

"Ay. She and the girl fled and fortunately met with one of the charity's supporters within hours of setting foot in London."

"They were lucky." Long before he had come to town himself, he knew of its dangers.

"The guardian is pursuing them."

"How could he find them? What could he do apart from notifying the magistrates and any friends the family has here?"

"Sketches he made of his cousins have been circulating, offering a guinea for news of their whereabouts, if correct. Someone is asking questions more discreetly in better areas about new servants."

Everard whistled. "Not many would resist such a windfall."

"No."

"If he is so free with his money, he will find the ladies sooner or later." Gossip and even casual talk traveled. "The law will be on his side."

"Not if we can conceal them until August. Under their father's will, once the older sister turns one-and-twenty, she will be the younger girl's guardian."

"Then we need not worry too much. He cannot have many resources apart from money to find two missing straws in London's haystack."

"I think he will not give up easily, as they are worth a great deal to him. He also possesses very useful connections here."

"Is he a nobleman, then?" A title was an invaluable assistance in getting one's own way.

"He is merely gentry, but he is remarkable in some ways."

Seeing Allan's expression, the man who was himself distinctly unusual said, "Consider what we know: he is searching for the young ladies with more thoroughness than one expects from an ordinary gentleman; he is plump in the pocket, judging from his ability to have his drawings printed and distributed and to offer a guinea reward. At Stanbury, he had the volume of correspondence you'd expect of a successful merchant, although the young ladies believed him to be a fashionable gentleman. Yet he has access to bullies and huffs to search for the young ladies. No magistrate in either the City or Westminster has been informed they were missing. I'd lay odds that would be an ordinary gentleman's first resort."

"Unless he feared making a scandal?"

Barlicorn quirked an eyebrow. "Would an ordinary gentleman know and employ bullies to search for misplaced young ladies?"

"No."

"I thought not."

"Then how can you locate the fellow?"

Barlicorn leaned forward. "I've seen a good likeness of Stanbury who looks like a man I was told runs an expensive brothel. Stanbury had in his possession a ring engraved with the insigne of a well-known bordello."

"The Devil fly away with him!" was Allan's first reaction. His second was to wonder, *How many clerks know the correct singular form of insignia?*

"Nothing called the place to my attention before. Now I have someone making inquiries."

Barlicorn was something other than what he appeared to be at first glance, as he himself was. But what?

Before he could follow that thought, Barlicorn said, "Stanbury's criminal connections introduce some danger into housing the ladies."

"If you mean to bring them here, the gates should provide enough security as long as they remain inside. 'Tis unlikely we will be besieged. This is not the Middle Ages, after all."

"I do think this is the safest refuge for them." His crooked-toothed smile invited Allan to share a joke. "By now they've been freed from their crates."

"What?"

"Moving household goods in made it easy to bring them here secretly, but we cannot count on Stanbury giving up his search for them. They cannot hide here forever, and this is not a fortress. Someone with criminals at his disposal, a sort of arch-rogue, could breach it."

"Is that what we are dealing with?" *We.* He had counted himself with the charity without a second thought. He did not merely live here: the property belonged to him. He was as much a landowner as any member of the landed gentry, if not as respectable.

"I doubt Stanbury himself is an arch-rogue." He laughed a little, inexplicably. "But he can hire bullies and bravoes as he has the money to employ a small army of men to pass out the drawings of the ladies."

The door opened, and the drayman stood, looking in their direction.

"Time for you to meet them," Barlicorn said.

The crates had been returned to the dray. The driver muttered "All's bob," as Barlicorn passed.

"Good. Thanks for your help. Mr. Simmons is arranging for the rest of the beds and bed-clothes, so your next delivery should be in a day or two. You'll have your usual mate to help, not a gent." Hayes, outside one of the rooms, laughed.

The man gave a gap-toothed grin, swung himself onto the seat, and gave the horses the office to move almost in one motion.

Barlicorn went to join Hayes, Allan following after.

The man of business said, "They're in this one."

Barlicorn said, "They'll be moved to a room on the other side. The furnishings are being stored in this wing so it made sense to unload them here."

At Hayes's knock and soft "Mistress?" a voice called, "You may enter."

A lady stood in the middle of the room, stopped in the act of pacing, perhaps, as she might have sat on one of the two chairs. "Mr. Hayes?"

She was the needle-witted female who had accompanied the curate and Simon Hayes on their inspection of the inn. The memory of her face and figure and her common sense tended to haunt him in the minutes before he fell asleep, together with the thought, *Where can I find one like her?*

A faerie-like miss perched on the bed, chewing her lower lip. At their entrance, she bounced to her feet.

"Ma'am, I know you met Mr. Everard earlier. Miss Hortense Milton, may I present Mr. Allan Everard?"

"Mr. Everard." Mistress Milton curtsied. She inclined her head and murmured, "Good morning," to Barlicorn. The younger girl echoed her greeting and curtsy, and added a smile.

The men bowed. Barlicorn's half bow, from a man who looked as if he might have been born and bred in London's meanest alleys, was graceful. "You'll be moving to a room on the other side, between the caretaker and his wife, and the matron." To Hayes, he added, "Chappell and I will move furniture into that one."

"I'll help," Allan volunteered without thinking. Why had he—? Perhaps for the same reason some landowners assisted in the harvest or sheep-shearing.

Certainly not because of the grave lady in her plain gown and round-eared cap or her nymph of a sister.

Mistress Milton's smile made the serious lady vanish. "Thank you. All of you. I have been so worried."

"Will we stay here always?" the young girl asked.

Barlicorn answered. "No, miss, only until we've made sure your cousin can't find you."

"We are more grateful than I can say for your help," Rose said. "But how can we ever be free? Even after I'm of age, someone who has seen our images may recognize us."

A swift glance passed between Barlicorn and Hayes. The question had occurred to Allan as well.

"We are exploring several possible solutions," Hayes replied. "At the moment, however, we will move you to the other wing."

The man of business did not scorn labor, either. The bed, a deal table, a pair of chairs, and a wash stand were soon in place in a room across the yard. The ladies carried their valises.

When they were done, Barlicorn muttered to Everard, "A word with you and Hayes before he leaves."

In the common room, Mistress Chappell brought ale to their table without being asked. The drink was welcome after the morning's revelations and exertion.

"Have you reconsidered your decision to stay here, Mr. Everard? Once the ladies are safe, you could return."

"I'm not leaving."

"The inconvenience and risk to you—"

"I will not abandon the inn. The Three Greyhounds or whatever you mean to call it."

"This is not a fight for a gentleman."

"You have mistaken me. I am only a bastard, not a

gentleman, though I suspect you may be and certainly Mr. Hayes is."

The man of business dipped his head in ironical acknowledgement. The other showed no reaction except to say, "I'm no gentleman. Why would you stay?"

"This is the only 'manor' I'll ever own. It makes me a landed by-blow," he added wryly.

The man barked a short laugh. "I see."

And Allan thought perhaps he did.

"Then perhaps we'll find a use for you."

Sensing he was about to be dismissed, an odd thought when as the son of a nobleman Allan must outrank Barlicorn in theory despite being illegitimate. However well-spoken he was, he was at home among the dregs of society.

"What is your plan to end the danger to Mistress Rose and her sister?"

"I cannot make one until I know more about their cousin. At worst, once she is of age, they should be out of danger."

Not precisely reassuring.

Chapter 11

Rose and Ory were the first to take up residence at the Three Greyhounds. After the clamor and crowding of Bethlehem House, the silent, empty rooms felt wrong, even though Rose had often longed for the peace of Stanbury Manor before their cousin's arrival. The first week, alone with the caretaker and his wife and Mr. Allan Everard, was like a protracted pause in the middle of a sentence, while the hearer waits for its ending. Barlicorn had warned her and her sister against going out. The admonition was unnecessary. At Bethlehem House, they had been too shaken by their initial experience of London and too frightened of the down-at-heel neighborhood to leave the charity's shelter. Since learning of Horace's intense search for them, Rose was happy to comply.

She gave as much help to Mistress Chappell as the woman would accept for lack of anything else to do. But Ory missed her friends at their first refuge and wandered through the rooms.

Crates containing a number of books were delivered, with a bookcase. This surprised her, considering the charity served so many who were unlikely to be able to read. On reflection, she might have expected it, as the charity was quite different from any other she had heard of. Ory unpacked and arranged them in the former passengers' waiting room, but slowly, as she tended to get lost in the pages of intriguing volumes.

They all sat around a scarred old table near the kitchen for meals: she and Ory, the Chappells, and Mr. Everard. He was on easy terms with the cook and caretaker, and Rose and Molly Chappell had been on first name terms by the second day, but Ory remained somewhat timid with adults she did not know well. At supper the fourth evening, when conversation momentarily failed, Mr. Everard asked what Ory found to interest her in her ramblings through the bare chambers.

Ory hesitated. Then words poured out like ale from a pitcher. "The inn has seen so much life. Our family has lived at St—our old home—for a long time, but nothing really interesting ever happened there."

"Only births and deaths and generations of our forebears' lives," Rose pointed out.

"That's what I'm saying, Rose. This place is full of memories of everyone who passed through it. Where were they going? Were they happy or sad or afraid? There's a window on the street side over the gate where someone etched something on one of the panes, I suppose with a diamond so he must have been wealthy. *I go to find my heart,* it said. Was he following the lady he loved? And in another there's one in a foreign language. It's in the big bedchamber in the southeast corner."

Everard's fork paused in the act of spearing a chunk of mutton. "The one that's engraved 'Paso por aquí de camino a Hampton Court 1554 Don Diego Anascote'?"

"Yes! I wish I knew what it meant."

"While I don't speak Spanish, when I saw it, I suspected it meant a Spaniard was on his way to

Hampton Court to attend upon King Philip II."

Her little sister's expression suggested she was searching her memory for a king of that name. Before she could give her a hint, Everard added, "Queen Mary Tudor's husband, you know."

Ory sighed. "How exciting it must have been to live in those times."

At fourteen or fifteen, Rose supposed she would have thought so, too, ignoring the horrid persecution of Protestants under Bloody Mary.

When they'd finished eating and the table was cleared, Ory went to find a book with a few engravings of historical figures from the period, meaning to draw them in some of the inn's rooms. Mistress Chappell retreated to the kitchen to begin washing dishes and her husband to the stable through the gate at the back of the inn where he was building a simple table and benches for the children's play room.

Rose remained at the table, almost too tired to move. She should help Molly with the dishes though the cook discouraged her from working in the kitchen. "There's not much trouble in washing so few dishes and pots with enough hot water, vinegar, ash, and brick dust. And you should be saving your hands." *For what?* Rose wondered.

She should take advantage of the summer evening's long light to finish inventorying the sheets, blankets, and coverlets which had arrived late in the afternoon, then distribute them to the rooms that had beds but no bedding. Everard had begun to rise, then dropped back onto the bench.

"You work too hard," he said. "If there's any way I can help, you've only to tell me."

"You're very kind to offer, sir, but you've already done so much for the charity by letting them have the stable as well as the inn and paying for the fireplace yourself. No one could expect a gentleman to do menial work."

"I'm not..." A pause. "I'm not so proud. I helped Chappell with the repairs to the Greyhounds. They took several months."

"Oh. It turned out very well." He must have had little money to fix the old inn. Perhaps he had spent nearly all he had to buy it.

"I enjoyed doing it. When I walked through it and saw the workmanship and the inscriptions in the windows, I felt as your sister does. There are six inscriptions in the windows and might have been more if some panes had not been broken and replaced."

"You fell in love with it."

"I did."

"I would not have expected a gentleman to buy or take an interest in an old inn."

His expression was unreadable. She must have offended him. Before leaving her home, she would not have forgotten the manners she had been taught, no matter what she thought. Except that she had around Cousin Horace, leading to his dislike of her. In her new situation, however, no one minced delicately around any subject.

"The inn was left to me by gift."

"You might have found it more convenient to receive funds, but 'twas well for us, the charity I mean, that you were given the inn."

Smiling, he said, "In fact, I find the inn was a far better gift. It has given me something interesting to do.

Money would not have made it possible for me to fit into good society."

"Whyever not?"

"I'm not a gentleman though my foster father raised me as one. I'm a by-blow. When my natural father died, I was banished from his property."

When she was still a gentlewoman, she never would have heard such an admission. "I suppose your father did the best he could, for I suppose he placed you with your foster father, who did well for you. And he gave you the inn. In any case, why should anyone know your origin?"

He sighed. "If I mingled in good society, sooner or later I might encounter someone who had visited my father or half brother or one of their servants and be recognized as the steward's assistant. I have made friends among gentlemen here who work for a living and are unlikely to ask about my family unless I request permission to court one of their sisters. They might not care about my origins, as long as I could prove I wasn't a fortune hunter."

"I had not thought of that. Of course one delves into a prospective spouse's history. Your problem is the same as mine, then. I cannot see a way my sister and I will ever be able to return to the life we were born to. But living and working here is better than whatever our cousin planned for us." She shivered. "Though I worry about Ory's future."

"Did you have no family or friends you could turn to when you escaped your guardian?"

"No. Our only remaining family is our grandfather and our uncle and his wife, who live with him. We were turned away by our aunt. She pretended not to recognize us and in any event, Grandpapa is seriously ill, as we have not received a letter from him since before Christmas."

"But then someone—Mr. Simmons, I think?— found you."

"We were sitting on the steps of St. George's, Hanover Square, and I was weeping like a ninny, wondering what we were to do." She swallowed a lump in her throat at the memory. "Thank goodness Ory took charge and told Mr. Simmons what had happened, for I was overset. I'd never have expected it of her, as she's always been rather shy. She's growing up."

"I cannot imagine you as a ninny, ma'am. You had every reason to be terrified and at a loss. Once you're of age, your difficulties will be over."

If only they might be.

****

Furnishings continued to arrive, and she and Ory, and Mr. Everard as well, made themselves useful by arranging furniture and hanging curtains. A number of the women at Bethlehem House had been busy sewing window coverings from heavy linen dowlas or from the coarse woolen cloth called bay.

The first few residents trickled in, some with children. Rose showed them to rooms according to a list written by Anne, and Ory kept the children amused and out of the way while their mothers settled into their temporary home.

Anne came to take her new post as matron of the Three Greyhounds. She continued to polish the behavior of aspiring servants in addition to her new duties. Rose taught children and women to write and instructed Anne's potential housekeepers in arithmetick and how to keep a ledger. Her days were now satisfyingly full, although in spare moments, her mind wandered to Allan Everard. Had he met any of his friends' sisters? More to the point, was he considering one of them as a bride? Not that it was any business of hers, of course.

Chapter 12

Before the Three Greyhounds was fully equipped, Allan had helped Chappell with gate duty and oversaw the disposition of the furnishings. With the last of the women moved in, he was left with nothing to do. He met with one or more of his acquaintances to play cards or to drink coffee or claret in the evening, but once he had seen the sights of London, the daylight hours hung heavily upon him. One morning, he met Solomon de Toledo by chance after leaving his bank. The moneylender asked how he was faring in London now the Three Greyhounds had been leased. Presumably Simon Hayes had told him. The transaction had not been a secret, after all. De Toledo invited him to his coffee house where they spent a pleasant hour chewing over the news. They would meet again, but like Allan's coffee house friends, de Toledo had his own business to tend during the day.

He must find some way to occupy himself. The question of what occupation he could engage in gave him pause. His foster father had written humorous verse in Latin, some of which had been printed. Could he take up writing? Under an assumed name, of course, as Lord Passevant's fury at seeing Everard's name in some publication was not to be thought of. No, he felt no urge to put down his thoughts on paper and no inkling of a notion of what he could write about. Buy a business he could oversee without having to work in it? The temptation to meddle, to make it more profitable or more efficient might be overwhelming. Investing in something over which he had no control, like ship cargoes, would be a form of gambling: too much depended on the expertise of others and on chance.

Before he reached any decision, however, he heard the matron and Rose discussing the latter's children's arithmetick class.

"It's not that there are so many; it's that there is such a wide variation in ages and abilities. Some of the boys are restless, too, and maybe resent being taught by a female."

"Perhaps Mr. Simmons can arrange for a man to come in and tutor them."

Everard interrupted, "I could do it. I'm already here, and I have time."

Both heads turned to stare at him.

"We should not impose on you," Anne said as Rose asked, "Would you really?"

"I'd be glad of something to do. I've never taught, but my own tutor made lessons understandable and sometimes even enjoyable. Before I came to London, I assisted the steward on a property that was not contemptible." He hoped Anne would not ask for a reference or for the estate's name.

"Would you consider teaching jointly with Rose for a few sessions, to see if you were willing to continue on your own?"

So Matron could determine whether he was competent and would stick to it? "Of course. That would give the boys time to get used to me. May I ask how many students there are in all? And can they all read at least their numbers?"

"The six youngest are learning to read. The other eleven can all read...to some degree."

"And what materials have you to teach with?"

She sighed, almost invisibly. "Any scraps of paper we can get. The street boys collect them for us. We use any blank space on discarded newssheets, the back of playbills, wrapping paper, and anything else they find. We use straws to work problems."

With a fair idea of what Mistress Milton and he had to deal with, he thanked her and bade her good day.

The following day did not see a great deal of arithmetick accomplished. Allan's presence alone accounted for some of the excitement, but when he unpacked the copies of *Cocker's Arithmetick* and the blank exercise books and pencils, Rose Milton sacrificed her planned lesson without a qualm.

"*Cocker's*." She paged through it reverently. "This will make it so much easier for the more advanced students. The less advanced will have to make do with the straw method."

"They'll move on to the books eventually. Do you think it would help them to write down their straw calculations in the exercise books? Seeing that two straws and three straws equal five is simple and practical, but writing it down in figures may reinforce the lesson."

"You would let them use the exercise books? They aren't only for your boys?"

"There are enough for the whole class, and extras for new students. And the donor will provide more as needed. They should write their names in them. A locking chest will be delivered later today. It's probably best they be kept there between lessons. I lost my first exercise book."

"Were you punished?"

"No. My foster father knew that small boys lose things, even books. But I felt guilty for years that I had disappointed him." Why had he shared that humiliation with her?

She thanked him warmly, ending, "I would never have thought of approaching someone to ask for a donation of anything. However did you find the donor?"

"He's just someone I know." She did not question his vague reply. She did ask where they could write to thank him.

"He prefers to, ah, do good by stealth."

When they parted, her step was sprightlier and her shoulders less tense. A very satisfactory beginning, he thought. Once he knew which of his students might profit from it, he would get a set of Napier's Bones for more complex calculations.

****

Allan was jotting notes on the boys' progress when a tap at the door interrupted his train of thought. "Come in," he called, reflecting too late that for a female to enter his chamber would give cause for talk. The door opened, admitting a gust of damp air. "Barlicorn?"

He was again wearing the concealing hat and coat, this time speckled with raindrops. He must have come with the wagon that had rattled into the yard a few minutes ago. His presence struck Allan as an omen of trouble.

At his invitation, Barlicorn draped his coat over a straight chair in front of the small hearth and hung his hat from a hook on the mantel to dry.

Allan offered claret. Barlicorn accepted but wasted no breath on idle chat.

"I set people to find Stanbury, which should not have been difficult. Instead it proved surprisingly hard."

"But you knew of his connection to a brothel. Could you not trace him from there?"

"You would think so, but until recently I had no success. A fashionable gentleman resident in London for some years should be found where such men amuse themselves. They attend the theater, masquerades at the Haymarket, and the usual gentlemen's entertainments. My people had no success in finding him or his direction. However, for the last week, several of my people have watched the Purring Cat. One of them passes as a beggar without the coin to hire a bed for the night. Another sells gingerbread. There are others, not always the same ones. In all, the brothel is watched day and night, at both the front door and the rear door on the alley. On Monday morning, Stanbury emerged with a pair of huffs—two of his men who deal with drunken or violent patrons. My watcher followed them to a bank. Stanbury went in. His guards waited outside and were dismissed when he came out. He went on to the Noble Cup, a coffee house on High Holborn before returning to the Purring Cat. Wednesday and today, he followed the same routine except he then returned immediately to the brothel. I suspect he follows the same pattern each week."

"Depositing the brothel's earnings every other day? That would make sense. He must live there, too, if your intelligencers haven't seen him go to lodgings."

"Ay."

The rogue's eyes gleamed with amusement. *Or something.*

"You've shown yourself a friend to the charity, Mr. Everard, so I will make bold to ask you to do us another favor. Monday at nine in the morning I'd like you to be in the Noble Cup."

"For what purpose?"

"Everything depends upon circumstances. You might be able to strike up an acquaintance with him. Or you might find he meets someone there. You'll be able to judge if it's a chance meeting or by arrangement. If the latter, I'd like you to follow Stanbury's associate to discover his name and where we can find him."

"Zounds, I would be happy to help if I thought I could be successful, but isn't this a job for someone more familiar with London and more sociable than I? Like you, mayhap?"

"You have one outstanding qualification for the purpose beyond intelligence. You have a way of making yourself inconspicuous. My face may be known to Stanbury as I recognized him as the owner of the Purring Cat from Miss Ory's drawing even though I'd only seen him once or twice. All of the men I'd usually use for such a task would be out of place at the Noble Cup."

"What sort of men does it attract?"

"Those who are genteel and have some money."

"Barlicorn, I would prefer not to mingle with the aristocracy." He needed to explain his reluctance while keeping the desperation out of his voice.

"You're not likely to meet them there. It's popular with gentlemen, some knights and baronets, maybe a few of the upper nobility, but they're likely to be still a-bed at that hour. Stanbury is there at the end of his day, not the beginning. There is a sprinkling of those who happen to be passing and stop for refreshment, so an unfamiliar face will not be conspicuous. Anything we can learn of the man may help Rose and her sister."

Oh, Hades.

****

Pausing inside the door, Allan breathed in the scent of roasting coffee and the tobacco from the pipes of two of the customers. The Noble Cup was better furnished than most of the coffee houses he had seen, with handsome tables, chairs rather than benches, and paintings on the walls. The cups and mugs bore the coffee house's sign, a crowned cup. A mere handful of men scattered the room. The hour was too early for those who did not work for a living.

From a table in a corner near the door, he pretended to consult his notebook while a brisk serving boy fetched his coffee. The knowledge this excursion was bound to fail chafed him. His life was already full of humiliation; he did not need the added shame of reporting his lack of success to Barlicorn, who might almost be a friend. He could not hide his education and his sometimes cultured speech. Like Allan, he was somehow caught between classes.

In Passevant Parva as a boy, the sons of the gentry scorned him. The children of laborers, tradesmen, and artisans stayed away from him because he was the son of a lord, even if he had been born on the wrong side of the blanket. Best to avoid giving offense to the earl's family either by familiarity with his by-blow or by snubbing him.

Augustus, Baron Passevant, had been kind to have him fostered by Raymond Willis, who had educated him almost like a gentleman (though he had been spared Greek and Latin, except for some useful law Latin). Yet in some ways his upbringing had been a mixed blessing. He had learned the importance of working hard, not making mistakes, humility, and of doing as he was bid. In short, of being better behaved than a gentleman while conducting himself like an upper servant. While his foster father would be horrified to hear him describe it thus, that was the truth.

Salt had taught him how to be a steward but as only an assistant. He was never permitted to make a decision without Salt's permission. Understandable when a mistake would reflect on Salt although when he proposed an action, Salt had almost always agreed to it. Nevertheless, now Allan was his own master, he hesitated to make any decision affecting others without approval.

His apparent study of the notebook kept anyone from joining him and provided an excuse for lingering. Hearing the door open, he glanced over the top of the book. The newcomer sauntered to an empty table at the other end of the room, giving the woman behind the serving counter a friendly nod and receiving a smile in reply. He seated himself facing the door.

Stanbury was instantly recognizable from the drawing Barlicorn had given him. He looked the part of a prosperous gentleman in a peacock-blue suit with bands of silver tape at the wide cuffs and edging the pocket flaps and neck. His cream silk waistcoat was embroidered with peacocks. Somewhat ostentatious for casual day wear. He was dressed for his night at the Purring Cat.

Allan had put on one of his new suits, to pass as a man of some means, golden-brown with a waistcoat of the same and matching thread buttons.

A boy came hurrying with a tray holding coffee and a bun and turned smartly at Stanbury's table. Impossible to hear if they exchanged words, and the boy's back blocked Allan's view so he could not even see whether they spoke at greater length than service would account for. Likely not, as he paused no longer than necessary to set coffee and bun before Stanbury and to receive a coin. When the server hastened away, Allan saw the brothel keeper breaking the seal on a letter.

Not good news: he frowned as he read it. Folding it and slipping it into his pocket, Stanbury addressed himself to his coffee and food. He did not remain long after finishing.

Allan looked up as Stanbury stalked out, then rose leisurely and approached the serving counter.

"Can I help you, sir?" the woman asked cheerfully, and he ceased to be nervous. No one had given him a second look. He had come here to play a role as in a play. Suddenly it felt natural.

"I noticed the man who left a moment ago, the one in a fine blue coat? I thought he looked like the cousin of a friend of mine from university, though I believed he was living at Carlisle. Can you tell me his name? I didn't like to run after him and make a fool of myself."

The woman smiled at this sheepish admission. "I saw him for the first time in early April, so mayhap he has moved to London, if 'tis your acquaintance. I recall it particularly because someone"—she blushed prettily—"gave me a bunch of bluebells that very morning, and they'd only just come into bloom. His name is Mr. Horace Stanbury. Would that be your friend's relative?"

Allan shook his head. "Alack, no. A different relative of his, possibly. I'll ask my friend when next I see him. Thank you, mistress. 'Tis a pleasant place you have here. I'll come again."

****

He went next day by appointment to Simon Hayes's office. Barlicorn did not like to be seen too often at the charities' houses. Allan did not ask why, remembering something he had said the first day he came to the Greyhounds: "…using my name would do the charity no favor." Neither, apparently, would his face. The man was as much of an enigma as Horace Stanbury.

Hayes showed him to a small room where Barlicorn was waiting, a sheaf of documents on the table before him. He rose, greeted Allan, and passed the papers to Hayes. "They're satisfactory," he said briefly. The man of business nodded and left them alone.

"I review the charity's business here," Barlicorn explained. Gesturing for Allan to sit, he asked, "What success did you have?"

"Very little. Stanbury arrived, was served without the necessity of ordering—"

"As if he were so predictable a customer they knew what he would want?"

"Indeed. He read a letter while he ate. He spoke to no one but the waiter."

Barlicorn stared at him as if Allan had said something startling. "He read a letter?"

"Ay, and when he had finished his coffee and pastry, he left."

"Where did he get the letter? Did he bring it with him or receive it at the coffee house?"

He summoned up the memory of Stanbury entering. "He had a walking stick in his right hand, nothing in his left."

"Could it have been in his pocket?"

"It might have been—"

But he had kept his eyes on the man continually from his arrival to his departure, despite the discomfort of pretending to stare at his notebook while focusing his eyes over it. "No, I don't think it could have been. He was sitting with his right side to me, and I could see his arm even when the waiter was standing beside the table. He did reach into his pocket once, before the boy served him, but he didn't take out a letter. It must have been a coin, because he paid the lad. And when the waiter left, Stanbury was opening the letter."

"So he receives some mail at the coffee house. That's useful. Presumably he receives other mail elsewhere. According to Mistress Rose, he sent and received a great many letters. Was there anything else you noticed, Everard?"

"The letter was not over-long, and it annoyed him. Oh, and although he was on good terms with the proprietress, he hasn't been their customer long. Only since April."

"Huh." Barlicorn seemed lost in thought. "I'm trying to remember something I was told about Stanbury. I think an interview with their family's former attorney is called for. You'll need a letter of introduction from Mistress Rose."

Chapter 13

He met Rose in the matron's office with Anne in attendance for propriety.

"Of course I'll write Mr. Brand. I wanted to send a message soon after we were rescued by Mr. Simmons, but I feared Cousin Horace or a magistrate would ask him about us and he would have to lie. If Horace has not already sought him out, I suppose he does not mean to. Our attorney may be able to help. I am already easier in my mind to know that Barlicorn is studying the problem…and you, too, I gather, Mr. Everard?"

Anne said, "There's paper in the upper left drawer. You may as well write your letter now while Mr. Everard tells us if there's been any progress in the matter."

"Not a great deal to report, I'm sorry to say, except that Barlicorn had him followed and discovered he has a certain routine three days a week. I observed him at his regular coffee house today. Barlicorn thought we might learn something from Brand. Your attorney is the one who found your unknown cousin?"

"Yes." Rose dipped the quill in the standish. "He discovered something in his files from years ago, long before I was born." She sanded the sheet and found a wafer seal in the drawer before tipping the sand back into its pot. She licked her thumb, moistened the seal, and pressed it down across the overlapping edge of the paper. "There! Not very ladylike of me, I fear."

Not very gentlemanly of him to find the sight of her tongue so arousing, but one's body's reactions were beyond one's conscious control. Later he remembered he had not told Rose about her cousin's connection to a brothel. Perhaps keeping that shocking news from her was the best course.

****

He told the clerk he had an urgent legal matter and would gladly pay for an hour of the attorney's time but needed to see him today if at all possible. Five minutes later, he was ushered into the man's office, and the door closed behind him.

"This is from Mistress Rosabel Stanbury."

Lucian Brand tore the letter open. Just as well the lady had written concisely, for after a minute or less, the attorney huffed out a breath. "Thank God they're safe. When I learned they had disappeared and heard nothing more—except a letter from Stanbury asking if I knew where they were—I began to be afraid for them. How can I help Mistress Rosabel?"

Allan had planned what he would say. Now he abandoned his prepared explanation in favor of bluntness. "We don't think we can wait for her to come of age to change the guardianship." He described the sketches being passed out and the lack of official involvement in the search for the girls. "Mayhap 'hunt' would be a better word."

Brand's eyebrows drew together. "Are you certain the men taking the drawings around are not simply whatever riff-raff he could hire cheaply rather than criminals? That he may be reserved and not easy to like, I can believe as he seemed to me to be rather strict in his views of morality. That he might take an inappropriate interest in Miss Oriana is not out of the question. Any man of law knows of men whose appearance of probity covers appalling faults of conduct."

"A friend of the charity has traced him to a brothel."

"Men do use such places," Brand pointed out.

"Indeed. But he has in his possession a ring with the emblem of the Purring Cat. I confess I am not yet familiar with all London's ways. Do men who frequent a bordello of the better sort all have them, as men who buy a season ticket to Vauxhall Gardens receive a token they show on entering?" Allan asked, equally dry, and went on, "He also lives on the premises."

"That is troubling. Are you are thinking the Court of Chancery might remove him as guardian for that reason?"

"Would they?"

"I would not depend upon it or even raise it as an issue unless there's something else. Owning a bawdy-house is no more illegal than selling vegetables or books."

"What would sway them?"

"Evidence of a crime."

What crime might Stanbury have committed? Barlicorn might have the resources to find out. "I have wandered from the reason I came. Will you tell me how you discovered Stanbury, with as much detail as you can?"

Brand sat back. "There's not much to tell. The firm has represented the Stanbury family since my grandfather's time. The Stanbury estate being entailed, Mr. Paul Stanbury's death meant I had to search for any possible heir, although I could not recall ever hearing of an heir presumptive. That led me to search through our records. Fortunately I had to go back no further than 1705." A rather smug smile. "In that year, the only brother of the girls' Stanbury grandfather died, and their grandfather became guardian of his only nephew, Horace Stanbury. In 1708, when Horace was turned eighteen, Grandfather Stanbury contributed a substantial amount of his own money to set up an annuity through my father, conditioned upon the money being paid out quarterly by Pimling's Bank here in London. He counted upon the difficulty of travel in those days being enough to keep the boy here, and I suppose too that the country held no interest for him. As I knew where the annuity was paid, I wrote to Pimling's asking them to give my enclosed letter to him when next he came in."

"When did you write?"

"Near the middle of March. Paul Stanbury died in February, and I learned of it a week later, but digging back through decades of documents and files took considerable time as such an important question could not be left to a clerk. Not even mine, though he's very good."

"And did Stanbury reply promptly? I have a reason for asking, sir."

"Not as promptly as I'd expect, given the size of the inheritance. I'd have expected he would draw his Lady Day payment out of Pimling's the day it was paid, but I did not hear from him until April."

According to the coffee house proprietress, he'd begun patronizing the place in April. He had wanted a place to receive Brand's mail other than the bank or the brothel. "The account of the annuity and why it was set up should cast some doubt about his fitness, shouldn't it?"

"Mr. Everard, did Mistress Rosabel tell you I no longer represent the Stanburys? Her cousin requested I transfer my files to his own lawyer."

"She did not."

"Perhaps he didn't tell her or mayhap she hoped I would help as a family friend. But in answer to your question, no, I don't think his wild youth more than thirty years ago would be enough to take away the guardianship."

"Our confounded luck! We need something we can use against him."

Brand coughed diffidently. "As it happens, while I did turn over the bulk of the files to his new attorney, I did not include the materials from Paul Stanbury's father's time and before. Subsequently I read the correspondence that led to the establishment of the annuity. I should have read everything relating to Horace before that date. A mistake on my part, I know. Horace began cheating at cards when he was still at school and did not improve after being expelled. There was some suspicion he was also a thief, although with no witness and nothing found in his possession or in his room, there was not enough to charge him. The elder Mr. Stanbury washed his hands of his nephew by setting up the annuity. However, even if I had seen the correspondence in which Horace was described as 'a hell-born babe' as they used to say, it would not necessarily prevent his being made guardian. Wild young men may improve with age."

And sometimes dishonest young men turn into old criminals.

"Rosabel was uneasy about him from the first, but I assumed that was because she is a young lady of, shall we say, firm opinions, which might lead to a battle of wills. Another misjudgment on my part."

Allan emerged from Brand's office where Chancery Lane met Cursitors Alley and came almost face-to-face with Julius Passevant.

"You!" his half brother snarled. "What are you doing here?"

"I live in London now." His momentary hesitation before replying, born of years of understanding his place at Passevant depended on not intruding himself upon the family's notice, went unremarked.

"Came out of some pettifogging lawyer's office, didn't you? You'll never get work there or anywhere else. I'll see to that." He started to push past Allan to enter Brand's office.

"You needn't bother Mr. Brand, my lord. He did not hire me."

"Be damned to you." The baron jerked open the door and stalked inside.

His heart pounding, Allan forced himself to stroll away rather than risk confronting Baron Passevant in a rage. And that was what he felt, rather than dread of what Julius Passevant could do. Fury was preferable to resignation, even if there was nothing he could do to strike back. He turned into the nearest coffee house to drink a glass of claret and contemplate the discovery that anger could be liberating.

He tossed off the last of his wine. He was no worse than many men, despite his birth. He was intelligent, hard-working, and as a man of property, entitled to vote. He could pass as a gentleman. If Rose could not find a way to re-enter the society into which she was born, she might be willing to marry him. He could support her comfortably in a suitable house in a respectable part of town. Her sister could make a decent match, if not the one birth entitled her to...Egad, where had that daydream come from? Both deserved to be restored to their rightful place, if Barlicorn could find a way to do it.

Tomorrow he would report to Barlicorn what he had learned from Brand and ask if there was some way of saving their reputations. He suspected the rogue's network of friends reached across social classes, given his air of assurance. If nothing could be done to salvage the Stanbury ladies' reputations...He suppressed that thought.

Chapter 14

One good had come from their new life: Ory's shyness was a thing of the past. She had begun to make a circle of friends at Bethlehem House, and now at the Three Greyhounds, she acquired two best friends.

Belinda was taken in only days after the Three Greyhounds opened despite not being a fugitive from a violent man or pimp. "We stretched a point to take her," Anne explained. "Fortunately, the board of governors interprets our rules liberally. As an orphan living on the street, she was at risk from many men. We thought we might as well catch her before she falls. As Mistress Chappell will need a kitchen maid once the house fills rather than just girls and women learning to cook or temporarily assigned to her, Belinda is a servant, not a charity case, although her duties are light, so she is also learning to read and write."

The girl's name conjured up an elegant young lady of the *beau monde*. Belinda was skinny and sharp-featured, a little younger than Ory, and quick-witted. That latter trait was better than elegance in Rose's opinion. *Wherever did her parents get such a literary name?* Rose had only ever encountered it in one of Mr. Pope's poems. Ory had adopted her as a little sister.

Fiona had fled from a bawdy house rather than a guardian. At seventeen, she was halfway between Ory and Rose in age and had become almost an adopted older

138

sister. After living in Bethlehem House, Rose was no longer startled that a pretty, well-spoken girl with red-gold hair could be abducted off the street while on an errand and end in prostitution. Apprenticed to a mantua-maker before the death of her Scottish mother and English father, she had been well brought up, thank goodness, and therefore was unlikely to teach Ory any more improper words. Like Ory, Fiona helped care for the children past infancy but too young for lessons.

The three were working at a table in the almost deserted common room. Ory was painting on a small sheet of stiff paper, no more than four inches by six. Belinda was fashioning a pin-pillow from a scrap of chintz and a bit of ribbon, and Fiona was embroidering a handkerchief.

Most of the people Rose had known would be horrified that Ory spent time with Fiona and would disapprove of Belinda. Rose thought her sister could have done worse. The girls Ory had met both at Bethlehem House and the Three Greyhounds were far more practical than Rose's carefully reared friends at that age.

That night she drifted toward sleep remembering the amusing problem Allan Everard had set for the boys that morning: something about an infantry regiment marching at such and such a rate from the Royal Arsenal at Woolwich while a cavalry regiment galloped toward them... *Allan Everard had a pleasant face, a body neither too slender nor heavily muscled, and a confidence in his movements that was a man's grace. He did not put himself forward, but any woman would notice him. And he was intelligent and kind.*

"Rose, can I talk to you?"

Her sister's voice jerked her out of her semi-dream. "What's wrong, Ory?"

"It's Fiona. She's worried for a friend. Fiona doesn't know what to do to help her, and she doesn't know who to ask and neither do I."

Any lingering thoughts of mathematicks and Allan dispersed like smoke in a high wind. "You're asking me. If I don't know, someone here will. What sort of assistance does Fiona's friend need?"

"When Fiona was…" Ory's voice faltered. "…where she was, the housekeeper was kind to her and sometimes they were able to talk because the women didn't all eat their meals at the same time if they were, ummmm, busy. Susan was almost like a mother to them all. Fiona told her she wanted to leave but didn't know where she could go."

"Oh?"

"Yes, and Susan went to a church near the house whenever she could and heard about Bethlehem House there. She told Fiona if she, Susan, I mean, could get away, she would, and she told Fiona to go." And Bethlehem House had passed her on to the Greyhounds.

"Fiona wanted Susan to come with her, but she couldn't because she's lame. Now Fiona can't stop worrying about her because she thinks Susan was afraid. One day she was herself, and the next, she seemed to be frightened. So-she-wants-to-help-Susan-but-doesn't-know-how," poured out.

"Someone here will know," Rose repeated.

Ory's only response was a mumbled, "Ummmm," as she fell asleep, her mind unburdened.

The following morning after breakfast, Rose drew Fiona aside. "My sister says you're concerned for someone where you were."

"I am. She was so good to me. I didn't want to be there, but the man who…"

"No need to explain about him."

"He left me there. They said I could leave or stay, and I didn't know what I could do but stay because where could I go then?"

"Everyone here understands how it is," Rose said. She understood what drove women to escape their husbands or lovers, as she had removed Ory from their guardian's power because she feared him. Rose had once believed no decent woman would prostitute herself. Since coming to Bethlehem House and the Greyhounds, she could no longer blame a woman for surviving or feeding her children by any means she could.

This thought was followed by another: what if Mr. Simmons had not found them on the church steps? How long would their morality have endured real hunger and no shelter? They might at last have been glad to go into a brothel.

"What help does your friend need?"

"She wants to get away, but she's afraid to try because she's halt. She walks to the market, but she's slow and she tires easily."

"Have you asked Matron if something can be done?"

The girl twisted a corner of her apron. "No. I'm lucky to be here, and I didn't want to make trouble because I'm new, and…" She was afraid she would be thrown out onto the street.

"We'll talk to Matron. The charity has some surprising resources." As she knew from the way she and Ory had been smuggled in and from being aware of the watchfulness of the street boys.

Anne asked the questions Rose had not thought of. "She told you she wanted to get away?"

"Ay. She said, 'Mayhap I'll never live to be old, but I think I'd live longer if I'm away from here.' Yet Susan was treated far better than any servant I've known. Sometimes she helped the cook as well as being the housekeeper. She had her own little room near the kitchen so she didn't have to climb the stairs to the attic, and a good bed with a pretty coverlet, an armchair, a table, and even a chest of drawers."

"Your friend wouldn't tell you why she was afraid, but can you guess why?"

"I think she saw or heard something," Fiona said hesitantly. "When I first came there, she seemed contented. But just before I left, she had dark circles under her eyes like she hadn't slept."

"I'll ask one of the charity's governors if anything can be done. Try not to worry."

Rose gave her sister the same advice.

Three days later, Rose and Ory went to the common room for a sisterly chat before Rose's writing class. Their talk was destined to be put off, as an excited group was gathered around one of the tables. Fiona was there with Anne, the Chappells, several of the residents, and a woman Rose did not recognize.

"Ory and Rose," Fiona called, "this is Susan. She's going to tell us how she was rescued."

The woman half rose from the bench and started to smile, her expression freezing as she saw them. She murmured a greeting and bobbed her head before sinking down again. Rose studied her, wondering at her reaction. The woman was younger than Rose had expected, perhaps not yet forty years, although poor women aged quickly. But her brown hair had only traces of gray, and her face was almost pretty. When she spoke, her diction and vocabulary were surprisingly good. She might once have come of decent family. Her casaquin and petticoat were of fine claret-red wool.

"I don't know how to begin, when I can scarcely believe I'm here. I do know I'm grateful for the help of those that brought me."

"Tell us how it happened," urged Patience, who oversaw the babies' and tots' care.

"I'd set out for the market to buy a few spices and herbs we needed for the kitchen today. But as I passed a little alley, someone said 'Susan,' and I was so startled I stopped and stood like a fool. The next thing I knew, I'd been picked up and lifted into a wagon, basket and all, and a canvas dropped over me. The fellow jumped up and sat in the wagon bed beside me and whispered, 'Fiona sent us.' And here I am."

The group broke up, some to return to their duties or chars, Anne to show Susan to a room on the ground floor because of her lameness. Fiona gave her friend a fierce hug before going off to help Patience. Ory had confided that when Fiona had first come to "that place," the woman had shown her sympathy, given her advice and little treats. She regarded Susan as a foster mother or beloved aunt. "Not like our Aunt Martha," Ory said.

Ory must long for more family than they had ever had, a lack Rose did not feel and so had not recognized in her sister. Perhaps she had always been too busy since their mother's death, or perhaps Oriana's nature was simply different from her own. At any rate, now in addition to treating Fiona and Belinda as adopted sisters, Ory might view Susan as an aunt.

Chapter 15

When he left the coffee house, Allan turned west on Holborn instead of east. A brisk half hour's walk took him to St. George's, Hanover Square. From the carriages and sedan chairs outside the church, a wedding must have been solemnized. Good. There should be someone within who could tell him where to find a general who was also a baronet and who lived nearby. If he had known what he meant to do before leaving Brand's office, he could no doubt have got the general's direction from him.

Minutes later, he was waiting in the hall while a footman padded off to see if Mistress Milton was at home, the general being indisposed at present. A long illness, then, and therefore likely fatal, as it had lasted half a year or more: Rose had not received a letter from him since before Christmas, and Midsummer Day was now past. Though if he had been too ill to reply to Rose's letter informing him of her father's death, why had his son or his daughter-in-law not written to her?

The lady of the house came rustling down the stairs. A plump, pretty girl with golden hair in her youth, no doubt, she had aged into plump, peevish, and faded. Her expression moderated slightly as she judged his suit: not a presuming tradesman, then.

"Mr. Everett?"

"Everard, ma'am. Do I understand General Sir

145

Oliver Milton is too ill to see me?"

"That is so. May I ask your business with my father-in-law?"

"It is something I must discuss with him." He frowned, thoughtfully, he hoped, as Salt had sometimes done: half annoyed and half perplexed. "Is he like to be able to receive me in a week? I must go to Edinburgh soon, but mayhap I could put off seeing Sir Oliver until I have visited the next person on my list, who resides in Bath."

"Surely someone else could assist you, as dear Sir Oliver is not well?"

"That may depend on how long you expect your father-in-law to be indisposed."

"He is quite old and has been confined to his room for several months."

"Perhaps your husband, as his nearest relation, would do."

"He is away on business."

"When will he return, Mistress Milton? Time is of the essence."

Her hands were clasped at her waist; the knuckles turned white. "I expect him with every ship arrival."

Eyebrows raised, Allan said, "*Every* ship arrival?"

"Every ship from New York in the American colonies, I should say. He went to look into a friend's investment opportunity. But he should return any day as I expected him back before this."

"That poses a problem. My instructions are to resolve the matter quickly." He heaved an exasperated sigh. Acting was not as difficult as he had supposed. "If I could verify that Sir Oliver is in fact alive, that would go some way to resolve my dilemma."

"But of course he is alive! Is this about a bequest?"

"I'm not empowered to discuss the matter with anyone except Sir Oliver, madam. If he is not well enough to talk with me, I must be able to confirm he is alive. Failing that…"

"I suppose there can be no harm in letting you just look in. He is so easily provoked that I must away keep all who might annoy him."

Despite her obvious reluctance, she led him up a flight of stairs to a room at the back of the house. At the door she paused and whispered, "Pray stand back a little. 'Twill be best if he does not see you."

He complied. She half opened the door and trilled, "Is there anything I can get for you, Papa-in-law?"

A man in his seventh decade sat propped up by numerous pillows in bed. Eagle-sharp eyes skewered her. "Damme, Martha, if I wanted something I'd call for my valet, not you. It'd likely be a chamber pot and neither of us would enjoy that."

Allan stepped directly behind the woman and waved his hand.

"Who's that behind you, hey?"

"Sir Oliver," Martha Milton protested.

"You, woman, out!"

"Please do not excite yourself when I only wish to spare you being disturbed in your recovery. I—"

"Out, Martha!" He reached for a small, thick book, rather battered, on his bedside stand. "And you, fellow, if you're not a doctor, come in."

She squeaked and brushed past Allan, scurrying toward the stair.

"I'm no physician." He entered and bowed. "My name is Allan Everard, and I've come to see you about—

"

"I don't give a fig if you've come to preach the Gospel to me. You're male, and you've thwarted my fool of a daughter-in-law. Close the door, and move that chair closer to the bed. Johnson!" he bellowed.

A head poked through a narrow gap in a door in the wall to the right. "Sir?"

"Didn't dare show your face to her, did you? Much good you are, man. Madeira?" he asked Allen. "I need the fortification, but if you'd prefer claret, Johnson will bring up a bottle of that as well."

"Madeira, by all means, sir."

"Good. Madeira and wiggs, too. I know Cook baked some today."

"At once, sir!" and the valet was gone.

"I should have had Johnson haul a chair over here for you. No sense in having to raise our voices as if we were at opposite ends of a long table."

"I can do it, Sir Oliver." He placed the nearest chair at an angle to the side of the bed where the general could see him without having to turn his head too much. Theirs was likely to be a long conversation.

The gimlet eyes focused on Allan. "Now, sir, what brings you here?"

"Your granddaughters were worried about you."

"Were they? Why? I wrote 'em early this month. I'm not one for scribbling a letter about every thought I have. Four times a year is enough when I haven't much to say. Not like a dispatch, you know, where there's information to be sent."

"They haven't heard from you since December. Their father died in February."

The old man's eyes widened in surprise. Before he

could speak, Johnson came in with a tray. He set it down on a small table by the window, then picked up the table and brought it to his master's bedside. He poured out two glasses of wine and waited for instructions.

"Good man. Off with you now." When the dressing room door closed, he demanded, "Stanbury dead? Why didn't Rose write? Have a bun." He waited until Allan had done so before taking one.

"She did. So did their attorney, Lucian Brand. They hoped you would agree to act as the girls' guardian."

Milton shook his head. "This is news to me. The mail isn't always reliable, but still, two missing letters is remarkable." He broke the wigg and dipped a piece into his wine.

"Three, if you wrote to them in March." Allan might have assumed he had forgotten to send his quarterly letter if the man had not so obviously had all his wits about him. A June letter might well be sitting at Stanbury Manor.

"Four, if they did not receive the one I sent around the middle of June. This goes beyond remarkable," he said grimly. "Johnson!"

The valet popped back into the room. "Sir?"

"I wrote my granddaughters this spring, didn't I?"

"Yes, sir, around Lady Day and then in midsummer as well, same as every year."

"I suppose I might not get a reply to the most recent one yet. What did you do with the March letter?"

"I gave it to the mistress, sir."

"Why? You usually take my letters to the general post office."

"Yes, sir, I used to, as there was always some errand I needed to do as well. But after you fell ill, I didn't feel

I could leave you as restless as you were, so I asked if Mistress Milton could have it sent by the footman."

"I see. And what of mail directed to me?"

"The mistress passes it out, as Mr. Milton would if he were at home, you being ill and confined to your chamber."

"Hmmm. In the future, you will take my letters to the post office yourself, and I will speak to Mistress Milton about letters that should come to me. Dismissed." Alone with Allan again, he added, "Well, well," in a tone that boded ill for his daughter-in-law. "It's time to crack the whip a little. That curst woman's got above herself. First the lung fever, damme, and I didn't begin to feel better until March. At the start of April I was finally well enough to leave my chamber and go downstairs. Wasn't as strong as I thought. I took a tumble on the stair and broke my leg, curse it. Now I've been cossetting myself. I walk around my room several times a day but recline on my bed like a vaporish woman part of the time. Martha's taken advantage, I suppose thinking she was taking care of me by keeping back my letters in case there was anything in them to excite me."

He took a long draught of madeira. "I'm sorry I did not learn of their father's death and will write both of them today. I trust they are well otherwise?"

"The situation is difficult. A distant cousin was appointed their guardian, and Mistress Rose felt it necessary that they remove themselves from their home. She did not feel she could trust him with Miss Oriana."

Sir Oliver ripped out a truly profane oath. "Why didn't they come here?"

"They did. Mistress Milton did not recognize them and turned them away."

"Hell-fire. She's gone too far with her pushing ways since my son's been gone. I'll soon cure her of that. Where did they go?"

"They're safe, but it's best I not tell you where they are, as their guardian is a greater danger to them than you know," he hurried on, seeing the man ready to erupt.

"Why? Who's the guardian?"

"One Horace Stanbury, a cousin of the late Paul Stanbury."

"That fellow? I'm surprised he's still alive. I'd have thought someone would have done for him by now or pox or the rope would have taken him."

"You know him?" Allan groped in his left coat pocket for one of Ory's sketches of Stanbury.

"Not personally"—Disappointing. Allan put the sheet down on the table—"but when old Stanbury, Paul's father, and I were working out the settlements before my daughter's marriage, he felt bound to reveal the family disgrace."

"Attorney Brand found papers about the creation of an annuity for him in 1708."

"I'd forgot the year, but I remember well enough old Stanbury set one up to keep the young scoundrel away from the rest of the family."

"Do you know what he'd done to merit being bought off?"

The baronet gave a crack of laughter. "What hadn't he done, from the time he was at grammar school on? He was lazy and learned as little as possible from his tutor and the school, but some ain't bookish. By the time he was eighteen, he was a hardened reprobate. He should have been packed off to the army with an ensign's commission, but his father hesitated to do it, as some of

151

the boy's failings might have seen him cashiered."

"That bad?" One need not be a pattern of virtue to be a soldier.

"He was expelled from school for cheating at cards. He had no interest in any profession his father or uncle proposed. He was suspected of stealing. When old Stanbury became his guardian, he did what he could with the boy, but by the time he was eighteen, he'd had enough. He funded the annuity, and Horace was never heard from again, as far as I know. Good riddance."

"He's back now, and the diocesan court appointed him guardian, rather than allowing Rose and Oriana to choose their own. Rose will become guardian once she's one-and-twenty, as specified in Paul Stanbury's will, but there's still a month or more until her birthday."

"She was born the third of August, 1719. My first grandchild. That's not so bad, then, if they're safe for now." He picked up the little pencil portrait of Stanbury and stared at it.

"There is another factor. Stanbury's associated with a brothel. He has criminals in his pay. There are indications…" He did not know how to phrase it so the next revelation did not bring on an apoplexy.

Milton was not slow of understanding. "Blast him straight to perdition." A mild oath, considering. He splashed more madeira into his glass and shoved the bottle closer to Allan. "What can I do? Are you sure the girls are safe enough or should they be brought here?"

"Their current location is more secure than a private house. We need a way to disqualify Stanbury as guardian in case he discovers their whereabouts before Rose's— Mistress Rose's—majority. What you've told me thus far is helpful, but I'd appreciate anything else you can add."

The general scowled. "I can't think of anything. By the time my son and Paul Stanbury's daughter were wishing to marry, Horace had been gone for years. I wouldn't recall him at all except Paul Stanberry's father was still hot as fire over the fellow being such a blot on the family escutcheon. You say the annuity commenced in 1708?"

"Yes."

"After considering it, neither Stanbury nor I saw any impediment in a scandalous connection out of sight and mind for ten years. If we had objected, I wouldn't have put it past Paul Stanbury to persuade my girl to elope."

Indeed, after so long, who would have expected him to reappear?

"I want to write Rose. Where can I send it?"

Allen suggested enclosing it in a letter directed to himself at the Green Tree Coffee House, Cornhill, near the Royal Exchange.

"I'll do so. Now, what's the name of the school of Venus which Stanbury infests? I'm not likely to know it, but I'll write to one or two of my younger former officers. Mayhap there's some tidbit to be gathered there."

"It's known as the Purring Cat."

"Zounds, I remember it from years ago. Not that I ever saw the inside, you understand," he added. "Expensive, I heard, and with some pretensions to whatever passes for gentility in a bordello. They had gambling too, informally, not like a gaming hell, and never a sharper, a friend told me. The owner was said to be particular about that. Horace Stanbury is involved in the business in some way?"

"As either the manager or the owner, we think."

"Hard to believe, given what I was told of him. Not that he would hesitate to be connected to a vaulting-school, but if he's in charge, I'm surprised he hasn't bankrupted it. For all our class's contempt for cits, it seems to me a good deal of hard work and intelligence is necessary to run a successful business." Sir Oliver still held Stanbury's likeness. "This is recent?"

"Miss Oriana drew it from memory within the past month, and one of the people trying to help the girls, who has seen Stanbury, recognized him."

The general harrumphed. "The blackguard must be flourishing like the green bay tree. He looks too young to be Stanbury. He must have been eight or ten years older than Paul Stanbury, and I believe he's one- or two-and-forty. Or was, when he died." He passed the sketch back to Allan.

As he rose to take his leave, Sir Oliver held up a hand. "I'm sorely missing male company these last months as I suspect Martha has convinced my friends I'm on my deathbed. Stay for supper, if you will."

"I'd be honored, sir."

"Johnson! Tell Cook I've a guest and we want real food, not that slop Martha's been sending up."

The manservant's head emerged from the dressing room again. "Yes, sir!"

"Do you play chess, by any chance, Everard?"

"I may be able to give you a fair game." His foster father had loved chess.

Chapter 16

While she could not but be glad her little sister had wrapped herself in a semblance of a family, Rose continued to be uneasy about Susan. The woman was friendly and cheerful and volunteered to work in the kitchen. Mistress Chappell was pleased to have a permanent helper with more than the usual skills.

"She's a better hand with pastry than I am," she reported when dinner was served that same day. "She knows dishes I've never heard of and has a mort of Frenchy receipts in her head. They must have served wonderful meals where she worked."

In Rose's anxious study of the kitchen maid, she saw worry in Susan's eyes when she looked at Rose and Ory and remembered the woman's expression when she first spied them. Should she talk to Anne? All she could tell her was that Susan had been as startled as if she recognized them.

Before she screwed up her courage to approach the matron, however, Susan sought Rose out after supper to ask for a word with her.

The library was empty and dim after the meal. Susan said, "I know you won't like me spending time with Miss Ory, but it will be hard to avoid with her and Fiona almost joined at the hip. Fiona is like a daughter to me, in spite of only knowing her for two months or a bit more."

"I can hardly object when we are sheltering here, too, with no reputation left. I'm glad my sister has a friend in Fiona and that you have stood Fiona's friend. But I've seen you uneasy when you look at Ory and me. Why is that?"

"That is the very thing I wanted to talk to you about, ma'am."

They sat in a pair of armchairs at angles only half facing each other, making it easy for Susan to avoid her eyes.

"It's God's grace that brought me here, and that's not something I would have said since I was a chit as young as Fiona. I wanted to tell someone when I first saw you, but I didn't know who was in charge. Anne's the matron and deals with matters here, but she's a woman and must have to answer to some man, and it's someone in authority I need. Only I need to know it's someone I can trust. So I've gone back and forth, thinking one thing one minute and another the next and couldn't make up my mind what to do for the best."

"I'm familiar with that feeling," Rose said in the ensuing pause.

Susan smiled faintly, acknowledging the comment. "Then I remembered what Fiona told me, about how she told Ory about me, and Ory told you, and you talked to Matron."

"Which proves that someone can help, Susan. The board of governors of the charity that oversees Bethlehem House and the Greyhounds is prodigious efficient. More sensible than I'd expect of men as a rule, too," she conceded.

"If I talk to Matron Anne, will you come with me?"

"Anne is not fearsome."

"I'm not afraid of her, but…what I have to say is about you and Ory. You're hiding here, like every other woman in this place, so you must know a man's hunting you. Did you know sheets with drawings of both of you are being shown and passed out all over London?"

"I did, and so does Anne and at least one of the men connected with the charity's governors."

Susan's shoulders sagged, tension draining away. She had been as straight-backed and stiff as if she were being interviewed for a servant's position.

"Oh! Then mayhap I needn't see her."

"How did you learn of the drawings? Did someone show you one when you were at the market?"

The woman picked at a bit of rough skin by her thumbnail. "No. I'd better see the matron after all so I only have to tell this once."

"She'll probably want the man who arranged to have you brought here present, too. He is trying to find a way to put an end to the search for us."

"Does he think he can?" Susan's incredulous tone surprised a laugh from Rose.

"I believe he does. Come, let's tell Anne so she can send a message to him."

****

Barlicorn rang the bell at the gate midway through the evening. Anne summoned Susan, who was sewing herself a shift, and Rose, who had been reading Defoe's novel *Colonel Jack*, which reminded her of *Moll Flanders*, the novel she had not finished. Now far less easily shocked, she found it quite interesting.

Allan Everard's absence from the meeting in the matron's office surprised her. She had expected he would be invited and said so.

"Chappell said he went to call upon an attorney," Anne said. "Something must have delayed him. I think we should not wait. The sooner we hear what Susan has to say, the better."

When Susan did not speak immediately, Barlicorn said, "The beginning is always a good place to start." Barlicorn's plain clothing and roguish smile put Susan at ease.

"It's a long tale that starts more than twenty years ago."

"We have time."

She took a deep breath. "I met Nick Winn in Tetbury, Gloucestershire, when he returned from the colonies. I was sixteen, and he may have been twenty. My father was a wool-stapler—" She broke off, seeing incomprehension on Rose's and Anne's faces. "He bought raw wool, graded it, and sold it to those that have it spun and woven. We had a fine house on Long Street, but I'd never met a man with such elegant manners as Nick had. I was as silly as most girls are, and I didn't much like my stepmother, so when Nick asked me to go to London with him, I did. He bought me a ring, and he said we'd be married there. I never thought of asking how he was supporting himself for he always had coin in his pockets."

Beside Rose, Anne sighed almost imperceptibly. She had probably heard similar stories before.

"We took rooms in a pleasant house where we had a bedchamber and a parlor, and the landlady would provide meals if we gave her notice. Mostly we ate in inns or bought food at cookshops because Nick wasn't always home for dinner or supper and not usually awake for breakfast. He was gone part of each day, and I understood he was looking for a profitable business to invest in, but he also spent evenings away sometimes.

"One day I was looking to see if he had another clean shirt or two, as the washerwoman had been ill and even with two girls helping her, she'd fallen behind. When I didn't find a fresh shirt in the clothes press, I thought I'd look in Nick's trunk. He hadn't opened it since he'd unpacked his clothing, but every stitch he had wouldn't have filled it. Maybe he had some older shirts in there and could make do until the others were done. I know this doesn't seem important but it is, I promise you."

John Barlicorn nodded encouragingly.

"There were two fine suits inside, and a pair of shirts, cuff ruffles, neckcloths with lace, everything a gentleman with plenty of money would wear. I was foolish, but being familiar with the wool and clothier's trades, I knew the suits and shirts were expensive. There was a box with sleeve links and a couple of rings and a pocket watch. I wondered Nick didn't use it, unless he feared it would be stolen. The cover was engraved inside 'To Horace Evan Stanbury in the hope he will make good use of time.' "

Rose gasped. If Susan's Nick had Horace Stanbury's belongings, their cousin had assumed another name. Before she could speak, Barlicorn raised a finger to his lips to bid her to be silent.

Susan took no notice of her listeners' reaction. She was lost in the past. "There were some papers, too, but I only glanced at them, and you may be sure I put everything back just as I'd found it, knowing Nick liked his privacy and wouldn't be pleased that I knew he was using a false name."

"You must have wondered why."

Susan chewed her lower lip. "If Nick had a fault, it was that he was so private and did not like being questioned. But I saw him dress in those clothes not long afterward, and he took some of the papers, too. When he came back he was in high good spirits and took me to the Drury Lane theater to celebrate finding a business to invest in. My gown wasn't near as good as his suit, and I suppose people thought I was his mistress. As I was," she added bitterly. "He wanted us to wait to marry until his business was profitable. That night I thought the wait was almost over."

Anne reached out and patted Susan's hand.

"The next day he went out in the morning and was back in the afternoon, saying he'd bought a business, though it needed some freshening: cleaning, new paint, and new furniture, and would I help him make it ready to open? I was happy to do anything I could." She sniffed, pulled a handkerchief from her pocket and held it to her eyes. "Something makes them smart something fierce," she muttered.

Anne rose and left the room, returning with a bottle and a tea bowl as Susan took a deep breath and clutched the handkerchief in her lap.

The matron filled the cup and passed it to her. "It's a mint-water cordial."

She sipped it gratefully.

"The business was around the corner from a square with handsome houses of fair size, the sort where well-inlaid folk would live. I asked Nick if he meant to rent out lodgings because it was a pleasant house that would be suitable for unmarried men who did not need a home for a family. He laughed and told me he meant it for a place where gentlemen could relax, play a hand of cards, or otherwise entertain themselves. I set about hiring charwomen to give the inside a proper cleaning, which was easy once the old furniture and rugs were taken out. Nick sold them to a dealer in old furniture. The rooms were painted in the colors he said were fashionable, and he took me with him to choose furniture. I did not think men would like the beds he bought, and anyway, if the place was not to be a lodging house, why would he need beds except cots for the servants? He'd an answer for that, too, claiming some men might stay overnight. It was lovely when all the work was finished."

"He took me to a good mantua-maker and paid for half a dozen gowns for me." She wiped her eyes again.

"Then he brought the women to the house. There were eight of them, all young and pretty, and they seemed genteel. Still, gullible as I'd been, I knew then what sort of business it was to be. I'd known for a while that Nick won money at cards and I accepted that, not that I liked it because if you win at cards you can also lose, which makes a very insecure living. But to open a hothouse or bagnio as such places were called when they weren't called worse! That made me wonder if I really knew Nick. But we lived there on the third floor, and I oversaw the housekeeping. 'Twas like being married, and I didn't mind so much."

The sudden memory of Horace Stanbury's sharp-eyed study of Oriana, very like the expression of a man examining a horse he might buy, and the phrase "…will pay you a good price for your filly…" drove the color from Rose's face. Barlicorn had said Horace Stanbury might have meant to sell Ory. Although Rose had been horrified, she had not really accepted the idea as a possibility until now. The news Cousin Horace owned a brothel made it real. Somehow there was not enough air to breathe.

She missed whatever Susan said next until she came back to herself and heard, "...lost one of the women, who accepted an offer from one of her customers. Times were hard just then. When Nick asked me to be the eighth female until he could find another, I refused at first. I thought I'd leave him, but how would I live? I hadn't the money to get back to Tetbury, even if my father would be willing to take me in, and I'd no skills but those expected of a prosperous tradesman's wife. Nick didn't threaten to throw me out if I didn't agree. He said it wouldn't be for long, only until he found another woman lovely and fresh enough to take the eighth room. And I couldn't bear to leave him." Her mouth twisted. "It was only a month or thereabouts, but it was never quite the same between us after that."

Anne listened, sympathetic but unmoved. She poured more cordial into the chipped tea bowl. Rose knew something of restorative drinks as Sally Howard was an advocate of them for all sorts of ailments and disordered humors. She hazarded a guess this one contained licorice, caraway seeds, and claret as well as mint. Small wonder Susan needed something to put heart in her to recount her sordid tale of love and betrayal.

Immersed in Susan's story, Rose could not imagine what more they could learn. However, Barlicorn's expression and posture reminded her of a cat waiting at a mouse hole: patient and hopeful.

"Seems as if it's taken as long to tell you the beginning as it took to live it, but we're near the end now. My Nick hasn't been a good man, but he's not all bad, either. Four years ago I fell and broke my ankle. Nick brought in a bonesetter and had a woman nurse me in a little storeroom he'd had cleared out until I healed. I couldn't climb the stairs easily anymore, so I stayed on in that room and continued to manage the house, which didn't take much time as the maids and butler I'd hired were well trained and seldom needed direction. I helped the cook sometimes, as I used to enjoy cooking at home. I haven't minded much. Nick runs the place well: no one's treated badly except men that cheat when they play cards, or that are rough with the women. I'd be there yet except—" She stopped speaking and dabbed at her eyes with her handkerchief.

"What changed?"

"The first was, he took Fiona from the man that had abducted and used her. The scoundrel owed him money. Nick had never done such a thing before and it bothered me, but Fiona had nowhere else to go. I could understand that. Then Nick went away in April and was gone near two months.

"When he came back, he was worried but wouldn't say why, nor where he'd been. 'A bit of old business that's gone bad and is taking some time,' he said." She took another sip of the cordial.

"Was there no clue at all to where he'd been or why?"

She frowned a little at Barlicorn's question. "Not as such. But the day he came home, I saw he had a different pocket watch. I almost asked about it before I recalled seeing it when I found the Horace Stanbury papers and watch in Nick's trunk. Then I was afraid to ask."

"Why were you afraid when you seem to have liked and trusted Winn?"

Barlicorn's sympathetic voice elicited a sad smile.

"Not long after Fiona came, I heard Nick tell one of the men who work for him that he was trying to find a pair of females, relatives of a customer of the Purring Cat. Their family name was Stanbury. The man was to have sheets of drawings of the girls passed out. I saw one of the papers, and I've a good memory. Later when Nick and I talked I said I was surprised a customer would ask him to help find the girls." She twisted the handkerchief in her lap. "Nick said, 'He's a country gentleman who comes here when he's in town. He doesn't know London well and thought I might know a discreet way of finding his wayward ladies, without the scandal of hiring a thief-taker.' He lied to me, which I don't think he'd ever done before, not intentionally anyway. And he told me more than he needed to, trying to make the tale more believable. His having been gone without telling me why, and the way he'd been distracted and irritable told me he was playing some deep game. I was the one he'd always confided in and asked for advice. If he'd stopped trusting me..."

She'd stopped trusting him.

Susan sighed. "I couldn't think what he was about, but I was worried about the girls he was hunting for." She sighed again and fell silent.

"So you decided to leave the Purring Cat?"

"Not then. When she came to trust me, Fiona told me she would not stay if she had anywhere to go, except the workhouse, maybe, which might be worse. I'd begun to go to church again, trying to settle my mind about Nick, and that's how I heard of Bethlehem House, so I sent her on her way. I'd have gone too, if I could, but I thought it best she should get away from the Cat as quick as possible. And the next thing I knew, she'd arranged for me to be taken away, too.

"I came close to swooning when I saw Mistress Rose and Miss Ory here. It seemed like the voice of God telling me I had to speak out. I hope I've given you something that will help protect Mistress Rose and Ory."

"You've confirmed things we suspected and added some useful details." Barlicorn showed no sign of being disappointed. "And now we know Horace Stanbury, who is Rose and Ory's guardian, is passing as your Nick Winn."

"You've got it the wrong way around," Susan said.

Chapter 17

"I think Stanbury's dead and that's how Nick came to have his belongings."

"But if he isn't our cousin—" Rose stopped before asking a stupid question. "Our attorney wrote to find him at the bank that pays out his annuity. I suppose I should ask instead why he would take on the trouble of the guardianship when it took him away from his own business for so long. I don't think he liked living in the country."

"Perhaps he thought refusing the guardianship would seem suspicious," Barlicorn said.

"Nick has always had an eye to the main chance. He would have expected to benefit from it."

"You know him well."

"For my sins, I do."

"But what makes you think Winn isn't Stanbury?"

"I guessed why he had those fine suits and the pocket watch about six years ago when Nick was knocked down by a customer while he and one of the men were trying to throw the man out. He wasn't hurt or said he wasn't, but for the rest of that night he was restless and spent more time leaning against a wall than walking or sitting. At the end of the night, he stayed downstairs to see to the closing, but a little later he waked me out of my first sleep. We were still sharing a room. He had a bottle of brandy which was not usual. Not a heavy drinker, is Nick. All he wanted was for me to bear him company for a while. He lay on our bed and sipped a little of the cognac. He wanted to talk but not about anything in particular, just chit-chat. After a while he sat up for a few minutes, then he stood and leaned against the wall, and then paced around the room a while. He drank more, standing and walking, then sitting, then lying down again. Nick talked about being sent to New York in the American colonies to live with his uncle when he was a boy. He didn't stay with him long. Somehow he became a servant to an officer for several years. Nick claimed he learned more from him than he ever did in school, but I think it was card sharping and gentleman's manners."

She shook her head over the memory. "I never saw him drunk before but I did that day, and for the next week or more he drank after closing, so I reckoned that fall had hurt him enough he had to deaden it somehow in order to sleep. He wouldn't take laudanum.

"Anyway, the officer saw something in an old London paper that made him say, 'It's safe to go home.' By then, Nick wasn't easy to understand, but from bits and pieces, I made out the officer had brawled with someone over cards. Now something in the newssheet gave him to understand he needn't worry about it anymore. So the officer decided to sell out and Nick came back with him as his manservant. When he mentioned the officer's name was Stanbury, I recognized it from the papers and watch I found in the trunk."

"Is it possible that Stanbury gave him some clothing?"

"I'd say so, as he was Stanbury's valet, except for the jewelry and the papers. Stanbury's name was on them and they looked important, not something you'd give or throw away."

"That argument convinces me, but we would need more evidence to prove 'Cousin Horace' is an imposter."

"A few more questions, if you're willing, Susan?"

"If I wasn't, I'd have kept mum. I owe you something for your help."

He gave a nod. "Did you ever meet Stanbury?"

"No. Nick had the trunk when I left for London with him."

"One more thing. Can you remember anything about the man Stanbury brawled with? If hearing of it caused Stanbury to decide it was safe to return to England, it might be important."

"I can't. I didn't understand all his ramblings. It was like he was talking to himself." Her forehead creased. "Except it had to be someone important, didn't it? Because you don't see ordinary folk in the newssheets unless they're criminals."

Barlicorn laughed aloud. "A point to you, Susan. I hadn't thought of that. We'll bear it in mind."

****

Allan used his key to get into the Three Greyhounds yard, glad he didn't have to use the bell to wake Chappell, and came face to face with Barlicorn and the matron.

"Everard, we learned something interesting tonight. I wish you'd been present. Mistress Anne and Mistress Rose took notes, but I can give you a summary if you aren't off to bed at once."

"I'll lock the gate if you mean to sit up," Anne said. "Mr. Everard, I trust you'll let Barlicorn out and lower the bar when you're done."

They sat in the library by the light of a single candle. Occasionally muted voices or the creak and rattle of a wagon or coach penetrated the shutters but hardly disturbed the room's tranquility. Barlicorn recounted the main points of the kitchen maid's tale.

"But if Stanbury's dead, that makes sense of something Sir Oliver said that I dismissed, thinking it was only an old man's faulty recollection. When he saw Stanbury's likeness, he thought he looked too young. Paul Stanbury was about two-and-forty when he died, and Milton believed Horace was older by as much as ten years, making him fifty or more."

"And the annuity was set up..." From his momentary abstraction Barlicorn must be calculating. "Two-and-thirty years ago. I'll cap downright Winn can't be much more than forty. The general has hit on a point. What did you learn from Brand?"

Allan related his visit to the attorney and concluded, "Horace Stanbury was slow to respond to Brand's letter to him. I wonder if that's because he only goes to Pimling's after the quarter days. Didn't you say your people trailed him to a bank?"

"It wasn't Pimling's. If I were he, I think I'd use a different bank for his Purring Cat business."

"And you never found any sign of Stanbury in London, so he may not have been using the Stanbury name until he heard about having inherited Stanbury Manor. Then he saw an opportunity and snatched it."

"And saw Oriana as another chance to enrich himself, with Rose as an added benefit. Everard, do you find yourself curious about Pimling's?"

"I do."

"Will you ask Attorney Brand if he is willing to pay

a call on Pimling's?"

"He's no longer the family attorney."

"But he is a representative of the law office that set up the annuity and may reasonably wish to assure himself as to its status now that another firm is handling the Stanbury affairs."

Thus must the Devil have whispered to Eve about the desirability of apples.

"He did hold back part of the Stanbury files and is concerned for Rose and Ory. It's worth trying."

"Perhaps he would permit you to accompany him as his clerk."

****

After teaching his class in the morning, Allan returned to Chancery Lane. This time he had to wait, as the attorney had a client in his office. He filled the time by reading the notes Rose had taken of Susan's revelations.

Finally, a door opened and he heard "...can't I allege that in my suit?" and Brand's voice replying, "You can allege it but you must have something, either a document or a credible witness's testimony, to support it. Without evidence, your contention falls into the realm of 'the faeries told me.' Not a winning argument in a court of law."

A red-faced, portly man blundered out, cursing under his breath.

Brand followed him. As the outer door slammed, he told his clerk, "We will not be taking his legal matter in hand." In the next breath he greeted Allan. "Has something happened?"

The worry in the lawyer's face confirmed what Allan already believed, that he cared for the Stanbury ladies' welfare rather than only their legal affairs.

"We've learned something new that may help."

"Come into my office."

Five minutes later, Brand put down the pencil with which he had been scribbling notes on the fraction of the desk not occupied by books, papers, and the tray holding the standish, quills, sealing wax, and a tinderbox.

"If Stanbury isn't Stanbury and has benefitted in any way from the estate, I am reasonably sure he has committed a felony. Whether or not he did away with the real Stanbury is immaterial unless the murder can be proven and even then, proving this Winn committed it?" He shrugged. "But proving he is not Stanbury will—more probably than not"—he qualified with a lawyer's caution—"cause him to be removed as guardian, especially as Sir Oliver is now prepared to be their guardian."

"Thank God."

"Or our patchwork legal code," Brand retorted. "However, even convincing a court that he is personating Stanbury will require proof. The testimony of a harlot who may be supposed to be acting out of spite will not suffice. The clothing and other possessions? Pooh. He might have come by them any number of ways: by gift from Stanbury or buying them or finding them by the side of the road."

Allan had been trying to think of a way to ask if he would visit Pimling's. However well-disposed toward Rose and Oriana the man might be, expecting him to present himself as the Stanburys' attorney might be one step too far.

"When I discussed this last evening with one of the people involved with the charity, he wondered whether

Pimling's might be able to supply further information about Stanbury."

"What sort of information?"

"He told you he had been living in London, didn't he?"

"He did."

"Did he give you an address, Mr. Brand?"

"I wrote him in care of his bank, and he replied, giving a coffee house as his direction for correspondence. I did not think to ask for more, being relieved to have found him at all."

"We could find no physical trace of him. If he has been living in London for years, his name should be known somewhere gentlemen congregate."

"Still, a gentleman of an austere disposition might not be found in such places. Are you suggesting I should attempt to tease out information about a bank's client?"

Hope of Brand's assistance faded. "I didn't think you'd like the idea."

"Under the circumstances, knowing he has engaged someone else to represent him, I cannot ethically pretend to be his attorney. Further, if the matter came to court, how could I testify about what I learned when acting as a spy? A pity, since someone might learn something useful by talking to the bank." He sighed heavily.

Someone might learn something useful? Was that a hint?

"It's possible he hasn't informed the bank he changed his attorney, if he only goes to Pimling's occasionally, as I understand is the case. Very likely no one would question the right of the law office that set up the annuity to inquire about its status, particularly in view of Paul Stanbury's death. I might well have sent my clerk to the bank to ask about it." He toyed idly with a quill.

Definitely a hint. "I suppose your clerk would have had a letter from you or from Horace Stanbury giving him authority to, er, audit the account."

"The annuity was funded over thirty years ago by this firm, under my father. I imagine if I sent my clerk there today, he would be accepted without question on the strength of his carrying a lawyer's bag and mentioning the law firm of Brand and Brand."

"I see." He had passed a stationer on his way to Brand's office.

"Thank you for letting me know what you have learned about our Horace. Now I must spend an hour or two researching the penalties for personation of another for financial gain." The attorney's helpfulness was at an end for the moment.

At the bank, Allan explained his errand to Samuel Wallace, the senior partner, who found nothing odd in his request.

"That account goes back to before I took over as managing director. Our head clerk, Inglestone, is the man for you. He's been with us since before Queen Anne, God bless her, took the throne." He dispatched a very young errand boy for Mr. Inglestone and himself escorted Everard to a small, untenanted office to wait. And wait. And wait.

Allan conceded to himself it hadn't really been that long; 'twas only his wish to find out whatever he could that made the time seem to drag. That, and anxiety occasioned by guilt at his deception. There was nothing to look at except a bare table with several straight chairs. From the green lawyer's bag Allan had bought, he took out a sheet of notes regarding provisions of the annuity, paper, and a well-sharpened pencil.

The head clerk entered with a rustling like a snake slithering over dry leaves, followed by the office boy bearing a ledger and a thin file. Inglestone, a thin, gray, dusty-looking man in his sixties, bowed slightly and gestured to the boy to set them before the seat at the head of the table.

"You may go, Griffin." The clerk sat down, opened the leather-bound volume to a page marked by a ribbon. "You wished to inquire about the annuity in place for Mr. Horace Evan Stanbury?"

"That is correct."

"Thirty pounds was paid into his account here on Midsummer Day for the current quarter. This sum has been paid into Mr. Stanbury's account regularly since the first installment came due at Michaelmas, September 29, 1708."

"I suppose he comes in promptly each time to collect it or have it transferred to his own bank?"

Inglestone frowned over the ledger and flipped back through the pages to the beginning. "There is a notation he came in before the first payment was due and informed us that we were to hold the funds."

"They weren't paid into another account elsewhere?"

"No, sir."

"I wonder how he survived, as he had no family but his uncle, who funded the annuity."

The clerk cleared his throat. "He spoke with one of our clerks, Mr. Totter, who died some years ago. He made a note that Stanbury had bought a commission. He added something the boy said, and I quote, 'By the time

I return from service in the colonies, I'll have a tidy sum waiting for me.' "

From what he'd learned from Brand, Allan doubted Stanbury's guardian had trusted him with another penny. He might have won enough at cards or hazard to buy a commission. But why do so? "Sensible of him. Did your clerk happen to note his appearance when he came in?"

"Certainly, sir. We take pains to be sure we are not gulled. 'Brown hair, blue eyes, average height, slender, eighteen years of age as of July 17 of this year 1708.' "

"When did he next return?"

Inglestone skipped ahead. "On April 14, 1718, and there was indeed a tidy sum with its accrued interest."

Almost ten years' worth of payments at thirty pounds per quarter would be over a thousand pounds. "After so long an absence, I suppose the bank must have verified his identity."

"Of course, sir. The clerk who dealt with him listed his proofs: a copy of the document which established the annuity, a pocket watch with an inscription from his father, several bills, and letters and documents addressed to Captain Horace Stanbury of the —th Foot. Ah, he must have earned or purchased a promotion. 'Hair, brown, eyes, gray, above average height, very lean, about twenty years of age.' " His voice faltered briefly before he added, "His signature matched the one in our file."

As Allan jotted down these particulars, he doubted the clerk could see his satisfaction. He made his voice hearty and spoke as Brand would have. "Very good, Mr. Inglestone. Pimling's clearly keeps excellent records. Has he come in regularly since?"

The head clerk ran a finger down the following

entries until he came to the last in the ledger.

"Not regularly but roughly once a month."

"How does he withdraw his funds?"

"He has not done so since his return."

"Then he did not make a withdrawal in 1718?"

"Ay, he did," Inglestone answered without hesitation.

"Ah. I asked because you said 'he has not done so since his return.' "

"I do ask your pardon, sir. I should have said, 'since his visit to the bank in 1718.' " He thumbed back through the book. "The note for that transaction states that he wished to take advantage of a business opportunity and withdrew four hundred and fifty pounds."

"It must have been successful if he has not drawn out money since. I suppose he comes in to see if he has received any letters."

"No, he comes in to make deposits to the account, although of course we would pass along to him anything that came for him."

Barlicorn had told him Winn deposited the brothel's earnings to a different bank. But his people had only been watching the man for a week or thereabouts. Allan would have liked to ask about the monthly deposits to Pimling's, but as they did not relate to the annuity, he could think of no justification for doing so.

"One last thing, then. We need a copy of the ledger. Inconvenient, I know, but as there's been no audit since Aldus Stanbury's death, it had best be from 1718 to date. I'll make the copy myself, if you wish, to spare your clerks effort."

"Quite unnecessary, sir, and inappropriate as I will have to authenticate the copy. I can have it delivered to

Attorney Brand or do you wish to return for it?"

"Oh, the latter, by all means. Would it be done today? I have other errands to do."

"It will be ready in three hours, sir."

Chapter 18

Barlicorn was to be found at a coffee house in St. Clement's Lane, Lombard Street, on Tuesday and Thursday afternoons. Today was Thursday. His decision made, Allan made straight for Job's Coffee House off Lombard Street.

He paused inside the door to peer through the fog of pipe smoke for Barlicorn among plain tables and benches occupied by artisans, clerks, several laborers, and two old men playing draughts. Job's extended its hospitality impartially, but he did not see Barlicorn either in his guise as a soberly dressed gentleman or as a laborer. At a table in the rear lefthand corner, a figure remarkable in a canary-yellow coat and a dark waistcoat beckoned. Good Lord!

When he reached the table where Barlicorn sat in solitary splendor, Allan eyed the purple vest uneasily.

Barlicorn gestured him to one of the chairs at the only table in the room that was furnished with them. "I should have mentioned my dress. It makes me easy to recognize, but 'tis a trifle jarring to those not expecting it. Have you news?"

Was his attention wandering? Barlicorn's gaze alternated between Allan and the entrance with an occasional sweep of the rest of the room.

"Brand was unwilling to mislead the bank, but he hinted that they were unlikely to question the authority of someone who looked like a law clerk."

"I'd give Brand my legal business if I had legal business." Barlicorn gave a faint, wry twist to the second "legal."

After recapitulating his meeting with Inglestone, he concluded, "Blue eyes and gray could be confused, but I've never heard of anyone aging only two years in ten. Besides, Winn could not be mistaken for average height."

"Did the clerk notice the discrepancy?"

"There's no question he did. He hastened to tell me the signature matched the one they had on file from 1708."

"Ha! If Winn can draw, he can forge a signature. Inglestone may be honest, but he wouldn't say anything to embarrass the bank if he thought you hadn't caught it. He may report it to the senior partner. I wonder if he'll investigate? A good day's work, Everard."

"I'm of two minds about telling Brand what I learned. He might prefer not to know."

"There's no need for him to find out, or not yet. We'll see what else we can dig up—" The man's casual glance at the door returned to Allan. He lowered his voice still more, though his table was some distance from its nearest neighbor. "No matter who you see or what I say, show no expression. You are an associate of mine."

Looking over the rim of his mug as he sipped, Allan beheld Nicholas Winn advancing toward them, face grim.

"Barlicorn."

"Ay." His voice had changed in seconds from a gentleman's to that of the lowest sort of Londoner.

"When you've finished your business with him"—

he jerked his head toward Allan—"I'd like to talk to you."

"He works for me and is in my confidence. Sit down and tell me why you've come."

Winn took the chair on Barlicorn's left. "A…friend of mine is missing."

"Ay? What of it?"

"I'm told you might be able to find her. I've tried, but…"

"I might. What do you want with her?"

"I want to know she's safe."

"Nothing more? You don't want her brought back by force? I know what your business is."

"Have you ever heard my women are forced to work for me? No. And she's not one of them. She's a friend, and I don't believe she'd have gone off without a word to me."

Barlicorn stared at him without speaking.

"Curse me, if she'd said she wanted to leave, I'd have made provision for her so I wouldn't have to worry she was starving or sleeping in some doorway."

Allan found himself thinking Winn was telling the truth.

"Then tell me anything you know about her. What she looks like, what she likes, her name, where her family is, when she disappeared."

The brothel keeper produced a sheet bearing an excellent likeness of Susan Freese and passed it to Barlicorn. "She's nine-and-thirty years of age. There's a sprinkling of gray in her hair, but most of it and her eyes are the color of brandy. She's lame in the right leg," he added as an afterthought. "One morning she set out to buy a few things we needed. Some spices and chocolate, nothing heavy, and the apothecary and shop aren't far away. She didn't come back. I had men ask along the route she'd have taken, ay, and on the streets nearby as well. No one saw anything. You've a reputation for performing miracles, Barlicorn. I won't haggle about the price."

"She may be dead."

His face bleak, he said, "I know. If she is, I'll have another job for you when you find who killed her."

"I'll see what I can learn."

Winn drew a purse from his pocket. Barlicorn shook his head. "I won't take your coin yet."

When he left them, Barlicorn asked, "What did you make of that, Everard?"

"Unless he's an actor to rival the best to tread the boards at Drury Lane, I think he was telling the truth."

"So did I. Still, even a complete scoundrel may be fond of someone. I believe it will take me some considerable time to search for Susan." The rogue grinned. "Now, there is another matter to discuss. Winn claimed the manor was not profitable. Could it be he'd looted the Stanbury account? Mistress Rose said her father banked at Fitchett's in Salisbury, as I recall. I would like to send an explorator or scout there as you have visited Pimling's, though I think we should not chance sending someone until we have taken, er, certain other steps. I wish we had access to her father's papers. If we knew where they're kept, a look at the estate ledger might prove helpful. Will you ask her? There are one or two other things you might inquire about, too."

"Of course." Any opportunity to speak with the pretty and intrepid Rose was welcome.

"In any event, someone must go to Stanbury to

speak with any of Mistress Rose's friends she trusts or servants who are loyal to her, for I am also curious to know how he has explained their absence."

"I could go."

"Thank you. You're the best choice for it: you know the facts, you're a gentleman, and you're inconspicuous. I'll make the arrangements."

From Barlicorn's lack of surprise, he had expected Allan to offer.

****

Rose's class was over and she was putting away the students' class materials when Everard entered the common room and stood at the other end. He did not approach until the women were streaming out the door. As soon as they were alone, he said, "I have news for you. If you have another class or duty, may I meet you at a convenient time? What I have to tell you should not be said in public. Mistress Anne will allow us the use of her office."

Nothing would have induced Rose to refuse the request. Since the previous day she had seen him only long enough to give him her notes of Susan's revelations. "I'm free for two hours. Thank you! A female is too often kept in the dark about the things that most concern her. Ory and I are fortunate to have so many friends willing to help us. One might expect it of Mr. Simmons and Barlicorn, who are associated with the charity, but you had no reason to involve yourself in our trouble."

"Yes, I did."

Rose felt herself blush under his intent study of her face. But they were outside the matron's office and she was able to chirp, "Here we are," to end the awkward moment.

The matron's office was stuffy with the door and window closed for privacy. Rose's smock grew damp in the warmth. She hoped the only odor Allan noticed was the soap she had washed with and pitied Everard, more heavily attired than she.

Rose had never seen a play, but surely few performances could be as enthralling as his narrative. She was not surprised by the discovery that the bank's records showed that the current "Horace Stanbury" could not be the real one, having been convinced by Susan's tale.

"If he's no relation to us…"

Allan's smile told her he understood her unvoiced thought. "Ay, it's an argument for the Court of Chancery replacing him as guardian."

Before she could take in the idea that they were almost out of danger, he continued, "We must prove him an imposter beyond any doubt. The Court of Chancery may be incorruptible, but it's best to plan for all contingencies."

"Why would he involve himself in our affairs? Wouldn't our little manor be too much trouble if his own business is profitable?"

"Being entailed, the estate would go to him whether he wanted it or not, once Brand found him. The tenancies would bring him a little more money or possibly a great deal more."

"But why burden himself with us? He remained at Stanbury Manor for some time, when I'm convinced he would rather have been in town."

"He may have wished to avoid raising any suspicion in someone who had your interests at heart, like Brand."

"I suppose he kept us from seeing our friends and

neighbors for the same reason. I did speak to two of our neighbors. One couple thought me headstrong to object to our cousin dismissing most of our servants and selling all our horses. Mistress Francis sympathized—" Something the widow had said now struck her as relevant. "—and from his speech she thought he must have grown up in a lower level of society, perhaps in Liverpool."

"He meant to cut you off from anyone who might assist you, yet still you succeeded in getting away." Allan's approval gave her a little thrill of satisfaction.

"We wouldn't have if our cook and her friend hadn't helped us."

"I'll mention to Barlicorn that Winn might speak like a Lancashire man. I didn't notice, but he may have done."

"Have you met him, then?"

"That's another part of my tale. I reported my findings to Barlicorn at a coffee house he uses as a sort of office. Only picture our surprise when Winn approached him there to ask him to find Susan."

At first Rose goggled at him, struck dumb with horror. "Oh, no. Winn must know we took refuge with the charity."

"I think not. Besides being one of the charity's governors, Barlicorn is known for, er, assisting others with problems, using his knowledge of London and a wide circle of friends."

This sounded like the sort of carefully edited explanation men often gave women to spare their tender feelings. Quite unnecessary here: Rose remembered her own and Ory's arrival at the Greyhounds in crates, and the efficiency with which Susan had been plucked off the street. "Her fear was justified, then. Did Barlicorn refuse?" He surely must have.

"Not outright. He let Winn think he agreed." Allan Everard's brow furrowed. "We both thought he was genuinely concerned for her safety."

"She couldn't quite believe he would ever hurt her," Rose said. "I thought it was because she is still fond of him."

"Is she? Then perhaps he still has some affection for her, unlikely as it seems." He smiled suddenly. "That's not the end of my story, either.

Hearing that Barlicorn meant to send someone to Stanbury, she exclaimed, "I'm glad! Perhaps his man will carry a message to Sally Howard for me, to let her know we're safe."

"I'm sure he would."

Her mind at ease, she took a sheet of paper and a pencil to write out answers to Barlicorn's questions, speaking as she did so.

"Of our own longtime servants, only our cook and our coachman, Henry Davis, were left when we departed. By now, Mistress Howard may have gone to work at the inn at High Stanbury. Mistress Ruth Francis has been almost a grandmother to me, and I think she will talk to Barlicorn's agent, if she is convinced he comes from me. I'll send a letter with him as an introduction."

She mused over Barlicorn's next question. "Getting at my father's ledger and bank documents may be impossible, even if no one is in the house. Our supposed cousin kept the study locked. He even took the key from the ring of duplicates." Her face heated. That statement revealed that she had been looking for the second key.

Allan received this with no sign of dismay, saying only, "I'll tell Barlicorn. Your father banked at Fitchett's in Salisbury?"

"He did."

"Do you know if your 'cousin' ever went there?"

Her head tilted as she strained to remember. "He never said so. He did ride out sometimes, though he was never away for long. I think he didn't like long rides, so I suspect he didn't go to Salisbury. I do know Mr. Brand sent Fitchett's a document to inform the bank Horace Stanbury had inherited the manor."

By the time she finished her note to Ruth Francis, a doubt set in. "Would Barlicorn know to send a man who wouldn't be conspicuous in the country, Mr. Everard?"

He cleared his throat. "Ah...I'm going." After the reluctant admission, he added, "I'm inconspicuous."

Inconspicuous? Not to any female, even though he was not strictly handsome by the standards of young girls or artists. Yet his features went together pleasingly and the intelligence and kindness in his face must attract any female of good sense.

"But that's not important. I spoke with your grandfather. Your letters were kept from him by your aunt as he was confined to his bed by illness and then with a broken leg. He is anxious to help you but agrees you are safer here until Stanbury is dealt with."

"Is Grandpapa well now?"

"He was well enough to threaten to throw a book at your aunt and to swear he would end her presumptuous ways. He invited me to sup with him and play a game of chess. That's why I was late getting back. I was sorry to miss hearing what Susan had to say, but I can't regret making Sir Oliver's acquaintance. He assured me he has not cast you off and stands ready to do anything he can to help, once 'tis safe for you to leave the Greyhounds."

She blinked away incipient tears. They had not lost all of their family, at least. She wished they might have lingered, perhaps to talk of other things, but they could not have remained closeted there longer with no chaperon even if Anne hadn't needed her office.

Chapter 19

What arrangements Barlicorn meant to make
became clear to Allan the next morning when he
received an early morning note bidding him to be packed
and ready to travel by ten. His trunk was corded and
sitting near the door in the common room when a clang
outside summoned Chappell.

The caretaker came in from answering the gate bell.
"There's a mortal fine traveling coach waiting for you,
Mr. Everard." The room was nearly empty, but when
Allan went out, Chappell following with his trunk, a
small crowd had gathered to peer out the grills in the
coach gate and the smaller entrance. To Allan's eyes, it
appeared that everyone who had business on Aldersgate
had stopped on the street to gape at the glossy carriage.
A lean, grizzled fellow dressed with the finicking care of
a valet held the horses' heads while the coachman helped
Chappell stow the trunk.

Allan Everard was to travel in a coach such as a
gentleman might own, in company with a valet instead
of on the common stage.

Higgs dressed the part though his manner was
unpolished. "Howsomever, I can care for a rum-cove's
clo'es good as any."

Allen hoped he would not converse too freely at the
inn. The fellow sounded like a hedge-bird.

"Mum's the word," Higgs agreed to this warning.

By contrast, Phelps, their coachman, a squarish man in his middle years, looked and sounded (when he spoke at all) just as he should.

They spent the night at the Maidenhead in Basingstoke and arrived at the Blue Boar in High Stanbury in the late afternoon of the second day. Allan enjoyed an excellent meal of roast chicken and potato pie, followed by a selection of tarts and cheesecakes. After finishing, with no one else waiting for a meal, he asked the maidservant to present his compliments to the cook and in particular to praise the bramble tarts.

As he had hoped, this brought her out of the kitchen. She might be in her forties and looked like Rose's description of Mistress Howard. As she approached, wiping her hands on her apron, her eyes raked him.

"You'll be the gentleman as liked my bramble tarts?"

"And the rest of the meal, too. I wonder you aren't cooking for a gentleman."

"I cooked for a gentleman's family, but after the master died, the heir did not live in the house long and so I took work here."

"But not before Mistress Rose and Miss Oriana departed, Mistress Howard." Allan lowered his voice though only two men remained in the room and they were at the other end and deep in an argument about equine bloodlines. "She told me to tell you she misses your bramble tarts and to ask if you remember the gown that was spotted all over the front with stains from the juice."

The woman gave a quick, emphatic nod. "Who might you be, sir?" Her gimlet eyes took in every detail of his face and dress.

"Allan Everard, mistress, at your and the Stanbury ladies' service. They're safe with friends who are trying to undo the guardianship."

"Good." She sniffed. "You seem gentlemanly enough if I may say so, but your man in t'other room is a poor advertisement for you. I'd take him for a pickpocket if I saw him on the street."

"He is not a credit to me in his manner, but my clothing is, so what would you?" Their overnight stay before arriving at the Blue Boar had proven Higgs an expert valet. "Besides, he is a constant source of amusement." He lowered his voice yet more. "I have come to take statements from you and some others about Horace Stanbury's behavior to Rose and Ory and about anything you may have noticed about him that seemed suspicious."

"I'll have to meet you in secret, sir. Tomorrow at seven after you sup, will you meet me in Oddford? It's only a little better than a mile west along the road. 'Twould be best if you walked. Taking your carriage or hiring a horse might cause talk and that Stanbury's got a man in the manor who spies for him. Our old coachman lives in Oddford now with his daughter at this end of the town, in the cottage with the hollyhocks. There's a path this side of it. Take that and go around to the back, not to the door on the street."

"Any man might take a stroll after a good supper," Allan agreed. "Can you tell me what servants are at the manor now? Is there a caretaker?"

"Wilks, who's supposed to be a groom and came after Horace Stanbury, is still there, and a simple fellow, and a female that does the cooking. Wilks and the woman sleep in the attic, the other fellow over the stable." Sally Howard snorted. "That woman's no better than Wilks, from what I've heard of her and seen with my own eyes when she comes to town. Slovenly, with her hair straggling and her kerchief not washed since I don't know when. I don't know what else she may do besides the cooking, but nothing good, if I'm any judge."

The innkeeper entered the dining room and paused to exchange a jocular greeting with the horsemen before approaching Allan's table.

"Here, now, sir, I hope you're not trying to hire Sally away from me."

"No, only complimenting her. You're lucky to have such a good cook."

"That's all right, then, for I can't spare her. I hope your chamber is to your liking?"

"I'll be going back to my kitchen, Jed." She dipped a curtsy to Allan and bustled away with a last, meaningful glance at Allan.

"Very comfortable."

The man probed delicately to discover his guest's business. Allan, wise in the ways of those who live in villages and take an interest in any stranger, admitted to traveling to find a part of the country not too far from London where he might buy a property, having recently come into an inheritance. "Not a big house, merely a country gentleman's home with six or eight bedchambers and stabling for as many horses."

"There's no properties for sale around here, sir."

"So I understand, but this makes a convenient stopping place while I explore all around Salisbury."

He excused himself, saying he needed a walk after hours in a coach and a heavy meal. *Just as well to establish it as a habit.* Strolling down the road well past the end of the village, a little way up a narrow lane and back, then down to the other end of High Stanbury after idling in the burying ground adjacent to the church brought him again to the Blue Boar.

Higgs bade him goodnight after taking his suit to brush and his shoes to polish, and setting out a clean shirt and stockings for the morning. Allan fell into bed gratefully after the day's travel and his exploration of the village.

The creak of a door awakened him in the depths of the night. Starting bolt upright, he threw back the covers and bedcurtains and swung his legs out of bed.

A hoarse whisper of "It's me, Higgs, sir."

"What the devil are you doing up?" Without thought, Allan kept his voice low. Steel struck flint; no answer came until Higgs had blown on the tinder to coax it to smolder and lit a candle.

"Don't be waking the house. I've been doin' a char for Barlicorn. I'll tell you tomorrow." The valet tiptoed past him to where a trundle bed had been made up for him. Through the bedcurtains, Allan heard a few rustlings as Higgs slipped out of his clothing and creaks as he lay down. Equal parts mystified and annoyed, Allan's last thought before sinking into sleep again was that he hoped Higgs was not ripe for the gallows as he rather liked the rascal.

****

Despite his active night, Higgs came in with hot water for washing as Allan opened his eyes.

"Eight o' the clock and a fine summer's day," his rascal announced, "if you happen to like the country, which I do. I'd move back to the fields and hedgerows of my youth if it wasn't so pestilent hard to make a living there. If you're meaning to stay more than another day, I'll see about having your shirts and neckcloths washed," he added inconsequentially.

"I need to speak to one of the Stanburys' neighbors. I'd hoped there might be more, but mourning and Horace Stanbury kept the ladies sequestered almost from the time he arrived. With luck, we'll leave tomorrow. How will you occupy yourself today?" For that matter, how did a valet fill his hours? Never having had one, Allan had no idea.

"I'll have a quiet talk with Phelps. He spent yesterday listening to the folk around here. Grooms and stable-hands mostly, but a few others as well. I'll write down what he learned. Don't forget to lock what you don't want to lose in your portmanteau. Countryside's not as wicked as town, but there's ding-boys everywhere."

"Says the Ding-boy General."

"Barlicorn said as you wouldn't cotton to it if you knew. But all went smooth as silk and we've got what he wanted." Higgs tucked a handkerchief into Allan's left coat pocket and his notebook and pencil into the right.

"If you'd been discovered, you'd be in front of the nearest magistrate now and on your way to be held for the next assizes soon after. How did Barlicorn think I'd explain having a felon for a servant?"

Higgs huffed. "Never happen. Barlicorn don't send out bumblers."

Which gave Allan pause; what sort of business was Barlicorn in, that Winn had known of him and gone to him for help in finding Susan?

"But what if the caretaker had waked and caught you?"

"Ho! He wasn't in the house, was he?"

"Wasn't he? How did you know?"

An eye roll. "A'cos him and me had been drinking together a'most until the pot-boy was ready to close. The bluffer gets up early so he has the ale-drawer stay late. It's not like there's much custom after ten o' the clock. The clodhoppers and hicks all go to bed early, so me and Wilks were the last ones there. When I see the lad start to latch the casements and shutter the windows, I'm ready. Wilks was pretty well disguised by then, and while I drew his attention to the boy, saying as we'd have to be going soon, I tipped a bit o' something into his mug, easy as can be. I sat there while Wilks was drinking down the last of his ale and waited for the pot-boy to be done with the windows, for there's a number of them.

"He says he's closing, and I say my friend would be the better able to walk if he could sit for a few minutes with nothing more to drink. 'Only while I clean up, mind, then you've got to go,' the lad says, and I tipped him a ha'penny and thanked him. He took our mugs and put them in a basket to carry to the kitchen for washing in the morning and busied himself wiping down the tables. By the time he was near ready to do ours, I had Wilks on his feet and staggering toward the door. I thanked the boy again and helped my suckey companion out, saying, 'Don't lock me out, I'm staying here with my master.'

"Wilks folded up onto one of the benches outside, but the drawer didn't notice, not as he'd have cared, being he was outside and the door locked and barred once I was inside again. I bade him goodnight and went up the front stairs to just beyond the landing and waited until the pot-boy passed on his way to the back stairs. Then I slipped down and unlatched a window and the shutters. Once I was out, I wedged the casement and shutters closed with wads of folded paper. As there was no wind I wasn't worried about them blowing open and banging."

His borrowed valet was born to hang. At least he had not been caught in the act of housebreaking.

"Wilks was still on the bench, so I dragged him up and marched him along. He'd had a'most too long for the dose I gave him to work, but I got him past the last cottages and a bit farther. He stopped to water the weeds and a little farther on he wanted to sit down and rest. Then he lay down and closed his eyes, saying the world was spinning something fierce. As soon as he was snoring, I went on my way to the manor."

"How did you get in?" Allan awaited the reply with foreboding. Wilks might report a broken window or forced lock to the nearest magistrate, and he would surely report it to his master, who might guess what it meant.

"Went in through the front door with the help o' my Kate."

"Kate?"

"My pick-lock, and a rum one she is, that's never failed me. I dubbed the gigger and was in easy as you please. I lit my dark lantern that I'd hid earlier in bushes by the gate posts and looked for a room with a desk."

"If you'd been heard—"

"The draggle-tail maid of all work sleeps up in the attic and the stable boy over the stable so I'd no fear o' that. I found the study, drew the curtains over the window, and went to work. 'Twasn't like the steward's office in a big estate" —*And how did he know that?*— "with shelves full of ledgers and drawers full of letters and bills and the like, but it was the same in a way, too. The books on the shelves was mostly just for reading, except for a row of old ledgers. The newest ledger was in the desk and the previous one under it, I suppose so that the master could compare recent costs to last year's. The bank book was there, too, under them. Gave me an idea, it did. I took the ledgers and the bank register and put two of the old ledgers in their place. I've put them in your portmanteau. You might take a look at them later. Near ruined my eyes trying to read by the dark-lantern."

Higgs's smug expression invited him to ask what he had discovered. Allan could not resist, despite being appalled at the theft of the bank book and ledgers. "Pray do not keep me in suspense, Higgs."

"From the ledger, they're not short of the rhino. *And*—there's no entry in the bank-book since two days after the Christmas quarter day. No entry in the ledger to show a bank visit after the last gent died, neither, nor any bank deposit from the Lady Day or Midsummer rents, though they're in the ledger, and some payments out for household expenses."

A man who owned a successful business wouldn't make a mistake in bookkeeping. Which must mean Winn had avoided the bank.

"That's uncommonly helpful. You got away with no trouble, then?"

"O'course. I'm a master o' my trade."

"You must be, if you've practiced it long. You didn't meet Wilks?"

"Passed him on my way back, sleeping like a babe where I'd left him."

"Thank you, Higgs."

"Glad to oblige."

Chapter 20

After securing Higgs's plunder in the lawyer's bag in his portmanteau, Allan fortified himself with a good breakfast and set off to see Ruth Francis. He arrived at a handsome brick house larger than he expected, set in extensive grounds. He had imagined Mistress Francis as living in a pleasant cottage with a servant or two, not poor but not wealthy, which was a lesson to him not to make assumptions with no evidence.

He gave the butler his letter of introduction and asked him to request his mistress receive him. The man returned almost before the lady could have had time to read the missive.

"Will you take tea?" The silver-haired lady was still holding the sheet and her posture and intent gaze told him the offer was the merest good manners.

"It's not necessary unless you customarily drink tea at this hour."

She smiled then. "Very good. No refreshments, Smithers." As soon as the door closed behind the butler, she waved him to a chair near her own, took a deep breath, and demanded, "Are they really safe?"

"As safe as anyone can be, and safer than most."

"Thank God. I've feared for Rose and Ory since their guardian put around that he'd sent them to stay with relatives. You wouldn't think I'd be the only one to wonder how they'd traveled. Their coachman was gone for near two weeks, but when he came back, I heard from my maid, who's Sally Howard's cousin, that he'd been sent to London on an errand to Horace Stanbury's lawyer and had to cool his heels while the man researched something. He was turned off soon after. Stanbury said he didn't need a coachman as he'd be returning to London for a time. But he gave him a reference to a friend in Bristol that he claimed needed a driver. Davis didn't trust him and went to live with his daughter in Oddford. He'd a pension from Paul Stanbury anyway."

"Got out of the way before anyone wondered where the Stanbury girls had gone," Allan remarked.

"I have come by another bit of information since they left Stanbury."

He could not quite imagine what a genteel elderly lady could have discovered about Horace Stanbury, who had held himself aloof from the local people.

"I told Rose I thought her cousin had been reared in or near Liverpool. My late husband was a student of accents and dialects, and I was perforce exposed to them for more than thirty years. Most would not have noticed Stanbury's speech. Recently I've recalled that Horace Stanbury's branch of the family lived near Crewkerne in Somerset, so why would he have sounded like a Lancashire man?"

Brand's old Stanbury documents should show where the real Horace's family lived, which would be some confirmation. "We may need a witness who can testify to his way of speaking."

"I can give you the names of two experts on English dialects. They were friends of my husband, and we still correspond. One lives in London, the other in Oxford, and I have no doubt either or both would be happy to display their scholarship. However, something more startling occurred after the girls disappeared which both reassured me and gave me greater concern for their safety."

She paused, then continued before he could prompt her. "After the Parish Poor Box meeting, I was going to the stable by the lane that runs along the side of the inn. The Blue Boar's taproom windows were open, the day being uncommon warm, and as I was passing, I heard a Londoner speaking. He said, '…on me way back to Rum-ville with the pitchures.' "

Allan's eyes opened wide at the lady's rendition of a man's coarse London accent.

"I found that interesting, so instead of walking on, I stopped a little beyond the window where I could still hear them. I pretended to be searching for something in my workbag so my loitering shouldn't seem odd if anyone noticed. Not," she commented, "that anyone does take notice of old ladies."

"That is their mistake, and we should be grateful for it."

Her mischievous smile hinted she had been captivating as a young woman.

"The other, whom I took to be that peculiar groom of Stanbury's, said, 'This fun o' wins wins the trick.' They laughed and he went on to say, 'I'd find a use for that guinea he's offering,' and the other said, 'I'd find a use for that dimber miss or t'other mort, come to that.' They were using criminal cant which I recognized from *A New Dictionary of the Terms Ancient and Modern of the Canting Crew*, one of my dear husband's favorite books. That was what drew my attention. Should I translate?"

"Please do, ma'am."

"Rum-ville is London. I didn't understand the reference to pitchers or perhaps pictures, and I confess I am not familiar with the phrase, 'fun o' wins' although 'fun' means a trick or cheat."

"I do: Stanbury also goes by the name of Winn in town. He has had sketches of the ladies handed out in London."

"I suppose one should expect that such a thorough reprobate would know criminals. 'Dimber' means pretty," she added as an afterthought.

"Will you put all of what you have told me in a statement to be used in evidence, Mistress Francis? If 'tis not too much trouble for you, I could collect it tomorrow and be on my way back to, er, Rum-ville. Your signature will have to be witnessed by a magistrate, however."

She agreed to write out a statement. "I am glad to do so, Mr. Everard. If you can stay to dine with me, I can write it out now and afterwards we can pay a call upon Sir Humphrey Baskins."

"Is he likely to speak of it to others?"

"I will have to explain about Rose and Oriana's absence if I ask him not to mention it."

"Having a magistrate here aware of this matter may be an advantage." Though news of Rose and Ory's plight might leak out, if Sir Humphrey were not exceeding careful around his family and servants. Still, the chances were that their reputations would be lost anyway. They could only roll the dice and hope for the best.

She gave orders to her butler, led Allan to the library, and invited him to find something to read while she wrote out her declaration, which ran to over three pages. She recopied it, and by then the butler informed them that dinner was ready to be served.

****

That evening he sauntered up the road to Oddford and the hollyhock cottage. Higgs had contrived to provide sheets of paper, a couple of quills, and a bottle of ink to Sally Howard, who would carry them in a basket with some gingerbread. Neither Higgs nor Allan had liked the idea of secreting the ink in his coat pocket.

They sat around the kitchen table, Allan, Sally, and the Stanbury coachman, whose name was Henry Davis. Davis's widowed daughter greeted Allan, expressed a hope that all would be well with the Stanbury ladies, and retreated to the parlor to sew.

"He let me go when he went back to London," Davis said, "and I was just as glad. That man of his, Wilks, wouldn't never have been hired in a decent gentleman's house. You'll laugh to hear I fitted a bolt to the door in my room over the stable, but I did so's I could sleep at night without fearing I'd not wake up in the morning. There's not much I'd put past that one. Or his master, either."

"Why would—?"

"See you, when the other servants who'd been with the family for years were turned off, Mistress Rose had the attorney, Mr. Brand, give them annuities, as her father intended. She told him to do the same for Sally, here, and me, even though we were still working because she saw the way the wind was blowing. But if either of us was to die, the money in the annuity would go back to the manor. Our young lady explained it to us, but I'm maybe not doing it as clear as what she did."

"No, you've done well enough. I understand how it would work."

"My door already had a lock on it," Mistress Howard said, "and glad I was of it."

Allan took down their statements. The coachman's amounted to little more than Stanbury's man being no more a valet, footman, or groom than he was King George.

"I've ripped out an oath, time and again, but the language he used made me blush like a maiden. He didn't know one end of a horse from the other and didn't do a stroke of work. 'Twas all left to the simple lad that was hired to do the gardening and muck out the stable and such though there's only the one hack there now, unless it's been sold. Wilks can't ride even as well as Stanbury did."

He frowned when Allan asked what he knew of Horace Stanbury. "Not so much. He wasn't one to visit the stable. He wasn't one for riding, neither, from the way he hauled himself aboard our old hack. He got better at it, but anyone could see he didn't really enjoy it nor like horses. And I had plenty of chances to watch him for Wilks couldn't saddle or bridle a horse to save his soul, so I was the one to do it."

"Did you ever drive him?"

"Ay. To church of a Sunday, of course, though it's not too far from the manor to walk, 'cepting in bad weather."

"Where did you take him other than church? Did he visit anyone in the area?"

"Not unless he did it when he went riding, though from what I heard from friends, he didn't call on anyone hereabouts. I took him to Bath. If we'd got an early start, we could have made it in a day, but we didn't, so it took two. He stayed there two full days, and with the return trip we were gone near a week. In the end, 'twas for the best, as that's when the ladies got away."

Sally Howard said, "Stanbury had been gone three days before Wilks discovered Mistress Rose and Miss Oriana weren't in the house, him not coming in any farther than my kitchen or the back stair to go up to the attic, and that was farther than I liked. Then he was in a taking and raged at me for not telling him they'd left until I thought I'd have to defend myself with my big frying pan. But I told him I understood his master had given them leave to stay with a friend in the neighborhood as was going to marry in a few weeks, so as to help her get ready. Worried as a fox in a kennel, he was, but daren't go to ask if the girls were there. Right afraid of Stanbury, I guess, for all that they talked so free and familiar together."

The cook tutted. "You should have heard the shouting and oaths when Stanbury returned and learned from his fellow they were gone. He tried that with me, and I told him what I'd told Wilks, that I understood from the mistress he'd given his permission, and her being an honest, sensible girl, I had no reason to question it. He was white with anger but had himself under control by then. He allowed as we'd been fooled and warned me and Henry that if anyone knew they'd run away, their reputations would be ruined. We were to say they'd gone to abide with connections of his where there were young ladies for company. Wilks was always going to and fro between the receiving office in Salisbury and here with letters for a few days, and then Stanbury said he was going to London to find the girls and gave Henry and me our notice."

"And glad we were," the coachman added.

"Do you know what Stanbury did in Bath?"

"He didn't tell me, o' course, but there not being much for me to do but talk with the stable hands and the inn servants at meals, I heard things. Stanbury spent hours with a gentleman as was staying at the inn. The waiter who served them thought they were talking about a filly that was for sale, and that they agreed though he wasn't clear who was selling and who was buying. But he said the other man was corky-brained to be wanting a horse to ride at his age and not steady on his own two feet. Some sort of lordling he was."

Allan could not think about what that discussion of buying a filly implied.

Allan and Davis's daughter witnessed their signatures. Allan and Ruth Francis's call upon the magistrate had been passed off as the widow introducing a friend's nephew to the magistrate, who was sworn to secrecy. The cook and coachman's declarations might not be enough to convince the Court of Chancery to change the girls' guardian but did cast a light upon Winn's character.

"Back to town in the morning, sir?" Higgs inquired. He sounded almost convincing as a valet this time, though clearly it was a strain.

"Not directly. We'll be stopping for a day on the way."

Chapter 21

Back in London, Allan delivered the originals of the statements to Brand. He kept the copies. He did not mention the ledgers and bank book. The attorney would be far happier not knowing of them. Certain other evidence he preferred not to think of, himself.

At his request, the attorney reviewed the correspondence relating to the annuity in the file and confirmed that Horace Stanbury had grown up on a manor in Somerset.

"Old ladies are the historians of our family life," he observed. "We still need more proof, unfortunately."

After that, he delivered to Hayes's office a carefully wrapped summary of Sally Howard, Henry Davis, and Ruth Francis's statements and copies of the relevant section of the current ledger and the bank book. As Higgs had presumably stolen them at Barlicorn's direction, he must want the information.

He returned to the Greyhounds by late morning, looking forward to seeing Rose. He had arrived too late the previous night to speak with anyone except one of the porters acting as night watchman, who scrutinized his face by the light of his bull's-eye lantern before wishing him a good night. Barlicorn had arranged for a small army of porters, all of them probably former soldiers. Woe betide an intruder!

He had missed Rose at breakfast, too, having

overslept as he'd stayed up late copying the Stanbury financial documents. He arrived on time to teach the boys' class, aware he was rather untidy. Her presence a few tables away with the younger children pulled at his attention throughout the lesson. After the first few minutes, he altered his plan. The boys had all had an opportunity to work one problem with the assistance of the set of Napier's Bones he had bought. Now he brought out the sets he had made and distributed them, with the scraps of waste paper on which he had written problems.

"Write your answer to each calculation and be sure to write your name at the top. You've until the end of the hour to finish."

Jeremy's eyes lit up. At thirteen, he would not have been admitted to the Greyhounds, but the board of governors had made an exception because he was lame. "He won't last a fortnight on the street," Barlicorn said. "He's too slow to make a few pence by running errands or to escape anyone who might steal anything he made by begging. But he does have a nimble brain. If he's taught, he can go for a clerk."

"Lads, I'll be using this time to plan another set of lessons for you. If anyone has a question about using the Bones, ask Jeremy. I know he'll know the answer." From the boy's glowing eyes, Allan might have given him a knighthood. Taking out Cocker's *Arithmetick*, Allan sat down at the next table to select story problems for future use and watch Rose.

After their classes ended, she would be at liberty and would want to hear what news he could bring her of her old home, and perhaps even be pleased to see him. A cat might look at a king—or a queen—but would the queen look at the cat?

****

She was delighted to see him, having only had glimpses of him between Susan's revelations and his departure for Stanbury. Not from any particular interest in Mr. Everard, of course, but to learn how Sally and Henry did after she and Ory fled. Had Stanbury taken reprisals against them?

"And Mistress Francis?"

"In good health, I believe, and good spirits once she knew you were among friends. Brand should be pleased with her account of your supposed cousin."

She asked about his journey, too, because that was only polite, not because she wished to prolong their meeting. Then the topic was exhausted and what more could she say?

"Mistress Rose, I was sorry not to be present for Susan's revelations about Winn, but I've read your notes and thought about them on my way to and from Stanbury. I wondered if you'd go over them with me."

Did her face treacherously reveal how happy she would be to do so? Fearing it did, she almost missed the way his eyes lit at her response. Reading over her notes, she described Susan's expressions and tones of voice.

"They convinced me, all of us, she was telling the truth."

"I don't doubt it, and what she said of Winn's age agrees with the bank's description of him when they saw him in 1718. But I wish we knew more of why the real Stanbury bought his commission when he could have lived on the annuity. What you took down seemed to imply he'd been involved in some sort of brawl. Not enough to send one post-haste to join the army, I'd think."

"Perhaps you should speak with Susan. Come, I'll introduce you. And remain while you talk with her," she added in a burst of inspiration, "as she may be wary around a strange man." Opportunities to spend time with Allan Everard came far too seldom.

Mistress Chappell had no objection to their borrowing her assistant though preparations for dinner were in progress. "The two girls we're training can manage well enough for now. Go along with you."

They chose the library for their talk to avoid being overheard in the common room by the little girls learning to sew and the woman teaching them.

As soon as they were alone and the door closed, Susan burst out, "I'm glad you've come to me, sir, for I've remembered more, from thinking on it. I didn't know if it would make any difference, but I meant to speak to Barlicorn the next time he was here."

"Once you told us the name of the officer Winn worked for, that was all I could think about and I suppose Barlicorn and Anne were the same," Rose said.

"Anything you can add now may help," Allan said.

In Rose's opinion, his smile and voice were as soothing as Barlicorn's.

"Bits and pieces of what Nick let slip began to make sense to me. Men do fight over cards even at the Purring Cat, though Nick puts a stop to it as soon as it starts, and he'll ban anyone caught cheating. No one else takes such fracases seriously unless there's a death or a nobleman's involved. So I think this Stanbury must have killed someone or thought he had and went into the army to get away."

"And eventually he came to believe he'd been mistaken?" Allan asked.

"Ay, someone had died or maybe married, I don't know what, except Nick said Stanbury took it as meaning he could go back. That's not much help, I know."

"In fact, it is, Susan. The man must be either titled or important in some way, for the marriages, births, and deaths of commoners are seldom published. And the fight likely took place in London, knowing what we do of Stanbury's youth."

And the annuity meant to keep him in London.

"That's not why I hoped to see Barlicorn and was glad you came to me. I've remembered his name or part of it. The man in the paper. 'St. Denys didn't die so the captain could go home,' Nick said and laughed. That stuck in my mind because I'd never heard of a saint or anyone called Denys, but I liked the sound of it. If I'd had a baby boy, I'd have chosen it for him. Just as well I never did have a child, all things considered."

"Susan, your price is above rubies."

"Then it's increased amazingly. When I was still young and fresh, 'twas a guinea."

Chapter 22

When Susan left them to return to the kitchen, Rose said, "St. Denys must be either a nobleman or a member of the beau monde. Would Barlicorn know, do you think?"

"He may, and I'll visit his man of business who may also know. If St. Denys can verify that the Stanbury he fought with isn't the current Winn, that should be enough to overturn the guardianship." Allan put his hand over hers where it lay on her lap. Mayhap she should have been affronted by the liberty. Instead she returned his smile with interest. Perhaps this evening they could talk more.

****

On summer evenings, the new benches around the outer edges of the yard made a pleasant place to sit. This evening, however, the yard was deserted, with everyone inside as a wind brawled around the eaves and windows. Many of the women had gathered in the common room to talk or sew or knit. She and Allan could have spent some time together there, in plain sight, but he was now tutoring his oldest student, Jeremy, hoping to fit him for some occupation in which his disability would pose no problem.

Ory and several of her friends were playing Pope Joan amid much glee over their cards. At a loose end, Rose paused in one of the classrooms where a woman recently admitted was making Honiton lace, with an audience of several women. If she could teach others to make bobbin lace, they'd have a valuable skill. Training the women and children to earn their own living so they need not depend on a man was an excellent notion. What a pity ladies were so hampered by society's expectations.

She would speak to Anne about it. The matron could sound out the lacemaker. Anne was not in her office or the common room or the classrooms. Could she have retreated to her bedchamber? She was usually available in case some difficulty arose. The only place left to look was the library.

She opened the door, saying, "Anne, do you think—"

The matron started up guiltily. Sitting opposite her was a man Rose had not seen before. He rose to his feet lithe as a cat and bowed to Anne, saying, "I had best be going," before making a slightly less deep bow to Rose.

"Wait, J—Mr. Dunham. Mistress Milton is my assistant and also the reason we need you and your porters."

Dunham halted and looked fully at Rose. When bowing to her he had kept his face half averted.

"Rose, this is James Dunham, our head porter. Mr. Dunham, Mistress Rose Milton."

"Ma'am."

"Mr. Dunham."

"Please stay, as Rose should know about Barlicorn's arrangements for her and her sister's safety. Rose, come and sit."

She had been aware they possessed several porters, more than seemed necessary, without giving it much thought before. They slept over the former stable and one or two were nearby whenever a delivery wagon was admitted to the yard. One went out with Mistress Chappell when she visited the market. Otherwise, they were seldom seen, even in the common room at meal times.

In the dim light of one candle and that one to Anne's right, near the shuttered window, she could not discern him more clearly than to see he was of average height and neither thin nor stocky. When Rose seated herself, he did not return to his previous chair but took one farther away from Anne and the candle. From the few words he had spoken, he was either a gentleman or had been well educated.

"Barlicorn provided us with some 'porters' as protection against violent men and added more because of your guardian. Most of them have had military experience or other experience with weapons and, mmm, fighting. James was an officer."

He made an impatient gesture, and Anne smiled at him with a warmth that stopped Rose's breath, confirming what she had suspected since entering. There was a bond between the two, or at least on Anne's side. Managing to find her voice, she said, "Knowing that we do not depend only on locked gates and bars over the lower windows makes me feel much safer. Thank you, Mr. Dunham."

A faint throat-clearing. "We try to keep out of sight except when one of us watches the gate or serves as an escort. Some of the women are shy of strange men. Others might think it indecent to have a number of men on the premises. Nor do we wish it known the Three Greyhounds is well defended. May I trust you will not speak of it to anyone? Except Barlicorn, of course, and the Chappells, who also know."

"I've seen Mistress Chappell go out to the stable," she said. Two or three times a day, in fact, on her way to the chicken shed. She brought in eggs and she must take out food for the birds but probably she also delivered provisions to the porters. "I won't say anything."

Dunham inclined his head. He turned to face Anne as he rose, exposing the right side of his face momentarily. "By your leave, I'll go now, Matron. I'm glad to have met you, ma'am," he added to Rose, his face again angled away.

"Goodnight," Anne called and Rose echoed her as he marched to the door as stiff as if he were on parade.

"How is it I've never seen Mr. Dunham before or heard anyone speak of a head porter, either?"

"He is on duty mostly at night. He isn't unfriendly. He is only reluctant to be seen by women or children who may be frightened." The matron went to the old stable sometimes to look in on the room where the children played in wet weather. Perhaps she also saw Dunham then.

"Because of the scars?"

Anne nodded. "He doesn't speak of it. I only know because Barlicorn told me before he brought James in. He ran into a burning tent to save another officer. His friend escaped with minor burns. James was lucky not to lose his eye. Have you ever seen a military review?"

"No."

"You wouldn't, I suppose, living in the country. Someone where I lived went into the army, and when he came home on leave he told us about some of his experiences, and having once attended a review myself since coming to London, I saw he was correct.

Appearance and style are important. When they assemble the men for a review, the tallest and best-looking men are put in front and on the sides of the column where they will be most visible and the shorter and less attractive where they'll be least noticed. James's commanding officer made some remark, mayhap several, about his appearance after the accident. His action made him a hero to others, but the colonel thought very little of scars not received in battle. Perhaps he began to feel his face reflected badly upon his company and the regiment, as eventually, James chose to sell his commission. I find it an odd response, but what woman can understand how men think?"

"What nonsense! But he is a gentleman, so why is he working here?"

"I don't know. I'm not sure Barlicorn knows. If he does, he didn't tell me."

Poor Anne. She had formed a *tendre* for the "head porter" and must wonder how it could prosper when he was so elusive and hid his feelings so well.

Rose now knew more of James Dunham's history than she did of Allan Everard's. Allan was a gentleman, she had no doubt of that, and well-educated. He seemed not to be poor, as he had paid for books and other educational materials, and his clothing was good though plain. He owned the Three Greyhounds as well. Why would he choose to live at the inn when he could afford decent lodgings? Where had his money come from and what family did he have?

"Did you wish to discuss some problem, Rose?"

This was the place to leave the subject both of Anne's cavalier and the man she wished were her own beau. "I only wanted to ask if you think the lacemaker from Devon might be willing to teach others."

****

"St. Denys is the family name of the Earl of Mountjoy." Simon Hayes added, "I probably know more about the peerage than Barlicorn does. He claims he knows nothing about our aristocrats except what he sees in the satirical prints displayed for sale. In any event, he's gone out of town."

"When will he return?"

"He was not sure. I've been his man of business eight years or more, and I've never known him to leave London. In fact, he was reluctant to do so but had no one else to whom he felt he could entrust the matter. He did say he had no doubt you were able to deal with the situation here. What do you wish to know about the family?"

Hayes listened to Allan's explanation and remarked, "Providence works in strange ways. Because Susan aided Fiona and Susan being brought to the Three Greyhounds at Fiona's urging, Winn may be brought down by his own act of kindness, if that was what it was, in keeping her on after their affair ended."

It might well have been some sort of solicitude as both he and Barlicorn had believed Winn was genuinely concerned about Susan.

"I am not going to question our good fortune. I do need to discover as much as I can about the fight or brawl or whatever it was that led to Stanbury abandoning our shores."

"I'm no help there, and as the incident occurred so long ago, few are likely to recall it, and those only the ones closely involved, like the family." Hayes stroked a jade figure of an animal, perhaps a Chinese dog or lion, sitting atop a stack of documents. "There is someone I can send you to. He may know something of the family or be able to find out. Ordinarily he gives information in return for information, but he owes me a favor. I'll write you a letter of introduction." He took a sheet of paper from a drawer, selected a quill, and uncapped the ink bottle. Allan admired his tidiness. Neither his foster father nor Salt had ever been able to keep a desk so neat.

If Hayes had not warned him Markham's home was located in a down-at-heels street, he might have thought he had been misdirected. Wych Street, west of St. Clement Danes and east of Drury Lane, was no sort of place for a gentleman to live. The tall, narrow houses might have antedated Queen Elizabeth; their ground floors held shops selling bedding and all manner of used household goods.

Halfway down the short street on the left, Allan stopped at a well-maintained house with a freshly painted door and rapped vigorously. The butler who answered might have worked for any prosperous family.

"I've a letter of introduction to Mr. Markham from Mr. Simon Hayes."

The man accepted it with a "Very good, sir. Please step in."

The door led directly into a room the width of the house. Several armchairs, a side table between two of them, a cabinet, and a bookcase made up the furnishings. A copy of *Lloyd's List* lay on the table. The butler vanished through the door on the far side of the room, closing it behind him. The sound of a bolt slid sharply into its staple was unmistakable.

To what sort of place had Hayes sent him? Then again, considering the location and what he knew of John

Barlicorn, perhaps the butler's caution was understandable. He'd bolted the street door, too, once Allan was inside. He wasn't trapped here. Too nervous to sit down, he stood and glanced through the shipping newsletter. Markham or his visitors, whoever they were, must have an interest in the shipping trade.

"Mr. Markham will see you, sir."

The butler led him up a narrow staircase beyond the door. Markham's study at the back of the house was full of books, not only on shelves but also piled on a table. Slips of paper poked out of some of them. The room reminded him of his foster father's library, instantly setting him at ease. A middle-aged man lacking the corpulence many acquired if they were sedentary turned from one of the windows overlooking a cramped yard at the back. From his face, his mind was also active.

"Mr. Everard, please be seated." He himself took the chair behind the desk. "You're seeking information relating to the Earl of Mountjoy's family. Why?"

"Will you keep what I tell you in confidence, sir?"

"Yes. I'm good with secrets."

Hayes's recommendation and his own sense of the man inclined Allan to trust him with most of the story. He withheld Rose's and Ory's location and details of how he had learned of the brawl and certain other matters.

"I seldom get so interesting a request. Ay, a pretty problem. Unfortunately, I have never heard of such an episode in connection with that family."

Allan, whose spirits had risen on meeting Roger Markham, plummeted. "I'm sorry for wasting your time, sir."

"Not at all. I found your narrative fascinating. Nor

have you wasted your time by coming to me. While I know nothing to help you, I am on good terms with the earl and will send you to him."

Chapter 23

Fifteen minutes later, he was on his way to Lord Mountjoy's home in Bloomsbury Square less than a mile in distance from Wych Street but a world of privilege and wealth apart. He need not have worried about his reception; Markham's letter saw him escorted to a comfortable salon to wait. A fine landscape over the mantel depicted someplace in foreign parts. Italy, perhaps, or France? He had not yet decided when a footman came to lead him to the earl's bookroom.

Allan bowed to the earl, a thickset man with a paunch and a neat bob wig rather than the old full-bottomed wig many men of his age still preferred. Mountjoy offered his hand to shake. This was condescension indeed from a nobleman.

"Markham asks me to answer your questions if I can, as—amazingly—for once he does not know the answers."

Seated and with a glass of claret Allan gave an abbreviated explanation of why he was looking into Stanbury's background.

When he finished, the earl frowned. "How did you come to hear of that tawdry old business? I'd take my oath the only ones who ever knew of it were the publican, the serving wench, my younger brother, myself, and the sharper, who'd hardly be likely to speak of it."

"Stanbury was indiscreet while in his cups, my

lord." Allan would not influence Mountjoy's answers or confuse the issue by telling him the current Stanbury was not the one who had taken part in the quarrel.

"A common failing. That affair has cast a long shadow. Do I have your word you'll not speak of it except to accomplish your purpose?"

"On my honor, I'll say no more than necessary to protect the man's wards from him."

"What do you wish to know?"

"I've been led to believe that no one died in the fight."

"Then you've been misinformed."

He juggled the fragments Susan had heard from Winn. "I was told Stanbury saw a St. Denys mentioned in a newspaper and he believed it would be safe to return to England. The implication seemed to be that he thought St. Denys had died."

"So that's why I couldn't find the scoundrel. Where had he gone?"

"To the American colonies with the army. He sold out in 1718." Assuming he was not already dead, his identity assumed by Winn.

"Damme. 1718? He might have seen the notice of my brother's marriage." The earl chewed his lip. "I suppose I must inform him of that cur's continued existence. You have no objection, I hope?"

"None. But if your brother didn't die, who did?"

"A cousin of ours. See here, I must inform Dunstan of this devilish resurrection. Do you wish to come with me? I'll order out my coach and explain the situation while we wait."

He shouted for the footman in the hall. The order given, he continued, "My brother's life was altered by the events of that night. For the better, as it happened, but it's left a mark. He was very close to Lawrence, our cousin, who was a few years older than Dunstan and figured in his eyes as the very pattern of a gentleman. He gambled deep, wenched, and was profane, a perfect libertine. Dunstan was eighteen and followed him like a puppy. I was new to my responsibilities, and he saw me still as his older brother, not as head of our family. As for Lawrence, he would not be ruled by anyone."

As the coach rumbled over the cobbles, Mountjoy said, "Duns went out that evening light-minded and careless and came back shocked and silent. He gave up his rakeshame friends, he gave up cards, he set himself to study law. I could not but be glad of the change while regretting he'd lost his sunny nature. The passing of time has restored some of his spirits, though I'm told some refer to him 'St. Dunstan.' "

The coach rolled to a halt, and the footman leapt down to open the door. The earl disdained to wait for the steps to be lowered, and Allan followed him. Inside, mild consternation among the clerks ensued. Allan hoped they were not going to disrupt Lord Dunstan St. Denys's day too much.

The attorney was alone in his office and welcomed his brother, closing and setting aside a book bristling with fragments of paper.

"Have you brought me a client, Mountjoy?"

"No." He introduced Allan, adding, "I've brought this gentleman to you because he can help us tie up those loose threads from Lawrence's death."

Hearing himself described as a gentleman still startled him if not as much as the reference to their cousin's death disconcerted the attorney.

"Sit down, please." St. Denys dropped into his own chair.

Explaining yet again that he was looking into Stanbury's background and that having heard he had fled England after killing a St. Denys, Allan had sought out the head of the family.

"Markham sent him," the earl murmured.

"The man who investigated Anna's dubious suitor?"

"Ay."

St. Denys nodded, satisfied.

"Everard learned of the unfortunate event from a female who knew Stanbury well. She had heard his drunken rambling about a fight over a game of chance and that he'd fled to the colonies for fear he'd killed a man."

"Lawrence was certainly dead."

"Then years later, he saw something in a newssheet that convinced him he was safe from a charge of murder, and he returned to our shores."

"He's here? And still alive?"

Allan nodded.

"The notice of your marriage brought him back, I suspect," the earl interjected, "though why he would think that made him safe, I can't imagine."

The attorney laughed ruefully. "He took no more notice of me than if I'd been a lapdog. I was with Lawrence that evening when we encountered Stanbury. He was my age or only a little older. I'd met him before in a group of my friends, so I introduced him to Lawrence, as he shared our cousin's passion for cards and dice. Stanbury wanted to play hazard, and Lawrence fell in with the idea. The coffee house refused to permit it, the proprietor claiming he would not allow men as young as Lawrence and me to ruin ourselves. Now I wonder if he suspected something about Stanbury, as he was no older than I. Lawrence took a pet over the refusal, but Stanbury knew a place where the brandy was good and we could play whatever game pleased us, or rather, he and Lawrence could. I would not play as I had no money to lose, having already lost my quarter's allowance and being unwilling to dig myself a deeper hole." He grinned at the earl. "My brother had threatened to cut off my allowance if he had to rescue me from a spunging house. If I'd played, Stanbury might have recalled me. Seeing our family name years later, he might have taken it to mean Lawrence." The attorney's lips compressed. "How can I help you?"

"Would you be willing to tell me what happened? Any new piece of information may be useful."

Dunstan slumped in his chair. "He took us to a public house not far from Custom House Quay. Shabby and not well supplied with customers. I wouldn't wonder if they had some other business than selling drink. They did have a private parlor and good brandy. Run in from France, no doubt." This admission came with a smile that quickly faded. "He and Lawrence settled down to play hazard." He rose from his seat, opened the door and called, "A jug of small beer, Peters."

He did not close the door but addressed Allan, "I trust you will prefer small beer to lemonade. I serve nothing stronger unless a client needs to be revived after bad news. It's more productive to discuss legal problems if no one's mood is too jovial."

One of the clerks brought in a tray and was dismissed. Private again and all of them with mugs, St. Denys took a long drink. "My cousin, Stanbury, and I were starting on a third bottle, though I hadn't drunk much and Stanbury hadn't, either, though more than I had. A good deal of it had gone down Lawrence's throat."

"Stanbury won a considerable amount as I thought of it then. Lawrence began to grow angry. 'Mighty lucky of you,' he said, and 'Mayhap I should ask the publican for fresh dice.' Stanbury only laughed and told him 'Winning streaks come and go. Yours will come in the next game or tomorrow.' My cousin rapped out, 'I say we'll have a new pair of dice and see how that changes my luck.' Stanbury laughed again and suggested Lawrence couldn't be an experienced gamester if he was so ignorant of how Lady Luck allots her favors. Lawrence fancied himself a knowing one—and at the time, I believed he was—so he didn't take that well, from a man half a dozen years younger than he.

" 'Split my windpipe,' snaps my coz, 'I'll have the innkeeper bring a hammer and we'll see if these dice are fair.' " St. Denys sat silent for a moment, lost in disturbing memories. Allan turned to the earl, wondering if the attorney would continue or whether remembering was too painful. But St. Denys sighed and went on.

"Stanbury had kept his temper to that point, but he began to look vexed. 'Lose like a man or don't play. Be damned to you.' He rose and started to pocket his winnings. My cousin ripped out a profanity I will not repeat and stood up so fast his chair tipped over. He smashed one of the empty bottles against the edge of the table. Stanbury swung around as Lawrence closed the distance between them with the broken bottle raised to strike. I stood like Lot's wife, unable to move or even voice a protest. Stanbury grabbed his wrist with one hand

and punched him hard with the other. The blow should have stretched Lawrence flat on his back if Stanbury hadn't still had hold of his wrist, but when Lawrence began to fall and the sharper released it, my cousin fell forward." The attorney blinked, grimacing as he relived the scene.

"He came down with the bottle under his throat and his blood spreading over the floor. I rolled him over, and it sprayed my clothing and my face. I was trying to tear off my neckcloth to stop the flow, but...Lawrence blinked once or twice and then he was gone. I recall thinking how uneven the floor was, as the blood ran toward one wall. Before I could gather my wits or move, Stanbury was scooping up his money and Lawrence's, too, and stuffing it into his pockets. I shouted at him and when he ran out the door, I called for help. Several minutes passed before someone came, and then 'twas only a maidservant who squeaked and threw her apron over her face before fleeing. I suppose she must have let it fall as she turned away, else she would have fallen down the stairs," he added with mordant humor. He took another draught from his mug.

"The publican came in a few more minutes and asked what I wanted done with the body. I gabbled something about sending for the Watch. He snorted as if the suggestion were too foolish to answer. I regained my wits at last and thought to tell him to send to Mountjoy to come and I even scribbled a note on one of the sheets they'd used to record the score. I drank a little brandy for I was almost sober, and a male servant came to mop up the blood. Eventually my brother came."

"You were fortunate to escape being suspected," Allan said.

Mountjoy spoke. "I knew when I set foot in that curst place the innkeeper wouldn't want a magistrate to hear of a violent death there. Come to that, I didn't want our family connected to such an occurrence or to make a spectacle at an inquest, so the fellow and I were of one mind. I'd come in my coach, and he offered to have a cart and driver take Lawrence's body wherever I pleased. He even supplied a sheet to wrap him in. When I took his coffined body home to his mother, I told her not to open the coffin as he'd died suddenly of the smallpox."

"You didn't pursue Stanbury?"

"I did, once I'd got the body to our house and given my orders. I reached his lodging by four in the morning, but he'd already gone. I had someone make inquiries, alleging I wanted to find him about an unpaid gambling debt. That he would go into the army never occurred to me."

"I hope this has been helpful to you," Dunstan said.

"I think it has. Could you recognize Stanbury if you saw him?"

"I'm sure I could. There's nothing about that night I've been able to forget, God help me."

Allan took Ory's drawing of "Cousin Horace" out of his notebook and passed it to Dunstan St. Denys, who stared at it furrow-browed for an eternity.

Mountjoy broke the silence finally. "Duns?"

The lawyer shook his head. "I'm not sure. This man is similar and yet not quite as I remember him. The passage of so many years may account for it, of course."

His brother rose and peered over his shoulder. "He was about your age which would make him about fifty years now. He would no more look like a youth than you do. Although he's held up well, considering his life."

"Better than I have, to be sure. I'd think him only forty or a little better." He squinted at Oriana's drawing. "Something else about the face is different. I don't recall the mole by his eye. If it is a mole?" he asked Allan.

"So I'm told."

"A mole might have grown after you knew him," his brother pointed out.

"It's not only the mole. I remember his face as less narrow. This man might be a relative, I suppose, as there is a resemblance. I can't swear this is Stanbury. I'm sorry. I was certain I'd know him out of a thousand men."

"Nevertheless, I appreciate your help, Lord Dunstan."

"What will you do now?"

"I'm not sure, though someone is pursuing another piece of evidence." Hayes had not known what had taken Barlicorn out of London. Allan hoped it related to Stanbury/Winn. "But the more we learn, the more threads there are to follow."

"Mr. Everard," Lord Dunstan ventured, "I would like to know more about your reasons for delving into Stanbury's past. This is not merely curiosity, I assure you. From certain things you have either said or not said, I conclude this is a far-reaching inquiry into Stanbury's past. Discretion is laudable, and as an attorney, I understand the need for it. I might be better able to help you if I knew more about the matter."

This was the kind of decision he dreaded making. In the past, he would have consulted his foster father or Salt. Recently he would have asked Barlicorn or Brand for their advice if not their permission. Today he must decide on his own and pray he was correct. The earl's lack of arrogance and his brother's sober manner and willingness to share his painful memories made the choice less difficult than it might have been.

"The reputation and safety of two young ladies is at stake. That's why I've been sparing with details."

"You may take it as given neither my brother nor I would say anything to harm a lady."

Lord Dunstan nodded agreement to the earl's statement.

"I am sure you would not, my lord, and mention it only because in this instance, discretion is vital." He cleared his throat. "Stanbury was appointed the ladies' guardian several months ago." They listened, fascinated: the ladies' surprise at discovering they had an unknown relative, Stanbury's odd behavior and their decision to go to their grandfather.

"Even that would be enough to cause damaging gossip, my lord, Mr. St. Denys. Unfortunately, there is worse to come."

"I thought there must be," the earl remarked dryly.

"They were refused shelter at their grandfather's home, through a mistake, no fault of his. If a clergyman with connections to various charities had not found them…"

Both men had been leaning forward slightly. Now they relaxed back in their chairs. "Indeed," St. Denys murmured. "But they are safe now?"

"For the moment, we hope. But their likenesses have been passed around town with the promise of a reward for information on their whereabouts."

"That would be a sensible way of finding a missing relative," the earl allowed.

"Except the ruffians passing them out are claiming

the older girl ran off with a man, taking her sister with her, not the way to quell talk. And Stanbury owns a brothel here under a different name."

"Damnation!"

"Merciful heaven." The attorney's utterance was more restrained than his brother's but equally heartfelt.

"Our goal is to have him removed as their guardian. Lucian Brand, who was the family's attorney until Stanbury hired another, thinks Stanbury's connection to a bordello would not be enough to sway the Court of Chancery."

"Brand is probably correct. I wish I could think of some way to assist you. But even if I could swear to the man being present when my cousin died, it would not help you. After I studied law, I realized that Stanbury would never have hanged for Lawrence's death, having acted in self-defense. Manslaughter is a clergyable offense, that is, one accused of it is permitted to claim the benefit of the clergy, and escape hanging. At most he might be branded in the thumb, but in practice, perhaps not even that."

"That does not seem reasonable to me, Mr. St. Denys."

"No, I am forced to agree to some extent, though it began with some sense to it. A member of the clergy who committed a crime had to be handed over to a church court, which would not impose the death sentence. As most lettered men were churchmen, any man who could read was assumed to qualify as clergy."

Curiosity forced Allan to ask, "How many criminals are literate?" He would not have thought it likely, but John Barlicorn was, for all his often uneducated speech. Allan's "manservant" during his stay in Stanbury could read, too. Barlicorn had some very peculiar associates.

"Very few. Now the ability to recite at least the first verse of the fifty-first Psalm is enough: 'Have mercy upon me, O God, according to thy loving-kindness: according unto the multitude of thy tender mercies blot out my transgressions.' Criminals commit it to memory and call it the neck verse. I cannot wholly disapprove. More and more crimes are made hanging offenses. If the crime is not clergyable, juries sometimes refuse to convict even when they know the defendant is guilty. Thus is the law's harshness somewhat mitigated."

"This is a pretty tangle, Everard. Please keep me informed. I'll be happy to help in any way I can, if we can only think of how. You receive your mail at the Green Tree Coffee House, Cornhill?"

"Ay. I go in most days as it's near where I lodge." Not that he received more than the occasional message there, having no correspondents but Brand and Barlicorn.

"I expect to be included among the ladies' faction. I want to hear the progress and ending of this matter. Besides, I may yet be able to do something for them. 'Tis an advantage to be a peer."

Chapter 24

The earl having asked where he would wish to be set down, Allan replied that if the earl were going directly home, that would be close to another call he meant to make. He had not actually thought of it until Mountjoy inquired, but he should visit Sir Oliver again. Hanover Square was an easy walk from Bloomsbury Square.

The footman made no attempt to turn him away or fetch the mistress this time. Nor did he lead him upstairs to the general's chamber. Instead, the man took him to a door opposite the dining room and tapped hesitantly.

"Come!" came the brusque response.

The footman opened the door and announced Allan.

The general was sitting at the desk in a small study or bookroom, less a place for reading than for getting away from others. When he heard Allan's name, he set down his quill and put aside the letter he had been writing.

"Everard, good to see you. Thomas, dismissed. I expect my guest will be willing to drink either claret or brandy."

Thomas bowed and removed himself.

"Which is it to be?"

"Claret, please, Sir Oliver. Your recovery appears to be proceeding."

"Anger is a fine encouragement. I'd become an old woman, keeping to my chamber and my bed. Not that there aren't old ladies who could whip a regiment into shape if given the chance. I've known a peer or two whose title might better have belonged to his mother or grandmother." With a wolfish grin, he admitted, "I do take Thomas's arm when I go up or down stairs. Don't want to fall again and break the other leg."

When they both had glasses, his host demanded to know what progress he'd made. Allan had written him before leaving for Stanbury about Susan's revelations and what he had discovered at Pimling's. The account of what he had learned in Stanbury and from Dunstan St. Denys and the earl outlasted two glasses of wine. Sir Oliver slapped his thigh on hearing about Ruth Francis's command of thieves' cant and laughed aloud to find he'd been correct about Stanbury being too young.

Abruptly he said, "If this Winn is masquerading as Stanbury, what became of the real one? His doxy assumed him dead, and Winn having his belongings may support her belief, but is it possible he is still alive? I may be able to learn something by writing Horse Guards. Some of those fellows may not be able to find their own backsides, but looking up a few service records shouldn't be beyond them."

They passed another few minutes speculating on who might be able to testify to Winn not being Stanbury. Conversation lapsed while they contemplated how to find such a person.

At length, the general said, "I must believe we will sort this out somehow. Still, once we have eliminated Winn as a threat, I am faced with another problem. What am I to do about Rose and Ory?" He hurried on, "Of course I'll take them into my home, though I fear Martha will not be kind to them even upon orders to do so. Rose will need a husband as will Ory when she is a few years older, and what if I die before one or both are provided for?"

"Rose—Mistress Rose—will be Miss Oriana's guardian in another month or so, when she turns one-and-twenty."

"That's all very well, but a woman on her own is defenseless. Consider this: when we prove Winn is not Stanbury, the estate will pass to the next nearest male Stanbury. If there isn't one, the property will revert to the Crown, leaving my granddaughters homeless and penniless as their father lost the money for their dowries. I can hardly blame him, though I'd like to, as more astute investors than he lost fortunes in the South Sea Bubble. My will makes some provision for them, but that's not enough to leave them secure or to find them suitable husbands when we may not be able to conceal that they were not living here after they left Stanbury. Thomas, the footman, knows they were turned away and very likely the rest of the servants as well, and Martha, blast her, might let it slip to her gossips. Unintentionally, of course." He scowled at Allan.

"I think I must look about for a man to marry Rose as soon as she's of age, which would remove her from Winn's power and Ory, too, as the court should support the child living with her sister rather than an unmarried male cousin who could not introduce her into society. At best, I am not sure I can secure them husbands of the class to which they were born."

Sighing inwardly, Allan agreed. Even quite a small dowry would be enough to persuade some young officer of the general's acquaintance to marry Rose.

****

Rose was tucking the ends of her neckerchief into her bodice when a double tap sounded at the door. Ory had already gone down to the common room to wait for breakfast with her particular friends. She would have burst in, all high spirits and no thought as to whether her sister might be only half dressed, not that Rose ever was in dishabille at this hour. Something must be terribly wrong.

She hurried the few steps to the door and jerked it open, expecting the worst without being able to imagine what it could be.

Allan stood there, his hair less tidy than usual and his neckcloth unevenly tied.

"Rose, will you come to Anne's office? She sent a boy with a note for me to see her and asked me to bring you. There's disquieting news."

"What?"

"I don't know, but it's not something to be discussed in public."

She stepped out and locked the door. The women needed the feeling of safety from being able to lock themselves in and from knowing that no one could slip in to steal their few possessions. They did not speak again until they were in the matron's office and the head porter closed the door.

Anne looked back and forth between the men. "Mr. Everard, have you and Mr. Dunham met?" Head shakes from both.

Flustered, she introduced them. By unspoken agreement, they dispensed with the standard civilities. This was not an assembly room.

"Mr. Dunham has news."

Something mighty serious: today Dunham had

forgotten his reluctance to show his face. "One of the street boys came to the alley door this morning just after dawn. He asked the man on duty for me. I know the lad and trust him. He's one of the sentinels Barlicorn provided. During the last two days, several men have been seen idling nearby, not always the same ones and not in the same places, but where they could see the gate. Hal waited until today to report because he wanted to be sure they were wrong 'uns. He had three of them followed when they went off duty. They all went to the same place: the back door of a brothel."

"The Purring Cat?" Allan asked.

"Ay."

They had felt safe here. Alarm brought on a sudden rush of heat and with it sweat that made her smock stick to her skin. "How could he have found us?" Her voice was steady, however. Somehow Allan Everard's presence only inches away comforted her.

"That's what I need to know," Dunham said. "There was no sign your whereabouts were known. Then Winn's bullies showed up."

"Is it possible Susan could have informed him?" Anne's hesitant question put into words Rose's own unwilling suspicion.

"She doesn't go out," Dunham responded. "She hasn't written anyone, if she can write. Mistress Chappell visits the market with one of my men to buy whatever can't be bought from the street sellers."

Hucksters came by in the morning with barrows of vegetables, fruit, and fish. Chappell opened the little gate and stood by while a porter went out with the cook. The precautions might seem excessive to someone who knew nothing of Nick Winn, but Rose found them reassuring.

"Who does go out besides Mistress Chappell and your porters?" she asked.

"I do."

"Besides you, Mr. Everard."

"Chappell does if he needs something for a repair. He and his wife go out together once in a while. I have no doubt of his honesty." He paused. "For many years, he was coachman for the family for whose steward I worked. He fell out of favor with Lady—with the lady of the house for being too forthright. Can any of us suspect Mistress Chappell?"

Dunham shook his head. "She is the mother or grandmother we all wish we had. She dispenses treats, advice, and admonishments to my men in equal quantities. And to me, too. It's embarrassing." His usual stern demeanor reappeared. "Sometimes one of the women goes with Mistress Chappell to buy supplies for her work."

Anne said, a note of apology in her tone, "Several of the women are very clever at sewing caps, infant clothing, neckerchiefs, and the like. They prefer to choose the linen and embroidery thread themselves. About once a month I go to Rag Fair with someone from Bethlehem House to buy for residents who arrive with only the clothing on their backs, and also for the seamstresses here who earn money by making over old clothes or using parts of them for new garments."

"But they don't go out to sell them."

"No. They're delivered to a friend of Bethlehem House who has a market stall."

The left side of Dunham's mouth quirked up. "I think we can acquit you of being Winn's informant."

Anne blushed. Rose offered up a silent prayer that

somehow things would work out for the pair. And for Ory and herself, though that seemed a forlorn hope.

Dunham conceded reluctantly, "None of the women could have passed word to Winn by any means I can think of. My men would have reported any conversation that didn't relate to a purchase. And I've been inspecting any letters that are taken to the post." Dunham continued, "The women—and ladies—sheltering here will go somewhere they can live and work in safety. None of them step outside the Greyhounds until then, except for the few who go a-shopping with the cook, and they go veiled, in full mourning. Before you ask," he added with a steely-eyed stare at Everard, "I trust my men. All of them come from within a few miles of my family's home, served with me and mustered out at the end of their enlistment."

"But if no one else goes out," Rose began, as Anne said, "Mistress Chappell takes Belinda, the little kitchen maid, with her to learn to recognize the freshest meat and fish and the best vegetables and fruit and how to bargain for them."

The head porter admitted, "I was forgetting her. She's little more than a child."

At Rose's shoulder, Everard stirred. "Something must have happened or changed. What goes on in an ordinary day here?"

Each of them described what they knew of the pattern of the Greyhounds' days.

Then Anne said, "That's six days a week. On Sunday, Mr. Simmons holds the service in the common room. There's no shopping done."

Rose could not imagine the curate as a suspect. Nor could anyone else.

"Something must have changed," Allan repeated. "In country life, there's a pattern. Planting in the spring, harvest in the fall—with a good deal of work in between—and ploughing at various times. But when these things take place depends on whether it's wet or dry, the kind of soil, the crop, even perhaps the kind of plough you have. At the Three Greyhounds, none of those affect the day's events, not even rain. Breakfast at a certain time, classes, dinner, more classes or various housekeeping tasks, supper, and amusements and leisure until it's time to go to bed. Does anyone seem to have more coin than you would expect? The women who sell the things they sew have a reason to have money—"

"Belinda," Anne interrupted. "She's been selling her pin-pillows while she's at the shops with Cook. She does very well with them. She began when one of the sewing women gave her some scraps of fabric and lace, too small to be useful. They're so pretty she always sells as many as she makes."

"Would your man have reported any talk she had with a customer?" Everard asked.

"Ay."

"I could more easily imagine Mr. Simmons had let something slip than Belinda," Anne said. "She's very shy, especially with men."

Yet she was comfortable with Ory, Fiona, and the other girls, and with women.

Allan pulled out his pocket watch. "We had better go to breakfast. Afterward we should talk to Mistress Chappell. She knows Belinda better than anyone else, I imagine."

Ory and Fiona probably knew her better, but Rose hesitated to say so. She did not want Ory upset by questions that might seem to cast suspicion on her friend.

They were late entering the common room, and Dunham's presence would have made them more conspicuous if everyone else had not been concentrating on their food and their conversations. They sat at an empty table at a distance from the kitchen but without speaking much.

When they were the only ones left in the room, Dunham began to rise, Anne forestalled him. "I'll ask Mistress Chappell to speak with us."

He sank back onto the bench.

When Anne returned with the cook and they were seated, the head porter asked her about the days she went to the shops, after explaining men had been seen outside the inn with no obvious reason to be loitering there.

"We wondered if you noticed any men, or any women, either, who seemed more interested in you than usual."

"No, sir. Though when I'm in a shop, my attention is on what I'm buying and whether the shopkeeper has his thumb on the scale."

"And does my porter go into the shop with you or stay outside?"

"If the place is full of customers, he might wait outside."

"And does Belinda stay by you?"

"Well, of course, as I'm teaching her to know how to deal with shopkeepers."

"So she's always attentive? I mean, she pays close attention?"

"Ay, when I point out the things she should look at and tell her what to watch for in bargaining."

"I hear she sells pin-pillows she makes."

"She does. Belinda's a hard worker and sharp with it. For all she's a bit shy, her little basket of wares empties quick."

In the pause before James Dunham could ask another question, Rose spoke, prompted by a certain memory. "How long has she been going to the shops with goods to sell?"

"She'd not been helping me more than a week before I knew she was worth training to be a cook, and I began bringing her with me. But it's only been the last three or four times she's had things to sell. They sold from the first though she's too timid to cry her wares." Sally Chappell shook her head and clucked. "Here's how clever she is: she put a pin-pillow or two and an embroidered handkerchief and a card with a picture of a flower or some such on the cloth covering the other things in the basket to draw people's eyes. You might think she'd'a lost one or two of them to some light-fingered lad, but not she! Belinda reckoned as how Mr. Dunham's porter being with us would keep the filchers away."

"I'm glad he was of service." Dunham's arid comment failed to mask a certain amusement. Rose would have shared it, but for the news that 'twas not only pin-pillows the girl sold.

"Does she embroider handkerchiefs and paint pictures, too?"

"Why—" Mistress Chappell hesitated. "I don't know as she ever said so. Come to that, I don't recall she mentioned anything but the pin-pillows."

Dunham, Allan, and Anne stared at Rose. She said apologetically, "I think we should talk to Belinda as well."

"I meant to do so." The head porter was not amused this time. "Thank you, Mistress Chappell. May we speak with her now?"

"I'll send her out to you. Don't be frightening her." She rose and marched back to her domain.

"Why did you ask about the other things, Mistress Rose?"

"When she mentioned them, I remembered seeing Belinda, Fiona, and my sister sitting together. Fiona was embroidering a handkerchief. Ory was painting. Mayhap someone else has a brush and a box of watercolors here, but I take leave to doubt it. Ory insisted on bringing hers from home." Her audience appeared puzzled. "Winn, our supposed cousin, is skilled at drawing. You saw the sheets with Ory's and my likenesses. Ory has always drawn, ever since she could hold a pencil. He gave her lessons. If one of her little paintings came to his notice, he might recognize her style."

"Like handwriting, I suppose," Allan ventured. "I've heard that artists sometimes know who created a painting by the brush strokes or other tricks of style."

Just then Belinda emerged from the kitchen, hands clasped at her waist. Her eyes flicked from Anne to Dunham to Everard, expecting to be scolded, no doubt. She smiled hesitantly at Rose, the only one she knew well.

"Sit down, Belinda." Anne beckoned her to the place the cook had occupied.

Dunham's smile, twisted by his scars, might not be reassuring, but his voice and eyes were kind. "We would like to hear about your success as a street seller."

"Oh…I'm sorry, I won't do it anymore if it's wrong."

"You're in no trouble. There's no rule against it. We weren't aware you were doing it and were pleased to hear you've been successful, and sell others' work as well."

"Pleased" did not describe Rose's sentiments.

"I give them the money for their things. Every farthing."

"No one thinks otherwise. You're all good friends, are you not? Friends don't cheat each other."

"They're like my sisters, sir, and teach me so much, as much as Mistress Chappell almost. I'd do almost anything to help them."

"Have you sold many of Fiona's handkerchiefs and Ory's little pictures?"

"All they've given me to take. Three of Fee's and seven of Ory's. She can draw and color faster than Fee can stitch. But the handkerchiefs are dearer than the painted cards."

He chatted with Belinda a few minutes longer before saying, "I think it will be necessary to stop Cook and you going out to buy at the shops for a while. There have been some men lurking nearby who may intend harm to someone here. They might abduct you or Mistress Chappell to be hostages. We won't risk that, but once the danger is past, you can continue your trade."

A relieved Belinda was sent back to the kitchen.

"I wonder how Winn could have seen one of my sister's pictures."

"We may never know. But if as you say he would recognize it as hers, that may explain why the Greyhounds is being watched. Mistress Anne, there must be no more visits to the shops for the moment. I'll speak with Chappell. Will you please inform Mistress Chappell and have her make a list of things she will need for the next week? I'll have a porter go out to order them and have them delivered. We'll have to depend mostly on bacon, hams, and salt cod except for what fresh meat or fish the hawkers bring around."

"Of course, Mr. Dunham."

Rose knew their formality was for her and Allan Everard's benefit. Allan might be deceived. Rose, having seen them together, was not. Nevertheless, the head porter's transformation from avuncular questioner of little girls to army officer was remarkable.

Anne hurried off to help the cook make her list of supplies. Rose cast Allan a glance that hinted she was reluctant to leave, but Dunham said, "A word with you, Everard," tilting his head toward the door.

Chapter 25

Dunham's office was over the former stable, between the porters' bedchambers and their parlor. They were able to cook or at least heat food. On duty in the middle of the night, a mug of soup or coffee would be a comfort.

The office contained a desk, two chairs, and a well-filled bookcase. The last was a surprise.

The head porter said, "As Barlicorn is away, I will rely on recommendations from my men to find other former soldiers who would be willing to join us for as long as necessary."

"You think Winn's huffs will not be content to watch?"

Dunham shook his head. "I wish they might, but I don't believe it. If I were Winn, I wouldn't. He's spent some coin on printing those sheets, paying for them to be passed around, and for the watchers. He has too much to gain from securing the ladies."

"By forcing them into prostitution in his bordello."

"Or by selling them to another or to a private purchaser who might pay a great deal more for Miss Oriana."

Sickened, Allan demanded, "What can I do to help you?"

"Barlicorn told me you refused to leave the Greyhounds despite being warned that there might be violence. As a gentleman, I suppose you can use sword and pistol."

"While I am not a gentleman by society's reckoning, being born a bastard, my foster father taught me taught me everything a gentleman should know. Most of it little use to me, when I was destined to be a steward." Why had he revealed his bitterness to a man he scarcely knew?

Dunham laughed ironically. "Better more education than you need than less. My father was a country gentleman. He trained my oldest brother to manage the property. The second and third were sent to a good grammar school and to university, one being meant for the law and the other for the church. I was to go into the army and had the benefit of my brothers' tutor until the last left for school, then several more years with an old parson nearby who had given up his parish because of infirmity. My father saw no need for a soldier to know more than how to read, write, cipher, ride, fence, and shoot. Why pay school fees when he would have to buy my commission?"

"Had your father any more education than that?"

His eyes fixed on the bookcase, Dunham did not answer at once. "Perhaps not. I never saw him read aught but a newspaper or mayhap a book about animal husbandry or agriculture. My sisters would never have learned to read or cipher if my mother had not believed it necessary for a lady to oversee her cook and housekeeper."

Everard said, "You're well read," inclining his head toward the bookcase.

"I enjoy reading."

"Even Caesar's commentaries on the Gallic war in Latin?"

"I learned a little Latin and tried to improve it. I still do. I believe John Barlicorn is better educated than I am, for all his rough speech. Never mind that. Are you willing to help if the Greyhounds comes under assault?"

"Yes." The old inn was his patrimony. Even if Rose and her sister had not existed he could not have turned his back on the other women and children living in his property.

"Thank you. The more men we have to defend the inn, the better. I'll need to assign two of my six men to night duty. That's when we're most likely to be attacked."

"What sort of attack do you anticipate?" He could not imagine how either of the gates could be breached. At some time, bars or heavy grills had been added to the ground floor windows. Mayhap crime had increased since the inn was built. All the windows had shutters, as well.

"If I were planning an attack, I'd break into the building that adjoins our north side. The shopkeeper's an old man who sleeps on the ground floor. He was a shoemaker but gave up the trade when he found it became too difficult for his arthritic hands. Now he's a cobbler and does well enough by it, this being an area where many have their shoes repaired. His joints ache, and the stairs are hard for him to climb. His daughter comes in during the day to bring him food and fetch down anything he needs from the upper floor."

As he spoke, Dunham sketched on a piece of wrapping paper salvaged from some purchase. The lines took form as the outline of the inn, the narrow alley to one side, the lane behind the stable, the cobbler's shop on the other side of the Greyhounds and less than half its depth. At the back of the shop, a yard separated it from the lane.

Dunham's pencil tapped the open space. "I'd bring in a ladder to reach one of the cobbler's first story windows. The daughter has enough to do at home and for her father that she doesn't shutter them. There's a hatch to the roof. Set the ladder up on the roof, and it would reach the Greyhound's eaves. Then I'd have my men on the inn's roof. There's no one sleeping in the attic, so they'd go in through the dormer windows. That would be the easiest way."

Allan had noticed the little shop adjoining the inn but missed its strategic importance.

"Do you have enough arms? I'll purchase whatever you need."

"We're well armed and can equip you."

"I've my own smallsword and a pistol."

They discussed plans for dealing with the hypothetical invading force a little longer.

Later, Everard took his smallsword and pistol out of the clothespress, hanging the former from a clothes peg in his bedchamber. Examining the pistol before cleaning it to be ready for use, he noticed the barrel and lock were steel and the restrained decorative metalwork was silver. The walnut butt was satin-smooth. The gunsmith's name on the barrel was *G. MacGavin.* In the excitement of receiving the pistol, he had not understood the flintlock was of the finest workmanship. So was the smallsword. How could Willis have afforded such expensive weapons?

Augustus, Baron Passevant. Allan's father must have supplied them, desiring his by-blow to be brought up as a gentleman because he would eventually have the means to live like one. Augustus Passevant's intention to have him educated and trained almost as if he were legitimate was as great a gift as the property and money. Greater, as it seemed to show he cared about Allan, rather than merely wishing to provide for him as a responsible man should settle his bastards in life. He had done it the only way he could, by stealth. Married to a harpy, he could not have sent Allan to university or done more than support him inconspicuously. And he had known Allan could receive the Three Greyhounds and its profits only after leaving Passevant as Allan would certainly do after the earl's death. If instead Allan had left his post with the steward, either Attorney Hart or Salt would have steered him to Peter Wilde anyway.

Allan finished inspecting and cleaning the pistol, and put it, the powder flask, and the box containing balls, patches, and spare flints in the drawer of the stand by his bed.

****

He went to the coffee house to see if he had received a letter from Sir Oliver with news from Horse Guards. Or perhaps Barlicorn had written him with more information about Stanbury or Winn. As he entered the Green Tree, Sir Oliver's voice greeted him with a cheerful "So-ho! I hardly hoped to find you, yet here you are." The baronet was seated at a table near the door in solitary splendor, a Malacca cane beside him. His valet sat uneasily at another table. "I delivered a letter for you to the charming female behind the counter. If you've the leisure to drink a cup with me, I'll give you my news."

At this remark, Everard almost forgot to bow. As he straightened from his regrettably casual gesture to deference, he said, "News?"

"I've had some luck."

Before he could say more, the serving boy hurried over with his tray of coffee and tea pots, a cup, and two letters. "Will you be sitting here, sir?"

"Ay." He took the chair opposite Sir Oliver, was given his correspondence and served with coffee.

When the lad moved on, the baronet spoke. "I've not yet received a reply from Horse Guards, but after I wrote, I remembered an old acquaintance of mine had been in New England during the time Stanbury was there, so I wrote to him as well."

"Did he know anything of him?"

"Nothing recent, but he referred me to a Major Grover, who also lives, or lived, I should say, in London." Sir Oliver did not keep him in suspense long. "He died a few months past. His widowed daughter and son-in-law lived with him, and they, on reading the letter, turned it over to the major's valet. Jones was his servant the whole of Grover's military service, nursed him in his last illness, and is still living there. Grover often said Jones was more sensible and more use than most officers, and even though he left the man a little pension, his daughter has kept him on as her husband is not in good health, and she wanted a reliable man in the house to oversee the footman and help her husband. If you've time to speak with Jones now, I'll send my man to ask the lady to let me borrow him. The house is not far."

While they waited, Everard described the situation at the Three Greyhounds as well as he could without mentioning its name or location.

****

Jones, a bulldog-squat little man, sat at attention.

"I never gossiped about officers or repeated

anything Major Grover said, sir, as I don't hold with that. But you tell me you have a reason to ask about Stanbury, and the major being dead, I've no objection to answering." A thin smile. "He'd want me to, God rest him. Couldn't abide the fellow, he couldn't."

They'd agreed beforehand that the general would ask the questions Everard had suggested and any others Sir Oliver could think of. Everard would take notes and interpose questions if needed.

"Not a good officer, eh?"

"No. A time or two he lost men because he didn't know how to lead or didn't care to. I'm sorry for speaking plain, but you did ask, sir."

"I meant for you not to shave the truth, Jones. There's many ways not to lead. Which did he fail at?"

"Some officers make the men feel valuable. Some don't. I reckon he was too full of his own importance to have any to spare for his company. And he never put his own self in danger. Still, there's officers like that."

Everard suspected Sir Oliver would have winced were it not for military stoicism. Instead he allowed, "Quite. More's the pity. The major wouldn't have had much patience for that."

"He didn't, but that's not all what he couldn't stomach about Captain Stanbury."

Milton's shaggy eyebrows raised. "There was something worse?"

"Ay. The major was right sure he cheated at cards. He admitted straight out he couldn't prove it and only said, 'No one's that lucky, and always against junior officers.' Stanbury got away with it because he was careful not to win too often from the knowing 'uns, but he'd fleece the young chubs."

"Sly."

"So the major thought. He spoke to one or two of his friends about it, but they'd noticed nothing, not having lost much to him. Stanbury won small sums from cup-shot lads, but there was a mort of them. Even if they suspected, they'd have been afraid to raise a question about his play."

"An experienced sharper, then. Do you know why he decided to sell out?"

"Some of the other officers finally began to wonder about his luck. He saw the way the wind was blowing, Major Grover reckoned, because he stopped winning so often. Then one day he says it's time for him to go home and take care of family matters."

"Did he mention what they were?"

"Not that I heard. The major thought it odd as he wasn't known to get letters from home and he'd never talked about his people. But my master said it was good riddance and didn't care why he was leaving."

Allan cleared his throat, a hint he had something to ask.

The general gave a crisp nod in Everard's direction.

"Did his servant talk about it? If he had a servant?"

"He did have one, but the fellow's lips were as closed as a fresh oyster's shell."

"Can you describe him? Or recognize him if you saw him again?"

"The captain's man? No. It's been a long time, and I don't have an eye for faces. If it hadn't been for the uniforms, I'd've had trouble knowing which officer was which, until I learned to recognize one feature on each. A nose or an ear, maybe. Got me in trouble, once or twice, it did."

"You didn't commit to memory any of Captain Stanbury's man's features?"

"I knew his voice. I didn't bother to know his face. His first name was Nick. I remember that because 'nick it' means to win at dice." With a grin that exposed a missing eye tooth, he added, "Stanbury had a way with the dice."

"Was Nick a cheat, too, then?"

"If he was, he was mighty careful about it, but he was Stanbury's manservant and tight with him, so I couldn't help but think 'like master, like man.' "

Jones's sudden intake of breath when Allan showed him the sketch took them all by surprise.

"Do you know him after all?" the general demanded.

"Not as such." He hesitated. "Like as I said, I'm not good at faces. But this phiz puts me in mind of the captain's manservant. Mayhap 'tis only because I was just speaking of Nick. Besides, this 'un's older, yet I a'most recollect Nick had a mole like that. If I heard him speak, now, I'd remember that. I've a good memory for voices. I wouldn't hang a dog on my word if it came to swearing to his face." After promising to testify if necessary, Jones was sent away with thanks and a gift for his trouble.

"Well, we now know Stanbury was a bad soldier and continued to be a cheat. As we cannot prove he's not Stanbury, we must hope Horse Guards or one of the men I've written can tell us he's dead."

Allan sat silent, brain toying with an idea as a cat plays with a ball of yarn.

"Eh, Everard? Why are you staring at your pencil?"

"I was woolgathering, sir. A possibility has occurred to me. I am not sure it would work, and in any case it depends upon someone else."

Chapter 26

In Chancery Lane, the clerk told him Brand was in court to watch a murder trial. "He wanted to see how the barrister did, so's to have another one to refer a client to, if he should need a case argued, our usual barrister being ready to retire from practice."

"I suppose I had better make an appointment, then."

The clerk heard the disappointment in Allan's voice. He glanced at the mahogany bracket clock mounted on the wall near his desk.

"No need, if you've a bit of time to wait. Mr. Brand left about an hour and three quarters since. I expect him back shortly."

"So soon?"

"A fifteen minute walk each way, mayhap another twenty minutes for the case to be called, thirty minutes for the trial, and another few more minutes to congratulate the barrister or condole with him."

"Half an hour for the trial?"

"Yes, as it's murder. They do take a little longer."

As he had not worked out the details, Allan used the time to jot down his plan as an aid to Brand, hoping he would not find deficiencies in it.

The clerk had been correct. Allan was re-reading the sheet to make sure nothing was left to chance when Brand entered, grinning. "Very neat work. The defendant's lawyer was wise to engage him. The sister-in-law was set on seeing the man hang, but Jamison's questioning of the servants brought out her antipathy to him and her sister's habit of taking laudanum. The husband had no idea how much of the stuff his wife was using." At this point he noticed Allan. "I beg your pardon, Everard. My enthusiasm for a good trial carried me away for a moment. What brings you here?"

"A possibility for resolving the situation we have been discussing."

"Ah. Come into my office. I haven't any client coming in for an hour or two, I think?"

"No, sir."

Brand read the sheet, then read it again, frowning. Setting it down in the middle of the desk halfway between them, he cleared his throat.

"That is my idea," Allan concluded a trifle uneasily. Would Brand consider it outrageous?

The attorney frowned. "Everard, you should have been trained up in the law."

With an inward wince, Allan concealed his chagrin at being reprimanded for his presumption. He knew a good deal about the law relating to land but almost nothing of other aspects of legal practice.

Brand said, "I know you hoped to wait out the time until Mistress Rose's birthday when she could petition to be made Miss Oriana's guardian as specified in her father's will. There would be no need to reveal Winn's imposture or his trade, which should have made it possible to conceal the most scandalous parts. This idea of yours is better. I consulted a member of the bar of the Court of Chancery, one I trust, who doubted Chancery would have agreed. Women are always held to need a man's guidance, and with the heir already in place as little Ory's guardian, the court would likely not change the guardianship."

Spinsters in Passevant Magna and Passevant Parva had got along without men. They'd had no choice. Perhaps having a male relative was as much a drawback as a benefit for a female. *Not a comfortable thought!*

"Your plan is well thought out, for the most part."

"Thank you, Mr. Brand."

"However, it depends first on the witness to the death cooperating. Do you think he will?"

"As he could not swear to recognize Stanbury—"

"Unsurprising," Brand remarked with a dry chuckle.

"Just so. But as the head of the family, could the earl not bring the charge?"

"He could. I have no objection to your notion if Mountjoy agrees. From what you have told me, he seems disposed to be helpful. Most noblemen would have declined to see you or at least not have been so forthcoming."

"I did have a letter of introduction from an acquaintance of the earl who had done him a favor. A Mr. Markham."

Brand's eyebrows rose. "A valuable resource. I do foresee one problem. What do you think will happen once you get the fellow before the magistrate and he denies being Stanbury, perhaps sending for witnesses to prove he's Winn?"

Feeling he had been turned back into a schoolboy, he replied cautiously. "I anticipate it will be noted in the record that he has proven himself to be Winn. We will request a copy be made to use in the Court of Chancery."

"And the letter in Winn's possession?"

" 'Stanbury' is not available to bring a prosecution

for theft of the letter, sir."

"The magistrate will want to know why Winn had Stanbury's letter, which is the earl's only proof of his being Stanbury. Then there is the advertisement, which we cannot suppress because otherwise Mountjoy could not explain how he discovered 'Stanbury' at the coffee house. That would certainly cause him to ask more questions. You will likely have to explain that you sent the letter to Stanbury at the Noble Cup because you had seen the sheet circulating with the girls' likenesses, and that you suspected Stanbury and Winn were the same man."

"Would such questions arise? I confess I've little experience with justices of the peace except in matters regarding poaching or the like. When we dragged a poacher before our local magistrate, we were not expected to tell him why we suspected him or how we guessed where he would be found. Surely a London magistrate will waste little time over our case under the circumstances."

"True, most would not delve so deeply, but the nearest magistrate to Winn's coffee house is painstaking."

"But that is all to the good, isn't it?"

"In part. But Winn cannot prove he was only picking the letter up on behalf of Stanbury if he cannot produce Stanbury. If Winn admits to using the Stanbury name, 'tis doubtful de Veil will let it rest there."

Noting Allan's raised eyebrows, he went on, "He has a well-deserved reputation as the most active justice of the peace in London. You could seek out a less careful one, but Thomas de Veil is honest, so Winn will not be able to bribe him, which is a great thing in a magistrate."

"Then do you advise we find a different magistrate? We can still use the other evidence in Chancery."

"Few things in law are that simple. If you seek out a magistrate who would limit the issue to Winn not being Stanbury, we will not have as easy a time in the Court of Chancery and you run the risk of Winn bribing the magistrate. Laying the whole matter before de Veil would wrap it up neatly for Chancery, so our petition does not stand shilly-shally there. Or we could take no action until Rose is of age in another month and then attempt to install her as guardian pursuant to her father's will. We might be lucky."

"I don't think we have a month to spare, Mr. Brand. Winn's ruffians are watching the place where Rose and Ory are sheltered."

"There's this to consider, Everard: whichever course we attempt, we cannot avoid all talk. If we reveal everything we know, the girls' reputations will suffer, but we prevent Winn's plans for them and make it possible for them to come out of hiding. However, the Purring Cat and Winn are well known in gentlemen's circles. His name alone will catch the attention of at least a few of those waiting in the court."

"But surely only a few, mostly not of the better classes, and present on their own business. Can it make a difference?"

"The room will be full of people, including perhaps a few of the better sort. One word about Winn being guardian to a pair of girls will run through the coffee houses and everywhere else men gather. And if some Grub Street scribbler is present to pick up whatever crumbs he can, Winn's connection to a brothel would be titillating enough to write about."

"In the newssheets?"

"Precisely. They might be relatively restrained, but the broadside ballads would spread a more highly colored version of the facts. There might also be satirical prints for sale. I shudder to think how they would portray this affair."

"Then they are ruined whatever we do." He had hoped to avoid scandal, both for the girls' sake and to smooth their move into Sir Oliver's household, where their aunt would not be sympathetic to their plight. When Oriana was old enough to enter society, the scandal would be far enough in the past to count for little and, given how very lovely she was, might not affect her matrimonial destiny. Rose's choices would be limited, even with whatever dowry Sir Oliver could provide. She should not have to settle for him...but what if he were preferable to the alternatives? He could support her comfortably at least, and she did not dislike him. Less promising marriages were made every day.

"You should ask Mistress Rose's opinion. I have a great respect for her sense."

"As do I," Allan said. "But I fear there's little time to debate the issue. I think we must put the whole of the evidence in the guardianship before de Veil and hope for the best. Mistress Rose and Miss Ory may be ruined in the eyes of society, but at least they won't be in a brothel."

Brand winced. "Yes, we must keep that in mind. Now, there's the second problem. How might I or perhaps Sir Oliver have learned of the earl's plan to arrest Stanbury? I cannot simply appear with the proofs we have collected as if by coincidence."

Since coming to London, Allan had sought to

remain inconspicuous, as he had been all but invisible on the Passevant property. If Brand was correct, their appearance before the magistrate might be reported in the newspapers. If the current Baron Passevant learned of his involvement…Well, and what if he did? He could blacken Everard's name making it impossible to court Rose…except that if the newssheets did destroy Rose's chances of marriage to a suitable man, might Sir Oliver accept Allan as the best match she could make? Would Rose care? Perhaps not, if she was not indifferent to him.

"Will the truth suffice, sir? As the landlord of the property where the Stanbury ladies lodge, I was concerned about their safety on hearing they were being sought by a man associated with a brothel. I searched into his background and spoke with Mountjoy when I learned of Stanbury's connection to the death of the earl's cousin. I also heard there was a question as to whether the current Stanbury was instead Winn. I informed you, the Stanbury family attorney, of my findings."

Brand scratched his temple at the edge of his wig. "When you present it like that, it sounds perfectly reasonable. But I think you did not want to appear publicly in this matter. Or any other?"

"I was trained not to put myself forward. But I'm no longer at an employer's mercy, and the ladies' safety counts for more than my embarrassment. I hope to tell you of the earl's decision to confront Stanbury in the very near future."

Brand studied his face thoughtfully. Allan gazed back at the attorney impassively.

"Very good. Then 'tis only a question of whether we have enough proof. The statements you obtained of the

Stanburys' servants and Mistress Francis will be useful. I would like to introduce the bank's descriptions of the real Stanbury and the one who presented himself in 1718, but introducing that evidence would put you in an awkward position."

"I did not claim to be the Stanburys' attorney. While I mentioned that the annuity was arranged by your father's firm, I did not identify myself as being your clerk."

Brand laughed suddenly. "Very true. Did the bank inquire as to whether I was still the family's attorney? No? They should have done. Pimling's procedures are a bit too careless for my liking."

"Mr. Brand, what is the penalty for perjury?"

"It's a capital crime although I have never heard of anyone being hanged for it. Still, I do not recommend it." The amusement faded from his face. "I do think we must have Winn's former mistress present to give her testimony."

"I dislike the idea of exposing her to his possible revenge. There's her affidavit."

"So do I. We might hold her in reserve against de Veil wanting more proof of Winn's identity. Well, then, you'll try to arrange it?"

"I will."

Chapter 27

A commotion at the gate sent Chappell striding out of the common room and distracted Rose's class. She could not blame them, for the pounding was loud and accompanied by shrill cries for help, easily audible as the windows and door had been left open to catch the breeze. A good deal of soot and dust also entered, but that was to be expected.

Chappell's deep voice layered over the woman's, which became less piercing. Anne hurried past from her office. Dunham and another porter ran across the yard toward the gate. To chide the class for inattention was impossible when Rose's mind was churning with apprehension. She gave in to it.

"Class, Betsy will call upon you to read aloud from your books." She gave the oldest girl an encouraging smile. While she was a little shy, Betsy had had plenty of experience in dealing with lively children.

Out in the yard, Anne and the three men were in heated debate, punctuated by a frantic female voice outside the gate. Rose heard Dunham declare, "I say no."

"But James—Mr. Dunham—" Anne began.

"Don't let him find me," the woman outside cried. "He'll kill me, he will, and my baby, too."

"It's a ruse," the head porter ground out.

"But if it isn't? Can we risk that?" Anne gazed up at Dunham's set face.

He would not wish to sacrifice her regard by what must seem like a callous refusal to help a terrified female. But Rose understood his reasoning. She said, "How did she know to come here?"

Four heads swiveled when Chappell spoke, "She says she heard a rumor the Greyhounds took in desperate women and children."

A baby wailed.

"If what she has told us is true, her situation is urgent. There's no time to send a message to Mr. Simmons or anyone else on the board of governors," Anne said.

"No one else can approve an admission in an emergency?"

Dunham's scowl did not improve his face. "I was instructed to rely on Everard's advice in most matters."

"But he's not here," Anne pointed out. The baby's whimpering and the woman's sobs made a counterpoint to their murmured discussion.

Dunham grunted something that sounded like a curse and turned to the porter standing silent at his shoulder and gave him some signal. Until swords appeared in their hands with no warning, Rose had not noticed they were wearing them.

He gave Anne a hard stare. "Ladies, retreat." Anne gazed back at him before taking Rose's arm and drawing her away. But they both glanced over their shoulders to see Chappell unlock the little gate and drag up the recently added reinforcing bar.

He tugged the little gate halfway open, and a thin, ragged woman darted in, a basket over one arm, clutching a small child to her chest. She froze, seeing two men with swords in hand, then sagged with relief when

Chappell slammed the door and dropped the bar before turning the key in the lock.

Dunham and the other man resheathed their weapons. The head porter turned his head toward Anne and beckoned.

Dunham addressed Anne with his usual courtesy. "I would like to hear her story. Will you and Mistress Rose join us?"

Rose found her class clustered around the windows, books forgotten on the table. Betsy, almost in tears, murmured, "I'm sorry, ma'am, I couldn't keep them at their work, no matter what."

"Never mind. I doubt I could have done any better, with everything topsy-turvy out there."

Rose dismissed her class for the day and herded them out of the common room. Anne sent Betsy scurrying off to arrange for a chamber for the woman, self-respect restored by having a duty to perform.

"I'll ask Cook for some food," Rose whispered to Anne and slipped off to the kitchen.

In the kitchen, she found Molly Chappell already cutting bread and cheese. "Chappell having said the woman and baby needed a bite," she explained.

Rose said, "There's one more thing. Could he build a pen today? Under the stairs by the coach gate would be best, I think, to provide some shelter."

"He could, there being plenty of bits and pieces left from the work here, but a pen for what?" she asked less confidently.

Rose told her and carried the tray out to the common room, satisfied that she had done what she could.

Anne fed little Hannah bread dipped in small beer while Gillian Gill ate bread and cheese as if she were starving. Her child was not chubby though she was better nourished than her mother, who had little flesh covering her bones.

Jill was the widow of a lumper, one of the men who unloaded cargo on the docks. The little money they'd saved ran out, and her efforts to earn coin by sewing and cleaning scarcely brought in enough to pay the rent, with little left over for food. "Luke did the best he could, running errands and holding horses, but it was never enough to help much."

"Luke?" Dunham asked.

"My son. He's almost eleven."

"Where is he?"

Her eyes filled with tears. "I knew you wouldn't take him in, seeing as he earns enough to keep himself." When she blinked them away, she told them her landlord gave her the choice of warming his bed or getting out.

"If it'd been only that, once in a while, I might've given in, but he wanted me to live with him so he could rent out our room. He gave me until today, when the rent was due. He's bad-tempered in drink, and I was afraid for Hannah and Luke and myself, too." She gazed at her child, now sleeping on Anne's lap, head against her shoulder.

So far the tale was common enough it might have been believable.

"How did you hear of the Three Greyhounds?" Dunham inquired casually.

"I slipped out early this morning afore he was up. I'd been asking around, quiet-like, for days, if anyone knew of somewhere better than the workhouse. A woman in Rag Fair had heard of this place."

"Did you apply to the parish?"

She blinked rapidly. "I couldn't prove we'd lived in the parish." She burst into tears.

Faint lines appeared in Anne's forehead, but Dunham gave no sign he disbelieved her. The sound of hammering out in the yard told Rose her idea was being put into effect.

The head porter asked whether she had family to whom she could go.

"We can arrange for you to travel to them, however far away they may be."

"My mam and dad died. My brothers both went to sea afore I married. I haven't seen them since. They'd not know where to find me."

"Well, you'll be safe here until we can find you a better situation. Mistress Anne, do you think a room is ready for Mistress Gill?"

Betsy had crept in and was sitting at a table some distance from theirs, darning a stocking. She looked up and nodded vigorously.

Rose and Anne settled mother and child in a room on the first floor. Anne promised to find more clothing for them and told Jill when meals were served. Tomorrow when she had recovered from her harrowing escape, she would be given a tour. She began to weep again, which started the little girl crying.

"You'll feel better tomorrow, Jill. This will all work out somehow."

"She did not seem to find that reassuring, Anne." They were out in the yard by then, but Rose kept her voice low.

"She didn't, did she? Perhaps she has been frightened so long that she has reached the limit of her endurance. Or James may be correct in his suspicion.

What is Chappell building under the stair by the stable yard gate?"

"Mistress Chappell thought she would like a place to keep a goose or two."

"Not with the chickens in the stable yard?"

"She thinks it better to keep them separate."

"Oh." Anne accepted the answer without question. She had lived in a town rather than the country, fortunately. "Rose, do you believe she heard about the Greyhounds as she claimed?"

"It's possible. Didn't people in Bishopsgate near Bethlehem House know what it was?"

"They did. But because the women here are in hiding, all of us have been warned not to talk about it. Still, someone might have let something slip. I think Jill came from Whitechapel. It's not above two miles, but I wouldn't think word of this place would travel so far."

"I don't recall she mentioned Whitechapel."

"Not by name, but she said something about doing mending for a Rag Fair dealer. You haven't been in London long—"

"Or seen much of it."

"—but Rag Fair is in Rosemary Lane, Whitechapel. I've gone there to buy clothing for both houses. But if her husband worked on the docks, I'd expect them to live closer to them. In either case, I'd not expect talk about the Greyhounds to spread that far. When we go to Rag Fair to buy clothing for Bethlehem House and here, we don't talk about the refuges, merely about a charity."

"Then she may be a spy for Winn."

"I'll speak to James in case he did not notice the reference."

Reluctantly, Rose said, "He looked angry."

"He was only letting me know that he knew best in this instance. James was right to think it might be a trick, but if it wasn't…there are so few men who will protect a woman, and so many who will take advantage of her or scorn her for her misfortune."

****

To his relief, the earl was at home and willing to receive him. With the threat of an attack on the Greyhounds, the sooner Winn was rendered powerless, the better.

Mountjoy's bookroom was still pleasant and untidy. As he had on his first visit, Allan wished he might be able to investigate the books shouldering each other for space on the shelves. The earl offered him a choice of tea or coffee "as the weather is chilly and you walked. Unless you'd prefer brandy?"

"Thank you, my lord. Tea would be welcome. Er, how did you know I walked?"

"Heh. I heard no carriage pull up."

They exchanged the ordinary civilities, waiting for the footman to bring their tea and depart. Then the earl said, "I perceive you have a bundle of news. Pray, share it with me. The young ladies must be safe, as you do not appear tense or agitated."

Despite the possible spy within their walls and the risk of attack, Allan found that with a job to do, he felt as confident as he did when going over estate accounts.

"We have a witness who can testify she has known the man we have been calling Stanbury ever since his return from America, but as Nicholas Winn. He had belongings with Stanbury's name. He has not lived as Stanbury in all that time: no lodgings and no address for receiving mail as Stanbury until the Stanbury attorney wrote to him at the bank where he received annuity payments from the family."

"Afraid to use his own name unless he could be sure he was not still in danger of being charged with something or else evading creditors?"

"One might suppose so." Allan took a deep breath of air scented with tobacco and old leather bindings. "Except he may not be Stanbury at all. The real Horace Stanbury bought his commission shortly before he was to begin receiving the annuity in 1708."

"Using the coin from that game of hazard," the earl suggested. "It was a goodly sum according to my brother, but he was not sure how much."

"At the bank, certain documents belonging to Stanbury were accepted as proof of identity when he came in on his return from America. The clerk took down details of his appearance but seems not to have verified them against the description from ten years before, or else he was careless. The Horace Stanbury of 1718 appeared hardly older than the one in 1708. Winn is about a decade younger than Stanbury. Or than Stanbury would be, if he were still alive, which I suspect he is not."

"Some age more quickly than others. Some seem to age but little," Mountjoy said cautiously. "I argue as an attorney would do, having heard my brother dissect a simple statement until two and two make five, or eighteen, or only one."

"We have hesitated to use Winn's woman to testify out of concern for her safety and because she might be considered to be acting out of spite. Now we have a second witness who can give some support to her testimony. He was manservant to an officer who knew

Stanbury. On seeing the sketch, he said it reminded him of Captain Stanbury's man." When the earl did not immediately respond, Allan raised his neglected cup to take a swallow. Evidently his persuasive powers were inadequate to the task.

Mountjoy sighed. "My brother talks about weighing the evidence. I find the sum of what you've told me convincing. We could place it before Duns, and he might agree that you've proven Stanbury—Winn, that is—an impostor. I imagine he would explain with a prim, lawyerly little smirk that this was why he could not swear to recognizing the picture. He would recommend a solicitor to deal with the Court of Chancery." He smiled indulgently at his brother's foibles.

"I did not expect Lord Dunstan to involve himself." Allan knew he would not like the plan given his scruples about identifying the drawing of the supposed Stanbury.

"Then you came only to advise me of your progress?"

"Well…no. May I ask, if you learned that the man who caused your cousin Lawrence's death was in London, what would you do?"

"I would either seek him out and challenge him if I were a hot-blooded young fellow or else drag the scoundrel before the magistrate, even though doing so would be pointless with the only witness refusing to identify him and even mild punishment unlikely."

"What if you could free the young ladies from his guardianship by doing so?"

"That would be worth doing. I am offended to my soul by such a blackguard having control over any young lady. My brother was also appalled to think of such a thing. But how could seeking his prosecution for

Lawrence's death accomplish that?"

"I believe he would deny being Stanbury and I dare say produce a witness or two to swear he's Nicholas Winn, owner of a business called the Purring Cat."

His listener appeared struck. "I'm cork-brained. Of course he would. And you have a witness to support his being Winn. The court might not take his mistress's testimony seriously, but with his own witnesses, his identity would be proven, and he would be safe from any charge relating to our cousin's death. I confess that however great a villain he may be, I could not want him punished for something he did not do." After a thoughtful pause, he added, "Even though my tutor held that if in fact I was not guilty of the thing I was being caned for, I had undoubtedly done something just as bad for which I had escaped retribution. It never seemed fair to me."

Allan agreed. "Our goal is only to force Winn to admit he's not Stanbury."

"Even a layman can see his own admission would cause the guardianship to be overturned. I'll help you. How do we proceed?"

"I need to speak with the young ladies' grandfather. As their remaining family, he should be in our confidence."

The earl nodded briskly. "As the head of their family he would be the most proper guardian, once Winn is eliminated. Pray, either call upon me tomorrow or write me if he is set against the project."

Instead of turning east on Theobalds Road when he left Mountjoy, Allan turned west, hoping Sir Oliver would be at home. The brisk fifteen-minute walk allowed him to mull over any objections Sir Oliver might make.

Chapter 28

"The idea that came to me earlier is workable, sir."

"I trust you now mean to tell me what it is rather than making me pry it out of you." Sir Oliver appeared amused rather than affronted by Allan's abrupt opening.

"That is the reason for my visit. While we had originally intended to wait until Mistress Rose was of age and attempt to change the guardianship, events are now moving too fast. And Brand thinks it would not necessarily have served anyway."

"What has changed to make the matter urgent?"

"Ruffians hired by Winn are watching the place where the ladies are hid."

"Damnation! What do you propose, then?"

"We need to force Winn to admit he is not Stanbury." Allan outlined his talk with Brand and the Earl of Mountjoy.

Sir Oliver guffawed and slapped his knee. "Damme, I believe 'tis checkmate in real life. Very good, my boy, very good indeed. I think you might pour us out a measure of brandy to celebrate. I salute the Earl of Mountjoy for his help and you for the idea. Come, clink your tumbler against mine, Everard. Have you never toasted before?"

"No, Sir Oliver. I have not come from a background where the custom was used."

Milton peered at him. "Not some sort of Dissenter

or Puritan, I hope?"

"No, sir." Apparently his foster-father had overlooked that gentlemanly custom, perhaps feeling it inappropriate in a boy destined for a life little better than that of an upper servant.

"Well, then, let us clink."

After their tumblers had kissed and they sipped, his host grew serious.

"You have been close-lipped about my granddaughters' whereabouts and who is sheltering them. I understand the reason for your reticence and even agree with it as if it came to Martha's ears she would bleat it everywhere. But do you have another cause for keeping silent? No, let me finish. I will stand by my girls no matter what has befallen them and no matter what circumstances they are in."

Rose and Ory were fortunate in their defenders. The earl might have preferred not to involve himself. They had their grandfather's support though most men would be appalled by the ladies having come to London unescorted and being concealed at an unknown location. *And among women of the lowest sort? Unthinkable!*

"They have come to no harm. After being turned away from your door, they got no farther than St. George's before a respectable clergyman took them to a place of safety. Since, they have been as protected from men as if they were immured in a convent." They had been exposed to women and language no gently brought up lady should ever encounter, but as long as no one in good society knew, that could not be held against them.

"Thank God. But Brand is correct that Winn's connection to a brothel will cause talk. You can imagine what kind." Sir Oliver grunted. "Society as a whole is hare-brained and will buzz with the story." He drank down the rest of his brandy. "My fool of a daughter-in-law claims a single unchaperoned meeting or a stolen kiss ruins a young lady. In the best of all possible worlds"—the baronet grinned wryly—"Winn would be struck by lightning or crushed under a pair of runaway cart horses. We must use your idea and avoid the consequences as best we can." His shoulders sagged. The relaxation of his military bearing spoke more plainly than his words.

"And I must make plans for their future. I know a lady, a good friend, who lives retired in Essex. I will ask Lady Helen if she will take Ory in. The matter may not be entirely forgotten by the time she is old enough to marry, but a decent fellow may be willing to overlook it for her beauty and her dowry. 'Tis already past time Rosabel should be married. A man with a title or near connection to one, or even a family of excellent lineage would have been my choice. None of those is likely for her now."

"I suppose you know of some young officer who needs a wife." A dowry and a general for a father-in-law should attract a selection of second or third sons embracing the military as a profession. Allan's suppressed sigh did not escape the general, though he kindly forbore to mention it.

"I do, as it happens, though none suitable. Of the ones who would be appropriate, some would not risk blighting their chances of advancement, if the rumors are widespread. I would not consider any man who would marry her merely for her dowry."

"Rose is not to blame for the actions of a scoundrel." His reply was too heated, and he had forgotten to speak of her formally.

"No, and yet society is judgmental. I confess I would hesitate to let a son of mine marry a lady about whom such gossip was certain to circulate unless I knew as a fact that it was false. Even then I would think twice or three times. Talk, however unfounded, is best avoided. I want a decent man who will not care about the scandal. A genteel cit might do; many of them possess better morals than men in 'good society' and are less concerned about the beau monde's opinions. Such a one might think connection to a baronet outweighed a few rumors."

"I hope both the ladies are not forced to marry men who do not, who are not…" He gathered his thoughts and continued, "Who do not respect and cherish them for themselves." Yet only the lowest sort of people married for love alone, as a rule.

"Those are my sentiments also. Besides those, I would require at least a smattering of gentility. I will not force her to accept any man, however acceptable to me."

This was a more enlightened attitude than Allan expected from a man of the general's age and profession. "That is kind of you, sir. No one who knows Mistress Rose could wish her to make an unhappy marriage however suitable it might be."

"I am glad you agree." The words might have sounded ironic if Milton had not smiled as he spoke them. "This brings me to the heart of the matter. You speak of Rose admiringly—"

"Sir, I—"

"Yes, yes, I know how it is. You have rendered the girls assistance far beyond what could be expected of a disinterested party. I know nothing about you except that you have the time and willingness to aid some sort of charitable endeavor and are a gentleman."

Allan sat mumchance, not daring to speak lest he be reading the wrong message in Milton's words.

"Very proper of you not to leap to a conclusion, Everard. May I ask you a few questions?"

"Assuredly, Sir Oliver."

"Has your family any say in your choice of a bride?"

He swallowed, torn between hope and honesty. "I have no family."

"Ah. Have you given thought to marrying to form one? You are of an age to do so. The wedded state can greatly increase one's comfort if one chooses wisely. My son did not, but he was old enough that I did not feel I could forbid him his choice."

"I have no family circle to welcome a bride. Family connections are valuable. Sometimes they are all that stands between a woman or her children and starvation."

"And sometimes they're a curst nuisance. Answer my question."

What was the question? His wits must have gone wandering.

Sir Oliver barked a laugh. "Have you thought of marrying?" His gimlet eyes and smile were not unsympathetic.

"I've thought of marriage. But I'm new to London and have no connections or friends to introduce me to suitable females."

The general snorted derisively. "Young men in my day would not have been balked by lack of an introduction or a hint. Use your initiative, man."

When he found himself on the street, he had no idea how he had taken his leave of Sir Oliver Milton. Bowed and wished him good day? His memory was a blank; had the baronet been suggesting he would consider Allan a suitor for Rose's hand? If so, he had been misled by Allan's reticence about his origins. He found a hackney stand and told the driver to take him to Aldersgate. He could have walked, but in his current state of mind, he might blunder into the path of a coach or wagon.

****

His brain was a-buzz when he returned to the Three Greyhounds.

Chappell, summoned by the bell to let him in, said, "Mr. Dunham would like to speak with you." His voice dropped. "About the safety of the inn and the young ladies. He's in the matron's office."

He found Dunham alone. "There have been developments since you went out this morning," the head porter began. He ended with, "I don't trust her. Her tale of hearing about the Greyhounds is a lie."

"You think she's a Trojan horse and you let her in?"

"With Mistress Anne and Mistress Rose there, I dare swear you would have done the same." His lips turned down. "And I might be wrong. However, we'll prepare for the worst."

"How do you think the woman can aid Winn, when she's shut up in here? Surely she can't raise the coach gate's bar unless she is a veritable Amazon. And the little gate is secured by the bar you installed as well as the key, so raising it would do no good."

"There's nothing to say she can't use a pick-lock or signal to Winn's crew once she'd unbarred the gate. One of them could use a betty to force the lock if he couldn't pick it."

"Does she seem like a doxy?"

Dunham shrugged a shoulder. "There's no way to

know. She dissolves in tears when you look at her. If she's honest, that may be natural enough, as from her account, she's been distressed by the loss of her husband and terrified by her landlord's demands. Or she could be shamming. Now, Chappell says he can use a blunderbuss and will help, giving us eight men to defend the Greyhounds. If you can stand a few watches for half the night, we'll be ready."

"I will." A thought occurred to him. "With a spy inside, the ruffians could easily find Rose and Ory, unbar the coach gate, and carry them out bound and gagged. They'd have a carriage or wagon waiting just beyond the inn."

"Ay, that's one of the things to watch for."

By then it was almost time for supper. Allan left Dunham meditating over his guard roster. He washed his face and hands and retied his hair ribbon before wandering down to the common room, hoping Rose might be present, as many congregated there before the meal.

Alas, she did not arrive until most had taken their seats and then slipped into a vacant place near Anne. He took a place at the boys' table. If he could not talk with Rose, he could at least keep the lads' natural exuberance under control.

When she bade a cheerful "good night" to her friends, Allan hastened after her.

Chapter 29

Behind her, a man murmured, "Mistress Rose."

'Twas vain to pretend she did not know who had spoken. She could not mistake Allan Everard's voice for that of anyone else.

"Good evening, Mr. Everard." She paused by the door.

"May I beg some of your time?"

"Certainly. Shall we sit? There's an empty table."

The room served as the inn's parlor after supper, with some women doing needlework or simply talking. Some children played games, sitting either at tables or on the floor, while others went outside to play in the yard.

"I have some news." He hesitated. "Perhaps we could discuss it in the library? For privacy."

She nodded. Had he meant he merely wished to spend time with her, he could have done that in the common room. After his morning class, he had been gone all day on some mysterious errand. To be apart with him in private would be scandalous if she had any reputation left to lose, but if he wished to discuss the situation with Winn, he would not want to be overheard.

The small room was dim with only the light from the window. When the door was closed and they were seated, he hesitated.

"Ma'am, I saw your grandfather today."

"Is he well?"

"He is though he's concerned about you and your sister. The Earl of Mountjoy will bring a charge against Winn for manslaughter. We believe Winn will deny he's Stanbury to escape being tried for the earl's relative's death."

"What a brilliant notion! Anyone would want to avoid trial."

"We think it sure to work as, when taken, Winn will have a letter addressed to Stanbury in his possession, making it difficult for him to claim he was not using that name."

"You will not take unnecessary chances, I hope," she said.

"I never do," he said easily, with a smile that went to her heart. Their eyes met for a long moment until he broke the spell by saying, "Your attorney foresaw one problem you must be aware of. In the country, we might meet in the justice of the peace's house with no one else present. Here in London there will be others waiting their turn before him, their accusers, officers of the court, and perhaps someone who writes for the newspapers. We cannot avoid notoriety whether we present all our evidence or only enough to force Winn to repudiate the Stanbury identity. Brand believes the magistrate is likely to take notice of any omissions in our testimony and question us about them. Are you willing to risk losing your and Ory's reputations entirely?"

"Sir, nothing can save us from ruin. If we could return to Stanbury where we are known, we might escape the worst of it, but we cannot do that even if Winn is proven not to be our cousin. With no other heir, the manor will go to the Crown." She made a wry *what would you?* face. "If Mr. Brand thinks there is a chance taking Winn to court will free us from his guardianship, let us do it."

He sighed deeply. "Very well. Your grandfather does not despair of easing you back into society."

"How?" In spite of her love and respect for Sir Oliver, she could not imagine how he could repair a broken reputation.

His delay in replying suggested embarrassment. "Ah…no need to discuss that until we know if it's necessary. Mayhap no one will pay attention to our little courtroom session."

Then he asked how Ory was doing, about Rose's classes, and finally, what she thought of Jill Gill. Soon after, she decided they must part. Their tête-à-tête might have escaped anyone's notice thus far, but they should not linger together longer, however much she might wish to do so.

****

Everard arrived earlier than was seemly and was left in the front hall while the footman inquired whether his lordship was able to receive him. The earl's raised voice carried from the back of the house: "Show him in, man, show him in."

Mountjoy was still at breakfast. Allan found himself pressed to eat a second meal, no hardship at all. Having stood watch with one of the porters from eight in the evening to two in the morning, he had asked Chappell to wake him an hour before his class. The Passevants' former coachman not only did so, he'd brought up hot water so Allan could wash and shave in comfort rather than in cold water from the previous evening. But that left time for no more than a day-old bun and a cup of tea before class. Aflame to speak with the earl, he glanced at the footman waiting to pour them more coffee or refill their plates. His host said, "We'll eat first, then talk in my bookroom. I make it a practice never to talk of important matters over a meal."

So Allan ate boiled eggs and cold sirloin and drank several cups of coffee while the earl commented on the latest news.

As soon as they were done, the earl gave orders he was not to be disturbed, unless there was news of his daughter's lying-in. "It's her first child," he explained, closing the study door. "I'd be in Berkshire by now, but my lady's at our daughter's home near Canterbury. We'll go to our estate after the baby's born."

"Congratulations."

Mountjoy nodded his thanks while asking, "What's your news? Does the girls' grandfather agree to your plan?"

"He does. Are you willing to set our plan in motion, my lord?"

"I am. It makes me mad as fire to think of ladies in such a rogue's power."

"Winn goes to a High Holborn coffee house one morning a week and receives any mail for Stanbury."

"There must be more to it than my waiting there with a burly footman to drag him before a magistrate."

"Are you free this morning to plan our course of action? I have come prepared to do so. Stanbury's next visit will be on Monday. The sooner this is resolved, the better."

"Nothing I have to do today is more important than this. What worries me most is whether I am sure to recognize him. To collar the wrong man would be a disaster. Embarrassing, too."

"I will be present to point him out and to make sure he does not escape. Having your coach nearby to carry him to the magistrate in Bow Street would be easier than taking him there on foot."

"Good! How did I come to hear of his presence in London and especially at that coffee house?"

Allan was content to let the earl ask his questions. More satisfying to Mountjoy and the method worked well with his own students. "He had a sheet with the girls' likenesses distributed. For the benefit of the literate, he added his name at the bottom and asked for replies to the Noble Cup."

"So I came upon one of those sheets?"

"I think only indirectly, as they are being given to servants, beggars, and miscreants of all sorts, not gentlemen. Perhaps one of your servants saw one and commented upon it as worthy of remarking?"

"My manservant has been with me since before Lawrence's death. He quite likely would remember the name if he saw it, as I'll remind him. I'll need one of those sheets."

"I'll give you one."

Mountjoy nodded abstractedly. "He'll deny being Stanbury, both to us and to the magistrate. How do I support my claim?"

"As his broadside invited anyone having information to write to him at the Noble Cup, I'll do so. The letter being in his possession should be persuasive."

"I'd suggest you not use your own name on the letter, Everard. Doing so would make your presence when we take him a trifle suspicious."

"I intend to use initials only and not my own, as any scoundrel would rather than put his name in writing, my lord."

"What if he maintains he is Stanbury, knowing he would be unlikely to face any significant punishment for Lawrence's death?"

"You know that because Lord Dunstan knows the law and told you. But when I was a steward's assistant I observed that many, from laborers to lords, are uninformed in most areas of the law. The laborers and tenants know the Black Act that governs poaching and the destruction of property on agricultural land. Lords are familiar with those and the legalities of marriage settlements and inheritance. Otherwise, law is left to attorneys and men of business."

The earl conceded the point with a snigger. "Exposed in all our ignorance." His amusement died. "You are sure he will be at the coffee house the day after tomorrow?"

"Yes. He visits it after going to his bank, which he will certainly do, having the money taken in over the weekend to deposit."

"Do you have your letter with you? If so, I'll have it delivered, rather than trusting it to the Penny Post, admirable though it is. Not by a footman in livery," he added, "which might cause a stir."

"I have not." He wrote it at the earl's desk with a pen that needed mending and made his handwriting ungainly.

They completed their plan to meet at the Noble Cup, with Mountjoy announcing he would inform his brother and ask if he had any advice. The earl thought he would be glad to have the matter laid to rest at last.

****

Rose lay awake for some time and then woke several

times from uneasy dreams. Allan's revelation that he and Lord Mountjoy planned to take Winn at a coffee house preyed upon her mind.

This time terrifying sounds jarred her into wakefulness. Ory did not stir; she would sleep through the Last Judgement. Only a moment passed before she recognized the racket as outraged geese. She flung back the bed covers, thrust her feet into her shoes, and snatched up her mantle on her way to the door.

Outside, the moon cast enough light that she could see a slight female figure shrinking in the middle of the yard. As Rose hesitated before her door, a bulky figure carrying a blunderbuss emerged from the Chappells' room and jogged past her, the birds' outcries covering the sound of his footfalls. Doors on the galleries opened and voices called out.

"What's that down there?"

" 'Ere, oo's making that noise?"

The caretaker turned around slowly, searching for threats. Rose, following his progress saw him pause, staring up at one corner of the gallery that ran around the upper level. Two notes from a whistle sounded over the clamor of the geese, and Chappell continued his scrutiny of the gallery and roof. Another whistle came from another direction.

A male voice snapped, "Identify yourself."

Someone in shirt, breeches, and shoes but no stockings, pelted down the stair diagonally across the yard from Rose, and called out, "Everard." Allan. Other footfalls thumped along the galleries.

The woman frozen in place wailed and folded to the ground. By then, Anne had popped out of her room, a blanket thrown over her night-rail. She reached Rose's side and grasped her arm before she could go toward that pitiful figure.

"Stay," she whispered. "In case—"

Dunham reached Chappell's side and evidently spoke to Chappell, who wheeled to face the gate and braced himself. Dunham strode to the woman, dragged her to her feet, and hauled her toward the common room, calling over his shoulder, "Matron, send the others back to their rooms. Chappell, porters, stay here. Everard, with me. Mistress Milton, you, too."

By the time Anne had calmed the women who had left their rooms, a branch of candles had been lit in the common room and Mistress Chappell was present, having thrown on a jacket and petticoat over her shift. Dunham's prisoner was still sobbing, a sodden handkerchief over her face.

With only the scarred side of his face faintly illuminated, the head porter was almost demonic.

"What were you doing in the yard?"

Jill, cringing, took several gasping breaths as she struggled to compose herself.

The cook, who had melted away unnoticed, returned with a tray holding a handkerchief, a bottle, and a cup. She pressed the former into the woman's hand and glanced to Dunham, raising her eyebrows and gesturing to the bottle. He nodded.

After she had been induced to drink a little brandy, Jill took a final, shuddering breath.

"You'll answer my questions."

Without raising her head or looking at any of them, she muttered, "I'm sorry."

He started to speak, but she continued, "I couldn't refuse without my Luke being killed."

After that, she answered whatever they asked. She knew only what a man she had never seen before told her: that he believed his wife was living at the inn and he wanted her back. She was to make sure they were there and then slip down to the small gate after everyone had gone to bed and wave her handkerchief out of the little grilled window. A friend of his was holding Luke, and if Jill did not help him, her son would die.

"Did he say who he wanted?"

"He had a drawing of two girls. He said the older one was his wife and he would take her little sister, as well, being as she was family. I'm sorry," she said again, without meeting Rose's eyes.

She was born and bred in London and hadn't known the geese would wake up and make noise.

A scratching at the door silenced them all. Dunham strode to the entrance, opened it, and listened. A dim figure beyond him moved away. He turned back, closing the door. "A night-man's cart that was stopped just beyond the inn is gone."

"They'll kill my boy."

"The threat may only have been to frighten you into obeying," Everard said.

Jill spoke without hope. "Mayhap that's so, but they might sell him to some captain as a cabin boy or powder monkey, and I'll never see him again."

Mistress Chappell poured out another dose of brandy and made her drink. When she had stopped coughing, Anne and the cook took her away to be locked in her room, though it seemed hardly necessary. She could not escape even if she had not had a small child to burden her.

Rose lingered in the hope of speaking with Allan.

She caught his glance and knew he wanted the same.

Dunham said, "The geese were a clever notion of yours, Mistress Rose. But tomorrow night—no, it's after midnight, so tonight—we must be ready for a full attack. Winn's crew won't try again tonight. Now I mean to go to my bed for a few hours. The rest of you should do the same."

James Dunham might have no moral objection to an unchaperoned meeting between a man and a woman, considering she had found him alone with Anne in the library once. But being alone with Allan in the middle of the night was a greater breach of conduct than Rose's conscience permitted. What if some wakeful Three Greyhounds resident saw them? Such scandalous behavior would reflect upon the charity. She bade the men goodnight with a wistful peek at Allan. He smiled crookedly and murmured, "Tomorrow is another day."

That boded well. She betook herself off to her room and fell asleep musing on her next meeting with Allan.

But Sunday was not the day of rest she had anticipated. One of the older kitchen helpers had taken Jill's breakfast to her, accompanied by a porter, and found her huddled on her bed, her little girl clinging to her. Jill did not look up when they entered or respond to Hannah's hopeful "Hungry, mamma." They left the tray of food but reported her lack of response to Anne, who asked Fiona and Ory to make sure the child was fed and cared for. Jill had spooned some oatmeal porridge into her daughter but had eaten nothing herself. When the girls suggested she should be taken to the nursery, her mother made no reply.

Mr. Simmons, the curate, visited her after the Sunday service and reported her too deep in grief to be comforted yet.

Allan spent much of the day in his own chamber, going over his plan for Monday, Rose guessed. Anne, worried about Jill, was searching in Mistress Chappell's cookery book for a remedy for her unnatural passivity. Rose had the fidgets and could not settle either to read or to do any sewing.

Almost too nervous to sit still, she was supervising half a dozen little girls who were making handkerchiefs. The activity was both suitable for Sunday and productive, as no matter how ill-stitched, handkerchiefs were always useful. Fortunately, given Rose's churning unease over tomorrow, Ory and her two bosom bows were present to help correct the children's stitching and untangle their thread.

When the door opened, her head snapped up. Allan Everard paused in the door and cast a wary look at the circle of little girls and young misses.

"Mistress Rose? I hoped to speak to you if you chanced to be free, but I see you are, er, engaged."

"We can watch the children," Ory chirped before she could reply. Fiona grinned. Belinda glanced at her older friends and smiled hesitantly, too young yet to be sure what their amusement signified.

Her presence was not required here, Rose conceded. "I know you can manage. I should not be gone long anyway," she mumbled to the three older girls.

A woman and two of the older boys, one of them Jeremy, were in the library, eliminating it as a place to speak privately. Games of leapfrog, marbles, and tag were in progress in the yard: not really proper on a Sunday, but neither the Greyhounds nor Bethlehem House would be considered decent by the standards of strict moralists.

"The stable?"

The ground floor room where the children played in bad weather was deserted. Rose sat on a bench as far from the open door as possible. Allan sat at the other end and cleared his throat.

"I wanted to reassure you about tomorrow's events."

"Do you really believe it may be over?" She hardly dared to repose any confidence in the plan.

"Ay." He did not meet her eyes. Did he have doubts? Heaven knew she had enough of her own. "Even if it isn't, you'll soon be of age, and Brand is ready to go to the Court of Chancery to make you your sister's guardian."

"I know. But that wouldn't keep Winn from abducting Ory." A thought which had occurred to her since they had last discussed her imminent emancipation.

"We hope for the best while preparing for the worst. If necessary, your grandfather will send Miss Ory to live in the country with a lady who is a friend of his. I don't doubt Barlicorn can arrange safe transport for her."

"That is something, of course. I'm of no real interest to Winn, as I'm not young or a beauty like Ory. The mare to her filly, according to that scrap of paper." Oh, dear. She sounded bitter.

Two vertical lines appeared between Everard's brows. What was he thinking of her display of pettishness?

"That is hardly a fair comparison, Mistress Rose."

"It may have been unkind, but my sister is a nonpareil." She lowered her gaze to her folded hands, which were still somewhat work-roughened. When she looked up again, Allan was smiling. What did that signify?

The smile faded. "Sir Oliver has an arrangement in mind for you."

"Oh. Does he?" Her voice flattened.

"He does." Now he was frowning again. "Mmmm…he thinks you should marry. I believe he is correct."

"Because marriage salvages a female's tattered reputation?"

"Well…yes. But there would be other advantages."

Rose raised her eyebrows in enquiry as if she did not know what they were.

Allan recited the reasons a woman should marry: a home of her own, perhaps children, the status of a married lady, a husband's protection. Rationally presented, they were strangely unappealing.

She could have added, avoidance of the fate of an aging spinster. Though even unmarried, she would have enough money to live on, assuming Winn had not looted the bank account. Allan had reported the bank register showed no withdrawals, but did that prove none had been made?

But even if there was money available, she would be alone once her grandfather died and Ory married. Some squire in the county where Grandpapa's friend lived would snap her sister up for her beauty and sweet nature, whether she had a dowry or not. Rose refused to become a dependent of her sister's husband, even if he were willing to take her in. A sigh she should have suppressed escaped her.

"Rose, what troubles you? I'll help in any way I can."

He could help, but if he did not know how, she could not tell him. "I am worried about tomorrow," she replied, managing a quirk of the lips that he might mistake for a smile.

Chapter 30

Monday came as a relief to all. No attack had come overnight, Jill Gill had roused enough to ask for Hannah, who had spent Sunday night in the nursery. The street vendors' cries began before breakfast, a welcome reminder of everyday life. Mistress Chappell bustled out to choose some fish, her husband following her, the end of a cudgel sticking out of one of his coat's deep pockets. A porter already stood by the small gate but out of sight of the window, hand on his sword's grip.

Anne and Rose paused in the yard to discuss Jill and what was to be done with her.

"I pity her, Rose, how can I not? What mother would refuse to do whatever she had to, to save her child? Similar bargains take place somewhere every day, as we know. I might have made a similar choice, but for Bethlehem House." She laughed bitterly.

"I know." Without money, mere survival was a desperate struggle in London. Or perhaps anywhere, though she thought life in the country was a little more forgiving. Guessing at the cause of the trouble she saw in her friend's face, Rose added, "I believe Mr. Dunham understands. Once this current problem is done with…" She did not know how to complete the thought.

Anne sighed. "He is kind, despite his stern manner. I'm sure you're correct."

Their heads jerked up at a shout from the gate. A

ragamuffin dashed toward the sally-port, as Dunham called it, only to fall on his backside when the guard stepped forward to block him. The porter's shrill whistle brought a second man down the nearest stair at a run to stand at the gate while the first collared the boy as he scrambled to his feet. He yelled, "Me mam's in here. Please, I got to tell her—" while he struggled to get free.

"Enough o' that, you little devil."

Out on the street, the Chappells, the fishmonger and his boy, and his other customers stood staring. The porter blocking the gate said, "Mistress, have you enough fish?"

Molly Chappell gave herself a shake, frowned at the heaped bushel basket at her feet and said, "I do." She counted out coins into the seller's hand, and Chappell hoisted the basket. The porter closed the door behind them as soon as they were inside and dropped the bar into the staples.

As the cook passed, she observed with a tilt of the head to the boy, "Needs feeding up, that one does," and marched into the common room, trailing her husband and the fish basket.

A handful of women stood whispering in the yard some distance behind Rose and the matron, while a few more watched from the galleries. Dunham loped up, his neckcloth askew.

"The common room," he told the guard holding the boy. In a softer voice he said, "If you can spare the time, Matron?" After a pause, he added, "And Mistress Rose?"

She did not resent her inclusion being an obvious afterthought, as Anne would naturally come first with him. Rose hoped they could find their way to happiness, almost as much as she wished for her own and for Ory's safety. She squashed the thought of her own future, which for all her daydreams did not look promising, and followed Anne.

Seated by himself on a bench with Rose and Anne on the other side of the table and Dunham and the porter standing, the lad was not an attractive object. Setting aside his dirty, torn clothing, he was thin and scowling.

"Mam needs to know I'm all right."

"First, tell us who you are."

"Luke Gill."

His eyes lit up, however, when Mistress Chappell returned from the kitchen with a tray holding a bowl of porridge left over from breakfast, a thick slice of bread and dripping, and a mug of small beer. Dunham opened his mouth to object as she set the food down in front of Luke. She met it with a baleful frown at which he threw up his hands, surrendering the point. "Mistress Chappell, will you send one of your helpers to summon Mr. Everard? He should be here, too."

Anne asked, "Shouldn't his mother be fetched?"

"I would rather hear what he has to say without exclamations, tears, and other distractions." To the boy he said, "Go on, eat. I'll expect answers from you when you finish."

Luke was already spooning up porridge as fast as he could.

Allan arrived as the bowl emptied. The bread was gone. The boy took a drink. "Thanks. I'd not had a bite since yestiddy morning."

Dunham was very good at drawing out information. "You came here looking for your mother?"

A nod. "Jill Gill. I was grabbed off the street to make her do an errand for a hedge-bird."

"Why don't you start with your being nabbed?"

"See, yestiddy I was on my way to see if anyone had any work or an errand for me to do, like ever' day. Someone drops a burlap bag over my head and picks me up like a sack o' grain and carries me off. Seemin'ly there was two of 'em, as somebody give me a cuff when I kicked and yelled, and he said I was a runaway 'prentice and they were taking me back where I belonged."

He thought he'd been taken to a house, a very poor, tumble-down place or one that was abandoned, from the odor of damp and mildew. "They carried me upstairs and shut me in a little room, a store-closet, one o' them called it. The door was locked. It'd have been dark as…well, right dark, 'cepting it was built so careless. There were a couple knot-holes in the floor boards and the room below must've had a window or two, for a little light come up through 'em. As it was, I could see a crate and I sat down on it, after looking to see what was in it, the lid not being nailed down. Bottles o'something. I broke the top off one. I'd been there for hours by then and I was thirsty. Wine, sour stuff, gone bad, I reckon. Cut my lip a little, finding out."

Mistress Chappell came out of the kitchen, poured more small beer into his cup and took away the bowl and plate. His smile might have belonged to a cherub if the cherub had yellow teeth and happened to be missing one.

"I sat worrying about what they wanted with me. Didn't think they'd sell me to a sweep. I'm too tall and too old. Nothing else I could think of was any better. 'Sides, Mam and my sis need me." He went silent and tight-lipped.

Dunham nodded to encourage him to go on.

"I spent a while feeling around to see if there was anything useful and I found a crow."

"A crow?" Rose voiced the question she was sure Anne shared, looking to Dunham.

Allan answered. "A bar to shift something heavy or pry things open. For taking up floor boards, for example."

"Ay, someone forgot it after opening the crate, I 'spect. That was good news as maybe I could use it to get out. But I felt people moving around, like when you feel someone's walking on the floor even if you can't hear them?"

"I know what you mean." Dunham unbent so far as to give a slight grin.

"So I knew I'd best wait. After a while, I fell asleep. There wasn't anything else to do. After I woke, I heard voices, pretty faint, coming up through the holes. I got down and pressed my ear to one."

Seeing his audience riveted by his account, Luke puffed out his chest as much as he could before admitting, "I couldn't hear everything. One was the cully that didn't carry me, but I couldn't make out much from him. He must not've been near the knot-holes. I did try both, but it wasn't no better. The cove I could hear best was a gent."

"What made you think so?"

"He talked like you and this other gen'leman." The lad tilted his chin toward Everard. "And he was giving the orders. He said, 'Go to the Three Greyhounds, Aldersgate. When you see the boy's mother wave something white, go to the gate. She'll tell you if the ladies are the ones I want. If they are, come to me as soon as it's morning, and I'll bring a magistrate.' There was a few mumbles I couldn't make out, as if they was moving around, and then they went out for they took the light with them. I didn't hear anything else, but he'd said my mam was here so that's where I had to go. Forcing the door didn't make much noise. I found the kitchen. Didn't even need to use the crow because the door was only barred. I meant to get to this here inn before the bully-rock did. Should'a been easy, because it was too early for them to be doing what they talked about 'cept I didn't know where I was. Took a while to find someplace I knew, and I was a fair way from here. I had to keep out of sight, too. Someone chased me and I got away, but I had to hide for a while, and I guess I fell asleep."

Women on their own were not the only ones at risk in London.

"Then I was lost and there wasn't no one to ask the way. I got here a little afore sunrise. I figured whatever was done was done." Blinking, he swallowed and lowered his eyes. "Is my mam here? Whatever they made her do, it must've been because they threatened her."

"She is here and maybe she can help us. The alarm was raised before she got to the gate. Matron, will you bring Mistress Gill down?"

"With pleasure, Mr. Dunham."

Luke let out a breath and slumped.

When the door opened and she saw her son, she gave a cry and ran to him. He jumped up so abruptly to meet her, he almost knocked over the bench. Jill threw one arm around him, sobbing, the little girl still held in the other. Luke's thin arms circled them both.

Rose's eyes prickled. Responsible for Ory's upbringing and safety for years, she understood the woman's feelings. If only she might have a child of her own someday. As well hope for a castle in Spain. That thought dried the threatening tears. Setting aside the difference of religion, Spain's climate was said to be hot and the food and customs would be alien. No, she would settle for enough money for food, coal, and clothing in a cottage, somewhere her ruin and Ory's was not known, but in England, of course.

Anne slipped away to the kitchen and returned with buns for Luke and Hannah. While the boy tore bits off his sister's treat for her, Jill admitted her tale about her landlord's persecution was a lie and that she lived in Wapping, though they were indeed likely to be evicted soon. A man in the neighborhood had offered her coin to do a favor for someone he knew, but she had balked when he would not tell her what it was. His reputation wasn't bad but it wasn't good, either, and she didn't want to do something that might end in a noose or transportation; what would become of her children? He came back a day later and told her he had her son. She could do as she was told or Luke's body would be returned to her for burial.

****

"We can't report this to a magistrate as he planned to use one to regain possession of the ladies. His magistrate would take the easy course, return them to him, and tell us to take our case to Chancery," Allan said.

Dunham added, "She doesn't know anything more about the man who snatched her son than the nickname, Hector, which may only be a nickname, a 'Hector' being a swaggerer who acts the part of a desperate fellow up for any villainy."

At length the head porter said, "If your ambush today succeeds, we can catch up on our sleep tonight. If it doesn't, I'll keep four men on duty, and I'll be awake as well."

Allan was counting the minutes until he could confront Winn. His attempt to court Rose had not gone well. She had not been responsive. Was it because she feared they would not succeed in eliminating Winn as guardian? Or because she did not care for him as a suitor? Mayhap once she was relieved of the danger from Winn, curse him, she would be amenable to a discussion of her future.

"I hope we'll have reason to celebrate," he said, and returned to his room to shave, wash, and dress for the meeting.

Chapter 31

Allan arrived early at the Noble Cup partly from impatience and partly from worry that this Monday Winn would come earlier than his habit and leave before the earl came. Unlikely: Barlicorn's watchers had reported the man deposited the weekend's earnings when his bank opened at nine o'clock. He would certainly not go to the coffee house first, laden with two nights' profits and trailing a pair of bodyguards. Presumably the time between the last patrons of the Purring Cat departing and Winn setting out with his escort were spent in counting the night's gain and whatever other tasks the end of the business day required.

He tried not to look up from his newssheet every time the door opened. The thought of postponing the capture roiled his gut. Another week of expecting an attack and fearing for Rose and her sister might turn his hair white.

Mountjoy strolled into the coffee house some fifteen minutes before they could reasonably expect Winn.

"Everard, good morning to you." He took the chair to Allan's left, and remarked in a lower voice, "Not many here yet. All the better, in my opinion."

"I agree." In a sentence or two, he sketched Sunday's excitement and its sequel this morning.

"Damme. And the geese were the lady's notion? She's got a head on her shoulders."

"She does." A pretty head on pretty shoulders and an enticing form. He sighed.

From the earl's amusement, he might have guessed the direction of Allan's thoughts. Mountjoy's next words, however, were a comment on the death two months previously of a former governor of the Virginia Colony. "Hadn't seen him in thirty years, since he went to the colonies, but we exchanged letters."

Apparently a gentleman could make conversation on any occasion, a skill Everard envied. It worked, as he found himself relaxing.

When Winn entered, Allan caught Mountjoy's eye and murmured, "At the table near the counter, in the green coat." Allan smiled, seeing the brothel keeper's expression of suppressed annoyance. His minion had reported his failure.

The server hurried to bring him coffee, a bun, and Allan's letter. Winn received them with a faint smile, a word, and a coin.

They had agreed to take action when Winn rose to leave.

The earl, dressed in an old suit he wore to ramble over his estate with his dogs, would approach him. Everard would prevent his escape.

Winn sipped coffee and ate the bun, eyes on the still unread letter. Did he mean to read it later? As long as he had it in his possession when he left the coffee house, it would prove he was passing as Stanbury.

Instead, having finished his food, he took up the letter and pried up the flap to read it.

"What did you write?"

"Only that I knew where the girls were living and could get them out with no difficulty, and would be here

Tuesdays and Thursdays at seven in the evening. He could recognize me by my yellow waistcoat."

Winn beckoned the serving boy, who hurried over with the coffee pot. Winn shook his head and spoke. The lad went to the counter, conferred with the woman, and hurried back again.

Another exchange; Winn dismissed the boy before refolding the sheet.

"It's the Bank of England to a farthing he asked who delivered the letter and when it came, my lord."

Their prey stood and secreted the letter in his pocket. The earl also rose and made his way toward the back of the room where a door opened onto an alley and a small yard with privies. Abreast of Winn, he cut between two tables to reach his side and block the way to the alley. Allan would keep the man from bolting out the street door.

"Mr. Stanbury, I believe." Mountjoy's normal speaking voice carried clearly.

Allan moved toward the door.

"I'm Stanbury." Winn's reply revealed no discernible emotion.

"I'm Mountjoy."

Winn's face showed no recognition of the name. Very likely he had not known of Lawrence St. Denys's connection to the earl.

Receiving no response but a blank look, Mountjoy continued, "My cousin died as a result of your fight after he accused you of cheating."

Something sharpened in Winn's expression. "I am no cheat. I seldom gamble, and I certainly do not remember dicing with anyone of your name."

"And yet you know the game was hazard."

Too bad the earl had noticed Winn's revelation and responded to it. Otherwise he might have accompanied them willingly.

"I assumed it to be so as weighted dice are a common way of cheating."

To Allan's surprise, he accompanied them without argument.

If he were a gamester, he might be willing to trust to luck and his wits to get him out of the scrape.

****

Susan was a-twitch with anxiety.

"How do I look?" she asked Rose.

"Neat, sensible, and respectable, like a good witness, if you're needed. And not a bit frightened."

"I'm not too pale?"

"No, you have a pretty color in your cheeks."

"I wish I didn't have these gray streaks in my hair."

"They won't show under your cap," Rose began, then noticed that it was not the plain round-eared cap Susan usually wore, but a smaller one of fine linen edged with the cheap Hanover lace.

Susan saw the direction of her gaze. "Fiona made it for me. She knew I wanted to look my best." She was adjusting its position when Dunham's voice from the other side of the door said, "Susan, the carriage is waiting."

Susan's appealing glance went to Rose's heart.

****

Winn had little to say during the brief coach ride to Bow Street and not much while they waited for the magistrate to finish with the cases before them. From his expression and bearing, he found the situation boring.

The long room at the back of the house, the

magistrate's "public office," was as yet thinly attended, the cases from the previous evening having been dealt with earlier. As they waited, one of the earl's two footmen approached him and whispered in his ear. Mountjoy gave a brisk nod and dismissed him. Allan followed the servant's progress toward the back of the room where Sir Oliver's height and Ramillies wig, its braid tied at top and bottom with black ribbon, made him easy to spot as he turned to speak to Brand.

The footman approached and waited until the baronet acknowledged him, before bowing and addressing Sir Oliver. He and Brand would come forward when the earl's party were summoned before the magistrate.

The current matter having been dispatched with a fine, de Veil looked up and raised his brows at the sight of Mountjoy. He spoke to one of the court's constables who hastened over to their group. And so they were taken out of order because of the earl's accident of birth.

"Lord Mountjoy? What brings you to my court?"

There was a faint stir among the people behind them. Allan stole a look over his shoulder. Sir Oliver and Brand hurried forward to join them.

Thomas de Veil gazed at the five of them. "All on the same matter?"

"Ay, sir," Mountjoy said. "This man, Horace Stanbury, caused the death of my cousin, Lawrence St. Denys. Lawrence accused him of cheating at dice and ended dying of a slashed throat."

The death had occurred over thirty years ago; it had not been possible to find Stanbury until recently. De Veil read Dunstan St. Denys's statement.

"What have you to say to this, Mr. Stanbury?"

The blankness of his expression and a certain tension around his eyes during the earl's account told Allan that Winn had heard only the barest facts from the real Stanbury. Winn hesitated before replying.

"I have no knowledge of the event Lord Mountjoy alleges."

"Do you deny you were present?"

"I do, Your Worship."

"And yet the witness's statement identifies you as having been present. It cannot be a modern forgery, as the paper is not new and the ink is fading. Do you claim you are being accused out of some malice of his lordship's that has lasted over thirty years?"

"I cannot know, sir, as his lordship and his family were unknown to me until he approached me in a coffee house and forced me to come with him to your court. Mayhap 'twas in mistake for some other man of the same name."

"I have any number of John Smiths brought before me, but I would wager there cannot be many Horace Stanburys. But what have you to say to this, Lord Mountjoy? Or have your companions, whose identities have not been made known to me, any evidence to give?"

"For that omission, I beg your pardon, Your Worship. This gentleman is General Sir Oliver Milton, baronet, and the other is Attorney Lucian Brand, both of whom have some knowledge of Horace Stanbury. Brand, the Stanbury family attorney, searched for the sole remaining heir to Stanbury Manor, near Salisbury, and located this Horace Stanbury."

Brand spoke. "This is the man with whom I met on his replying to my letter addressed to Horace Stanbury at the only address I could find for him, Pimling's Bank, where an annuity had been established for him in 1708 by the late Paul Stanbury's father. As a result of the young Horace's conduct," he added primly.

Allan watched Winn's face. He showed no unease, no sign of anything beyond the mild curiosity of an uninvolved party.

"Is that true?"

With De Veil's sharp eyes on him, Winn said, "It is, sir. However, I know nothing of the death of Lord Mountjoy's connection. Perhaps some other man made use of my name, knowing I had bought a commission and been sent to the American colonies." He smiled ruefully. "I confess I had some rakehelly acquaintances in my youth and was something of a rascal myself. Hence the annuity."

"Lord Mountjoy, can you offer any evidence that this Horace Stanbury is the man with whom your cousin gambled? Why is your brother not here, when he witnessed the fight?"

The hearing had taken an unexpected turn when Winn failed to deny he was Stanbury. Dunstan St. Denys would not identify him. Before Brand could respond, Sir Oliver elbowed Brand.

"Sir Oliver, have you something to add? For thus far, I am ignorant of your purpose here."

Brand spoke. "Your worship, if I may answer for the baronet, as I am in some way acting for him in this?"

"Go on, then."

"The guardianship of Sir Oliver's granddaughters, Mistress Rosabel Stanbury and Miss Oriana Stanbury, was given to Horace Stanbury, despite the young ladies having named me as their preferred choice. I subsequently learned certain facts which make his appointment as guardian unconscionable."

"You are aware that is a matter for the Court of Chancery, Mr. Brand."

"Sir, I would agree if 'twere merely a matter of his ownership of a brothel—"

The magistrate's eyes opened wide. He stared at Stanbury. "I thought I was tolerably familiar with the names of most of London's bordello owners, yet no Stanbury comes to my mind."

"That is the point, Your Worship. This man is not Horace Stanbury, and I have evidence to prove it."

De Veil sat back and clasped his hands on the table. "You came here to try to lay a charge against one Horace Stanbury and now are asserting he is not that gentleman but rather another, as yet unnamed. I should censure you, Mr. Brand, but I am curious. And I like to dispatch problems when I can rather than defer them or pass them on. Present your evidence."

The attorney pulled a sheaf of paper out of his green lawyer's bag. "Item, a sworn statement from Susan Freese explaining how she met Nicholas Winn in 1718 and discovered he possessed goods and documents belonging to a Horace Stanbury. Later, while in his cups he spoke of knowing Stanbury in the colonies…"

On Sunday, Susan had written an account of how she knew Winn and his possession of Stanbury's belongings and identified a copy of Oriana's drawing of Stanbury. Mr. Simmons, clergyman, and James Dunham, formerly a captain in the —Foot made respectable witnesses. Susan would be waiting with Dunham near Bow Street if her testimony was required.

Something changed in Winn's expression, the first sign of emotion Allan had seen, and even that was so slight someone who had not been watching hawk-eyed might have missed it. Oddly, it seemed more like relief than worry.

After reading Susan's declaration, the magistrate said, "Have you anything more?"

Brand presented another handful of sheets. "Affidavits by Mistress Ruth Francis, gentlewoman, who is a friend of the Stanburys and lives near Stanbury Manor, Sally Howard, the Stanburys' cook, and Henry Davis, the Stanburys' coachman. And an advertisement seeking information on the whereabouts of Rose and Oriana Stanbury."

Another silence while the justice of the peace reviewed them, frowning. Finally he set them on top of Susan's affidavit. "I have a few questions before I reach a decision. While ordinarily I would not question the authenticity of an affidavit, the issues here are unusual. But I will address the last deficiency later." He fixed a basilisk gaze on Winn. "Do you maintain you are Horace Stanbury? Or are you Nicholas Winn, owner of the Purring Cat?"

His face revealed nothing, an advantage to a gamester. "I have represented myself to be Stanbury since receiving Attorney Brand's letter."

Allan admired his sang-froid under the magistrate's glare.

"How did it happen you received Stanbury's letter, Winn?" De Veil's voice was mild, which Allan would not have found reassuring were he standing in Winn's shoes.

For once, the brothel keeper showed a trace of discomfort. "I knew of Horace Stanbury's annuity, having been his servant in the army. When I returned from the colonies, I visited Pimling's Bank to see if I could borrow money to set up in business, identifying myself as Stanbury. The banker suggested it would make more sense to use some of the accumulated funds in the annuity, which I did. In April of this year, on going into Pimling's to make a deposit, I received a letter from Brand which he had sent there. He told me I was the heir under the entail. I didn't want or need a manor, but I did not feel I could admit I wasn't Stanbury. The guardianship of the young ladies didn't come into it at all as Attorney Brand said they'd requested their grandfather or Attorney Brand be named their guardian. To have the consistory court make me their guardian came as an unpleasant shock."

The magistrate pursed his lips. "Very fine sentiments. How did you think to get away with your imposture? Where is Stanbury now?"

"Dead."

Chapter 32

"I trust you mean to expand upon Stanbury's fate."

Winn blew out a breath. "He slipped on stepping down from the coach at an inn that was hardly more than a hedge tavern. It wasn't a stage on the coach road. But rain was pouring down, 'twas dark and the horses were fetlock deep in mud. A rider coming from the other direction told our driver the bridge had washed out, and he decided we had to stop. Stanbury hit his head on the step up to the door. By the time we got him to a bedchamber, he was right enough except for the bump on his head and being vexed his clothes were mucky. When I went to his room in the morning to shave him, he was dead and cold."

With an impatient hand, de Veil gestured for him to continue.

"I told the landlord. After he felt for breath and a heartbeat and found none, he said there was no need to send for a doctor as there was none nearby. Stanbury was dead."

As an assistant steward, Allan had had some experience with liars and some lessons from Salt on how to recognize them. He had expected Winn to lie, but the man's account had the ring of truth.

"And then?"

"The landlord sent his boy to the nearest magistrate, and the crowner's court was held that same morning, though the squire complained at having to come out, for it was still raining. The death was brought in as being the result of Stanbury hitting his head when he slipped in the mud, as the coachman and the only other passenger, a governess on her way to a new post, testified."

"The name of the inn and the village?"

"I don't know I ever heard the first, and I can't remember the place's name now. It was no more than the inn, which made its coin selling ale, cider, and a bit of bread and cheese to the local folk, and a few cottages. I do recall it was sixteen or twenty miles out of Bristol."

"The magistrate's name?"

"It's more than twenty years ago. All I remember now is that it was a common one."

"I suppose Stanbury was buried nearby?"

"You could toss a stone from the inn's door to the churchyard. Ay, and the church was St. Aethelwine."

The chances of a liar using such an uncommon saint's name for a church were slight. The magistrate sat scowling. At length he remarked, "According to the statement of one Susan Freese, you had certain belongings and documents in Stanbury's name."

"I don't deny it, Your Worship."

"How did you come to have them?"

"Stanbury was dead, and I was sorry 'twas so, partly because I was grateful to him and partly because it meant I had no employment. He'd paid my fare, but I'd not enough gelt to eat on the way or to live until I found work."

"Go on."

"It started out an innocent mistake. When the squire came, the landlord introduced me as Stanbury. He'd met us on his threshold with Stanbury unconscious, and as we carried him upstairs, he asked our names. I told him, 'Stanbury and Winn.' He must have thought I gave my name first, but he never addressed either of us as anything but 'sir.' The girl who served our supper called us both 'master.' So the first I knew of it was that introduction."

"And you did not correct his error."

"Believe it or not as you wish, sir, I opened my mouth to do so and stopped myself from speaking just in time. Stanbury had no family or none he admitted to, so what would happen to his money and clothes? I'd already settled our shot from his purse the night before. I didn't think he'd grudge me taking his things, especially when it was the innkeeper's mistake. He'd have laughed."

"You stole his belongings, however you try to justify it."

"Easy to be high-minded when you've got food and shelter."

Allan acknowledged a certain sympathy for Winn's long ago predicament. Without family or money, the line between survival and starvation could be very thin. He wondered if he would have dared make such a dry retort, which might have angered the justice. Apparently not, for de Veil only replied, "Very true."

Winn smiled; no wonder Susan had found him charming, and Miss Ory, too, at first. His speech was as refined as that of most country gentlemen, but—

"Could the publican not tell you were a servant by your dress?" Discovering he was the focus of all eyes, Allan's face heated. The magistrate might ask questions; Allan had no right to speak except to answer if questioned. To his surprise, Winn answered.

"I was wearing an old suit of Stanbury's, and he wasn't dressed fine either, as we were traveling. Besides, it was so covered in mud that only a sharp eye would see it was newer and better than mine."

Now de Veil's attention was on Allan. "You have not been identified to me. Your name, sir."

"Allan Everard, Your Worship."

"What is your connection with this case?"

"I was at the coffee house when Lord Mountjoy apprehended Nicholas Winn. I beg your pardon for interrupting, sir," he muttered.

"Hmmf. I may permit a degree of informality in my court, but do not think to push it too far, Mr. Everard."

"No, sir."

"Nevertheless, the answer goes some way to explain how the suspect was mistaken for his master. However, Lord Mountjoy is not prosecuting him for the theft of Stanbury's effects. The charge in question was whether the death of Lawrence St. Denys was homicide. From what I have heard, had there been an inquest, as there should have been"—and he paused after emphasizing the last phrase, staring at the earl—"I do not believe the jury would have brought in any verdict but misadventure. In any event, my lord, if this man is not Stanbury, which the evidence has proven, your case is stillborn."

"I believe we all agree that is true, sir, but does not Sir Oliver have a case against Mr. Winn for personation of Horace Stanbury?"

"Sir Oliver?"

The baronet bared his teeth. He may have meant it for a grin. "I do indeed wish to charge Winn with personating Stanbury. For my granddaughters to be in the power of a man who…" Brand, beside him, must have given him some subtle hint, for he continued, "They should have been placed in my charge or Attorney Brand's, if I was thought too old. More to the point, the money that should go to Rose and Oriana is now under his control, leaving them disinherited. And another thing: what of Stanbury's bank account and the annuity Winn has embezzled?"

Winn stiffened.

Brand spoke. "Horace Stanbury's annuity has been going to Mr. Winn since he returned in 1718. As the Stanbury family attorney, I am familiar with the documents setting up the annuity. In the event of Stanbury's death, the funds should have reverted to his uncle or his uncle's heirs and therefore to the young ladies. There is also the decedent, Paul Stanbury's, bank account. Whatever monies Winn has withdrawn from the date of his becoming the ladies' guardian are owed to them."

All Allan and Brand had hoped for was Winn's admission he was not Stanbury. They had accomplished that. The baronet having brought up the financial issues meant Winn might suffer some consequences but might also complicate matters. *Will the magistrate want the bank records?*

There had been a subdued murmur in the background from those waiting. At some point it had lessened without Allan being aware that those nearest the magistrate's desk had fallen silent.

"Ay, that would be a cause of action," de Veil agreed. "Have you an accounting from the banks of the amounts in question?"

"Sir, I have not, Mr. Winn having chosen other representation."

"Your Worship?" Allan ventured. He had no choice.

The magistrate stared at him. "Apart from having been present at the coffee house, what is your connection with this case?"

"I own the property where the Stanbury ladies have been lodging and learned of their problem from Mistress Rosabel Stanbury."

Some disturbance roiled the room near the door as several people pushed forward.

"I'm right sorry, Your Worship," one of the court officers said, reaching de Veil's side. He tilted his head toward Brand. "They wouldn't listen, and I couldn't lay hands on decent females, and them in mourning."

Allan looked to the attorney. Two women in black gowns, faces veiled, stood behind him. With a sinking feeling in his gut, Allan knew who the second lady was before they raised the black crape concealing their faces to drape it back. An edge of white lace showed under the edge of Susan's veil.

"Who might you be and what is your interest in this proceeding?" De Veil's compressed lips suggested he was losing patience.

The fat's in the fire now.

"I might be—that is, I am—Rosabel Stanbury, Your Worship, and this is Susan Freese, who has known Nicholas Winn since 1718. I apologize for our bursting in, but as the parties most deeply concerned, I thought our testimony should be heard."

Rose met de Veil's gaze, showing no discomfort at her surroundings. Neither did Susan, but perhaps that was because she was gazing at Winn, terrible pain in her eyes. After a single glance at him, Allan looked away as Winn sighed, "Sukey."

Heaven preserve me from ever revealing so much of my heart.

"Mistress Freese, do you affirm that you have known this man Winn since that time, and did you sign this declaration?" De Veil shuffled through the stack of documents and offered her the sheet.

"I do and I did, sir."

With great deliberation, he removed his pocket clock, opened the cover, and set it upon the table. "Most trials for murder would be concluded in less time than we have already spent upon this one affair. Let me sum up the issues."

The constable was still hovering to one side. De Veil waved him away irritably.

"Mr. Winn, as you are not Horace Stanbury, the death of Lord Mountjoy's cousin, however regrettable, is irrelevant. Do you agree, my lord?"

"I am satisfied that Winn had nothing to do with my cousin's death, Your Worship."

"Thank you, Lord Mountjoy. That's one item disposed of. Next: Winn, you should be removed as guardian of the Stanbury young ladies. That—"

Winn tore his attention away from Susan, interrupting de Veil. "Yes, please, your Worship. I never wanted the guardianship."

"I have no power in the matter, which must be taken to the Court of Chancery. If you resign your guardianship, that court will no doubt act quickly."

"I'll be happy to do so."

"You will swear out a statement in, hmmm, triplicate: one for yourself, one for Attorney Brand, and one to be entered in my court's record."

"Ay, sir."

"Attorney Brand, there is the question of any Stanbury monies or property which have been under Winn's control for the last several months. As you have no accounting or other evidence of embezzlement, there is nothing I can do at this time."

Allan squared his shoulders. The moment was upon him. "Your Worship?"

"Mr. Everard?"

"I have a statement from Fitchett's Bank in Salisbury regarding the Stanbury account."

"How does that come about?"

Brand said, "Your Worship, Everard has been acting as a sort of clerk for me, gathering evidence which required travel."

The justice of the peace raised his eyebrows. "This evidence? You did state you had no accounting."

"Sir, I went to Fitchett's without Mr. Brand's knowledge."

"Personating his clerk, eh?"

"Yes, Your Worship."

"Hand it over, then." The brusque request was accompanied by a glance at the pocket watch. "Hmmpf! A letter from the owner of Fitchett's Bank affirming he was aware of Horace Stanbury having inherited, to which is attached a copy of activity in the account from the month before Paul Stanbury's death to ten days ago. No deposits or withdrawals since the death, and the heir has not visited the bank. No embezzlement there."

"Your Worship, there should have been deposits of the Lady Day and the Midsummer Day rents," Rose said.

"Winn?"

"The rents came in. I kept them in the strongbox in Stanbury's office and paid the manor's bills out of them."

"Why did you not deposit them and write out cheques for any substantial expenses?"

"Your Worship, forgery is a capital crime."

Allan held out another sheet. "Here is another accounting, this one from Pimling's Bank regarding the annuity from 1718 almost to the present, Your Worship."

The magistrate tutted irritably. "Brand, did you know of this one?"

"No, sir. I had spoken with Everard, regretting that as I was now only taking an interest in the young ladies' welfare as a family friend, I could not represent myself to the bank as having a right to any information."

"Everard, I fear you are something of a rogue. What is your interest in the Stanburys' affairs that you do not scruple to exceed your limits as Attorney Brand's assistant?"

"I am deeply concerned for the safety and welfare of Mistress Rose and Miss Oriana Stanbury."

"Hmmpf!" De Veil scrutinized the first sheet, the corners of his mouth turning down. His index finger ran down the following sheets at greater speed.

"Winn, I see a withdrawal of four hundred and fifty pounds in the year of your return to England and no withdrawals but many deposits thereafter. Is that correct?"

"Ay, sir. Ninety guineas for the first year's lease on the house the Purring Cat occupies, and the rest for the furnishing of it and funds to live on until it made a profit, which it soon did."

"As you still operate that establishment, I conclude you are prospering despite the small deposits you have made to the Pimling's account."

"I am, sir, but I put my profits into my account at another bank and pay out costs from there."

"I see." He blew out a breath. "Has anyone any more allegations or evidence?"

Mountjoy, Brand, and Sir Oliver glanced around their half circle in silent inquiry. Allan cleared his throat.

"Sir, while it may not be a chargeable offense, Mr. Winn has had ruffians posted outside my property, I believe in the hope of abducting Mistress Rose and Miss Oriana if they should venture out or of breaking in to abduct them. We want them withdrawn and some surety Winn will not continue his attempts to secure them…for whatever purpose."

"What say you, Winn?"

Allan was glad not to be the object of de Veil's glacial stare.

"I will do so as soon as I am at liberty to give the order."

"If you are not at liberty, I shall certainly arrange for it to be given."

Winn bowed by way of acknowledgement.

"Have any of you anything to add?"

Sir Oliver had been observing with an eagle eye. Now he said, "What of the damage to my granddaughters' reputation? They were forced to flee their home for fear of Winn, and I can see no way of concealing that they have not been living in London under the protection of their family."

"That is a good point, Sir Oliver. Winn, you will wish to compensate the young ladies by agreement with Sir Oliver and Attorney Brand. You will also arrange for repayment of the amounts from Pimling's and reimburse Fitchett's the amount of the rents less the amount of the bills paid. I suggest you adjourn to the nearest coffee house to work out the details. I feel sure Everard will be useful for copying. When you are finished, return and advise my clerk that you are in agreement on all points. If you are not, I will decide.

"And Winn? Be sure to withdraw whatever scoundrels you have watching the mousehole, or I shall have to pay attention to your place of business. The Purring Cat has not previously been a source of trouble, but as bordellos in general tend to disturbances and infractions of the law, the watch might be instructed to keep an eye on it. Next case."

The clerk who had been writing notes of the proceeding as quick as he could wilted with relief.

Chapter 33

As they left the public office, James Dunham fell into step behind them. He had been standing at the back of the room after accompanying Rose and Susan. "Mistress Rose insisted on coming," he muttered to Allan as they emerged onto the street opposite the Theatre Royal. "Do you want me to take her and Susan home?"

Rose, arm in arm with her grandfather, looked over her shoulder, not for the first time, though on this occasion at Allan rather than farther back in their procession. Who had she been glancing at before?

She said, "I intend to be present for your discussion with Mr. Winn."

"Rose, my girl," the baronet began.

Brand said, "We have been considering where to conduct our talk. There is a coffee house around the corner, but ladies do not attend such places, so you cannot be present, Mistress Rose."

"It seems to me that my sister and I are the ones most nearly concerned, and as such, I will not be shunted aside."

Winn had taken Susan's arm when they left the court and matched his pace to hers. She was listening intently as he spoke close by her ear. Allan caught a few murmured words: "...nearly went mad when you vanished..."

They halted in a cluster to the inconvenience of passersby. The Earl of Mountjoy said, "My home is no farther than half a mile or so. Sir Oliver, if we secure a sedan chair for you, we could walk it in fifteen minutes and be there well before my coach could convey us. We would have privacy, refreshments, and all we need to prepare whatever documents are necessary." He pursed his lips and studied Susan, whose limp had been apparent. "I'll have my coachman take Mistress Freese to her destination."

A chorus of "Noes" greeted this suggestion.

"My granddaughter should not be left without a chaperon."

Dunham said, "That's very kind of you, my lord, but Mistress Freese's direction must be kept secret. I can escort her."

"I want her with me." Winn looked down at Susan, who was biting her lower lip, clearly embarrassed to be the center of attention. "I'd have some things between us settled and though they do not concern the guardianship, I'd like witnesses so my Sukey—Susan—feels safe. And I hope, Mr. Brand, that you will offer her your advice."

How would the earl greet the idea of having a magdalen in his house?

Without so much as a raised eyebrow, Mountjoy beckoned his footman. "Two sedan chairs, quick as you can. We won't need the coach."

"What do you want me to do?" Dunham asked Allan.

Rose spoke before he could answer. "My lord, although we have not been formally introduced, may I suggest Mr. Dunham accompany us as there may be a good deal of copying to be done. He is a gentleman and writes an excellent hand."

"A good idea, ma'am. With two copyists, the work will be completed sooner."

"I fear we are trespassing on your hospitality, Lord Mountjoy," Brand commented apologetically.

"Not at all. Since Everard first approached me, I have wanted to know the end of this tale."

Left unsaid was Allan's thought that an earl's presence would provide some restraint if tempers ran high.

Twenty minutes later, they were seated at the table in the small dining room in which Allan had breakfasted with the earl.

Agreeing on the wording of Winn's renunciation of the guardianship took less than half an hour.

"A record for preparation of a legal document," Brand said. "Very good, indeed. 'On the grounds of my lack of a wife, inexperience with young ladies needing to be introduced into society, the press of my business commitments, and their grandfather, Sir Oliver Milton's closer connection and regained health,' et cetera, et cetera. Sign it, Everard and Dunham will copy it, and 'tis done but for submitting it."

"As for the signature," Allan began hesitantly, "perhaps that should be put off until after the copies are made and the other matters considered."

"That is more efficient," the attorney agreed. "Let us move on to the financial matters. The estate ledger shows two quarter days' rents of 366 pounds each, and a total of, er, 92 pounds in expenses, so 366 times 2…"

"Is 732 pounds. That amount minus the 92 is 640 pounds," Winn said.

"You're very fast, Winn. Is that amount still in the

strongbox at Stanbury Manor?"

"I'm good at figures. Leave that sum in an almost empty house where a few shillings might be a temptation? No, I took it to London with me. I will write a draft on my bank, Andres & Barlow, for that amount." He added, "And any others I may owe."

"Very well. The annuity is easy enough to resolve with your accounting from Pimling's. A withdrawal of four hundred and fifty pounds."

"It didn't seem like stealing from anyone, Stanbury being dead."

"I see. Minus some deposits thereafter. Everard, can you total them?"

"I already have. Er, they add up to 2,650 pounds, but that does not include the interest they earned."

"That much?" Brand's exclamation seemed to express the others' surprise, except for Allan and Winn. "Do you agree that amount is correct, Winn?"

"Yes."

"So you should receive a payment from the account of 2,200 pounds and the interest thereon."

"I want it deposited to an account for Susan Freese. I was putting it aside for Sukey. Susan." His face colored as Susan stared at him.

Silence reigned while several pens scratched on paper. When they were done, Brand continued, "I hope you excel at calculating interest. I don't have my copy of Castaing's *Interest Book* with me."

Winn gave a crack of laughter at Brand's deprecating smile. "For simplicity, let us ignore the interest."

"Thank you. That deals with the financial aspects."

"All very well," Sir Oliver grumbled, "but what of

Rose's and Ory's reputations?"

"An amount is not easily calculated for that, when we do not know how damaged they may be."

Allan said, "I fear many of those nearest us at Bow Street heard enough to make gossip inevitable."

The baronet grunted. "And if they didn't, I may not be able muzzle my daughter-in-law."

"You meant to sell my sister into, into…" Rose's sharp voice trailed off, unable to complete that thought, and finished "so you must have spread the word somehow."

"I was trying to make a marriage for Oriana with a wealthy old viscount who would have taken her with no dowry at all. I knew his tastes, and that he was looking for a wife. She'd have been Lady—well, never mind who—and a wealthy widow in a few years."

"Over my dead body," she snapped.

"How is that different from a girl's father repairing his fortune by wedding her to some man willing to pay for the privilege?" Winn inquired. "Her future would have been secured. I would have seen you suitably married, too, Rosabel, though that appeared to be a more challenging project. I'd have provided a dowry for you, using the viscount's settlement and adding whatever more was needed."

Rose looked to Brand and Mountjoy for their reaction to this outrageous attitude. Their faces bore an identical studied blankness.

Brand said, "Such transactions are not unknown."

The earl agreed. "That is the way of the world, Mistress Rosabel, much as those of high principles may deplore turning one's daughter into merchandise. Or one's son; for young men are sometimes also forced to marry females for their family's and their own gain. My marriage was arranged thus, and it has turned out well enough."

Rosabel snapped, "Whatever the world may tolerate, there is the matter of Mistress Gill. You hired criminals to abduct a child to force his mother to spy for you at the Three Greyhounds. You cannot explain that away." Glaring was not ladylike, and her poor mama would have claimed it caused wrinkles, but Rose did not care. Winn was entirely too plausible.

Winn's brows came together. "I hired a fool. I needed a respectable female to get inside to make sure you and Oriana were present. Then I'd have come with a magistrate to get you out. The viscount would still have taken Oriana, and the settlement would have gone to provide a dowry for you. Rather than pay the woman to do the task, the bottle-head kept the gelt to force her do it for nothing and meant to take you and your sister out with the help of a couple of his brothers. Thought I'd be pleased. I'm heartily sorry for it—and he is, as well. You can take my being gulled as proof I don't use criminals as a rule."

Winn exhaled abruptly. "Sir Oliver, will it satisfy you if I contribute to their dowries?" He named a figure.

"Each?" Surprise was writ large on the baronet's face. Rose hoped her own was less expressive.

"Of course."

"You can afford that much?" Allan asked.

"My business is profitable, even given that the Purring Cat does not pander to the more depraved tastes." The corners of his lips turned down. "Consider it my just punishment for not refusing the guardianship in the first place."

Brand whispered something close to Sir Oliver's ear. Milton gave a curt nod. "Your offer is accepted."

Winn had already penned the draft for the monies owed to the Stanbury account. He pulled another sheet toward him and took up his quill.

"An easier settlement than I expected," Mountjoy remarked. "I believe refreshments are in order."

"There's one last thing. Pimling's must be notified of Stanbury's death and the cessation of the annuity. As 'Stanbury' has had no real presence in London except for Winn's brief use of his identity, a letter to the bank should suffice. I hope," Brand added. "If the management took note of their faulty identification of Stanbury in 1718, they might be more diligent in verifying his death."

"Pimling's might prefer not to stir the pond lest their earlier lack of diligence be discovered," Allan pointed out. "Before we notify Pimling's, however, I've had an idea. What is to happen to Stanbury Manor?"

"It will pass to the Crown," Mountjoy stated, and Brand added, "With no heir, there's nothing else to be done."

"How will the Crown find out he's dead?"

They all stared at Allan. Rose suspected he was beginning to have second thoughts about his notion.

"Why…" Brand stopped short. "That's a very good question," he said slowly. "A nobleman's death is always widely known as is the existence of or search for an heir. In the case of a private gentleman, his death might not come to the Crown's attention…except that some officious person who knew the family might report it if they and a dishonest attorney tried to pass the property to someone not in the line of succession."

Allan Everard glanced around the table, his gaze resting on Rose a moment longer than the rest. "Winn's request to be released as guardian is based on his unsuitability as a guardian of young ladies and their grandfather and Mr. Brand being both suitable and willing. Nowhere does it state he is not Horace Stanbury."

Rose said, "He admitted at the magistrate's court he was not our cousin. Surely the clerk entered that in the records."

"As the matter was not referred for trial, why would anyone bother to read it?"

"But the magistrate knows."

"The ownership of the manor did not come up, and de Veil ordered us to sort out the financial matters. When we report that we have done so to everyone's satisfaction, I doubt he will inquire further."

"If there were any way to keep the manor out of the Crown's grasping hands, I would be in favor of it," Sir Oliver declared roundly. "We are taxed for our land, windows, coal, the poor, and foreign goods. But if doing so is merely to benefit Winn, here, I'm against it."

"My idea wouldn't benefit him, or not very much."

"Good. I do not care for country life. And the Purring Cat's profits are far more than the manor's."

"Who would it benefit?" Rose inquired. "Ory and I may not need its income, but I wouldn't want it held by someone who would mismanage it or treat the tenants badly."

"I'm associated with a charity which always needs funds. Part of the manor's profit would be welcome." Surely there would continue to be a need for refuges and to pay for apprenticeships and who knew what else?

Barlicorn, no doubt.

"What kind of charity?" Winn asked.

Everyone else at the table knew.

Dunham scowled at Allan, presumably warning him not to be too free with his tongue.

"It aids indigent women, their children, and orphans, keeps them out of the workhouse, and prepares them for employment."

"Worthwhile goals," the brothel keeper allowed, and no one disagreed with him.

"The manor would need a good bailiff."

"One could be hired, Mistress Rosabel. 'Twould be a fraud upon the Crown, of course, but the charity would be able to help more unfortunates, though only until Winn departs this life. Assuming he agreed to continuing his imposture," Brand qualified.

"Unless he has a legitimate male heir under the Stanbury name." Sir Oliver studied Winn speculatively.

"I don't. Nor an illegitimate one, neither."

Allan coughed apologetically. "That might not be an insurmountable problem."

"Everard, I hope you are not suggesting I marry some fertile young widow to beget a son to inherit the property I am not entitled to in the first place. He could hardly set up as county gentry while also running the Purring Cat."

Susan, seated beside Winn and seemingly lost in contemplation, sat up straighter and was taking notice. Allan stole a wary glance at her, perhaps wondering as Rose was whether Susan was primed to explode. For all she had feared about him, she seemed fond of Winn.

"If you had married while you were in the colonies—"

"I didn't." Nick Winn's eyes sought Susan.

"That is not necessarily an obstacle." Allan toyed with his quill. "Er, have you told anyone you never married? You might be a widower and still have an heir."

"The question never arose until Oriana asked."

Rose remembered that strange conversation. Ory should be warned not to speak of it again.

Mountjoy watched as if enjoying an excellent play.

Sir Oliver squinted at Everard. "What is the point of inventing a marriage and an heir? Ay, ay, I understand it would ensure support for your charity, and I'm grateful it has sheltered my granddaughters, for that is the benevolent institution you've mentioned, isn't it?"

"Yes."

"But when Winn is no more and the heir cannot be found, the property will escheat anyway."

"The heir I am thinking of would probably be available to inherit."

"This isn't meant only to help your asylum, is it?"

"No. There's a boy we've kept past the usual age, hoping to educate him to be a clerk. He has a deformed foot, so there's no future for him as a servant or laborer. The charity can't send him to university, but we hope to see him in some situation where his intelligence isn't thrown away. He understood Napier's Bones at the first explanation."

"Did he? How old is he?" Winn asked.

Susan Freese turned her head and gazed at Winn.

"He thinks he may be thirteen."

"No family or anyone who'd know his history?"

"He doesn't remember any man being present before his mother died. We got him before he'd been on the streets very long."

Rose liked the way Allan spoke of "our" charity and "we."

"You're speaking of Jeremy, aren't you?" For the first time, Susan spoke in Mountjoy House.

Rose was surprised she had paid any attention to him. On second thought, they were both lame and that might have made a bond, even so quickly.

"You know the boy, Sukey?"

"I do. He's a good lad. Quick-witted and well spoken."

"I wouldn't mind having an heir." Winn brooded. "I'm not sure the Cat would be a suitable home."

Susan gave a choke of laughter.

The earl said, "If a boy's going to inherit a country property, he should be raised on it. If he's not at a public school, and I wouldn't advise one for him if he's not able to fight, he should have a good tutor to prepare him for university. As it happens, the son of one of my cousins is looking for a position. He's hoping to find one with a quiet, studious boy as he's not fond of vigorous sports himself."

Winn's sharp gaze fixed on Allan. "How would you prove a marriage and birth?"

"If you'd married in America, you'd have something in writing from some clergyman over there and perhaps a letter from some respectable citizen congratulating you on your marriage—"

"I knew a fellow well placed in the Colonies, who is now dead, who might have written you such a letter," Mountjoy remarked.

"—and as the parish register wouldn't be available for inspection here, that might suffice."

Brand had been leaning forward intently. "In fact, it

almost certainly would. The search for an heir is left to the family or the family's man of law. If there's a title, the heir's proofs would probably be studied carefully. That's not the case here, and you've already been accepted as Paul Stanbury's heir. If the family were to accept your hypothetical son, who will quibble? There's no rival heir."

Winn studied each face around the table. "Is no one here offended by Everard's suggestion? My lord? Sir Oliver? Mistress Rosabel?"

"You're a reprobate, Winn, and you frightened my granddaughters. But if the choice were between you and the real Horace Stanbury, you'd have my vote. From what I heard of him, he was the greatest rogue unhung. And I don't mind Everard's women's and children's shelter benefitting, or that crippled orphan."

"It's not mine—"

"You're associated with it somehow, and it saved my granddaughters. That's good enough for me. I can't stomach the sanctimonious pap mouthed by most philanthropists. Very little love of mankind among them!" He gave a brisk nod.

Mountjoy grinned. "I never met you myself until today, Winn, but I know something of your business. The play at the tables is honest, I've never heard of a brawl or unpleasantness at the Purring Cat, the women are wholesome...or so I've heard," he ended hastily before dipping his head in Rose's direction. "I do beg your pardon for speaking so freely in a lady's company."

"Accepted, my lord. My innocent little ears have recently heard much worse."

"As a peer of the realm, I must uphold the law and moral standards as the majority of my fellow peers do, so I find no fault with Everard's proposal." He lounged in his high-backed chair very much at ease. "Dunham? You're the last man here. What do you say?"

"Family is important, my lord. I think this is the family's business and no one else's."

"Well, then," Mountjoy began.

"No one has asked my opinion or Susan's."

"And we should have asked you first." Allan's rueful admission banished her pique.

Now she had a chance to speak, Rose found it uncommonly difficult. Her dislike and distrust of Winn remained, but on the other hand, she had seen how Susan looked at him and heard of his kindness to her. He had been kind to Ory, even if his plan to arrange a marriage for her had been wrong-headed. There were the tenants to consider, too, and the opportunity Jeremy would be given. They were all waiting for her to cast her vote.

"Would you manage Stanbury Manor yourself?" she asked Winn.

"I'd hire a bailiff to deal with the day-to-day questions. I can manage a business, but country estates are a closed book to me, though I tried to get an idea of how yours worked. Perhaps Everard and Lord Mountjoy would advise me on how to choose a trustworthy man."

"I have no objections as long as you treat the tenants fairly."

"Might I consult you regarding tenant matters as you know them?"

"Yes." She turned toward Allan.

Winn said, "Sukey? What do you think?"

Their eyes met. Rose almost felt she was intruding upon a private moment, but she could not look away.

"I believe it answers a great many needs. Though I

don't like the idea of a boy living alone except for a tutor and servants, if Jeremy's to be brought up there."

"You could live there, too, Sukey. The house isn't as fine as the one you grew up in, but the scenery is pleasant. There's a housekeeper's room on the ground floor, so you wouldn't have to climb stairs."

"I'd be the housekeeper, then?"

"No, you'd be the lady of the house."

"You'll have to tell me what you mean by that, but we shouldn't be taking Mistress Rose's and his lordship's and the gentlemen's time."

"Devil take it, let's deal with it now. Marry me."

"Do you mean it, Nick?"

"Ay. I should have married you as soon as the Cat was making a profit. But I wanted everything to be perfect."

"And nothing ever is." They were staring at each other so intently the others might not have been in the room. The other men in the room distanced themselves by attentive study of their notes or the documents. Rose did her best to disguise her fascination by folding and re-folding her handkerchief.

"Will we be living at the manor?"

"We will. Todd had no trouble managing the house during the months I was at Stanbury. I could return to town for a few days every month to make it clear I'm still in control. Not perfect, maybe, but can you accept it?"

"Yes. Though I know you prefer town life."

"I was like a fish out of water at Stanbury, never having known any county gentry, but I'll learn to like it. Will you want banns?"

Susan gave a peal of laughter, startling them all. "A license would be better, under the circumstances."

Brand remarked, "Many marry in the precincts of the Fleet Prison. There's no license or waiting required."

Allan cleared his throat. "If you intend to save Stanbury Manor, your marriage now must be concealed in order that Jeremy appear to be your legitimate heir."

"Perhaps he is my son by an earlier marriage?"

Dunham hemmed. "As it happens, I know how you could marry under the Rules of the Fleet but with an earlier date on the certificate and in the register."

Rose suspected Barlicorn would be involved somehow.

"Sukey?"

"That would be acceptable. Many couples marry there because it's cheap and quick, and I think both the haste and the privacy would be desirable."

Given that Nicholas Winn was well known in certain circles, Rose thought, amused. *What a day of surprises!*

Half an hour later, with all documents copied, signed and witnessed, the Earl of Mountjoy sent for a sedan chair for Sir Oliver and ordered his carriage to return Rose, Susan, Dunham, and Allan to the Three Greyhounds as only Brand, Winn, and Sir Oliver were needed to report to the magistrate's court.

Chapter 34

Chapell shut the gate behind them, and Dunham strode off to the stable to let his men know they were no longer on alert.

Rose sighed. She still felt uneasy about Susan marrying Winn, though she had seen another side of him. Still, she said, "I wish we had time to buy or make you a dress for tomorrow, Susan."

"Oh, Rose, I don't care about that. It's who—"

Allan, behind them, interrupted, a breach of manners she would not have expected.

"We forgot to ask the opinion and permission of the one who is most affected by the arrangement."

Rose and Susan stopped and looked back at him.

"Jeremy," he said.

Rose waited, a sinking feeling in her middle, while Allan went to find the boy. "I hope he won't be upset. Or refuse."

Jeremy, apprised of the plans for his future, asked, "Will I have to change my name?"

"Your last name would have to be Stanbury."

Seeing the worry in Allan's face, she wondered if reluctance to give up his family name would doom their plan.

"Even if Jeremy refuses to live in the country and pretend to be our son, the money from the manor will still send him to university when he's ready. I'll see to that," Susan said.

The boy's unexpectedly sweet smile flashed. "I don't mind about my name. I don't think Smith was mam's real name anyway."

Three covert sighs of relief until Jeremy's next question. "Will I like Mr. Stanbury?"

Rose and Allan kept silent. Susan gave the boy a quick hug, saying, "Many people do."

"That's all right, then."

****

Before they parted after their meeting at Mountjoy's house, Sir Oliver had asked that he bring Rosabel and Oriana to his home the following afternoon. He had added, ominously in Allan's opinion, "I'll want to discuss certain matters with you."

At the Three Greyhounds, once they had made sure Jeremy had no objections to acquiring a new name and family, Rose and Susan had disappeared into Anne's office with Fiona. Allan retreated to his chamber to write a report of the day's events and their outcome and made a copy of it. That took almost until supper. On his way to the common room, he went to the gate and whistled for one of the street boys to carry the letter to Simon Hayes.

There was no chance to sit at the same table with Rose; a chattering covey of women and girls surrounded her and Susan and carried them away after the meal. But what could he have said to her anyway? Better to wait and see what Sir Oliver had to say. He did not sleep well that night.

In the morning he had scarcely finished washing and shaving himself using the jug of water he had brought up the night before, when a knock at his door forced him to throw his banyan on over his breeches for decency.

"Sorry to call so early," Dunham said, "but Barlicorn's in my office, asking for you."

Allan flung on the rest of his clothing to follow Dunham to the stable, where the "head porter" left him alone in his office.

"A tidy piece of work, Everard."

"Thank you, but it was mostly luck."

"While luck may have played a role, all the other parts would not have come together without you. Would the earl and his brother have been so helpful if they'd been approached by someone else? Would Mistress Francis? Both banks cooperated with you and gave you accountings when approaching them came at some risk to yourself. I'd like you to sit on our board of governors."

"What, all of them at once?" The flippant retort slipped out. Inwardly Allan writhed with embarrassment and to cover it, said, "Wouldn't they have to vote on me?"

Barlicorn's crooked white teeth flashed in a grin. "No. Every man on the board was chosen by me, and I trust them in charitable work but not to choose another board member. They've led lives too sheltered to suspect the motives of others. I've no intention of letting the board of the charities under the St. Dismas Charitable Foundation turn into the sort that meets to eat and drink and congratulate themselves on their charity in helping the poor. And we need someone like you: a man with a pleasant, trustworthy manner who's not afraid to take action, and who is as generous with your time as with your money. I should mention there's no honorarium involved."

"I don't need the money." He had nothing better to

do. He was already deeply involved with the Three Greyhounds. "Very well, I accept."

"Being on the board does come with a certain dignity. The St. Dismas charity is well known for aiding the indigent and the deserving poor fallen on hard times, though the exact nature of our efforts is not. We do not give tours of our sanctuaries to potential donors, there being a general prejudice against aiding fallen women, children who have had to live by thieving, and the like. We rely on testimonials by those who have hired our, er, alumni. The board meets the first day of each month at Hayes's office unless 'tis a Sunday. He'll introduce you."

"Won't you be present?"

"The board members are chosen for their compassion and common sense, but they do not need to know me. I am only the founder and anonymous benefactor they never see. Some of them might be appalled to know that some of the donations come from criminals, courtesans, and even the occasional bawdy-house owner."

Before they parted, Allan commented, "I hope whatever problem took you out of London is resolved."

"It is. I foresaw that Nick Winn would haunt me at Job's until I located Susan Freese. So I told him I was pursuing a clue that she had left London and would write as soon as I had found her. I thought I was returning to speak with Susan about her wishes and discovered instead that you'd sorted everything out as I was sure you would."

****

Rose, Oriana, Allan, Susan, Jeremy, and Dunham met Winn at Brand's office, Chancery Lane, the most convenient meeting place near the Fleet. Susan and Oriana were the only ones apart from Brand who showed no sign of uneasiness. Allan had been late to breakfast, and his neckcloth was a trifle less neatly tied than usual.

The faint tension around Winn's eyes vanished when he shook hands with Jeremy and received a shy smile.

"You both brought your luggage?"

"Such as it is, Nick."

"I packed your things from the Cat. They're already on the coach. Jeremy, we'll order you some clothes, but we can do that from the manor."

"Will you be able to spend some time there while we grow accustomed?"

"For a month or so, Sukey. Then I'll go into town for a week or less to review the ledger and see if there are any problems."

Dunham had arranged for the marriage to be solemnized before an elderly and rather doddering ecclesiastic in his daughter's lodging outside the prison but within the Liberties of the Fleet, under the jurisdiction of the prison rather than the City of London. He had to be reminded of their names but otherwise performed the service without hesitation and without having to read it.

Dunham had instructed them as to what they must do. "He has years' worth of registers of marriages. While you talk to him before he begins, I'll offer to fetch the register and I'll make sure it's one with a place where this marriage can be written in before the boy could have been born. Because his sight is bad and his hand shakes so 'tis hard for him to write, I'll offer to fill in the register and make out the certificate and have him sign. He won't notice the date is wrong. Be generous with his fee, if you would. He does few marriages now, and his daughter struggles to support him."

Allan produced a basket with delicacies and bottles of wine for a celebration. Rose's heart swelled: there would be enough food left over to supply the old man and his daughter with treats for several days, and she had seen Allan slip a purse into the bottom of the basket, too. She struggled not to frown when she saw Winn thank the churchman and give him a coin for his fee. Then he turned to the woman who was setting out Allan's offerings and pressed a plump purse into her hand as he spoke to her. Feeling it, her eyes widened, and she stammered her thanks.

They drank claret out of an assortment of tumblers and mugs before Susan, Winn, and Jeremy departed in a hackney for the livery stable where their traveling coach waited. Rose said a silent prayer that the oddly assorted new family would be happy and that all would work out for the best. After a moment, she hoped the same for Anne and Dunham before adding a wish on her own behalf.

****

Ory threw herself into her grandfather's arms. When he released her, Rose returned his hug with more dignity but also a murmured, "Thank you," in a voice that betrayed incipient tears. She fought them back, and smiled mistily.

"You should be thanking Everard, my girl."

"I do." She turned to Allan who was standing apart, reluctant to intrude on their meeting. Martha Milton stood yet farther away, hands clasped tightly at her waist. Grandpapa must have terrified her into that blank face or

343

she would appear to be sucking a lemon.

"You have been more than kind, Mr. Everard."

"I hope he will be," Sir Oliver grunted. "Martha, show my granddaughters to their chambers. Rosabel, you and Oriana will join me in the parlor once you've seen your rooms. Everard, my study."

The footman was already carrying their valises upstairs. Worried by her grandfather's abrupt order to Allan, Rose cast an apologetic glance at him. He smiled uneasily and followed his host.

"They'll take a little time to wash their faces and hands and tidy their hair," Sir Oliver said, gesturing him to one of the two chairs by the fireplace. "Claret or sherry?"

"Claret, please, sir."

When they were both seated, the former general demanded, "Have you thought about our discussion before Bow Street?"

"Sir, I have been afraid to read anything into what you said, because you know almost nothing about me. Though I have thought of little else."

"I know you are a gentleman and have saved my granddaughters."

Now it must all come out. "Sir Oliver, I am the base-born son of a baron. My half brother is the sixth Baron Passevant. Given my irregular birth, I cannot see how I could court any lady."

The baronet raised his eyebrows. "You are a gentleman by nature if not by birth. William the Conqueror was born a bastard. If her family has no objection and the lady herself is willing, I see no difficulty."

His mouth had gone dry. "That would make a

difference. If you would allow it, sir?"

The general must often have shown the same face to some officer under his command who had asked an epically stupid question. "Damme, boy, your lack of presumption may do you credit, but I know from your ability at chess you're sharp enough to take my meaning. If Rose will have you, I'll welcome you into the family. Perhaps you should ask her opinion. She's a sensible girl." He smiled, thin-lipped. "From the letter I received from her, I imagine she would not be offended. I'll give you the opportunity to speak with her in private after supper, for which you will of course stay."

"Thank you, sir. I am deeply appreciative of your tolerance."

"Pshaw. I was a successful officer because I never worried much about what was appropriate or expected. The results usually justified me. I have a great respect for your intelligence and character, and I like you. Also I've needed a good chess partner since the former one died."

Had he explained he could maintain a wife in comfort? Allan thought not. "There is one more thing. I have investments. According to my man of business, at a conservative estimate of my earnings, I can afford to lease a house, provide comfortably for a wife and children, send the boys—if any—to school and university, and dower the girls."

"So much the better. We can talk about the settlements after Rose accepts you. Now let us join the ladies for a sherry before supper."

Most of the talk was among Sir Oliver, Rose, and Ory until supper was over and they all returned to the parlor.

"Rose, I believe Everard wishes to speak to you.

You may make use of my bookroom. The footman's been instructed to make sure there are candles lit and the fire is tended."

Rose's eyes widened, and she stole a peek at Allan. He smiled, he hoped in an encouraging manner, and offered his arm.

"Papa-in-law, I protest. For Rosabel to be going off in private with a strange man is an offense against decency."

"Enough, woman. They have my permission. Twenty minutes should be adequate, Everard. Go."

"Ay, sir." He swept her out the door with perhaps more haste than grace.

"Allan?"

"Wait. A servant may pop out at any moment."

In the bookroom with the door closed, he discovered its one lack. There was neither sofa nor settee. Allan could not quite imagine paying his addresses to Rose while they sat primly in separate armchairs. He also could not envision making a cod's head of himself by dropping to one knee, possessing himself of her hand, and blurting out the Question. He had not courted her, even if he had known how to do so. And in the Three Greyhounds, such attentions to a lady would have been inappropriate.

****

Rose waited while Allan stood there staring at her. Grandpapa must have encouraged or persuaded him to offer for her. Or, heaven help them both, ordered him to do so. Was that the plan to salvage her reputation Allan had spoken of? How humiliating for both of them. She would assure him he need not sacrifice himself...but what if this tête-à-tête was about something else? She stared mutely back. She had had the courage or the foolishness to abandon her home with her little sister. Reverting now to the well-bred girl she had been was ridiculous.

"If there is much to discuss, perhaps we should begin before Aunt Martha interrupts us."

His smile lit his face. Her heart had often been melted by it when he was teaching the boys. "Rose, I have esteemed you ever since you tested the window grills and asked about the arrangements for dealing with slops at the inn. I could not tell you whilst you and Oriana feared for your safety even if it had not seemed wrong when we both lived there and you could not get away from me if my admiration was unwelcome." He drew breath. "Sir Oliver is not opposed to my offering you marriage. But he and I are in agreement that you must not feel any compulsion either from him or from me."

"He did not order you to ask for my hand? He can be very forceful, but you are not one of his officers."

"No, thank God! I'd be terrified to serve under him. But I've thought and dreamed about you for weeks and wished I dared tell you. But I was not sure such a confidence would be welcome."

"And I wanted you to court me." She waited expectantly.

"First, there is something I must confess to you. I won't ask you to marry me under false pretenses." He tensed.

Her heart, already beating fast, pounded with apprehension.

"Rose, I was born to my father's mistress."

"You did tell me you were illegitimate."

"Did I? What was I thinking, to burden you with that

when there could be no excuse for it then?"

"I have no idea, but it did not matter to me then and it does not matter to me now. I suppose you told Grandpapa?"

"Of course."

An unladylike snort escaped Rose. Living at the Greyhounds had coarsened her, she feared. "If my grandfather did not object, Allan, please ask me to marry you. If he did, which I do not believe, we will wait until I am of age."

"I will. I am, but let me assure you I can support you in comfort. While I was working on the repairs, I found a hoard of old jewels which provided me funds to invest, so we can have a house and servants and educate our children—"

"I'd marry you if we had to live at the Greyhounds, though I admit 'twould be more comfortable to have a place of our own. Please just ask me so I need not feel I'm proposing to you."

"Rose, will you marry me?"

"Yes, yes, a thousand times yes! I thought you were not indifferent to me, but I could never be sure. And I could not show I was interested in you without embarrassing both of us because you were unlikely to want a female with a scandalous reputation."

"The pot calling the kettle black, my dear, as it happens. Shall I apply for a license? Or would you rather the banns were read?"

"I'd marry you tomorrow under the Rules of the Fleet, but I think Grandpapa would prefer banns so it does not look as if we are marrying in haste. I would like to invite our particular friends."

Somehow while they talked they had moved from

two or three feet apart until only inches separated them now.

"Agreed. I love you, Rose. May I claim a kiss?"

"Yes." She threw her arms around his neck and bussed him right heartily, like a wanton. His arms encircling her promised support and protection and—

A sharp rap at the door interrupted a delightful thought.

"Everard, you've had twenty-three minutes. Have you good news for me? If you haven't settled the business by now, you are a clodpate and I despair of you."

They sprang apart guiltily. Their eyes met, shining with merriment. Allan stepped forward to open the door.

"We do, Sir Oliver. Rose has accepted my hand."

"Excellent. There's champagne in the parlor," her old rogue of a grandfather said smugly.

A word about the author...

Kathleen Buckley has loved writing ever since she learned to read. After a career which included light bookkeeping, working as a paralegal, and a stint as a security officer , she began to write as a second career, rather than as a hobby. She is now the author of ten published Georgian romances and is inthe final throes of revising the eleventh.

Warning: no bodices are ripped in her romances, which might be described as "powder & patch & peril" rather than Jane Austen drawingroom. They contain no explicit sex, but do contain mild bad language, as the situations in which her characters find themselves sometimes call for an oath a little stronger than "Zounds!" http://18thcenturyromance.wordpress.com

Thank you for purchasing
this publication of The Wild Rose Press, Inc.

For questions or more information
contact us at
info@thewildrosepress.com.

The Wild Rose Press, Inc.
www.thewildrosepress.com